Highest Praise for Leo J. Maloney and His Thrillers

BLACK SKIES

"Smart, savvy, and told with the pace and nuance that only a former spook could bring to the page, *Black Skies* is a tour de force novel of twenty-first-century espionage and a great geopolitical thriller. Maloney is the new master of the modern spy game, and this is first-rate storytelling."
—**Mark Sullivan**

"*Black Skies* is rough, tough, and entertaining. Leo J. Maloney has written a ripping story."
—**Meg Gardiner**

SILENT ASSASSIN

"Leo Maloney has done it again. Real life often overshadows fiction and *Silent Assassin* is both: a terrifyingly thrilling story of a man on a clandestine mission to save us all from a madman hell bent on murder, written by a man who knows that world all too well."
—**Michele McPhee**

"From the bloody, ripped-from-the-headlines opening sequence, *Silent Assassin* grabs you and doesn't let go. *Silent Assassin* has everything a thriller reader wants—nasty villains, twists and turns, and a hero—Cobra—who just plain kicks ass."
—**Ben Coes**

"Dan Morgan, a former Black Ops agent, is called out of retirement and back into a secretive world of politics and deceit to stop a madman."
—*The Stoneham Independent*

TERMINATION ORDERS

"Leo J. Maloney is the new voice to be reckoned with. *Termination Orders* rings with the authenticity that can only come from an insider. This is one outstanding thriller!"
—John Gilstrap

"Taut, tense, and terrifying! You'll cross your fingers it's fiction—in this high-powered, action-packed thriller, Leo Maloney proves he clearly knows his stuff."
—Hank Phillippi Ryan

"A new must-read action thriller that features a double-crossing CIA and Congress, vengeful foreign agents, a corporate drug ring, the Taliban, and narco-terrorists . . . a you-are-there account of torture, assassination, and double-agents, where 'nothing is as it seems.' "
—Jon Renaud

"Leo J. Maloney is a real-life Jason Bourne."
—Josh Zwylen, *Wicked Local Stoneham*

"A masterly blend of Black Ops intrigue, cleverly interwoven with imaginative sequences of fiction. The reader must guess which accounts are real and which are merely storytelling."
—Chris Treece, *The Chris Treece Show*

"A deep-ops story presented in an epic style that takes fact mixed with a bit of fiction to create a spy thriller that takes the reader deep into secret spy missions."
—Cy Hilterman, *Best Sellers World*

"For fans of spy thrillers seeking a bit of realism mixed into their novels, *Termination Orders* will prove to be an excellent and recommended pick."
—*Midwest Book Reviews*

ALSO BY LEO J. MALONEY

Termination Orders

Silent Assassin

Black Skies

LEO J. MALONEY

PINNACLE
Kensington Publishing Corp.
www.kensingtonbooks.com

PINNACLE BOOKS are published by

Kensington Publishing Corp.
119 West 40th Street
New York, NY 10018

All Kensington titles, imprints, and distributed lines are available at special quantity discounts for bulk purchases for sales promotions, premiums, fund-raising, educational, or institutional use. Special book excerpts or customized printings can also be created to fit specific needs. For details, write or phone the office of the Kensington special sales manager: Kensington Publishing Corp., 119 West 40th Street, New York, NY 10018, attn: Special Sales Department; phone 1-800-221-2647.

PUBLISHER'S NOTE
This book is a work of fiction. Names, characters, businesses, organizations, places, events, and incidents either are the product of the author's imagination or are used fictitiously. Any resemblance to actual persons, living or dead, events, or locales is entirely coincidental.

First electronic edition: September 2014

ISBN-13: 978-0-7860-3610-3
ISBN-10: 0-7860-3610-9

First print edition: September 2014

ISBN-13: 978-0-7860-3611-0
ISBN-10: 0-7860-3611-7

Printed in the United States of America

To my dear friend Dr. Rodney Jones,
who has spent timeless hours listening to me running
ideas by him . . .

And to my wife, Lynn,
who is always there to listen to me, and to support me in every way
possible. Without her support and encouragement, I don't think I
would have ever finished my first novel. I love you, Lynn.

Chapter 1

May 23
Federally Administered Tribal Areas, Pakistan

The Night Stalker Black Hawk flew low over a sea of darkness that reached up in jagged peaks along the horizon into a leaden sky. The sleek black chariot of death flew completely dark, keeping radio silence even here in the middle of nowhere in the tribal areas of Pakistan. Alberto Medina's muscles were tense with anticipation.

The Pakistani government was on board with the op, so radar detection and antiaircraft missiles from the local military weren't among their concerns. But there were still the Martyr's Brigade and the Pakistani Taliban to worry about. The countryside was riddled with them. They were known to stock surface-to-air missiles and wouldn't think twice about trying to bring down a Black Hawk helicopter if they saw it coming.

Since talking without radio over the scream of the engine was a nonstarter, Medina and the rest of SEAL Team Six Gold Squadron sat in silence cheek by jowl in the cabin, one in each seat and two on the floor along with their two Belgian Malinois, Boomer and Roscoe, wearing their harnesses.

Not that there was anything to say. This was hardly their first time around the block. Medina had lost count of how many operations they had run together in the past five years. It had been a whirlwind tour through Africa, the Middle East, and South Asia, whose physical and mental demands left Medina used to living at the edge of his tether.

This was different, though. They had taken out countless militants and low-ranking members of terrorist groups, but today they were going to decapitate the Martyr's Brigade. Today, they were going after Haider Raza, code-named Phage for this operation. He was a young man, Medina had seen in his file, just over thirty with a strong nose and the intense glare of the true believer. Under his leadership, the Martyr's Brigade had killed untold numbers of civilians in Pakistan, and Raza had, according to intelligence reports, masterminded a series of suicide bombings that had killed dozens in France, England, and Germany. All that was before the bombing of the US Embassy in Islamabad a month before.

In the wordless roar in the chopper, Medina's mind wandered to an image of Michelle, her smooth brown skin, her dark eyes, that beautiful long neck made vivid by the heightened senses that came with the adrenaline rush of the mission. He had promised her that he'd leave after this tour of duty, and that woman deserved to have a man by her side. He had already let her down once, he thought with a sting of shame. He'd signed on for another two years out of duty and camaraderie—the bond of the Navy SEALs was not one easily broken.

Medina shook those thoughts out of his head and clutched his HK MP5, as if to anchor himself. He focused on the mission, going over in his head the carefully choreographed attack that they had planned in under twenty-four hours after the intel had come in. He pictured the floor plan of the compound, his positions as they would move in. He remembered the contours of the faces of the people suspected to be in there, one by one, until he formed the picture of Haider Raza clearly in his mind.

If he was lucky, Medina would be the one to gun him down.

"Five minutes to target," the pilot said over the radio. Medina felt energy surge through his body, his muscles twitching in anticipation. He chambered a round into his MP5, and heard the others doing likewise with their weapons. O'Connor knelt by the still-closed door of the chopper, ready to throw out the rope when they reached their target, the four-tube night-vision goggles raised above his helmet.

"Stand by to deploy," said Moody through their communicators. Medina checked his watch, clicking on its built-in light. It was just shy of 3 A.M. He felt it in his stomach as the chopper slowed down its horizontal movement, then began to descend. Shortly thereafter, the aircraft drew to a standstill in the air. Medina slipped on his heavy gloves, flexing his hands to accommodate them to the leather. They had worn in nicely by now, and didn't make his movements quite so stiff. It was a small comfort.

"Go, go, go!"

Sykes opened the door, letting a rush of air into the chopper. He unrolled the fast-rope off the edge and went over first, tethered to Roscoe, and O'Connor went next with Boomer. Medina pulled his night-vision goggles over his eyes, and the interior of the chopper was revealed from the darkness in shades of green. Each member of the nine-man team followed the two down in turn. Medina climbed down last, leaving the standard ten feet between himself and the man below him. Cool air blasted him as he emerged from the chopper door, holding on to the thick braided rope with his gloved hands and thighs.

Faint and irregular lights spread out on the town below, bright green spots in a green landscape. His hands grew hot from the friction with the rope, and his MP5 swung gently against his back for the few seconds he was in the air, and then his heavy boots connected with the hard, dusty ground of the complex backyard. His eyes followed the outline of the outer wall that encircled them, by now intimately familiar to him from satellite and aerial drone pictures.

He ran after the rest of the team for cover, where the wall shadowed the moonlight, pulling off his fast-rope gloves as he did. King, Sykes, and Hinton, their demolition team, had already run ahead to plant the C4 on the hinges of the back door and of the iron security gate. Medina and the remaining five stood by, guns against their shoulders, ready to move in, taking cover against the blast.

In a flash and a puff of smoke, the gate broke loose from its hinges and crashed onto the concrete in front of it.

Three men fanned out into the downstairs floor and secured the outside while the demolition team moved on. Medina led the other three in a charge upstairs, where they expected to find Raza. He would have been alerted to the noise by now, but with any luck he wouldn't be able to arm himself fast enough.

"Outside clear," came a voice through the communicator.

"Ground floor clear," came another.

Something's not right. The house was supposed to be occupied. The misgiving had barely registered in his mind when he kicked open the door to the room reported to be Raza's bedroom. Raza was not there. Instead, he saw a young man with a short beard and wild fear in his eyes. He was wearing a *shalwar khameez,* under which Medina recognized the familiar bulk of the suicide bomber's vest. In a split second, too surprised to act, his eyes followed the man's arm to his hand, where he was holding a detonator.

Hands trembling, the young man pushed the button.

Medina never heard the blast that took out his entire team. His last thought, barely formed, was of Michelle, of that lovely spot where her neck met her hair.

Chapter 2

May 24
Boston

"So what's the story on the Raza mission?" asked Morgan, navigating the narrow streets of South Boston in his Ford Shelby GT 500 Mustang. It was evening and the sky was lead-gray with overhanging clouds that on occasion smoldered with lightning. It had snowed lightly earlier, and then it had rained, and every time Morgan edged the car near the curb the right tires were bogged down in thick slush.

"The story is, nobody knows what the hell the story is." The speaker was Peter Conley, Morgan's old Black Ops partner, riding shotgun. Conley, thin and tall with a bony face and high forehead, had an almost professorial look. He was careful and deliberate and picked up languages like others pick up bad habits. As a man of action, Morgan would give him grief for his thoughtful approach, but there was no one he'd rather have at his side in the line of fire.

"Come on, you gotta know something," said Morgan. He knew, of course, everything that had been on the news. The raid on the house in the tribal areas of Pakistan where Haider Raza was supposedly staying. House was rigged with explosives, with a suicide bomber to set it all off. No survivors among the SEAL Team, not even the chopper, which had stalled and crashed after being pummeled with flying debris. But Conley had active assets all over the globe, contacts who kept him up to speed on everything. He was bound to know more than CNN.

"Only the rumor that someone tipped him off," said Conley.

"You could count on your fingers and toes the number of people who knew about the op in the US government. But once they cleared it with the Pakistani leaders . . . Well, we know Raza has friends in high places, and it only takes one."

"What I'd do if I got my hands on that bastard," said Morgan, his knuckles going white on the steering wheel.

"You and me both," said Conley.

"Meanwhile, we're stuck doing grunt work in Southie," said Morgan, with an irritated gesture of his hand.

"You know how the game works," said Conley, running his fingers deftly on the touch-sensitive screen of a tablet computer. "We keep the Zeta sponsors happy with a couple of errands here and there, they keep us financed with a smile, and we keep fighting the good fight."

"I'm just here because I'd rather do this than have Bloch on my case about it for the next two weeks," said Morgan. "Plus," he said, feeling an electric excitement in his muscles, "I could use the exercise."

"Are you sure you know where you're going? This thing has GPS, you know."

Morgan brought the Shelby to a halt at the curb on a street corner. "Yeah, I know where we're going." He cut the engine.

"This the place?" Conley asked.

"Over in the corner," said Morgan, pointing with his hand still on the steering wheel. It was a low brick building, whose white façade was tinged blue by the evening light. It sported a wooden sign in faded green Celtic letters. MACAULEY'S.

"Why do these bastards always have to meet in pubs?" asked Conley, retying his bootlaces.

"They're Irish," said Morgan. "Where else are they going to meet?"

Conley checked his tablet computer once more.

"Police?" asked Morgan.

"We're clear," said Conley, turning off the computer and stowing it in the glove compartment.

"We going in armed or not?"

"I say no," said Conley. "We go in packing, and they start shooting as soon as they see us."

"If they start shooting, don't we want to shoot back?"

"Let's try to keep this one low profile, shall we?" said Conley.

"All right," said Morgan as he unstrapped his shoulder holster and laid it on the floor of the car at his feet. "But you let me do the talking, all right?"

Morgan got out of the car and moved with purpose to the door of the bar, sinking his boot into the slush as he crossed the deserted street. The air was chilly, and Morgan had worn only a short-sleeved shirt for mobility. But tension kept him from feeling the cold.

They reached the door of the bar together, and Morgan made eye contact with Conley for half a second. After years of working together, it was all the go-ahead he needed. Morgan pushed open the door and was greeted by the acrid smell of cigarette smoke—the NO SMOKING sign next to the door, Morgan noted, was covered in rude sharpie drawings. The main bar room was long and narrow. The bar itself ran three quarters of its length, with bottles of booze lining the wall. The half dozen working class stiffs on faded yellow pleather barstools or small circular tables that lined the wall opposite the bar were illuminated by dim, hanging yellow lights.

Morgan led Conley though the hostile stares of the regulars to a couple of stools at the bar. The waitress, a skinny, aging redhead whose thick skin seemed both figurative and literal, shot them the stink eye. Morgan could practically see what she was thinking plastered on her face. *Plainclothes cops.*

She should be so lucky.

"What'll it be, ladies?" she rasped, wiping the counter in front of them with a rag.

"Grey Goose Rasmopolitan," said Conley. "With a twist"

The barmaid raised a disbelieving eyebrow. Morgan suppressed a laugh.

"Aperol Spritz? Mai Tai?"

"He'd like a pint," Morgan cut in before the barmaid lost what little temper she had. "Whatever you have. Water for me, if you've got that on tap."

"Cute," she said without a smile.

"You got a bathroom in this place?" asked Morgan.

"In the back," she said, tilting a pint glass against the tap.

"How about an ATM?" asked Conley.

"Next to the bathroom."

They both stood up and made their way to the back of the bar, feeling the patrons' eyes burning holes the backs of their heads. A short, dark hallway led to the bathroom in the back, and a grimy old ATM stood there as promised. But they were interested in another door, on their right, an old-fashioned door with a glass window that was obscured by dirty, bent venetian blinds on the other side.

"Let's try to be subtle about this," Conley whispered. "I'd rather not fight a bar full of surly drunk Irishmen."

Morgan tried the door, which was locked. Then he knocked.

"Bathroom's the otha dooh!" a man's voice came from inside.

Morgan looked at Conley and shrugged. He took a step back and kicked in the door. A chunk of wood and a spray of splinters flew into the cramped room inside.

Time slowed down as Morgan assessed the situation. Three young men and a blond woman huddled around a small table, two men on his right and other man and the girl to his left. A snub-nosed revolver lay on the table, in front of the man on his immediate right, sharing the surface with bags of crystal meth and stacks of money. The blond hair and fair skin advertised the girl as their target.

The man's hand went straight for the gun. Morgan grabbed his arm and twisted until he heard a crack, while taking the gun in his left hand. Morgan released the man's arm and kicked him in the chest with a heavy wet winter boot, tipping his chair so that his head banged against the wall. The man next to him just sat petrified. Morgan heard the thump of the other man hitting the ground.

"Stay," Morgan ordered the last seated man, pointing the revolver at his chest. "You can keep your junk and your money. We're here for the girl."

She was shrieking and cussing, her pretty face contorted and red with rage. "We're here from your father," Conley told her. "We're taking you home."

"That goddamn Nazi can go to hell!" She landed a right hook on Conley's cheek, and Morgan winced. That was going to leave a mark. She then picked up a baseball bat and retreated against the wall, brandishing it wildly to keep Conley away.

Morgan could tell Conley was at a loss for how to deal with the girl, and they had seconds before the rest of the bar was drawn to the screaming. He turned his attention to the man Conley had laid out, who was now trying to stand. Morgan pulled him up by his lapel and laid him on the table, money and bags of meth spilling on the floor. He was red-haired with finely freckled skin, and his green eyes were dazed and blinking from Conley's blow.

"Is this your boyfriend?" Morgan asked the girl, still holding him by the lapel.

Her anger now turned to Morgan. "Don't you lay a finger on him!"

"Then let's do this the easy way, all right?" Morgan said. She held up the baseball bat. Morgan took the middle finger of her boyfriend's left hand and pulled it back with a *crack*. This woke him from his daze and he screamed in pain, writhing on the table and clutching his hand.

"Now be good and come with us," said Morgan, "and I'll stop." He forced the boyfriend's palm against the table and wrapped his muscular hand against his ring finger. "Your choice."

She let the bat tumble to the floor and leaned over the red-headed kid. "Baby, are you okay?"

"He'll live," said Morgan. "Now come, or he might not." He looked at the kid, contorting in pain on the table, square in the eyes. "And *you*," he said. "Come after her and Daddy is going to do a lot worse than a broken finger, you hear?"

"Come on," Conley said, playing good cop. "We won't hurt you."

She let herself be led by Conley. Morgan took the lead out of the back room, the man's revolver in his right hand. He emerged to a bar where every single patron was frozen still, looking at him. The barmaid, standing behind the bar, had a shotgun with a sawed-off handle pointed at his chest.

"Honey, we're leaving with the girl," said Morgan, gun trained on the woman. "We didn't hurt anyone. Much. And we're not taking any of the drugs or the money. Let's not turn this into a bloodbath, all right? Same goes for everyone else in here."

There was a tense silence as Morgan took his first steps out, slow but showing no sign of hesitation. She kept the shotgun on him, and he kept the revolver on her. The room watched as Morgan traversed its length with Conley and the girl in tow. Morgan was by the door when someone cleared his throat.

"Anyone got something to say?" Morgan demanded, booming voice filling the bar. No one answered.

"Please carry on then," said Conley, and they walked out the door and into the chilly street. This seemed to wake up the girl, who struggled against Conley until he carried her and put her in the cramped backseat of the Shelby. Morgan tossed the gun into a water drain and got into the driver's seat. Conley got in the backseat with the girl.

"Get away from me," she spat.

"Sit tight," said Conley, and Morgan peeled out. "And buckle up. This guy's a maniac behind the wheel."

She struggled, kicking Morgan's seat back, and then, apparently realizing there was no good exit, Morgan saw through the rearview mirror, she sat back and cast down her eyes.

"Can I ask you something?" Morgan said. She showed no sign of having heard him. "What the hell has gotten into your head to get involved with some lowlife in a two-bit drug running operation?"

"What are you, my dad?" she said, looking out the window.

"No," said Morgan. "*Your dad* has more money than God."

"Like I can just get any whenever I want. He controls me like I'm under house arrest."

"And your way to prove him wrong is to carry meth for a worthless gangster of a brother?"

"Who said anything about proving him wrong?" she said. "I just wanted the money."

Morgan drove on the rest of the way to their meeting point, the empty parking garage of a certain downtown office building, where her father was waiting for her with a couple of burly bodyguards. Her old man, an industrialist whose name and face were recognizable to anyone who cracked open a *Wall Street Journal*, ordered her into his car. He nodded at Morgan and Conley, and took off without a word.

"You going home?" Morgan asked Conley as they settled back in the car.

"I'm on the clock all weekend," said Conley. "Just drop me at headquarters."

"You'll let me know if there's anything new on Raza, won't you?" Morgan put the car into gear and rode out of the garage.

"Believe it," said Conley. "Are you working today?"

"Nah, I've got a thing I'm doing with the kid," said Morgan. "I bet you're glad you never had any, after dealing with this daddy's little princess, huh?"

"Sure am," said Conley, but Morgan wasn't sure he believed it.

Chapter 3

"Our condolences are, of course, with our American allies," said Pakistani Foreign Minister Salman Mangi. "The brave men of SEAL Team Six did not deserve such a death."

US Secretary of State Lee Irwin Wolfe, sitting across from him at a bulky antique hardwood table with thick tapered legs, furrowed his brow in shared concern. From his corner, however, Diplomatic Security Service Agent Philip Lawson thought that he detected the hint of a scowl.

"I thank you for your sincere distress at our loss," said Wolfe, bowing his head, showing his balding scalp and hiding his boyish face from the view of Lawson, who was standing up, to his right. "We, for our part, regret the civilian casualties that resulted from the suicide bombing that occurred during the operation." He was going through the motions of the diplomatic gestures, but Lawson knew they were empty in either case. Regrets had been previously expressed, and this meeting was, as they were with Wolfe, about business. Wolfe's taut lips and his poise, leaning just slightly too far forward, betrayed his impatience. This time, they had skipped the meet and greet in front of the press with the flags and the fancy chairs. It was time for brass tacks.

"This is not good for the relations between our countries," said Wolfe, leaning forward, arms resting on the table. "In fact, this is very goddamn bad, Salman."

Lawson surveyed the room one more time. Standing with his back against a wall covered in gold leaf designs and making no sign of understanding any of the words that were spoken—his role was that of a fly on the wall, springing into action only if the Secretary's life were in danger. He did not expect trouble here, in the heart of the Ministry of Foreign Affairs, but paranoia was a healthy attribute of a man in his position. Three bodyguards present watched over the Foreign Minister, a heavy man with a trimmed and well-kept beard, temples graying but still sporting a full head of hair. He sat alone on his side of the table, facing Wolfe with round gold-framed spectacles, which he adjusted compulsively. Lawson had two of his guys against the wall behind the Secretary of State, who sat next to his Chief of Staff, Nadine Prince, who was taking notes on a yellow legal pad.

"We gave you permission to run this operation in our territory," said Mangi, throwing up his hands. "We have been more than friendly to our ally the United States in this matter. Tragedies aside, I do not see why this should negate what was an act of friendship on our side."

Wolfe's face contorted into a near scoff, but he seemed to check himself. "This is not the time to count feathers in your cap. Washington is not happy, and you need to think about how to make this right."

Mangi pressed his lips together in consternation. His tone was more than a little impatient. "We have been forthcoming with any intelligence we might have regarding the unfortunate events of this past week. We have given your people access to the scene." Exasperation built in his voice. "What more do you expect from us, Mr. Secretary?"

"A lot of people in your government have been less than friendly in talking about our country. Some might even say they've been inflaming the people's anti-Americanism. Do you think that's a fair assessment?"

"The people are angry, Mr. Secretary. They are angry at your country. That is no news to you or anyone in Washington."

"Government officials are fanning the flames," Wolfe pointed out matter-of-factly. Prince, at his side, noted Mangi's every reaction with sharp darting eyes.

"They are worried for their positions!" Mangi said, wiping the lens of his glasses with his sleeve and putting them on again. "Some for their lives. It does not pay to be pro-American in Pakistan. You were aware of the possibility of this kind of reaction to this mission. Do not tell me you were not. Now, are you really here to discuss public relations?"

Wolfe leaned back in his chair and took a deep breath. "How do you think Haider Raza knew we were coming?"

Mangi's eyes widened in surprise for only a split second, but Lawson noticed, and Wolfe would have, too. "Raza is a clever man," he said. "He has eluded all attempts to capture or kill him, and you know well enough the effort that has gone into that."

"I do know," said Wolfe. "The President knows, too. And we know that he has been two steps ahead of us at any given time. So tell me, how exactly has he managed to do that? Does he have supernatural powers?"

"I admit that sometimes it seems so," said Mangi, confused at the sudden turn in the conversation.

"Or maybe he's always two steps ahead of us because someone is tipping him off."

Realization seemed to dawn on Mangi's face, and then his forehead grew lined with dismay. "So you mean that you suspect one of ours has been passing along information to Raza."

"Not only me, Salman. The concern is shared among the Joint Chiefs. Your intelligence services have been compromised. Heads are going to have to roll over this."

"Whose heads?" said Mangi, adjusting his glasses on his face.

"It's time to draw battle lines inside your government," he said. "There are people on the side of the terrorists. People who are protecting Raza and enabling the Martyrs Brigade." Mangi made as if to speak, but Wolfe interrupted them. "Don't deny it." He pointed an accusatory finger. "Don't you dare goddamn deny it. Washington is tired of this, and so am I. We've been sinking millions in helping you deal with the Zafar Network and the Taliban, fighting them both in Afghanistan and here in Pakistan. Now, say we pull our resources from the Pakistani side—to respect your sovereignty, of course, and the right of your people not to be meddled with by Americans—and ramp up the pressure on the Afghan side. How many antigovernment terrorists are going to pour over to your side of the border?"

The Pakistani foreign minister drew himself up in alarm. "We have been loyal allies! We will not be threatened this way!"

"Consider this a test of your loyalty. Tell the President and the PM. It's time to get your ship in order." He assumed a businesslike, diplomatic manner as if by flipping a switch. "I think we're done here. Thank you for your time, Minister." Wolfe stood up and extended his hand.

Mangi shook his hand. "Thank you, Mr. Secretary. I shall relay your position to others in the government of Pakistan. I feel certain that we can come to some equitable agreement on the issue."

"I'm sure we will," said Wolfe.

Nadine Prince shook the Minister's hand as well, and both turned to go. Lawson walked behind them, forming the rear guard of his security detail. "Dovetail is on the move," he said into his comm. "Copy," came the voice of Agent Hemmer. The Secretary leaned to speak to Prince as he walked.

"What's your take?" he asked.

"Honestly?" said Prince. "Still what I told you before. Mangi's got no power to do anything about this, and I have serious doubts about the President and the Prime Minister, too. Not unless they get the generals on board. And I mean *all* of them."

"It's a start," he said. "Only an opening salvo. It'll be a long, drawn-out process. But we'll get results. Get in touch with the President and give him the thirty-second version."

Prince made the call as they walked through the low, drab hallway and into the indoor garage, where Hemmer was already waiting at the car, with the three other identical black sedans that made up the Secretary's convoy. He motioned the Secretary toward his vehicle, and settled into the passenger seat, thanking God for air-conditioning.

"Moving out," he said into the communicator. "Airport. Marsh, you take the lead."

As the cars pulled out into the street and the scorching sun, Lawson drew his sunglasses from his breast pocket, feeling the gun holstered under his suit jacket, and rested them on his ears and the bridge of his nose, brushing up against his forehead as he did so and finding it drenched in sweat.

Christ, it was hot.

It was a short drive to the airport, which they took with an escort of Pakistani motorcycle police. Wolfe and Prince conferred in low voices in the back as Lawson communicated constantly with his people in the other cars and at the airport, meanwhile keeping a watchful eye on the streets around them. The procession drew curious looks from people on the street. The grim thought came to Lawson that the curiosity would be replaced by rage if they knew who was in that car.

They pulled into the airport not twenty minutes after setting off. The Secretary's assistants had taken care of the paperwork so that by the time they arrived at their destination, the convoy was waved through the airport gates, bypassing all usual travel procedures and going straight to the tarmac, toward their plane.

The Secretary of State's Boeing 757, its US flag proudly displayed on the tail, was waiting there, glinting under the punishing sun.

"Nightingale," said Lawson into his comm to their people on the airplane, "approaching you now. Report in."

"We're ready for you, Oriole."

"Then let's get ready to blow this town," said Lawson. "Over."

"Amen," said the secretary from the backseat. Then, to Nadine Prince, "Ready to get out of here?"

The three cars in the motorcade drew to a halt near the airplane. Hemmer and Lawson opened their doors, then the Secretary's. Lawson heard a familiar whoosh that caught him in the pit of his stomach before his brain could properly process it.

Rocket.

Mayhem came swiftly after. He saw the projectile flying in from their left and broadsiding the car in front of them. The big sedan went up in flames, spewing thick smoke. Hot air hit him in the face. He shut his eyes reflexively, feeling them burn like he'd poured lemon juice on them. There was another explosion, and the vehicle behind them burst into a bloom of orange and black.

Lawson turned back to check on the Secretary when he heard the faint buzz a split second before it hit. He looked up just in time to see Agent Marsh's head erupt in a pink mist. Before he could react, two more agents were shot and dropped to the ground.

"Secretary, back in the car!

But Hemmer had already ushered him in. Lawson got back in the car and looked at the driver, Welch, who was slumped over the steering wheel. The back of his head was a bloody mess, and blood and brains dripped down the wheel and onto the floor. The word *sniper* had just formed in his head when Hemmer fell against the door, blood smearing and running down the window.

"Secretary, Ms. Prince, *down!*"

Lawson ran around the car, crouching down and moving erratically, hoping to avoid fire. He pulled Welch out of the car through the open door. The driver's body tumbled out onto the tarmac. Lawson climbed in as a bullet sailed inches from his head, hitting the window on the passenger seat. The window cracked into a spiderweb pattern. Keeping his head low, he pulled the door shut and peeled off, passing through the thick smoke of the wreckage of the car ahead of him.

"Need backup *now!*" he screamed into his comm.

He turned the car around, back toward the airport, and saw the two military Jeeps converging on the door to the building. Men in Pakistani civilian garb stood in their seats, faces covered by handkerchiefs, killing their way onto the tarmac with a barrage of Kalashnikov fire. Lawson made a sharp right.

"Hang in there, Mr. Secretary!"

Turning parallel to the airport building, he saw another two Jeeps ahead of him, approaching fast. He made a 180-degree turn, and the car drew to a halt at the point of convergence of four enemy vehicles. And then he heard the whipping sound of the sniper's bullet.

He hardly felt the impact on his neck, but blood gushed out almost at once. He put his hand up, trying to stanch it, while reaching for his gun with the other. The blood seeped out around his fingers, a torrent that couldn't be held back. He tried to talk to the Secretary, tell him to run, but a gurgling came out.

The car shook and Lawson heard the awful sound of warping metal. With all his strength he turned to see two men in face masks reaching inside the car. There were two gun reports, still deafening despite Lawson's fading senses. Nadine Prince clutched her abdomen as the bullet wounds stained her white blouse crimson.

"Come in, Deadbolt," said a voice on his comm, sounding so far away. "Report Status. Come in, Deadbolt, I repeat, come in."

The world darkened around him. The last thing he saw was Secretary Wolfe, hands tied and a burlap sack over his head, being manhandled into an enemy vehicle.

Chapter 4

May 27
Ashburn, Virginia

Philip Chapman opened his eyes to darkness with the first ring of his phone and picked up before the second so as not to wake Rose, his wife. He staggered to his feet and said in a hushed, groggy tone, "Chapman."

"You're gonna need to come in, Buck," said Cynthia Gillespie.

"What's new," he grumbled, pulling on the white button-down shirt he'd laid out before he'd gone to bed. "What's going on?"

"Secretary of State's been abducted in Islamabad."

"Jesus," he said, missing a beat.

"Lucky I was here, or it might have taken us hours before everyone on the team was notified."

"When are you not there?" he said. She was a confirmed workaholic, and would often stay at the office late into the night if she had caught on to any lead she thought might pan out. "I'll be right in." He pulled on his pants and leaned over Rose, kissing her forehead. The gesture was not without ambivalence. He still harbored anger from the screaming match they had the night before. He couldn't even remember what about, although it had devolved into the usual—he spent too much time at a grinding, thankless job.

He walked over to the crib, where baby Ella was sleeping. He touched his fingers to his lips and then to her head, and then ran his hand lightly over her wispy blond hair. She was growing. Soon it would be time for her to get her own bed, which meant her own room, which meant getting a new place.

The thought of fitting that into their budget gave him a sinking sensation, but the emergency at hand overrode everything else. As he put on his suit jacket and walked down the narrow staircase, he went over a list of organizations that might possibly be responsible. Grabbing a PowerBar in the kitchen, he went into the garage and got into his gray Corolla beater, a ten-year-old car that he had kept for more than just sentimental reasons.

As he pulled out onto the driveway, he took out his second cell phone, the one he'd been given for this very purpose, and dialed. The familiar voice picked up after three rings, level and deep, with no trace of drowsiness. "Smith here." The sheer impersonality of the voice, its all-business tone, always left Chapman slightly unnerved.

"Something's happened," said Chapman. He related the news to the man on the other line.

"Is that all you know?" he asked.

"Haven't even been in yet," said Chapman. "All I have is the bare outline. Thought I'd let you know right away. You'd better get your people on it."

"Thank you, Mr. Chapman," said Smith. "Call me when you have more. I will let you know if anything turns up on our end."

Chapman hung up and put away the phone. Leaking Smith sensitive information had become routine, so much so that he barely even thought about what kind of betrayal that entailed. But he was convinced that Smith was on the side of the angels, at least to the extent that anyone could be in this sordid business. As far as Chapman could figure out, Smith worked for, or maybe ran, a clandestine intelligence outfit, something called Aegis. So far, sharing information with them had been fruitful, but like with any asset, he kept himself at a distance, wary of how they used what he gave them.

Chapman consoled himself with the fact that he'd never taken a red cent from Smith, and never would, and then thought about Rose and Ella and felt terrible about it. He scrolled through the contacts on his phone as he made his way along the dark winding streets in the direction of CIA headquarters in Langley, wondering who he was going to call first. It was going to be a long day.

Chapter 5

May 27
Boston

Diana Bloch pulled into the parking spot next to the navy blue BMW 3 series—an older model, used but without a scratch on it. She had never seen it before, but then again, Smith hardly ever drove the same car for more than a week. The garage, which served a local mall, was sparsely occupied, which reduced chances of bystanders spotting them, but it was still full enough so that the two cars parked next to each other in the dark corner would not attract attention.

The driver's-side window of the BMW rolled down as her car came to a halt. At the wheel was *he*. The man with no name, no identity, who for his plain brown hair and blank face might as well have been an empty suit. Smith, he called himself. An alias, of course—although Bloch sometimes wondered whether it wouldn't be the ultimate joke if that were his real name.

"You're late," he said.

"It's six-thirty now," she said.

"If you arrive on time, you're late."

Christ. She was not in the mood. She said, in a cool voice, "If you're done being a prick, we can get to business. As I understand, there's something a little more important than my punctuality that needs our attention."

"The Secretary of State—"

"Kidnapped," she cut him off. "I heard. My sources are not quite as incompetent as you might think."

"Well, then you should have told me immediately," he said, in his stony, even voice.

"I assumed that's what this meeting was about, and it seemed redundant."

"Do not assume," he said. "What do you make of it?"

"What do you mean, what do I make of it? It's a catastrophe, that's what I make of it. It's enough to put everything else on hold. It's going to mean the mobilization of every intelligence operation between here and Islamabad. And if we don't get him back alive, this might very well mean war against a nuclear power."

"Then we'd best try to avoid that, shouldn't we?"

"Yes, we'd *best*," she grimaced.

"Don't be flip," he said. "Lee Irwin Wolfe is a *very* important man."

"I know, Smith, he's the goddamn Secretary of State."

"He's more than that," said Smith, leaving a pregnant pause that let Bloch know the significance of the statement.

Bloch's brow furrowed. "He's . . ." Clarity dawned on her. "He's involved in Aegis."

"The Secretary of State is operationally important to us," said Smith. "That is the extent of what you need to know."

"Are you kidding me?" said Bloch. "What if his kidnapping is connected to his involvement in Aegis? If you want me to find him, you're going to have to throw me a bone here, Smith."

"I'm sure that you will do fine with the extensive resources at your disposal."

She huffed through gritted teeth. "Fine. I've already called in the troops, and they should be coming in over the course of the morning. I haven't told them anything yet, but it doesn't matter. It'll be all over the news within the hour."

"It's a start," he said.

"I've sent Conley to Islamabad, too, although he's going to have a hell of a time getting there, with the airport closed. And he'll need credentials to access the scene."

"He'll have them. I will send you the rendezvous information within the hour so that you can relay it to him. Is *that* acceptable to you, Ms. Bloch?"

He didn't stick around for her answer. His tone would have been enough to tell her the conversation was over even if he hadn't rolled up his window and pulled out.

Chapter 6

Dan Morgan jogged up the hill, rifle slung on his back, boots sinking an inch into the soggy ground with every step, fresh, rain-washed air whipping his face. His right knee ached dully from an old injury that had never entirely healed. The woods around him were still, extending out, he knew, far past his line of sight limited by the foliage. Lots of places where she could be hiding, lots of directions to go in. But running wasn't her style—it wasn't *fun* enough for her.

He would find her. They'd played this game before, and he knew the way she played. She would go for the high ground, stake a defensive position. She had given away her position the previous night by building a fire, though she'd had enough sense to leave before he got there. Maybe she even meant for him to see it. She was smart, so it was plausible. But he was sure that she would go up the ridge and lie in wait. He got a few hours' sleep about a half-mile from the remains of her fire, and had awakened at the break of dawn to make his way up.

It took him the better part of an hour to get up to the top. The air was getting stale, and he was sweating. The woods thinned out and gave way to rocky ground ahead, out into the bright, blinding sun. He lingered behind the tree line, taking his rifle into his hands, and scanned the scene. She would be in a place that was easy to defend, a strong position with good visibility. An outcropping ahead was bordered by a grove on the far side.

Bingo. If she was up here, that's where she would be.

Morgan walked back into the woods fifty yards and circled

around toward the outcropping, taking slow, deliberate steps, moving his upper body as little as possible and keeping his attention open to any sound or stirring. He reached the point at which the gap between the woods and the grove was only some ten yards. He crouched and examined the scene. Everything was quiet. He looked down. The ground had been disturbed by footsteps, and flecks of dried mud speckled the rocky ground ahead. She had been there, and not long before.

He lay in wait for five minutes, and then ran across the open ground, hiding himself with his back flat against the trunk of a thick sycamore as soon as he reached the other side. He froze and listened again. Once he was satisfied that he hadn't been spotted and that she wasn't moving around him, he moved again.

He crept around the edge of the outcropping, along a smooth boulder that was about half as big as his house. The ground here was drier, and loose twigs and a few dead leaves crunched lightly under his feet. He skulked on, focused like a predator listening for its prey, treading as lightly as he could so as not to alert her of his presence.

He perked up at the crack of a breaking stick in the direction of a thicket of trees and bushes just ahead. A flash of camo moved through the foliage. He lunged forward, getting in position to flank the figure that he had glimpsed. When he reached a point where he could get a clear view into the thicket, he found her camo jacket there, tied to a long piece of twine hanging from a branch, swinging lazily from side to side. He had an instant of confusion as he looked at the jacket—one that proved fatal.

"Toss your weapon and put your hands up," he heard, a voice clear, commanding, and triumphant, coming from behind him. Exhaling, he complied, letting the rifle fall by his right foot with a muted clatter in the dirt.

"Gotcha," she said.

He couldn't help smiling. He turned and saw his daughter, Alex, grinning back at him, all brown-haired five-foot-three of her in a dirty moss-green T-shirt and holding up her paintball rifle, trained at his chest.

"That you did," he said, chuckling.

"Do you give?" she said.

"I—" but before he could finish, she had let loose two paint pellets, which hit him painfully in the rib cage. "Why, you little—" he said, with mock anger.

"Don't make me shoot you again," she said, laughing. "You lost, old man."

He picked up his rifle. "So that makes it what, two to six?"

"You're just bitter that you lost!" she teased. "Although, to be fair, I did learn it all from you."

"I don't remember teaching you that trick with the jacket," he said as she used her pocket knife to saw through the twine that held it to the log.

"But you did teach me to work with what I had. Not to mention misdirection, and using the environment to my advantage. It was all in your lessons." The twine gave, and she draped the jacket on her back.

"Look at you. Pretty soon you'll be as good as any of the pros."

"Well, then, maybe—"

"No," Morgan said curtly. He knew what she wanted—that she wanted to join the army, the Navy SEALs, or worse—the CIA.

"But Dad—"

"No buts," he cut her off. "That's out of the question. Now how about you tell me how you got the idea to rig that trap?" She made like she was going to protest, but didn't press the issue. The two of them climbed onto the tallest boulder of the outcropping, set their packs down, and ate jerky and granola bars while they exchanged their respective sides of the weekend's game, each trying to determine where the other had been at any given time, and whether there had been any close calls.

Afterward, father and daughter made the long trek back to the car together, talking animatedly as they went. Three hours later, when it was already past noon, they reached his Shelby GT 500, which was parked on the side of an old dirt road a couple of miles off the freeway. They were dead tired, and Morgan felt a satisfying ache in his muscles.

Morgan unlocked the car and sat down in the driver's seat. The first thing he did was to turn on his phone. There were about a dozen calls and half as many messages. His thoughts flashed to his wife, Jenny, but he didn't have to get past the first to find out that it was another sort of emergency altogether. The message was from Diana Bloch, time-stamped six hours before. It said, "We have a code red. Get your ass to the office right now."

Chapter 7

Buck Chapman rubbed his temples as he pored over transcripts of recordings from the Secretary of State's security team while at the same time listening to audio of preliminary eyewitness interviews obtained by Pakistani intelligence, but realized that his Urdu was not nearly up to the task. He called Cynthia Gillespie through the intercom. He saw her coming through the half-open blinds on the windows of his office. Behind her, the rest of the team was working, most at their computers, two putting pictures up on the corkboard. She walked in to find him grinding his teeth in frustration.

"You look like hell," she said. Chapman looked up from the sheet at her. She somehow looked the opposite of hell. Even though she had been in the office for at least twelve hours now, she looked alert and composed. While he was pasty with bags under his eyes and unkempt hair from lack of sleep, her dark brown skin looked as healthy as if she'd just had breakfast after a long night's sleep. Her black hair was pulled back into a neat ponytail, with not one hair out of place.

"Thanks," he said. He almost told her she looked beautiful, but held it in. She looked at him—she'd noticed his hesitation. "What can I do for you?" he added, and knew she had noted his haste in that, too.

"You asked me to update you every thirty minutes," she said with a smile.

"Right, right." He rubbed the rheum out of his eyes. "Can we talk while I get coffee?"

"I could use some myself," she said, motioning toward his office door.

He stood up. "Can we get a translator to transcribe the eyewitness accounts?" he asked. He was about to walk out the door when he doubled back to grab the mug off his desk.

"Agency translators are all backed up," she said, following him out the door. "Although I'm sure those are on the to-do list."

"Can we get freelance?" he asked.

"With security clearance?"

"Why not?"

They had a pot of coffee in the corner of the outer office, but Chapman was dismayed to discover that it was out.

"I can check," said Gillespie, taking notes on a small notepad. "You know, the first webcam was set up to monitor a coffee brewer, so that people would know whenever there was a fresh pot?"

"You'd think that would come standard nowadays. You know, I'm not in the mood to wait. Vending machine?"

"You got it." They made for the outer hallway. "We might be able to push this through, but *you* get to go upstairs and ask Carr."

"The webcam?" he asked, puzzled.

Gillespie laughed. "The translator, Buck. Jeez, you're really out of it, aren't you?"

"Oh, right," he said, scratching the back of his head. "I guess I am. Long day. Yeah, I'll do it."

"Also, we're not budgeted for that," she said.

"I'll use my discretionary fund. Hell, at this point, I'd be happy enough to pay out of pocket. How's the team doing? Any update on our status?"

"Well, Mel and Donna are monitoring online chatter," she said. "The extremist message boards and chat rooms are blowing up, of course. But so far it's all fantasy and speculation on that end. A lot of talk about executing the oppressor and bringing the American empire to its knees, but that's all it is. Talk."

"There's never anything good on chatter," he said. They turned into the alcove that held the vending machines. "And no idea who's behind this yet?"

"Nothing solid, but there's only one man we know who would have the cojones to pull off something like this."

"Haider Raza," said Chapman. He took a Styrofoam cup and set it on the machine.

"I'd put twenty-to-one odds on it."

"What are you having?" he asked her. "I'm buying."

"Oh, that's all right, I—"

"Don't be ridiculous," he said. "I said I'm buying."

"Espresso, then."

"Have we gotten a list of sensitive information that's been compromised by the abduction?" he asked, inserting his employee card and pushing the button. The machine whirred and rumbled. "Things the Secretary was privy to?"

"The interagency liaison is supposed to forward that to us, but they're dragging their feet on it. My guess is they need to sort through security clearances to figure out what's going where." The thick black liquid poured into her cup, and he handed it to her. He set another one and pushed the button for a cappuccino.

"You want some balls to go with that?" she said, sipping her espresso through a grin.

He flipped her the bird as he took his drink from the machine. "Meantime," he began as they walked, "fingers crossed that Raza doesn't get anything sensitive out of him in time to do something about it."

"Is there any word on the field team?" she asked. "This investigation is going to be a whole different animal once we've got boots on the ground." He took his cappuccino, and they started making their way back to the office.

"The field team's setting up shop over at the airport in Islamabad," he said. "We've got seven people on site so far."

"Is the Pakistani government being accommodating?" she asked.

"No complaints from any of our guys yet."

"What about our assets in the city?" she asked. There were other sources that the department cultivated in the city—a handful of policemen, government functionaries, a few businessmen who performed some key services, all handled by field agents.

"Scrambling," he said. "No word on anything useful yet. But who knows. Something might turn up. If anything does, it'll come straight to me."

They reached his office, and he sat down behind his desk. It suddenly seemed as though he were short of breath. He obviously showed it, because Gillespie had a worried look on her face.

"Buck," said Gillespie, walking toward him, her voice softening. "Are you doing okay?" She put her hand on his shoulder. It was warm and comforting.

"I'm fine," he said. "Just—another one of those days."

"I hear you," she said. She withdrew her hand and crossed her arms. "Do you need a nap or something? I'm sure the rest of us can cover you for fifteen, twenty minutes."

He stared at the middle distance, then said, "No, this needs my attention."

"There's no end of things that need your attention, Buck. You need to rest at some point."

"You don't, apparently."

She smiled her broad, pearly white smile. "Don't you think I take whatever naps I can whenever I can find the time? Why shouldn't you, too?"

"Can't," he said. "But thanks for the concern."

She shrugged. "Oh, hey, we're getting Chinese delivered. Wanna pitch in?"

He reached into the pocket of his jacket, which was draped on the back of his chair, and pulled out a crumpled ten. He tossed it on the table in front of her. "You know what I like."

"General Tso's. You got it." She took the bill and turned to leave.

"See what you can do about that translator!" he called out as she walked out his door.

He looked at his watch. Smith had called with a request earlier, and now it was time to follow through on it. He picked up his phone and dialed.

"This is Philip Chapman, Crisis Response Team Leader at Langley," he said, then sipped his cappuccino. It was still too hot. "Who am I speaking to?"

"This is Special Agent Pacheco."

"Listen, Pacheco," said Chapman. "I need a favor. I'm going to need you to put a name on your guest list. This does not go in the logs, you understand?"

Chapter 8

May 27
Boston

Dan Morgan pulled his Mustang into the garage of the Hampton Building in downtown Boston and went to the lowest level of the garage, to a northeast corner far from any stairwell or elevator. He got out, locked his car, and walked to an unassuming plain off-white door in the concrete wall, with a simple key card reader mounted on the wall next to it.

He swiped his card and was admitted into a pitch-black room. Once the door was closed, fluorescent lights came on, revealing a small chamber, all in concrete to match the parking lot, with a reinforced steel door ahead of him. He opened a breaker box next to the door, then unfastened the breaker panel via a hidden latch. The panel swung open to reveal a retinal and fingerprint scanner. He laid his hand on the panel then put his eyes up to the scanner. The machine beeped, and the door unlocked.

Morgan shivered as he entered the air-conditioned environment. There was a short, brightly lit corridor, wood-paneled and carpeted in a way that seemed to call for ambient Muzak. The corridor led to the top of a staircase which in turn led down into the War Room. The vast chamber, with its long conference table and walls lined with monitors, had three corridors going off into the various recesses of the facility, which took up several levels and the entire breadth of the building under which it had been built. There were offices, debriefing rooms, living quarters complete with kitchen and gym, and even an engineering lab for their genius-in-residence, Eugenia Barrett. This was the heart of Zeta Division, where everything came together. And above it all, opposite the big screen, up a curving flight of open steel and glass stairs, overseeing everything, was Diana Bloch's office, suspended from the ceiling and closed off by glass walls that could become opaque if she wanted them to.

Half a dozen people occupied the War Room. Of these, Morgan only knew three well. At the table engrossed in something on his laptop was Lincoln Shepard, their computer security wiz, pale like he rarely, if ever, saw the sun, with permanent red eyes, his blond hair standing up at every angle like he had just gotten out of bed, wearing jeans and a rumpled red T-shirt with some sort of old video game character on it.

Standing next to him and looking on his screen was Karen O'Neal, a lean, petite half-Vietnamese woman of about thirty, dressed, as usual, professionally but always, Morgan noted, with a casual flair. Talking at the foot of the stairs to her office was the capo herself, Diana Bloch. She was an impeccable woman, always dressed like she was going to meet the President, hair in a tight bun and always bearing an expression of steely professionalism. She was with Paul Kirby and a woman he did not recognize. The operation had grown significantly in the past year, and gave them a good deal more resources while still keeping the team small and agile. It had been a good year for them.

"Morgan." Bloch had spotted him, and was walking toward him. As she drew closer, Morgan noticed that her hair was not as precise as it had seemed, and she had bags under her eyes. "What took you so long?" He opened his mouth to speak, but she didn't let him, cutting in with the terse, clipped tone that she adopted whenever she was in a hurry. "Never mind, I don't care. Kirby," she said to the analyst who had followed her over, "fill him in. I need to check in with our contacts in Washington. Oh, and Morgan," she added, "this here is Louise Dietz. She's new. I'll let you make your own introductions. And don't go easy on her. She may be shy, but she knows what she's doing." Bloch walked off in the direction of Lincoln Shepard and Karen O'Neal.

"So, this is Louise Dietz," Kirby repeated, barely raising his eyes from the file he had in his left hand, waving his right in halfhearted introduction. Paul Kirby was one of the newcomers. His head was large and oval, with a receding hairline that only accentuated the effect, a thin pointed nose and small eyes that gave him a vaguely weasel-like aspect. He was meticulous and precise, which was in itself an asset in his work, but tended to rub Morgan the wrong way.

"Nice to meet you," said Dietz, shaking his hand, trying to hide her nervousness. She was slightly taller than Morgan, but she still had the body language of a scholar, quiet and introverted, with shoulder-length brown hair and plain clothes in muted colors that said that she groomed and dressed to be presentable but to call as little attention to herself as possible.

"Dietz does criminal psychology and profiling," Kirby said.

"Terrorism, mostly," she said. "I wrote my PhD thesis on Haider Raza."

"Well, you should feel right at home, then," said Morgan, raising an eyebrow.

"It's a trial by fire, of sorts," she said with a half smile.

"Hell of a first day." He turned to Kirby. "What did I miss?"

"Come on, walk with me. What do you know?"

"Only what was on the radio," said Morgan as they walked down a corridor, with Dietz following. "The Secretary of State's motorcade attacked in Islamabad. At the airport. Apparently there were explosions, and the Secretary of State is missing, but they've not been generous with the details. Whatever else there is, it's not being broadcast to the public."

"In here," said Kirby. He turned into an office and Morgan followed. It was a medium-sized office, windowless like the rest of Zeta, but with bright, yellow lights designed to mimic sunlight— something to do with making people more alert, according to Barrett. A printer, a scanner, and two monitors were neatly aligned on a desk that stood against the wall. He sat down on a leather-upholstered office chair, and motioned for Dietz to sit beside him.

Morgan pulled up a chair on the other side of Kirby. "We've got some preliminary surveillance footage," he said. "It came in through our CIA contact, from the team they have in place at the airport." He pulled the video up on the screen, black and white and jerky, showing a line of black cars moving along the tarmac toward a large airplane—Secretary Wolfe's convoy. "It's not exactly high-definition video."

"Not going to be easy to see anything useful in these," said Morgan.

"We might be able to get some better quality video from the local press, but for now, this is what we have. Watch. Here's when the first rocket hits." The rocket itself was a blurred blip on a single frame of video. Following that there was a bright flash of white on the lead car, which resolved itself into flames in about two seconds. "And the next." A few seconds after that, there was another flash—the third car was hit. "As you can see, this isn't a random attack. They knew which cars to hit, and which to spare."

"That spells leak," said Morgan.

"Maybe," said Kirby. "But I prefer to have all the facts before coming to a conclusion like that."

Morgan turned to Dietz. "What's your professional opinion?"

She stammered, drawing her hands to herself in alarm. "S-successful terror attacks tend to show a great degree of planning, but I think you're right in this case. The video seems to show that they have information they shouldn't be privy to."

"We're working on getting a list of people who had access to the details of the Secretary's protocols from the Diplomatic Security Service," said Kirby. "We're also getting regular updates from our contacts in the CIA, NSA, and Pakistani intelligence. I don't see any reason why we shouldn't let them do the heavy lifting on this."

"Not unless you want to make sure it's done right," said Morgan, still eying the video. A member of the Secretary's security detail had gotten out of the car and was taken out by a sniper.

Kirby ignored him. "No one has yet claimed responsibility, but—"

"But there's a name on everyone's mind," said Morgan. "Haider Raza. Do you think he'll claim the attack?"

"That's *assuming* he didn't take the Secretary just to extract whatever he could get out of him," said Kirby testily.

"Actually, information is probably not the reason they abducted him," broke in Dietz. She seemed to be surprised by her own boldness. She opened her mouth to continue speaking but faltered. She started up again, animatedly now. "The Secretary of State is at too high a level to have information immediately useful to a terror cell. He might know about general strategies, and maybe they get lucky if he has knowledge of a surprise attack, but mostly it would be useless to Raza. Usually, terrorists prefer targets that provide a tactical advantage. Commanders out in the field who will know about particular troop positions and movements—that kind of thing. With the Secretary of State, it's more likely that they will have demands."

She cast her eyes down, as though she suddenly remembered she was supposed to be shy. "At least that's what I think."

"I think you're gonna do fine here," said Morgan, impressed. "In any case, I wouldn't want to be in the poor bastard's shoes." Then, to Kirby, "So what can I do?"

"For now?" said Kirby. "Look at the tapes, and whatever else comes in. We could use expert eyes on everything we've got. That goes for you too, Louise. Plus, you want to know whatever you can if you're called on to spring into action. Meanwhile, we're working on getting our own man on the ground. Bloch tells me you know him. Guy named Cougar."

"You could say that I do," said Morgan. Code Name Cougar was Peter Conley's alias in the field.

"Is he good?" asked Kirby.

"Almost as good as I am."

Chapter 9

May 27
Over the Gulf of Oman

Peter Conley had not taken his eyes from his laptop computer as he traveled on the Cessna Citation X that had brought him from Yemen, where he'd been touching base with Zeta assets on the ground, looking into Raza's possible sources of funding. Updates came in constantly, compiled in real time by people at Zeta from their key people in various intelligence agencies.

Conley knew he looked incongruous in the luxurious aircraft, wearing his khaki shirt, denim, and sneakers, but he wasn't the type to dress up when he could avoid it. He certainly had no time to enjoy the amenities that the aircraft boasted—it was a loan from a Yemeni businessman friendly with Zeta—except maybe the wide, comfortable leather seats. And yet even those beckoned him to sleep, something he was craving after a few recent sleepless nights, but that was out of the question. The work he had to do now was too urgent.

From the bar fully stocked with the most expensive alcohol in the world, he only drank water and one cup of coffee on boarding. He barely looked twice at the statuesque, bored-looking blonde who was serving drinks—he wasn't rich enough to warrant the all-smiles treatment. Normally, he'd be planting the seeds that would get her to come back to his hotel room at their destination. Ruefully, he thought, casting a quick glance in her direction, there'd be no time for that today.

Instead, Peter Conley kept his eyes on the pictures of the site of the attack, which were already circulating in the intelligence community—official cars spewing heavy smoke, the ground strewn with dead bodies, blood darkening the tarmac, and the airplane, whose flames reached up to twice its own height. Two hours into his four-hour flight, the sun was already low in the sky, and the people on the ground had only begun to sort out all the evidence.

The President appeared on TV and made the official announcement to the nation. Conley followed the closed captioning, the video on silent. The speech was short and dry, stating that the Secretary of State had been abducted by unknown terrorists, and that the entire US Intelligence community was mobilizing en masse in response to the crisis.

New information was coming in at a trickle, and nothing much worth noting, so he spent most of the rest of his time on the plane catching up on the latest developments of the major players in Pakistan. He struggled to keep awake as time ticked by slowly, until something came up on his screen. A video, taken by a member of the press that had been near the airplane when the convoy was approaching. It showed the cars coming near, and then jolted from the explosion on the airplane.

The videographer took cover, the camera bucking wildly as he ran, but then he turned back to the scene. It focused on the attackers' Jeep—the closest one, then another, off to the right. It showed as they pursued the Secretary's car and mowed down several of the Diplomatic Security Servicemen. Some of them shot back, however, managing to take cover from sniper fire near the burning airplane. As the attackers left their Jeep to take the Secretary, two were shot as they ran toward the car, then a third straggler was shot going back. It cut off a few seconds after they disappeared out of the airport. Conley watched the video carefully, again and again, taking note of every detail, as the sun dipped in the sky and evening approached.

The Cessna touched down on a private airfield outside Islamabad. The main airport had been shut down following the attack. Conley knew it had taken significant connections to secure even this landing—if he'd been less lucky, he might have ended up in Peshawar or Nowshera, both at least an hour and a half away from the Pakistani capital.

Harun Syed, a local asset with whom Conley had worked before, was already waiting for him on the edge of the runway. They embraced like old friends. Conley had this effect on people, an ability to make people like him almost instantly, which was one of his greatest advantages as a field operative. They walked together to Harun's car, an ugly, boxy silver Daihatsu, and set off on the congested N5 National Highway toward the airport.

"So, what is the word?" asked Harun, in English. He was a balding man, almost forty, with a handsome, friendly face, a close-cropped black beard and thick eyebrows that almost met in the middle.

"You tell me," said Conley. Harun worked for the FIA, the Pakistani version of the FBI, in their counterterrorism division. His working with Conley was tacitly condoned by his superiors, as Conley made sure to supply them with morsels of valuable intelligence from time to time—the kind that was mutually beneficial to share, of course.

"Our headquarters is in a panic," said Harun "The Americans are breathing down our necks. Accusations are flying free. They think our government had something to do with the abduction."

"And did you?" Conley asked. Harun's lips grew taut and he tightened his grip on the wheel.

"Do you think I would stand silently by as my country committed suicide by doing this? No, Cougar. There is no great government conspiracy."

"That you know of," Conley pushed.

"I would know of it!" he exclaimed. "Look, we are giving you Americans free rein to conduct your investigations in our country. We want to know who did this as much as any of you. We have nothing to hide." Harun looked forward, fuming at the suggestion.

Conley sighed. It was no use alienating him. "I'm sorry, Harun. I had to ask."

"Of course you did," he said. "You're an intelligence asshole, just like me." He laughed, the tension between them dissipating.

"Not as big an asshole as you, though," said Conley, chuckling. "How is your wife?"

"A mother, and I a father!" he said with pride. "A little girl. Najiya."

"That's great news, Harun. Congratulations!" He patted the Pakistani on the shoulder. "We need to celebrate."

"After the mission," he said.

"And what is the mission?" asked Conley. "I thought you were just dropping me off."

"What am I, your driver?" said Harun. "Not a chance. I am coming with you. You are stuck with me, my friend."

They passed rows of palm trees along the darkening road. Then Harun asked, all the energy and enthusiasm gone, "Do you think there will be war?"

"If they find any evidence that someone—and I mean *anyone* at all—in your government was involved in this, all bets are off. Next year's an election year, and hawks win elections. Rhetoric's going to fly high, and candidates are going to try to one-up one another. All politics is going to be pushing the President to war. At the very least, heads will have to roll."

"Supposing there *is* someone in the government involved," Harun said grudgingly, "it is entirely likely they would be protected by certain powerful factions in our nation."

"Then let's make sure we do our job right," said Conley.

It was night by the time they arrived at Benazir Bhutto International Airport. They elbowed their way past the press, national and international, many of whom had camped out outside the airport. They kept a respectful and prudent distance from the cordon of armed guards, whom Conley and Harun approached. Harun flashed his identity and spoke quietly to the guard, then motioned for Conley to approach.

"Someone's coming to admit us to the scene," said Harun. "Let's see if your people managed to get you a ticket inside." It was several minutes before the contact appeared, a heavyset, dark bearded man with a stiff, suspicious face. He and Harun exchanged a few words in Urdu, identifying themselves. Then the man said, looking at Conley, "And who is the American?"

"Peter Brewer, CIA Counterterrorism Center," he said, flashing his ID for that particular alias. He used his real first name—common enough not to give him away—in order to avoid blowing his cover. A person's reaction to his first name is deeply ingrained, and could be enough to tip off an enemy to the false identity.

"Naseer Awan," said the man. "FIA. Come with me, I'll take you to where the Americans are coordinating."

"I didn't schlep all the way out here for you to tell me what I can see on a computer screen," said Conley. "Roger wants eyes and ears that he trusts on the ground," he said, referring to the head of Counterintelligence by his code name.

"I've already given the CIA man the tour," he said. "Your people are setting up in there. You can coordinate with them, and they can give you the information you need."

"I don't play well with others," said Conley. "And I'm not here to work with the other suits."

"All right, all right," Awan said, waving his hand for them to follow. "Whatever you say. Come in, I can show you around."

They walked toward the site of the attack. The air grew acrid with suspended smoke as they approached, and Conley's eyes watered. He heard intermittent coughing around them, and felt the tickle in his own throat. The fire from the airplane was still smoldering, and the tarmac was blackened in various spots. Enormous floodlights lit up everything, while dozens of men bustled about, scouring every inch of the area. Awan led Conley and Harun through the scene.

"Here is the Secretary's car," he said. It was in largely good shape, structurally, but for the broken window on the passenger's side and the back door, which was bent where it had been forced open. The front seats and passenger's-side window, however, were covered in blood.

"They came prepared," said Conley, pointing to where the Secretary's door had been pried open. The thick metal had been bent. "Hydraulic tools. These guys knew exactly what they were doing." He turned to Awan. "Have you found where the snipers were located?" asked Conley.

"Two spots along the roof," said Awan. "We found the mats they left behind. Nothing significant, apart from their locations."

"How'd they get up there?" Conley asked.

"Surveillance showed they got in dressed as maintenance workers. You can check that out with your people."

"Do you have any idea if they got any inside help?"

"All airport personnel have been taken aside for questioning," Awan said, pissy at the implication. "As you see, gentlemen, there isn't too much here," he said. "You can wait for forensics. They will be able to tell you more. Meanwhile, the surveillance video has already been turned over to all investigating agencies, including the CIA."

"Can I talk to the survivors?" asked Conley.

"They have already been removed to the embassy," said Awan. "Speak to your own people if you wish to have access to them."

"How about the attackers?"

"We've laid them out over here. Come on." Morgan and Harun followed him a few dozen feet where two bodies lay on the ground in open body bags. They were young men, one bearded and the other clean-shaven. Their clothes were simple, typical for the city and well worn.

"No identification, of course. No personal effects, except cheap digital watches. We are running them through every database we have. I believe the CIA is doing the same."

"Where's the third?" asked Conley.

Awan looked at him suspiciously. "Where did you hear about a third?"

"I saw video of the abduction," said Conley. "Three men were left behind. Do you know where he is?"

"He was alive," said Awan. "He was sent to the hospital."

"That wasn't in the field reports," said Conley. "Why wasn't this shared with the other agencies? Having a living witness would have—"

"He died," cut in Awan. "On the way. In the ambulance."

"Was he gravely injured?" asked Conley.

"The first people on the scene did not think so," said Awan. "He did not go in the first ambulances, which were reserved for the victims, specifically those more gravely injured. But perhaps it was worse than they thought."

Conley frowned. Important as victims were, having one of the attackers alive in their hands could lead them to the people behind this—and to the Secretary. "Do you know where his body was taken?" he asked. "I'd like to get a picture and an autopsy report."

"That information will be shared with the agencies in time," said Awan.

"Maybe I can get a head start if I—"

"I have things to do now if you don't mind, gentlemen. I suggest you check in with your people and ask them for whatever you need from now on." Awan walked away, motioning to an investigator who was leaning over the Secretary's car.

"So what do you make of it?" asked Harun once Awan was out of earshot.

"The attacker. The one who survived. I'm not buying the story on his death. There's something about it . . ."

"Do you think Awan was lying?"

"I don't know." Conley rubbed his chin between his thumb and index finger. "But someone is. There was one living person left here who could tell us who was behind this. One key to finding the Secretary. And that person conveniently died before anyone got to interrogate him."

"You are grasping at straws, my friend," said Harun. "There is no significance to his death. Just a man who took a little longer to die than the rest."

"Say what you like, Harun, but I've got a hunch. How many people to an ambulance in the city?"

"Islamabad? Could be three, I don't know, but for an emergency like this? It is probably just the driver and a paramedic."

"Then we need to find them," said Conley. "Yesterday."

"That's a lot of work for a hunch," said Harun.

"I've been at this a long time, Harun. You know what it's like when you get that feeling. Like you just *know* you have a lead. You *know* which way you need to go."

"It will take hours, Cougar. And these are hours we cannot spare."

"If I'm right, then we have even less time to track them down," Conley insisted. "The Agency boys have the other bases covered. Look, you can argue with me, but I'm gonna do this."

"You're as stubborn as a mule, you know that?" said Harun. "Of course I'm coming with you. Let's see what to make of this *hunch,* then, shall we?"

"Let's," said Conley. "And let's move fast. I get the feeling that those guys aren't going to last very long."

Chapter 10

May 28
Andover, Massachusetts

Morgan drove home to his sleepy suburban neighborhood well past midnight. He was a wreck. He'd hardly gotten any sleep during his game with Alex, and then had spent a grueling, frustrating day going over intel that led nowhere and making phone calls that got him nothing.

He parked his Shelby Mustang on the driveway and got out of the car. A cool, soothing breeze riffled his hair, and the moon and stars were bright in the cloudless night sky. He looked up, feeling some of the frustration flow out of his body as he breathed deeply. He then turned toward the house.

Through the window, out of the corner of his eye, he saw a faint bluish light coming from the living room, like from a computer or TV screen. His thoughts turned to his wife, Jenny. She'd often stay up waiting for him when he was out late, no matter how many times he asked her not to worry, to go to bed. He felt a twinge of guilt. She had known about his work as a spy for years, and she had come to support him and believe in what he did.

Still, fiercely loyal and strong as she was, she had a sensitive soul. It was part of her strength, the way she could lend comfort to people in need—the way she could make Morgan himself feel whole and fully human while working in a business that could be dehumanizing. All the same, it was something that he knew caused her more than a little suffering.

Morgan walked into the garage and opened the kitchen door. His German shepherd, Nieka, gave him her usual enthusiastic greeting.

He ruffled the fur on her neck and petted her head. He walked into the warm kitchen, which had been put together by Jenny, who was an interior decorator, to be elegant and at the same time cozy. It was always the first place he walked into when he got home. The copper pots hanging from the wallpapered walls and the old-fashioned white cabinets were a welcome sight.

Nieka followed him to the living room, where he found not Jenny but his daughter, Alex, sitting on the couch in pajama pants and T-shirt, hair up in an unfussy ponytail, her face lit up by her laptop computer.

"Hey, kid," he said. "What are you still doing up?"

"Couldn't sleep," she said, setting her computer aside and crossing her skinny legs on the couch. "To be honest, I hit the hay pretty hard when we got back in the morning. But I saw the news about the Secretary online when I woke up, and now . . . I just keep thinking about what's happening, you know? I keep looking for the latest news online." She motioned her head toward the computer. "That, and what people are saying about it."

Morgan sat down on an ottoman facing her. He understood. The pundits had been crawling over themselves, speculating about the events, its causes and outcomes. Not that he ever read any of it—you'd get better predictions flipping a coin than listening to any of them. "Are you scared?"

"No. I mean, not for myself. I know things might get ugly, that there might be more to come, but I can handle myself. And things are safe here at home. At least for now. Right?" This last word came with a sudden tone of insecurity. "But I—I mean . . ." she continued. "I know you're out there, doing your part, and I feel so helpless here. I just feel like I maybe I could be doing something, anything, to help out. Like I should be."

"Alex, it isn't your time yet," said Morgan. He drew the ottoman closer to her, so that she was within arm's length. "I understand how you feel, you know, kiddo? That feeling like you've got to take action. It's been that way for me all my life. Jesus, you really are my daughter, you know?" He grinned and put his arm on her shoulder. She smiled back. "But you can't rush thing sort of thing. Your time will come, I promise. Right now, you need to focus on staying sharp and getting strong, because you will be needed. We need kids like you to be better adults than us in the future. But for now, it's for others to take care of. People who are prepared. Trust me."

"I do, Dad," she said, looking away. "I always do." He didn't buy it.

"All right, kid. Go get some sleep. It's late." He embraced her and gave her a kiss.

"You too, Dad. Are you going out again tomorrow?"

"Before you wake up, probably," he replied, standing up with a slight grunt. "We're in crisis mode I might have to stay over a few nights after tonight, depending on how it goes."

"Do you think you might have to go away? Like, overseas?"

"It's a possibility," he said.

"You'll come say good-bye if you do, right?" Her voice was faltering. He knew what kind of good-bye she was afraid of.

"I'll be back before you know it, kid. And I'll call you tomorrow, okay?"

"Okay," she said, trying to conceal the fact that she was tearing up. "Good night, Dad."

Morgan crept upstairs and opened the door to his room. The lamp on Jenny's side of the bed was lit. She was asleep, propped up on her pillow with an historical novel resting on her chest, reading glasses balanced on the tip of her delicate nose and her short brown hair fallen over her closed eyes. The careless way in which her bathrobe exposed her legs and just a sliver of her red panties made him bite his lower lip. God, that woman. She stirred as he walked toward the bed, and her eyes fluttered open.

"Dan." Her voice could somehow combine tenderness, pain, and reproach, all at once.

"Hi, honey. How're you doing?" He leaned down and kissed her soft lips.

She kissed him back and sleepily pushed herself up and sat back against the headboard, rubbing her eyes. "All right. A bit tired, I guess. How are you?"

"Pooped," said Morgan. "Hell of a day. It's shaping up to be one of those weeks."

"One of *those?*" she asked pointedly, and he knew exactly what she meant. She was asking if he was going to go off on a mission, put himself in danger.

"I can't say," said Morgan. "We'll have to wait and see."

She winced. They'd had this argument too many times before. She did understand the importance of what he did, why he persisted even at great risk of injury and death. But while she accepted it, she sure didn't like it. "Alex has a pretty bad case of poison ivy," she said. "Plus a few ugly scratches. Dan, I swear, I don't know what you two get up to out there."

"Just a bit of fun," he said, going into the bathroom to wash his face. "Nobody ever died from a little poison ivy."

"Dan . . ." she admonished. "And that motorcycle you bought for her . . ." Alex had pleaded with him for a motorcycle for the better part of a year. A month ago, Morgan relented and took her into town to the dealerships. She spent the better part of the day test-driving every model, but finally settled on the Ducati Streetfighter. Morgan had never seen her so happy in his life as when she was tearing out of the lot on her new bike, leaving him to trail behind in his car. Jenny, on the other hand, had not been pleased. "I'm afraid she's taking after you in the worst way, Dan. All this risk-taking. Thrill-seeking, even. It makes me sick with worry."

"The girl is *fine*," he said, toweling off as he walked back into the room. "She's tough. She can take care of herself."

"She's saying she doesn't want to go to college now." Jenny said it as if Alex were running off to join the Hell's Angels.

"Is that right?" he asked.

"Dan . . ."

"What?" he asked. "She doesn't need to go to college if she doesn't want to. Plenty of people don't, and they do just fine."

"They end up unemployed or at dead-end jobs."

"Or they end up owning their own companies and becoming millionaires," said Morgan. "Let her find her thing. A girl like that? Not having a college degree isn't going to hold her back from anything she wants to do. And if she ends up wanting to become a doctor or something, she can always go back."

Jenny looked miffed. "I don't want you encouraging this sort of thing. It won't end well, I know it."

"Let her learn that her actions have consequences, then," said Morgan. "That's a more important lesson than anything she'll learn in college."

"She's not you, Dan. I think sometimes you forget how young

she is. And how sensitive, deep down. I'm glad you two are bonding and having fun together, I really am. But couldn't you go fishing or something, for once?"

"She's old enough to make her own decisions, Jen."

"Is she? She's eighteen. I'm not saying she's not mature. But you don't have to encourage this kind of thing."

"Why not, if that's what makes her happy?" asked Morgan. "I always did, and look where it got me."

She cast him a sharp sidelong glance. "That's exactly it, Dan. It's hard enough having *one* of you in my life. All I need right now is another member of this family to worry myself sick over. But let's not talk about it, okay? I just want to be near you."

Morgan fell asleep with his wife in his arms. For that moment, at least, everything was right in the world. In the morning, he would rejoin the fray.

Chapter 11

Alex Morgan had set her alarm for 3:30 in the morning. Her eyes opened when it rang, and she deactivated before it had rung twice. Getting out of bed, she pulled on the sweatpants and T-shirt she had laid out the night before. She didn't know when her father would leave, so she lay in her bed, listening for signs of stirring in the house. She took the opportunity to browse the news on her phone. Every outlet was blowing up with stories about the abduction of the Secretary of State. Alex hadn't known much about the man before, but there was no lack of information now.

Secretary of State Lee Erwin Wolfe had been a hero of the Gulf War, collecting medals and, more important, the respect of his men and of his superiors. He'd been conducting his duties as Secretary of State with his characteristic boldness and self-assuredness. His tenure had so far been effective in garnering cooperation from many countries to hunt terrorists and other enemies of the United States. He was friendly when possible, tough when necessary. He was one of those rare figures who was admired on both sides of the aisle.

Alex remained under the covers reading the news until her father got up at five. She heard the sounds of the shower first, then of him going downstairs. After a few minutes she heard the rumble of his car's engine pulling out of the driveway and moving down the street.

She didn't hurry—she didn't need to. She knew her father was going to take I-93 down to Boston, so she might as well catch up with him there. Plus, she didn't want him to spot her tailing him through the narrow suburban streets that led to the highway. She waited for two minutes to elapse—she had been training herself to count time in her head, and was within twenty seconds when she checked her phone—and then walked downstairs, treading lightly so as to avoid waking up her mother.

She made her way to the garage and got on her Ducati Street-fighter. It was a graphite sports cycle, sleek and aerodynamic, and it felt bulky and powerful between her legs, like a thoroughbred horse she had once ridden on a trip she'd taken with a friend. Her father had given her a pink helmet to wear, which Alex suspected he did precisely so that he could spot her if she ever tried to do what she was planning at that very moment, but Alex had secretly bought a second helmet, all black, for the exact opposite purpose.

She took the black helmet out of its hiding spot in a box of her old stuffed animals. She then unhooked the chain from the garage door motor and pulled it open, revealing the gray light of dawn outside and letting in a gust of chill air that broke against her leather jacket. She guided the bike out, closed the garage door, and walked it about one hundred yards from the house. Satisfied that doing so would avoid waking her mother, she hopped on and turned the ignition.

The bike rumbled underneath her. She set out, slowly at first until she was far enough from the house, and then she unleashed.

Alex Morgan's experiences had taught her to use the phrase *life-changing* carefully, but getting the motorcycle nearly justified it. She loved her newfound mobility, the speed and flexibility of the vehicle. Sometimes she'd take the motorcycle out on the highway at night to see how fast she could go. She was working up to asking her father for stunt-riding lessons (asking her mother would have been a waste of breath), but in the meantime she had to be content with looking up videos and instructions on the Internet and trying them out in empty lots and deserted country roads.

Alex cut corners and pushed the throttle as far as she could while making the curves until she reached the highway. There, she matched her speed to the fast lane, keeping an eye out for her father. She spotted his Mustang by its stripes and slowed down to keep a safe distance from him. Lately, he'd been teaching her how to tail a car without getting seen, and she applied the principles he had taught her

He had, of course, warned her against doing this very thing, but curiosity had gotten the best of her. She wondered about where he worked, what exactly he did. She fantasized about going on missions both with him and alone. Also—and she had taken after him in this way—she wasn't the sort to take that kind of warning to heart.

When her father, in the Shelby, signaled and took the off-ramp to downtown Boston, she followed suit, making careful mental notes of each of the turns he took. Eventually, she turned a corner and saw his car disappear into a building's garage. She found a parking spot on the street and dismounted in time to see the garage door begin to descend.

Leaving her helmet with the motorcycle, she ran to the door and crouched, squeezing under it into the garage. There was an additional gate for cars that didn't keep pedestrians out. She sneaked farther in, running along the wall and down a ramp. She followed the faint growl of her father's muscle car reverberating through the garage, then the *tut tut tut* of idling, and then the noise cut off. He had parked.

Alex continued downward. Halfway down the ramp to the third floor underground, the wall ended in an opening to her right. She stood flat against a corner and peered out into a seemingly forgotten parking sconce that fit maybe twenty-five cars. She saw her father shutting the door to the Shelby. He walked to a nondescript door in the corner and disappeared into it.

Bingo.

Alex ran back up to street level. She found a button to open the garage door and walked out into the brisk early morning air. Very satisfied, she got back on her motorcycle and rode away, the roar of the motor echoing between the sheer faces of tall buildings. She had found the place. For the time being, that would be enough.

Chapter 12

"This is it," said Harun. He turned the Daihatsu into the parking lot of a low-cost apartment block, not a mile away from one of the city slums. It was a dark night. Working streetlights were few and far between, and there was no one to be seen out on the street.

"Are you sure?" asked Conley.

"That's the address for Parvez Nutkani." Harun had made some phone calls to the city hospitals. It took him three hours, but he got the names of the driver and the emergency responder who had been in the ambulance that carried away the injured attacker. An additional call had gotten their addresses.

"He is in building number four," Harun added. It took them a few minutes to determine which building was which. It was dark, and the numbers that weren't missing were hardly visibly placed. Luckily, there was no security to speak of, and they had the run of the place. Still, the whole operation was sloppy and rushed. They might have waited to get together a tactical team and run a well-organized op, but in a race against time, Conley knew you had to work with what you had. And what they had was just the two of them in a Daihatsu beater.

Harun found a spot and parked, and they skulked along the shadows to the outer gate to the apartment building. Conley slipped his lock-pick tools from the pocket of his khakis. He inserted the lock pick and the torsion wrench. His fingers moved deftly as he nudged the pins into place, getting the lock open in just under twenty seconds.

He opened the gate and stepped aside to let Harun in. He put in a piece of duct tape to keep the gate from locking behind them and pulled it shut. They walked up the stairs as fast as they could without being audible to any of the residents. They stopped at the landing of the fourth floor and crept to the door of their quarry's apartment.

"You're sure he lives alone, right?" whispered Conley, pulling out his tools once more and inserting the torsion wrench into the lock, working as quietly as he could.

"That is what his file said," Harun responded, shrugging.

The lock gave, and Conley very slowly turned the knob. He pushed it open, and then met with a sudden resistance. There was a security chain on the door. Conley took two short paces back, drew his gun, and kicked the door in. He took the lead and ran inside, with Harun close behind him.

It was a small apartment, dark except for the dim yellow light coming in from the streetlights outside. They were in a combination kitchen and dining room. There were two doors, and one led to a bathroom. Conley ran ahead to the other, to the bedroom, which he opened and found Parvez Nutkani, young, wiry, with longish hair on his head and no hair on his face, wearing tan cotton pajamas that were moist with sweat. The man woke up with a start, eyes wide, looking around like a terrified animal. Harun talked to him in Urdu.

"Stay. Do not move. We will not hurt you if you cooperate."

Conley clicked on the light. The room was cramped, with a narrow single bed in its center. There, Nutkani lay cowering, wide-eyed. Harun had his gun pointed straight at the man's face a few inches away.

"Will you keep still?" Harun asked.

"I will," Nutkani responded weakly, in Urdu.

"Good," said Harun, lowering his gun, but making sure to keep it in Nutkani's line of sight. "We just want to ask you some questions."

This seemed to make Nutkani even more nervous, but he didn't move. His wide eyes remained fixed on the gun. "What—what do you want to ask me about?"

"You were in the ambulance that took a man from the airport today after the attack," said Harun. "Is that correct? Yes or no is enough."

"Yes," he said.

"Was the man one of the ones who took the American Secretary of State?" asked Harun.

"Yes," Nutkani stammered.

"How did he die?"

The man's face seemed to sink. He must have expected the question, but there was obviously something there. He was terrified, and but he wasn't looking at the gun anymore.

"I, uh . . . he was wounded when we picked him up." His voice was shaking. "He bled out in the ambulance. There was nothing we could do to save him."

"Do not lie to us," Harun said. "If you lie to us again, we will kill you. Did the patient you were transporting die from the gunshot he took during the attack?"

Tears welled up in Nutkani's eyes. "Please. Please. Don't make me talk."

"There is something to say, then?" asked Harun.

"Please," he said, crying, the pitch of his voice rising. "They will kill me. They will kill my parents. Please don't make me talk."

"You won't convince me to let you go," said Harun. "The best chance you have now to survive is to tell us everything you know, and pray to Allah that we find the people who are threatening you before they come to kill you."

"Please," he said.

"My friend here?" said Harun, motioning with his head toward Conley. "The one who looks foreign? American. He's *CIA.* Maybe I can give you to *him,* and we can see what you tell him. And then you spend the next twenty years in Guantanamo Bay, if you are *lucky.* Now, start talking. Did you kill the prisoner, Nutkani?"

"I—I did not," he said, still trying to hold back his tears. "I did not kill him myself."

"Tell me what happened," Harun commanded him, his voice menacingly cold.

"We were hailed by an official vehicle," he said. "The driver pulled over and the back door was opened. I was ordered at gunpoint to get out of the ambulance and turn away. The driver, too. Afterward, they told us to get on our way and left. When I got back into the ambulance, the man was dead. Suffocated, I believe."

"Who did this?"

"I do not know," he said. "They were two men with handguns. They were dressed in suits. They looked like government types."

Conley shot Harun a glance, but the Pakistani did not look up from the man on the bed. "Can you describe them?"

"I do not know. They looked normal. Clean-shaven. One had his hair slicked back."

"You'll have to do better than that," said Harun.

"Please!" He cried, his hands linking in a supplicating gesture. "I do not know! It happened very quickly, and I could not see his face well! There is nothing more I can tell you!"

Harun looked up at Conley, and Conley gestured toward the door

"Do not tell anyone we were here," said Harun. "We know where you live, and we will come back for you if you tell anyone."

Connor and Harun slinked out of the apartment and walked downstairs. Conley pulled the duct tape from the outer gate as they exited. They were halfway to the car when Conley spoke.

"Now do you accept there are elements of your government involved?"

"Bastards," Harun said with pure hate. "Sons of a whore!"

"We need to find whoever is behind this, or there could be war."

"I will find him and kill him," Harun said. His pace picked up with the intensity in his voice.

"Easy there," said Conley. "Slow down. Whoever it is, we need to focus on finding the Secretary first. That's our number-one priority. Things can still be salvaged if we find the Secretary alive. But if we don't—"

"We will find him," said Harun. "We have a lead."

"Well, it's not a lot to go on. All we have is two men—"

"And a government car," said Harun. "If we find the ambulance driver, perhaps he will give us enough information to track down—" He stopped short, his eyes focusing somewhere over to Conley's right. "Quick, into the shadow!"

Conley heard the car approaching before he saw it. It was coming in fast, tires squealing as it turned a corner in the apartment complex parking garage. They walked into the shadow of a nearby tree, which in the lack of electric light enveloped them in pitch-black. Conley strained to see the car. Its green license plate told him that it was a government vehicle. The car came to a screeching halt in front of Nutkani's building. Two men emerged from the car carrying semiautomatic rifles. They stopped at the gate. It took them a minute to open it and disappear inside.

Conley and Harun looked at each other, and knew what was happening. They ran after the men, retracing their previous steps, and through the gate, which had been left open. Conley stopped Harun before he started up the stairwell, and pointed to his shoes.

"Take them off."

Conley hastily undid the knots on his bootlaces and pulled them off. They sprinted up the stairs, Conley taking the lead. The tiles were cold beneath his feet, and he almost lost his footing twice in his hurry. He could hear the footsteps of the men above, at least two floors above Conley and Harun.

Without shoes, they were moving silently enough that they wouldn't be heard. They pressed on, two steps at a time, Conley's legs burning with the effort after two flights. The pattern of the footsteps above changed, and Conley knew they had reached the fourth-floor landing.

There was a loud crash upstairs—*that would be the door being kicked in,* Conley thought. Seconds later, Conley and Harun reached Nutkani's floor. Just as they made the landing, Conley heard four shots coming from a poorly suppressed handgun. *Too late for poor Nutkani,* he thought.

Conley tapped Harun, who had obviously heard it, too, to get his attention. He motioned toward the door to the apartment, and then positioned himself on one side of it. Harun stood on the other side, a tactical knife in his right hand.

They didn't have to wait too long. The first man emerged from the door, looking straight ahead, in too much of a rush to notice the two standing flat against the wall. As soon as the second came out the door, Harun grabbed his head and slit his throat ear to ear. Lunging forward, Conley caught up with the first man and kicked in his left leg while reaching forward and grabbing for his gun. The man cried out and contorted in pain. Conley relieved him of his gun as the man tipped over and fell on the tiled floor.

"Cougar," said Harun. "There were gunshots. Someone will have heard. We need to get out of here. The police will come."

"Well then," said Conley. "We'll just take him with us."

Conley bent down to pick the man up by the armpits. The man's hand went to his pocket. Conley saw the flash of metal: a switch-blade, being thrust up at his torso. Conley dodged the knife, then took the man's wrist in his hand and twisted his arm until the blade clattered on the floor. He continued to twist until he heard the man's arm snap. He then picked up the blade from the floor and stabbed it deep into the man's bicep. The man roared in pain.

"Try something like that again," said Conley, "and it goes in your eye." The man looked at him with eyes of pure fury. "Ah, you speak English, then. That'll make this whole process easier."

"Eat shit, you CIA pig!"

"Not CIA. Good guess, though." He punched the man in the face. Blood trickled from his nose. "Now, we're getting out of here." He looked at the man's leg, which bulged visibly even through his pants on the spot where Conley had kicked him. "Your leg is broken, but this will still be a lot easier if you're conscious. Your choice."

The man looked at his companion, who was crumpled at the threshold of Nutkani's apartment, a pool of blood blooming around him. He screamed for help in Urdu, but held his tongue when Conley held the switchblade within an inch of his left eye.

"I need you alive. But I don't need you whole."

There was movement in the apartment across the hall from Nutkani's. Conley saw the man's eyes, unfocused from the pain, cast a glance at the door.

"Don't even think about it," said Conley.

Gritting his teeth, the man held his tongue.

"Good boy," said Conley. "Now, up we go. Harun, a little help here?"

The two of them bent down and helped the man up. He tried to put his weight on his broken leg and yelled in pain. He nearly fell to the ground, but Conley and Harun held him up. They started down the stairs.

"You will regret this," said the man, in English, in a slow, pained drawl.

"Shut up," said Conley. Then he asked Harun, "Should we be worried that we'll get caught by the police?"

"With their response time? We'll be long gone before they arrive." Harun grunted from the weight of the man they were carrying. "The only thing to be worried about right now is the residents.

But they're afraid and won't come out. For all they know, we *are* the authorities."

They huffed and grunted as they carried the man to Harun's Daihatsu. Conley supported him as Harun opened the trunk. Conley lowered him into the trunk, where the man clutched his leg and groaned in pain. Harun stood over him, so that to the man in the trunk he must have been nothing more than a dark, looming silhouette.

"Who do you work for?" Harun demanded in Urdu.

"Screw you."

Harun slammed the trunk shut. Conley looked at him in the dim light that filtered from a streetlight through a nearby tree. Harun was covered in blood from their prisoner's arm, which had been bleeding from the stab wound. Conley looked down at his own clothes, which were not much more presentable. "What now?"

"Now we need to get him out of here." Harun made for the driver's side door, and Conley walked around to the passenger side.

"Into custody?"

"No," said Harun. "I don't know who I can trust."

"So it's just us then?"

"Come on. I know a place."

Harun drove for twenty minutes to an empty house in a remote residential neighborhood. It was flat-roofed like all the others, with no yard, a tall wall with a wooden gate and barred windows. The sky was going from black to dark gray as dawn drew near. Conley got out to open the gate with a key provided by Harun, then closed it behind them.

The floor of the garage was tiled black and white, the walls bearing white cracking paint. Harun got out of the car and both of them made their way around to the back.

Harun popped the trunk, and the man swung out his good arm with something that flashed in the dim light. Conley felt a sharp pain in his left forearm. He instinctively slapped the weapon out of the man's hand and then backhanded him across the face. He looked down and saw that it was a screwdriver that had been stored somewhere in the trunk.

"Bad move, buddy," said Conley. He and Harun took him out of the trunk. He was struggling, but with a broken arm and a leg, there was little he could do to get free. They took him, limping, through a dusty, unfurnished parlor and into a room that had been chillingly repurposed for what might euphemistically be called interrogation: The floor was all linoleum, with a large drain right in the middle, and a steel chair with straps for hands and legs. There were hooks on the ceiling and walls. It was a room made for brutal acts. Conley would not hesitate to use violence in self-defense or to neutralize a target, if the mission called for it. He was no pacifist. But this level of cold and calculated cruelty rattled him.

They sat the man down on the chair and strapped him in, dripping with sweat that mingled with the dried blood on his shirt. "Please," he was moaning in Urdu, but Conley and Harun made no acknowledgment of him. He cried out as they secured his injured arm and leg. Once he was tightly bound, Conley and Harun left the room, turning off the light and closing the door behind them. The man shouted as they walked out, but once the door was closed, all sounds from within were wholly muffled.

They sat down on wooden chairs, the only furniture in the kitchen dimly lit by the rising sun. "So," Harun said first, "what is the strategy?"

"Let him sweat for half an hour or so," said Conley. "Leave him in the dark and let his imagination go wild."

"We don't have time!" cried Harun. "We are racing the clock! If the Secretary dies, our countries could go to war!"

"Rushing the interrogation won't help anything," said Conley. "If we start pulling out fingernails, he's just going to tell us whatever he can to make us stop. He might tell us the truth, but we'll have no way of knowing that."

"We need to be aggressive, Cougar."

"We will," he said. "Leave it to me. I have a plan."

"This better be good," said Harun, taking off his bloody shirt to put on a spare button-down he'd brought from the car. "If we are not interrogating him right now, I'm going to get us something to eat. Can you handle him on your own?"

"Yeah," said Conley. "I'm going to make some phone calls while you're out."

Conley dialed his satellite phone as Harun pulled out of the garage in his Daihatsu. He checked in with a few of his intelligence contacts, who had nothing new to report. Next he dialed Diana Bloch.

"Give me some good news," she said. "Did your hunch pan out?"

"With a vengeance," he said. He filled her in on what was happening.

"This looks promising," she said. "Don't screw it up. And for Christ's sake, keep the body count down."

"I'll do what I can," he said, and hung up.

Conley then scanned the day's headlines on his tablet computer. The media circus continued, but there was nothing notable. Washington was controlling the messaging well, doling out enough information to keep the hounds hungry and coming back for more.

He read the news for a few minutes until he heard Harun's car pulling into the garage. The Pakistani walked in with a plastic bag with three paper packages in it.

"Bun kebabs," he said, laying them on the dusty kitchen counter. "I brought one for our guest, in case he's feeling helpful now. Did he give you any trouble while I was out?"

"None at all," said Conley, unwrapping one of the sandwiches. He bit into it. Spicy savory lamb in a fried bun and the kick of raw onions. He was hungrier than he'd thought. The two men devoured their meal in silence.

"So, are we ready to do what we're here to do?" asked Harun, still chewing the last morsel of his sandwich. "Just take my lead," said Conley, wiping his hands on the flimsy paper napkins Harun had brought in the bag.

They walked together to the door of the holding cell. Conley slammed the door open and they stepped in. The man raised his head with a start.

"Morning, sunshine!" said Conley loudly in English. "Time to wake up!" He took the man's head in his hands and shook it. "You're going to tell us who your boss is." Harun leaned against the wall and lit a cigarette.

"Go to hell, American," the captive spat, looking up at Conley. "I'm not telling you shit."

"I know," said Conley. "You're afraid of the people you work for. Every two-bit flunky is. You all know you're expendable, that your employer will get rid of your ass like a tick on a fingernail if they think you ratted them out. But the person you ought to be afraid of right now, buddy, is *me*."

The man laughed, but Conley could tell it was false. He was trying to put up a brave front. "Afraid of you? No chance." He was forcing a grin that was just a little too wide and stiff. Here was a man who was scared. *Good,* thought Conley. It was something he could work with.

"You're not convincing anyone, buddy."

"The people I work for are powerful," he said. "They will kill you both, and I will spit on your bodies before they are buried in an unmarked grave."

Conley chuckled—and his was actually relaxed, with that nonchalant menacing quality of someone who has absolutely all the power. "Here's the score. Nobody—and I mean *nobody*—knows you're here except me and my friend over there. We found you by a fluke. Total accident. No one even knew we were there. So you see, no one will know to look for you here. You're on your own, my friend. It's just you—and *us.*"

"Bullshit," he said. "The other one—him—he is Pakistani. Someone will know. Someone will find out."

"No, but you are getting closer to what I need to know," said Conley. "So your boss has ties in Pakistani intelligence?"

He just looked at Conley with seething anger. "You killed Rashid," he said.

"Rashid? Is that your friend, that we took out back there?" asked Conley. "Actually, it was my buddy who killed him. But I'd have done it myself in a heartbeat."

"Bastard!"

"I don't think you're half as choked up about that poor EMT the two of you murdered back there."

Conley held the man's gaze. He had wide eyes and flared nostrils, sweat dripping off the tip of his nose.

"Look, you have two options here. You can talk, and take your chances out there with the people you work for. Or you can keep your mouth shut, and die for sure."

"You are lying," he said. "Americans never let anyone go. You will send me to some hellhole until the day I die—"

"I'm not the CIA," said Conley. "I don't give a crap if cheap muscle is running around Islamabad. *I don't care about you.* Talk, and I won't only let you go, I'll pay for your cab fare to anywhere in the greater Islamabad area. But you only get to go if you tell me everything."

"You will have to kill me," he said, all bluster.

"See," said Conley, with a tight smile on his lips, "we won't kill you exactly. We'll just—leave. No one ever comes in this house. And the walls? They're soundproof like you wouldn't believe. You can scream your guts out and it won't do a bit of good. No neighbors are going to come snooping around."

The man tried to put up a front of pure anger, but fear was showing in his eyes.

"Look, man, you're not a true believer. I can see that. You're here because they're going to toss a few bucks your way, which you can blow on hookers and a tricked-out car. You don't give a shit about anyone but yourself, so don't start with this loyalty crap now, all right?"

Conley studied the man's face. He had on a mask of arrogance, his chin up, lips in a light pout.

"Do you know what it's like to die of dehydration?" asked Conley. "That means dying of thirst, in case they didn't teach that at goon school. So, do you? It's not pretty. You're going to get hot, because you can't sweat. How hot do you think this room is going to get if we shut you up in it for a couple of days, do you think? You'll get delirious, too. See things that aren't there. That, and the constant nausea, and dry heaving because you've got nothing left to vomit. You're going to be consumed by your desire for water. You'll gnaw on your tongue just to feel the moisture of your own blood in your mouth. Your skin will look like that of an old man. You'll be praying for death, but it won't come quickly enough. It never does when you really want it."

The man looked down. He was sweating profusely, and his brow was furrowed in a look of abject terror.

"Now, is this really what you want your next week to look like?"

He swallowed hard, and broke down. "What do you want to know?"

Chapter 13

It was past midnight when Buck Chapman signed in through security at the Pentagon. Despite the late hour, a steady trickle of people went in and out, each with the same glum, tired expression that Chapman knew so well. There was no quitting time in a crisis.

He walked down a long corridor under grating fluorescent lights that, in his exhaustion, seemed to be pulsing. Time hardly seemed to pass at all, and the hall had a hypnotic sameness to it, so much so that he almost missed his turn. When he arrived outside William Schroeder's office, he could remember nothing about the way over. There was no one to admit him, so he knocked on the door.

"It's open."

He let himself in. Schroeder was sitting behind his desk. His office, to which Chapman had been a great many times, was as cluttered as ever with a smorgasbord of fishing trophies, gun paraphernalia, and pictures of his family, not only of his wife and three kids but old pictures going back to the beginning of the twentieth century.

"Close the door, Buck," he said. "Take a seat."

"So," said Chapman. "You rang?"

"Things are mayhem here," he said. "The State Department's a mess. We're struggling just to get our bearings."

"Things aren't much better at the Agency," said Chapman.

"Cigar?" Schroeder held out a Cuban to him. Chapman declined by holding up his hand. Schroeder snipped off the tip with a guillotine and lit it, puffing without relish. "I'm not supposed to be smoking in here, but screw it." He took a puff and let the smoke billow out of his mouth. "The President personally went to talk to Wolfe's family. Wife, two college-aged girls." He puffed on his cigar again. "Did you know him?"

"Can't say that I did," said Chapman. "I don't think I've ever even been in the same room as him."

"He was one of the good ones," said Schroeder. "He got sidelined for the presidency, you know? Some party bullshit. It could have been him in that Oval Office. He'd have been good. He'd have been a hell of a commander in chief. A real man in the White House." His maroon leather chair creaked as he leaned back. "It's been a hell of a day."

"That it has," said Chapman. "I'd kill to be able to spend a few hours in my bed."

"Let's get to business then," said Schroeder. "The sooner we're done with this, the sooner I can spend some quality time with a bottle of single malt and Frank Sinatra records." He punctuated the thought with a series of shallow puffs to his cigar. "I need to know how close we are, Buck. Are we going to get him back?"

"It's been a day, Bill."

"Which means they've had the goddamn Secretary of State for a whole twenty-four goddamn hours!" he said. "That's twenty-four too many and you know it."

"We're chasing every lead. We've got three SEAL teams ready to drop in anywhere within two hundred miles of Islamabad in less than two hours. As soon as we get a location, it won't be long."

"*If* you get a location," said Schroeder, tapping his cigar on an ash tray. The acrid smoke was permeating the room and making Chapman's eyes water.

"We've got people on the ground, and information's trickling in. I know it's not much right now—"

"Goddamn it, Buck, we can't afford this kind of black eye. We can't lose to the terrorists. Haider Raza can't beat us like this *again*."

"We're doing everything we can."

"We're not," said Schroeder. "Not everything."

Chapman stiffened in his chair. "What are you saying?"

"I'm saying there are more drastic avenues that we, the government of the United States, can pursue."

Chapman leaned forward in disbelief. "You can't mean— "

"The possibility of military operations has been kicking around in the upper echelons," said Schroeder.

"Look, the captors haven't come forward. We haven't received any demands yet! Christ, Bill, it's only been a day. Can we give it a little longer before we go into worst-case scenarios?"

"This is a worst-case scenario already," said Schroeder. "We've got a member of the Cabinet of the President in the hands of the enemy. We won't negotiate, because we don't negotiate with goddamn terrorists. Any minute now, they could leak a video of his beheading on the Internet. A good man dead, and the terrorists coming out on top, showing that we're weak and emboldening a new generation to come out and blow themselves up for Allah. So tell me, do you still think ground troops are a goddamn overreaction?"

Chapman's mouth was left slightly agape. "You've got a delicate situation. Invasion is taking a mallet to it. There's no way the Secretary lives if Raza sees the US Army coming for him."

"It would show that we're not cowed by these bastards," he said. Then, in a measured tone, he asked, "How do you think the Pakistani government would take it?"

"I think the words 'international incident' would be a bit of an understatement," said Chapman. "I think the term you're looking for here is 'disaster.' "

"Drastic circumstances call for drastic measures," said Schroeder. "It might be the lesser of two evils."

"They're a nuclear power, Bill. Are we really going to kick that hornet's nest?"

"Ultimately, it's not my call," he said. "I just wanted your honest opinion."

"Well, you've got it," said Chapman, standing up. "It's goddamn suicide. Now, if you'll excuse me, I'm going to do everything I can to get us to step away from the ledge."

Chapter 14

May 29
Islamabad

The sun had risen high in the sky when Harun pulled into his own parking space in the Intelligence Bureau. They walked a few blocks toward their destination. Conley felt the clothes he'd changed into back at the house already getting damp with sweat.

The street was moderately crowded, and a nervous energy pulsed through the people. Driving over there, they had passed a protest in front of a government building, maybe a hundred mostly young men full of rage that they couldn't contain. Anti-American signs abounded, and Conley felt nervous for his safety. Although it helped to be with Harun, he wasn't exactly blending into his surroundings, and tensions were high.

The information they had gotten out of their prisoner was disheartening, but it was a lead. The man who had hired them was a Deputy Director of the Ministry of Narcotics Control, a man by the name of Iftikhar Ali. Harun had confirmed that the man was at work that day, but hadn't made an appointment—they'd decided it was best to show up without advance warning. No need to give the bastard time to disappear before they could get to him.

Within fifteen minutes they reached the ministry, an unimpressive squat whitewashed building. Harun flashed his badge and exchanged words with the man at reception, and they were waved in without ceremony. Harun led the way down dimly lit halls to the office marked as Ali's. They walked in, paying no mind to the admonishment of a secretary who was sitting at a desk by the door, and Conley closed the door behind them.

Iftikhar Ali sat behind a large, ornate wooden desk in a large office. He got up in alarm as he found the two strange men in his office, his waxed moustache twitching and his bald head glistening with sweat. "You do not have an appointment," he stammered in Urdu. "What is this?"

Conley sat down in a heavy hardwood chair. "We need you to answer some questions," said Harun, sitting down next to him.

Ali raised a bushy eyebrow. "You are in *my* office, you answer *my* questions." He looked at Conley and narrowed his eyes. "American?"

"Yes," Conley answered in Urdu. This seemed to surprise Ali.

"It would be in everyone's best interest if you cooperated," said Harun.

"I'm sure it would," said Ali, shaking in an apparent mixture of rage and anxiety. "But you see, I am not in the mood for questions from a man from the Intelligence Bureau today. I am in even less of a mood to talk to an American. Good day, gentlemen."

"I really think it would be best if you answered our questions," said Harun, leaning over Ali's desk to match his eye level.

Ali stood up. "I will not hear threats in my own office," he said.

"Look, I don't have time for bullshit," Conley said in English, "so we're going to have to make this quick."

"What is this?" Ali replied in English, outraged. "You come into *my* office and talk to me this way? Get out! Get out now!"

"Like I said, not a lot of time," said Conley. "The American Secretary of State," he said. "I want to know what you know, and I want to know in the next five minutes."

"I know nothing about the abduction of the Secretary!" he said, his anxiety replaced by pure righteous indignation.

"Now, you and I both know that's not true."

"I will not stand for these allegations!" he exclaimed.

"I don't care if you stand or sit," said Conley, "just listen. I know you're involved. You haven't called security yet, because you want to know how much we know. I can tell you that. Your man, who you sent to kill the ambulance driver and the EMT? He talked. I know— can't find good goons anywhere these days. Anyway, look, I don't really care about you. You're not a big enough fish in this. You're not the one who planned this, and you don't have the American Secretary of State. But I think you know who took him. As I see it, you've got two choices here. I can share this information with the CIA and everyone in Pakistani intelligence, and you can bet that the rest of your life will be nasty and short. Or, you can cooperate, and I give you the chance to get lost. Disappear and never come back. And then no one finds out your dirty little secret. Are we understood?"

"You have nothing on me," he said. "The word of a hired gun? Ha! No one will believe it. Not for a second."

"Maybe not by itself," said Conley. "But it sure will be enough to get people interested. Poking around your affairs. Now, I ask you, how well did you cover your tracks? Well enough that the combined efforts of the CIA and Pakistani intelligence won't be able to find a scrap against you? Seriously now, how long do you really think you'll last in the spotlight?"

"You are bluffing," he said derisively.

Conley took out his cell phone. "This city is crawling with American intelligence personnel. I know of at least two who are close personal friends of mine. I think they'd be very interested to hear what I have to say." He picked a name at random from the contact list on his phone and made a call.

"No!" Ali was sweating now, looking down at his desk. He was perfectly motionless. Conley knew he had gotten to him.

Conley turned the phone for Ali to see, and ended the call. "Your turn to talk, then."

"If I tell you what I know . . ." Ali said.

"You step down, tell everyone you want to spend more time with your family, disappear from public life, and scout's honor, nobody finds out," said Conley. "Added bonus is that you never see me again. Do we have a deal?"

"Why should I trust you?"

"You thought you were having a nice swim in the ocean, but you got dragged away from shore by the undertow and now you're about to drown, Ali. I just threw you a life jacket."

Ali sat back down on his chair, deflated. "Okay," he said, exhaling heavily, shoulders slumping. "I will take your deal. I will give you what I know."

"I'm all ears, Mr. Ali."

Ali drew nervous circles with a pencil on a pad of paper and spoke without looking either Conley or Harun in the eye. "The

United States Secretary of State is being held in a compound outside the city of Zhob."

"Where exactly?" asked Conley.

"I do not know!" he exclaimed, throwing up his hands. "I did not make these arrangements, all I know is that they were headed there."

"Okay," said Conley. "I'll take that. But if it doesn't pan out, if I discover you're lying to me . . ."

"I swear that I am not! I do not play games with men who have swords poised over my head, ready to strike."

"Wise man," said Conley

"So are you satisfied?" asked Ali nervously. Conley could tell there was something he was afraid Conley would ask. And Conley knew what it had to be.

"Not quite," he said. "This abduction was not your idea. We know you didn't plan any of this. I want your boss. The person you did this for."

Ali swallowed hard, and seemed to go paler than before. "I have already told you what you wanted to know."

"Ali," Harun said menacingly in Urdu. "Answer the question."

Ali seemed to be on the verge of getting sick. "I have a family," he said weakly.

"Imagine how much they would suffer if this became known," said Harun.

"Please. They will be killed. It was just money." Ali's voice was cracking, and he was nearly in tears.

Conley pulled on his partner's arm. "Come on, Harun, let's get out of here."

Harun looked at him with irritated surprise, as if to ask, *What are you doing?*

"He's not going to talk," Conley whispered. "Or he'll lie."

"He'll break," Harun insisted.

"He's obviously more scared of whoever is behind this than he's scared of us. Just look at him."

That seemed to convince Harun, who bit his lip and gritted his teeth. "All right," he said to Ali. "We're going to go."

"You stick around," said Conley. "We want to be able to reach you if we have any more questions. And if I find out you lied to me, the CIA will be the least of your worries. Do you understand?"

Ali nodded, pale.

Harun and Conley walked out of Ali's office, leaving him behind, stunned. They walked out of the Ministry building and into the bright afternoon sun.

"Do you think he told the truth?" Conley asked Harun.

"You don't get as far as he did without learning how to lie like it's your mother tongue," said Harun. "But I think you were very persuasive. What now?"

"Now we go check out this lead," he said. "After I get this information to my people."

They reached Harun's car and drove back to the safe house. Conley called Zeta and asked for Bloch.

"I have a lead," he said. "Possible location for the Secretary. I'm going to go check it out."

"Who's your source?" she asked.

"Local bureaucrat," he said. "Just a flunkie, and he wouldn't tell us who his boss was. He's worth looking into—you might find a connection. I'll send whatever I have on him as soon as I hang up. In the meantime, we're going after Wolfe and the people who took him."

"Nonsense," said Bloch. "There are SEAL teams standing by, it's just a matter of giving them a target."

"We need confirmation," said Conley. "We'll call less attention to ourselves if it's just me and Harun."

"Okay. See what you can find, but *go no further.* I don't want you getting yourself killed over this."

"I know what the risks are," he said.

"I know you do. I'm telling you not to take them."

Chapter 15

May 29
Langley

Chapman woke with a start from uneasy dreams and realized he was in his office. There was a gentle but persistent knock on his door. He looked at his watch. 8 A.M. He'd slept for four hours. When he went to sleep, all he could see through the half-closed blinds of the windows to the outer office were the screens of other night owls tapping away at their keyboards, but now it was bustling with activity. He felt a vague sense of dread, and then remembered the conversation he'd had with Schroeder the night before. It made him sick to his stomach.

"Come in!" he called out. It was Cynthia Gillespie. "Morning, Cyn." He rubbed his eyes, and couldn't mask the sleepy thickness of his voice. "What's up?" She was wearing a button-down shirt with one button too many undone, and he shamed himself into looking intently into her eyes to the point that she had to hold up a file in her hands for him to notice that that's what she was bringing him.

"The dead attackers," she said, dropping a thin packet of papers on his desk where his head had been resting, covering up what he had noticed too late was saliva that had dribbled from his mouth in his sleep. "We've got positive IDs on two of them. Martyr's Brigade. Looks like Raza's definitely our guy."

"Is this for sure?" asked Chapman as he leafed through the translated rap sheets and scanned IDs. "Where's it coming from?"

"The Pakistanis had them in a database. They were both arrested in connection with terrorist acts with Raza's group a couple years back. Both got broken out of prison last year, presumably by Raza's people."

"All right, this confirms what we already knew," he said, rubbing his eyes. "What does this change, then? Our efforts were already on finding Raza."

"At least we know we're not barking up the wrong tree," she said. "That's something, right?"

His phone rang.

Chapman fumbled for the phone. His regular cell was sitting on the desk in front of him, silent as a stone. It was the other one, then. "I gotta take this," he said, and she edged out of the room. He found the phone in the pocket of his jacket, which was draped over the back of his chair.

"Chapman," he then said, picking up.

Smith began speaking without hesitation, in his usual deliberate voice. "I need you to look into someone. I will be sending you the name and what personal information I have."

"Look into?"

"He is a functionary in the Pakistani government," he said. "We believe he may be involved in recent events. We need you to find out whatever you can about him. Pay special attention to financial transactions. Money is likely his motivation in this case. I need whatever documents you can get your hands on."

"All right," said Chapman, jotting things down on a yellow legal pad as Smith spoke. "What kind of involvement are we talking about?"

"He ordered the death of the surviving attacker," said Smith. "And the witnesses to that assassination. You will receive the information on your telephone in less than one minute."

Smith hung up without another word. Chapman swore silently to himself. His phone beeped, and he looked down at the screen. The message had arrived. He opened it, and at the top of it saw the name *Iftikhar Ali.* It was something. A silver lining.

He got up with sudden resolve. There was work to be done. He emerged from his office and yelled out to the twenty-two people who composed his taskforce. "Listen up! We've got a lead! I'm tossing a name into the network. I want everyone who's not putting out a fire to get on this. Pull up whatever we already have on him, and work on getting what we don't. I want assets, bank statements, travel visas, family, known associates, and the name of his childhood pet."

"Can we coordinate with Pakistani Intelligence?" asked Gillespie from her workstation, loud enough for the entire room to hear.

"No. He's a government official. We have to fly under their radar. This needs to be fast and quiet."

"That's practically our motto," said Gillespie.

Chapter 16

Conley sat in the passenger seat of Harun's car, trying and failing to sleep. The sun was rising, but he knew that he'd had to take the wheel again in a couple hours. He and Harun were making the nine-hour drive from Islamabad to Zhob in one go, so it was important to get whatever rest he could. The highway was well-kept enough, running through rocky terrain that was not particularly interesting to look at, and so favored sleep.

Harun had loaned Conley some of his own clothes, which were a bit short, tight and itchy, but were convincing enough as his own. He always avoided getting new clothes when he had to blend in. Someone in all brand-new clothes was an unusual sight, and a trained eye could spot it a mile away. He had also made a fake beard for himself—he'd had enough practice to be able to make it very convincing—to mask his features and thus his identity as an American.

Conley watched the uniform terrain and felt his consciousness fading. When he came to again, they were in a town, surrounded by mud-brick buildings, and the sun was nearing its high point in the sky. "We are here," said Harun.

"I thought I was supposed to drive for a few hours," said Conley.

"You were sleeping like a baby," Harun said with a laugh. "I felt sorry to wake you. We are coming up on the police station now. We will begin our investigation there."

Harun stopped a couple of times to ask locals for directions.

Conley had been to this kind of town before, and it always made him nervous. It was a bad place for him, as a Westerner.

They soon reached the police station, which was small and dingy. "Now you don't say a word," said Harun. "Just let me do the talking. They don't like strangers here, and they will suspicious of you if you speak."

The police station was a small, low building with an even lower wall around it, and seemed like a repurposed home. They walked through the iron gate and into the front door. Behind the desk, were two men in the gray uniforms with the standard police caps on their heads. One was young and skinny, with an incipient beard and large Bambi eyes, while the other was just bordering on the status of "old."

Harun greeted them and introduced himself. When Harun showed him his ID, the younger policeman straightened up and grew rigid. Conley didn't imagine they got many intelligence types so far out from the capital, and it seemed to have made an impact. The older one was less impressed, but seemed to welcome them nonetheless.

"We're looking for outsiders who might have come here," said Harun. "From Islamabad, probably. There would be at least ten."

"We do get trucks coming in and out," said the older policeman. "Not too many, but some. That's the only outsiders that we see around here, usually. But I don't know. The town is not so small that we would always know when a stranger arrives."

"It would not be a passing truck," said Harun, "though they might have come in a truck. They would need a house. A compound, actually. Walls, lots of space, not too many nosy neighbors."

"I don't know if I can help you . . ." said the policeman. "Perhaps you should talk to the chief. Today is his day off, but he will be back tomorrow."

"I will do that," said Harun. "Thank you for your help."

Harun turned to go, and Conley followed, trying to imitate everything about the Pakistani's body language—another dead giveaway to the trained eye.

"One more thing," said Harun, turning back toward the policemen. "Where can we lodge around here?"

The older policemen sent Harun and Conley to a guest house that was run by his cousin. It was a simple two-story house where the three upstairs bedrooms were available for rent. They were greeted at the door by Khalol, the owner of the house, and his wife, both of whom smiled and waved them inside. Conley kept silent, merely making the gestures of greeting without the accompanying words. Harun asked to take dinner in their room, to save Conley from having to speak and giving himself away. If he had to speak, they had already gotten their stories straight that Conley was originally from India, and hope that the interlocutor could not recognize an American accent.

Harun asked if they could borrow a radio for their room, and their host happily obliged. Harun tuned it to a local pop station. It was a small radio, so he had to set the volume almost all the way up to get the effect he wanted. He then closed the door. Conley stretched out on the bed's cheap foam mattress, resting his muscles, which ached from the prolonged journey.

"So what's the plan?" he asked Harun as the Pakistani sat on his own bed. They spoke in Urdu. Even with the music, they couldn't take the risk of someone picking up the cadences of the English language in their speech.

"Let's rest a while," he said. "But before dawn, we take the car and get the lay of the land and map the likely locations for their safe house. Going out at night will make our hosts suspicious, but that can't be helped. We need to get out there as soon as possible. But the first order of business is dinner."

Conley noticed the smell of stewing meat wafting into the room from under the door and realized how hungry he was. He hadn't eaten since morning, and even then just a pastry. The mere thought of whatever was on the stove made his mouth salivate and his stomach growl.

Their hosts served hard flat bread and stewed lamb. Harun told Khalol that they would be going out very early in the morning, while it was still dark, explaining that they would be scouting properties for possible real estate ventures. Khalol seemed satisfied with this, and so Conley and Harun turned in. Harun opened the window to the warm night air, and they fell asleep to the silence of the small Balochi town.

Conley awoke to Harun's gentle nudging. "It is past four," he whispered. "Time for us to go."

They left the house and drove off in Harun's car. He drove down the empty narrow streets, along rows of storefronts with their grates down, while Conley navigated with a satellite map on a tablet computer. He marked down a few locations that might have been but probably weren't what they were looking for, and soon they left the urban limits of the town. On the satellite photos, Conley identified six possible locations where the Secretary of State might have been held.

They parked at a safe distance from each and ran surveillance with night-vision binoculars. They ruled out the first two and fourth locations, while listing the third as a possibility. They then made their way to the fifth house on their list. Harun parked about a mile away, on slightly higher ground in the cover of an outcropping of rock. They exited the car. Conley, with the binoculars in his hand, and with his body partly obscured behind a stone, surveyed the house. This was a large country villa with high white walls. All the lights were off, but over the wall, Conley could make out the roofs of two Jeeps.

"I think this is it," said Conley. "Take a look." He held out the binoculars for Harun.

"That is definitely the one," he said. "What do we do about it?"

"Call it in," said Conley. "Let's send in the cavalry."

Chapter 17

Buck Chapman was on his way home, where Rose had promised him her famous spaghetti and meatballs and a relaxing night away from work. He was lost in this daydream when Smith's phone rang, and he swore, with a mixture of irritation and anticipation.

"Chapman," he said, picking up.

"My people may have located the Secretary of State," said Smith.

"Holy shit," said Chapman, making a highly illegal U-turn that drew angry honks, his tires squealing as he turned back toward Langley. "Where?"

"The Balochistan province of Pakistan," said Smith. "Outside the town of Zhob. I will send you the coordinates presently. I don't think I have to impress the urgency of this upon you, do I?"

Chapman hung up and called Schroeder's office. Getting voice mail, he called his cell.

"Tell me this is good news," said Schroeder.

"It's the best kind," said Chapman. "We've got a tip on a possible location. I'm getting in touch with my team next to get satellite imagery. How fast can you mobilize the SEAL teams?"

"They're on standby," said Schroeder.

"Good. I'll send you the coordinates. Have them formulate a plan of attack. Let's get those bastards!"

Chapman then called Cynthia, who was in charge of the team in his absence. "Put everything on the back burner. I need satellite imaging on this." He gave her the coordinates Smith had sent him. He hung up and clutched the steering wheel white-knuckled and bit

his lower lip in nervous anticipation, his foot heavy on the accelerator. Smith might be a prick, but when he delivered, goddamn did
that man deliver.

He practically ran into the task force office and nearly knocked
down Gillespie, who smiled as she saw him. "We've got satellite
images of the location whose coordinates you sent," she said. "I
have to say, it looks promising."

"You," he said affectionately. "I could kiss you, you know?"

It was supposed to be just part of their usual banter, but there
was an awkward beat after he said this, a slight hesitation on her
part that faded almost immediately.

"Look, here," she said, clearing her throat. "It's up on the monitor."

She showed him the images of a large compound on rocky
ground speckled with green cedars. There were two Jeeps parked in
the courtyard.

"Those look awfully similar to the ones used in the attack," said
Chapman.

"Do they ever. I have Ingram working on identifying them—"

"We've got a match!" yelled out Ingram, from three workstations
over. He was an overweight, pasty man with curly brown hair and
permanent pit stains who, through thick glasses, never missed a thing
on the monitor.

"We have positive identification on the vehicles, boss," he said.
"These are definitely the ones that were used in the abduction."

"Hot damn," said Chapman, euphoric. "We found him."

"Looks that way," said Gillespie with a grin. "Where did you get
this tip, anyway?"

"I've got people," he said.

"I should know better than to ask," she said with a knowing
smile. "Do you think this is conclusive enough for us to take action?"

"Not my call," he said. "I need to get Schroeder. Excuse me." He
touched her shoulder, and there it was again, that awkward beat.
She giggled and punched him in the arm to break the discomfort.
He was too excited to give it a second thought. He walked straight
into his office and dialed Schroeder's cell.

"Talk to me, Buck," he said.

"We've confirmed that the cars used in the abduction are there,"
he said. "Tell me that's good enough."

There was a pause as Schroeder considered it. "Okay," he said. "I'm convinced. I just need to get the President's approval on this, but he's already said he's willing to do whatever it takes. He'll do it on my recommendation. Let's pull the trigger on this. We're getting the Secretary home."

Chapter 18

Morning had come as Conley and Harun made their way back into Zhob, revealing the deep green of the cedar trees that speckled the city. They reached their lodging and were admitted back inside by Khalol. Conley got the call from Smith about an hour later telling him that an operation would be launched imminently. Now, all they could do was wait.

An agonizing hour passed, during which neither man said much. Both listened for the sound of an approaching Black Hawk helicopter and the ringing of the phone. For a time, Conley tried looking out the window, but he found that he couldn't help scanning the skies, so he opted for lying in bed and staring at the ceiling instead.

It was in this state of tense expectation that Conley first heard shouting downstairs. He and Harun both stood up at once. Conley reached into his bag for his handgun, and Harun did likewise. Heavy footsteps sounded on the stairs, three men, at least.

"The odds are against us," said Conley. "We can't fight our way out of this one." He looked around the room, and his eyes fell on the window. "Help me get the bed up against the door!"

They dragged Conley's bed so that its length was pressed against the threshold. They pulled Harun's bed next, between Conley's and the far wall so that they were wedged tightly and the door couldn't be opened. Someone on the other side turned the knob and pushed, but the barrier held.

"All right, out the window!" Conley yelled. He grabbed his bag and jumped out, rolling as he hit the ground. He leapt out of the way for Harun, who hung from the window ledge before dropping down and hitting the ground with a graceless tumble. Conley heard the familiar sound of gunfire from an AK-47 coming from upstairs.

"That door's not going to hold," said Harun.

"How many people do you think they left guarding the front?"

They looked at each other with tacit understanding, then ran around the side of the house, guns drawn. A narrow alley led from the front to the backyard. Conley rounded the corner and found a man on the sidewalk, leaning against a beat-up Jeep that he recognized as one used in the attack, holding an AK-47. The man hardly had time to react before Conley double-tapped him in the chest at close range.

"Your keys, Harun!" The Pakistani took them from his trouser pocket and unlocked his car. Conley could hear the men coming back downstairs, drawn by the gunfire.

"Get moving!" he cried out to Harun, and shot out the Jeep's front tires. He ran to the passenger door to Harun's Daihatsu and jumped into the car as it was already moving. The men in the house had emerged on the sidewalk. They opened fire as Conley and Harun tore down the street as fast as the old car would run.

"They're going to come after us," said Conley.

"I know," said Harun. The tires screeched as they went around corners, putting as much distance between themselves and their attackers as they could.

"Is there anywhere in town where we can hide?"

"If they found us once, they will find us again," said Harun.

"Let's get the hell out of Dodge."

They drove in silence as Conley looked anxiously at the rearview mirror for any sign of pursuit. As they left the city limit, something nagged at the back of his mind, but he couldn't quite put his finger on it. Suddenly it drew into focus: the sound of the rotating blades of an approaching Black Hawk helicopter.

The op!

Conley took out his cell phone from his pack.

"What are you doing?" asked Harun.

"They know we're here," said Conley. He speed-dialed Bloch. "They're going to know that the SEALs are coming. They'll be waiting. If they reach that house, they're all dead."

"Cougar," came Bloch's voice after three rings, "the operation is going down right now, I don't—"

"Call it off," he said. "Do it now."

His tone brooked no argument, and Bloch said only, "Okay, stay on the line." He heard Bloch speak, then yell something he couldn't make out, but could very much imagine. He looked for the aircraft, and saw that it would pass right over them.

"Stop the car!" he yelled to Harun, who, startled, hit the brakes hard, pushing Conley's body against his seat belt painfully until the car came to a complete halt on the dusty shoulder of the road. Conley released the seat belt clasp and got out. He waved frantically at the helicopter as it passed over them, with no sign of stopping. In a desperate effort, he drew his gun from his bag in the car and fired shots into the air, but the chopper crew took no notice.

Harun got out of the car, his eyes on the chopper as well. Conley could only watch as it approached the house. He picked up the phone, which he had dropped onto his seat. After some commotion on the line, he heard Bloch saying, "Cougar?"

"Here," he said.

"I've sent word to the Pentagon. The abort order should be coming through."

Conley took the binoculars from his pack and found the chopper through them, steadying his hands against the roof of the car. It had reached the villa and was hovering, slowly descending low enough for the team to rappel down. Conley couldn't look away. It stopped, and a rope went over the edge.

"No," he whispered.

And then the chopper began to pull up. It was hardly perceptible at first, but it picked up speed as it rose higher into the air. A sudden movement from below caught his eye: a surface-to-air missile, hurtling toward the chopper. Conley's heart sank. It was over.

But the chopper banked, and the rocket sailed past, hitting the mountain behind it and sending up a plume of smoke and fire. In another moment, the Black Hawk was far enough to be out of harm's way.

"Let's get the hell out of here," he told Harun.

Chapter 19

Silence hung in the air as Buck Chapman watched the monitor in dismay. They had been getting a live feed from the helmet-mounted cameras of the SEAL team, following in anticipation the raid on the Pakistani villa. Without warning, the mission had been aborted.

"What was that?" said one of the analysts.

A full discussion broke out, a din of voices expressing their anger, frustration, grief and attempts at understanding. Chapman felt his phone vibrate. It was Schroeder.

"What the hell happened?" Chapman asked.

"We got a tip that it was a trap," said Schroeder. "You'd better thank your lucky stars, Bucky boy. If this operation had gone south, it would've been your ass."

Chapman had to get out. He slipped away from the crowd and closed himself in his office, pulling down all the blinds. The thought of being responsible for the deaths of a team of Navy SEALs made him short of breath, and nausea was coming in increasing waves. He didn't want anyone to see him like this. He put his hand on the desk and tried to suppress imminent dry heaving when his door opened behind him and Cynthia Gillespie came into the office.

"Buck," she said. "It didn't happen. They didn't die." Even though he didn't turn to face her, her presence had a stabilizing effect on him, and he could feel his feet more firmly on the floor.

"Who cares?" he said. "It was my call, and I made the wrong one. It nearly got good men killed."

"It wasn't your call in the end," she said. "You're not in charge of this operation. You didn't have the authority to do it. You were acting on the best information you had." Her voice was faltering now. It was clear that the guilt was getting to her, too.

"Except now, we're back at square one," he said. "This was supposed to be a slam dunk, and it was a bust. What the hell do we do next?"

"We're not at square one," she said. "Not exactly. We know the captors were in Zhob. It narrows down the radius of the search. Plus, there's something else."

He turned around to face her, half sitting on his desk. "What?"

"I know it's not much," she said. "But that guy? Iftikhar Ali? We got his bank records. I didn't tell you because, well, this was more important at the time."

"It really isn't much," he said.

"But it's something."

"Yeah," he said. "It's something."

She moved in closer to him. "Look, Buck . . ." She put her hand on his shoulder, and her touch felt electric. She drew in her breath when she touched him too, and for a long moment frozen in time, they stared into each other's eyes.

Everything in Chapman's mind had been exhaustion, frustration, and despair. This sudden sweet longing welled up inside of him. All his energy drained, he gave himself up to this feeling, and leaned in. Their lips met with a sensation he had not felt in years, and he pulled her close. His only thought was of her.

He couldn't have said how long it lasted, but they broke apart and the haze lifted. He could only regard her in shock. She looked like a deer in headlights.

She blinked twice, shaking her head with eyes downcast as if to jog herself awake. She cleared her throat. "I should . . ."

"Yeah . . ." he said, turning his back and moving to put his desk between them. He turned back just in time to see the door closing behind her as she left the office.

Chapter 20

May 31
Boston

Dan Morgan, along with Kirby, Shepard, O'Neal, Dietz, and Bishop, the Head of Tactical, had been waiting for news of the operation in Pakistan in the Zeta War Room when Conley's call came. "It was a trap," Bloch had told them after relaying the news to Smith. "The Secretary wasn't there. The SEAL team was attacked, but the chopper made it out."

Morgan's first thought was about Conley. "Do you have word from Cougar?" he asked.

"He told me he was getting out of Zhob," said Bloch. "I'm going to stand by for more information. I'll pass it along to you as it comes."

Morgan sank in his chair. "God*damn it,*" he said through gritted teeth. O'Neal exhaled a whispered curse.

Bloch emerged from her office again, phone in hand. "It's Cougar," she said. "He's on his way back to Islamabad. Shepard, could you come up here for a second?" Shepard got up and started heavily up the stairs. "Meanwhile, the rest of you, our job is not done. This setback means that our work has really only started. I want everyone focused on trying to find Raza and the Secretary." She rubbed her palm against her face in consternation. "Now!"

She and Shepard disappeared into her office, and she shut the door.

Kirby, Dietz, and Bishop shuffled off in different directions, leaving Morgan, who didn't have a permanent workstation, and Karen O'Neal, their resident financial analyst, who usually preferred to work out there. Morgan pulled out his laptop at the War Room table and went over the field reports one more time with his eyes glazed over. He always hated this part—he was a field agent, not an analyst, but right now, the order was "all hands on deck." He had experience with foreign intelligence, and he might catch something that others would miss. He also needed to be up to date on the situation in case he was called into action.

Lincoln Shepard emerged from Diana Bloch's office with purpose in his step. As he passed the table, he said, "O'Neal," in a quiet tone that was completely uncharacteristic of him. "Come with me. There's something that we need to look at."

O'Neal stood up to follow him.

"Mind if I tag along?" asked Morgan. "If you've got something new, I'd love to take a look."

"The more the merrier," Shepard said glumly. Morgan followed the two young analysts to Shepard's office, where he had a multi-screen setup at his desk, a Space Invaders poster on the wall, and a mini-fridge full of snacks and energy drinks. He whistled, and the screens, which had previously been running a screensaver in which comets would whoosh by from screen to screen, were restored to show the programs that were running.

"Do you like that?" he asked Morgan. "Programmed it myself. Responds only when I do it." He whistled again, and it went back to the screensaver. "Try it." Morgan whistled, trying to hit the same pitch, but nothing happened. "Cool, isn't it?"

"Oh, please," said O'Neal. "A three-year-old could do that." She laid her laptop on a desk along the side wall and turned it on.

"Could have fooled me," said Morgan, shrugging.

"Could we get to it?" said O'Neal. "We do kind of have a national emergency on our hands."

"Forgive me," said Shepard. "What we have is information on one Mr. Iftikhar Ali, the Pakistani government official who tipped Cougar off about the house in Zhob. We suspect he was receiving bribes from whoever is behind this, and the hope is we can find out who that is."

"Has anyone thought about picking him up and interrogating him?" asked Morgan.

"It seems," said Shepard, "that our Mr. Ali has disappeared. According to bank records, he took his money and, as best we can presume, hightailed it for greener pastures. He wouldn't have been an easy man to take, at any rate. He was a public servant. The Pakistani government might resent someone other than them taking him into custody."

"We don't need interrogation," said O'Neal. "Data tells us everything we need to know"

Karen O'Neal had been one of the quant, or quantitative analyst, whiz kids on Wall Street, making investment predictions based on mathematical models and mountains of data. She had brought her considerable talents to Zeta after an SEC investigation put her in hot water with federal authorities.

"To me," said Morgan, "it's people who tell you things."

"People can lie," said O'Neal. "They can deceive themselves. They can just get the facts plain wrong. But data doesn't lie. Lay it all out in front of you, know how to tease and prod it, and you can unravel all the secrets of the universe."

Shepard scoffed as he ran through items in a complicated file management system, dense with text.

"It's a wonder you ever find anything," said O'Neal.

"Does baby need a nice user interface to hold her hand?" Shepard mocked. He brought up what seemed to be what he was looking for.

"Toss that over to me," said O'Neal. In moments, she had the same file on her laptop screen. "Jeez, you'd think they would at least have it in a spreadsheet format. What have we got here, checking and savings accounts, credit card bills, receipts and income tax returns . . ." She clicked through the documents one by one.

"Is this what you did on Wall Street?" Morgan asked.

"Not quite," she said as she laid out the numbers in a grid. "You know how short-term trading works these days? Like, on stocks and bonds and commodities?"

"I imagine my mental image of people yelling on the floor of the New York Stock Exchange is a little outdated."

O'Neal chuckled. "And how. Everything's electronic these days." She continued to manipulate the numbers on the screen as she spoke. "You've got your dinosaurs who do it old school still, putting in orders to buy and sell based on hunches. And then you have people like me, who let computers do the work for us. We write programs that do thousands of trades *per second.*"

Morgan raised his eyebrows.

"Yeah," she said. "It *is* impressive. And instead of running on gut feelings, these programs run on *data*. No fallible human judgment, just predictions based on the numbers. You get reams of data on stock market fluctuations and run a regression analysis—"

Morgan blinked.

"Are you all right, Cobra?" asked O'Neal. He realized, embarrassed, that he had fallen asleep in his chair.

"I think I need a break," he said, rubbing his eyes. "I'm going home. I'll be back in later."

Chapter 21

June 1
Boston

Lincoln Shepard's eyes flitted from monitor to monitor as he typed feverishly, constantly taking sips of an energy drink. He was running several different programs at the same time, searching databases, analyzing data and testing electronic security for weak spots. He worked best when his attention was divided, and he alternated between tasks about every thirty seconds, whenever some process took more than a few seconds to complete.

He was in the zone, which is where he liked to be. Computers were the air he breathed, and had been ever since he was a young teen. He hadn't ever been a good student, never been popular, and, though he might fit the *nerd chic* mold that had come into vogue of late, had not been particularly attractive to the opposite sex in his formative years. But he had had computers, and he sank hours into them.

He got into hacking young, at thirteen. At first he was what the community called a *script kiddie,* a term for someone who uses premade hacking programs to do general vandalism on the Web, by changing the content of sites and stealing passwords. He soon graduated to more advanced hacking, joining a group who did online stunts as a form of protest. Having gotten in too deep, he got a visit from the FBI, and Diana Bloch offered him a choice. She could make the criminal charges go away if he came to work for her.

"What *are* you doing?" asked Karen O'Neal, still sitting at the same desk across the office from him behind her far more modest laptop computer. "You're typing like a maniac."

Diana Bloch walked into the room, cool and composed as always. "Updates," she demanded.

"Someone made a transfer of one hundred thousand euros from a Swiss bank account into Ali's," said Shepard. "That was early last year. It's the only thing that seems out of the ordinary."

"A recent lump sum?" she asked. "That doesn't square with the theory that he's been in someone's pocket for a long time. He's in drug enforcement. The natural supposition is that someone is paying him to look the other way on drug trafficking. If that's right, then this doesn't make any sense."

"Maybe," said O'Neal. "But a lot of that money was cashed out almost immediately. And if we look at his previous statements, we see that money was slowly draining out of his account, and would have reached zero in short order."

"What does that mean?" asked Bloch, crossing her arms.

"Think about it," said O'Neal. "He got that much money, right when he needed it. He was gushing money on something—drugs, gambling, whatever. Suddenly he saw that he had run through his savings, and he had racked up serious debt."

"You still haven't answered my question."

"What I think is that the money was *his* to begin with," said Shepard, leaning back in his chair, gloating. "That's his Swiss bank account, money that was deposited by whoever is bribing him. He kept it there to avoid getting caught or having to pay taxes on it. Maybe he was thinking of retiring as soon as he'd amassed enough. But when he ran up those debts, he had to dip into that fund."

Bloch touched a finger to her chin. "That makes sense."

"Now we're working on finding whoever put the money into that Swiss account," said Shepard. "On the assumption that that's the person behind the abduction."

"Good work," said Bloch. "I want reports whenever you find anything. I want you to nail this bastard."

"Will do, boss," said Shepard, whose attention had already shifted back to his computer. The clicks of Bloch's heels on the wooden floor receded as she walked away.

"I think I have a way to figure out who was paying off Ali," said O'Neal.

"I do too," said Shepard. "It's called 'hacking into a Swiss bank's customer database.' "

"Good luck with *that*," she said.

"Watch me," he said. "What are you going to do?"

"I'm going to sift the data and find relevant trends," she said. "That should tell us everything we need to know."

"Oh, please," he said.

"Care to make it interesting?" she asked with a sly grin.

"Shepard, wake up," said O'Neal.

Lincoln Shepard babbled, and then opened his eyes to Clapton blaring on the stereo. He grumbled—that would not have been his choice, nor was it what was playing before he had fallen asleep in his chair, in front of his computer. His neck hurt like a bitch, and his mouth was dry. He took a sip of lukewarm energy drink—breakfast of champions—and yawned. "What time is it?" he asked.

"Who knows," said O'Neal. "It's always night down here. But you've been out for like two hours. You always have too much caffeine and then crash. You should know by now that it's all about the endurance, bud."

"I run on a strict regimen of highs and crashes." He munched on stale tortilla chips from an open bag, wiping his hands on his shirt. "Keeps my body working like a well-oiled machine."

"Shut up and look here, will you? I think I found something."

"Can you just tell me?" he drawled, stretching out his arms above his head. He looked back at her, hair frizzled and messy, but sitting on the edge of her seat.

"Get your ass over here, Linc."

He stood up out of his chair and made a show of dragging it next to her, all of which she ignored, because, as he knew, she was used to it. "Okay," he said. I'm all eyes and ears. Tell me what you have."

She turned sideways in her chair to face him. Her makeup was smudged around the eyes, but there was an enthusiastic glow about them. "So, we know that at some point in the past, this guy Ali started to get bribes. Big bribes, probably regular."

"Yes. I was the one who told you that, remember?"

"Well," she continued, "what would you do if you suddenly started receiving hundreds of thousands of dollars in offshore accounts? You can't spend that money now, okay, but one thing you're definitely *not* doing is saving for retirement. Is that fair to say?"

"I suppose it is," Shepard said, yawning. "What of it?"

"Look." She brought onto her screen a graph that showed a line, ascending in relatively small increments with a sudden drop within the past two years, after which the graph remained near zero. "This is his savings. Up until about three years ago, he was putting money in the bank pretty regularly, at least a little every month. We see a few dips in the graph, where he made some big purchases, but overall, he was a pretty steady saver." She moved her mouse cursor to the highest peak in the graph. "Now, at this point, he stops, completely, and starts spending it. Precipitously, I might add."

"Okay," said Shepard, frowning. There was something to it, but he couldn't quite figure it out. It always peeved him when O'Neal outsmarted him, and he had to admit to himself that it happened far more often than he'd like. "What does it mean?"

"Well, why do you start spending all the money you saved for retirement?" She was speaking fast, almost euphorically.

"Well," he said, thinking to himself. "Maybe he didn't expect to live that long—"

"Which would mean medical bills," she said.

"Would explain the depletion of the savings," he said.

"It could, but I checked. No hospital bills. What we have is a nice car, electronics and a whole lot of cash withdrawals. How do you explain that?"

He racked his brain. "Okay, I give," he said. "Tell me."

"When do you spend your whole retirement fund?" she asked. "When you have a whole other, *bigger* one stashed away in a Swiss bank account. I think he started spending that money when he started receiving bribes."

Shepard thought. It made sense. "Okay, let's say that explains it. How does that help us? We still have no idea where that money's coming from."

"Correlation, correlation, correlation," she said. God, she could be smug sometimes. "We look at other data sets, news reports contemporary with that time, specifically those pertaining to foreign trade. And what do we find?"

She hit enter again, and a news story popped up—a small note from the *Wall Street Journal*. "This article says that, during this very period, a certain company, a German shipping company called the Himmel Corporation, seriously expanded its operations in Pakistan, nearly doubling its business there."

"Come on, Karen," said Shepard. "I know you believe in this stuff, but you have to admit, it's pretty thin."

"That's just the beginning," she said, her voice sounding more breathless. "Ali has been to Zurich three times in this time. Now, who do you think was staying at the same hotel, every single one of those times?"

"The pope?" said Shepard. She could tell he was trying hard to act nonchalant now.

"The goddamn president of Himmel Corp!" she exclaimed, with a snap of her fingers. "Tell me, who cracked this now?"

He shrugged. "I suppose there's a possibility—"

She punched him in the shoulder. "Tell me I beat you. Tell me I'm better than you." She punched him again. "Say it, nerd!"

"Ow! All right, all right. You won this time."

"Damn right," she gloated.

"Ow," he repeated, clutching his shoulder.

Chapter 22

Chapman opened the door to his home to find no one there. Rose would be at work for several hours, and baby Ella would be at Rose's mother's. The silence and stillness in the middle of the afternoon were ominous to him, and being alone with his thoughts was probably not a good idea. The extent to which he craved a drink frightened him, and he wished that Rose were there to give him some comfort and restraint. But whenever he thought of Rose, he remembered Cynthia, and what had happened—that kiss—and all he could feel was terrible, crippling guilt.

Ah, but he felt fear, too. And anger.

"I'm not going down for this," Bill Schroeder had told him in a phone. "If this comes back to bite anyone, it's going to be your ass. You and your anonymous source."

"You're a real goddamn piece of work," Chapman had told him back. It hadn't been Chapman's decision alone—in fact, Chapman didn't have any decision-making authority at all. Still, he knew that if he tried to make a stink, there'd be a probe that would investigate his source, and the possibility that they might uncover where he got his information . . .

He plodded upstairs and fell forward into his bed without taking off his shirt or shoes. Tired as he was, he couldn't fall asleep. He tossed and turned, and the sliver of light filtering through the curtains felt like a flashlight shining right at his face. He couldn't get that one thing out of his mind. He shook his head against the pillow to get rid of the thought.

Back downstairs, he poured himself a glass of whiskey and collapsed onto the armchair that cramped the corner of the living room—"cozy," they insisted on calling it after the manner of the real estate agent, without irony when they were on good terms and with bitter sarcasm otherwise. He took a long draught from the glass, trying to forget the current state of his marriage.

It did no good to think like that. Nor about the kiss. It had been a fluke, a moment of weakness. A confluence of events and circumstance, never to happen again. He had no reason to feel bad about it, then. Because that was all it had been—nothing, really. He was going to get some rest, resist drinking himself into a stupor, and wait for Rose to get home. He'd get a good night's sleep, and then the next day—

He heard the door open, and saw Rose carrying baby Ella in one arm and a brown bag of groceries in the other, her keys held awkwardly in her left hand. She gestured with her head until he took the cue and rushed to help her by relieving her of the groceries and taking them into the kitchen.

"I got you those corn muffins you like," she said, with the half-hurt but tentatively cheerful tone she took after a fight.

"Thanks."

His cell rang. It was Smith. Chapman resisted the urge to throw the phone across the room. Instead, he just turned off the ringer and vibrate function, and put it in the pocket of his jacket, hanging on a coatrack by the door.

"Could you take her for a second?" she said, bouncing Ella gently in her arms. He did. The baby's face was cold, with a red nose, but her eyes were wide and curious, and she seemed happy to be in his arms. "Thanks. My back is killing me. Who was that just now?"

"Just work," he said. He couldn't deal with giving her answers longer than a couple syllables. The whiskey sat uncomfortably in his stomach. He played with his daughter, dangling his keys in front of her mostly to avoid having to make eye contact with his wife.

He walked upstairs and put Ella in her crib. He heard Rose coming up the stairs as he tucked Ella in, and turned to see her standing at the door. Her face was all tenderness, and was that the glimmer of a tear in her eye?

"Hey," he said softly, trying not to be cold or distant, and failing. She walked over to him and kissed him anyway.

"I love you for who you are and what you do," she said. She always knew how to cut right to the heart—to his.

"I love you, too," he said, and knew that the utterance was not nearly up to the task that was assigned to it. She hid her disappointment in a wan smile and he told her he probably should go pick up his phone and see what that call was about.

He walked back downstairs and reached into his coat pocket. Unlocking the phone screen, he dismissed the several missed calls and found one message. He went into the kitchen and closed the door before looking at it.

We know who is behind the attacks. Call ASAP for more information. S.

"Shit," Chapman said out loud, and then said it again. Then he called Smith.

"I was concerned about you," said Smith. "You didn't pick up."

"Screw you. You come in, cause trouble, and act like nothing happened."

"I gave you information," said Smith. "Good information, as far as it went. I did not tell you to act immediately on it."

"So you wash your hands of it, you smug, serene bastard?"

"I don't think you called me for recriminations," said Smith, evenly as ever. "You called because you want to know."

"It's Haider Raza," he said. "We know that already."

"Haider planned and executed the attack, but he was not behind it."

Chapman paced back and forth in his *cozy* kitchen, which was really not built for pacing. "Not behind it? Raza is the one who calls the shots in the Martyr's Brigade. He's masterminded plenty of complex, coordinated attacks."

"He didn't mastermind this one."

Chapman took out a knife and played with it, twirling it. "Just tell me. What did you find?"

"Gunther Weinberg."

The knife clattered onto the kitchen counter. "S-say that again, I think I must have heard you wrong."

"You heard me correctly," said Smith. "German tycoon Gunther Weinberg."

"You're *kidding* me," said Chapman.

"I don't *kid,* Mr. Chapman."

That really went without saying. "What do you have to back it up?"

"Circumstantial evidence, so far," said Smith. "All I intend is to bring him to your attention. It will be your job to prove the link."

"My *job* is to find the Secretary of State."

"Weinberg may be the key," said Smith. "Our goals are the same, Mr. Chapman. Don't forget that."

Smith hung up and Chapman was left standing, without knowing what to do. He yelled out an obscenity and grabbed his coat. Duty called, and as little as he wanted to, he had to obey. He ran up to the bedroom. Rose was in bed, lying as she did when she was about to take a nap.

"I gotta go," he said. "All this craziness." He gestured at the air, as if it was present right there in the room.

She pulled a blanket over herself. "Should I expect you later?"

"I really don't know."

She shut her eyes. He walked over to her and kissed her forehead, and she smiled without opening her eyes.

He arrived at the office after 7 P.M., secretly hoping that Cynthia Gillespie had already left, but it was hard to win a bet against her dedication to her work. He found her at her computer, scrolling through photos of the house in Zhob over a box of *yakisoba,* the whites of her big, beautiful eyes standing out starkly in the darkness of the room, with a green sweater draper over her shoulders. She turned around, startled, when she heard the door shut behind him. When she saw that it was him, she quickly set down the box of food and stood up, wiping her hands on a napkin.

"Hi," she said, obviously trying to suppress her discomfit. "I, uh, thought you had gone for the day." Her eyes wouldn't meet his as she spoke.

He had to say something. They had to address what had happened. "Look, uh . . ." There was a pause during which she looked at him expectantly. Chapman lost his nerve. "I got a tip. I don't know if it's really something, but I want whatever we have on file for Gunther Weinberg, the German billionaire."

Surprise offset whatever awkwardness had existed. "Weinberg? Where the hell did you hear that?"

"Let's call it an anonymous tip," said Chapman.

"I get it, your goose that lays the golden eggs is shy. But if you ever get promoted to upper management or quit the business, I get dibs on your assets. So what's the deal?"

"Just that he might have ordered the abduction," he said.

"Sounds sketchy," she said. "Should we check out the trilateral conspiracy, too? Maybe the Fed's in on it, or the Rothschilds."

He felt embarrassed for bringing it up, and chuckled hollowly. "It's not a conspiracy theory. It's a lead from a solid source."

"Still, a German billionaire contracting with a Pakistani terrorist to kidnap the American Secretary of State?"

"I know how it sounds." He couldn't help smiling at the absurdity as he laid it all out. "But stranger things have happened."

"You're the boss," she said. "Do you want the team on it?"

"Let's keep the focus on Raza," he said. "But keep tabs on Weinberg. Anything that shows up. Financial transactions, travel. I want this on the DL. You and, let's say, Les set this up and get me what you know when you know it."

"I'm going to need you to sign off on some of that intelligence gathering."

"Will do," he said. "I'm going to make some phone calls and look over whatever we have in the database on Weinberg already. Talk to you in, oh, forty and we'll compare notes?"

"You got it."

Chapter 23

The man known as Smith pretended to read a newspaper while parked at an out-of-the-way DC street in his latest car, a Hyundai Azera. The sedan was a tad too big and clumsy to maneuver, but it was powerful and reliable. For a man who lived constantly on the move, the choice of vehicle was an important one. He had to switch every other week, of course, and he tried not to show a preference for any particular make or model—any regularity was a potential weakness that could be exploited by his enemies. Randomness was what kept him secret and safe.

Smith saw the man he was waiting for approaching by a sidelong glance at the rearview mirror. Ken Figueroa. He could clearly make out the bald head, thin face with a moustache and a permanently incipient beard. He was in his gray suit, as usual, with a red-striped tie. Smith watched as the man circled around the car. He unlocked the passenger door in time for Figueroa to open it and come inside.

"You're late," said Smith, pulling out.

"You are a pain in the ass," said Figueroa. Beads of sweat had formed on his brow. It was not hot outside—there was a cool, perhaps even chilly breeze. But he had walked over.

"You said you had something for me," said Smith.

"I do," he said. "It's big. I've got a possible location on Haider Raza."

"We've had a few of those, of late," said Smith. "They have, as a rule, not panned out."

"This one might be different," said Figueroa.

"I'm listening."

"A little birdie at the Agency thought he was on to something with a lead on Raza. A relative of his owns a house in the tribal areas . . . Anyway, apparently his section leader has it in for him and shut him down, sent him on another assignment. He got disgruntled and he came to sing to us. I think there might be something to it."

"Think?" Smith tested.

"We've got satellite surveillance on the place," he said. "There's been some activity there recently."

"Is it reliable, in your opinion?"

"I think it's worth checking out."

Smith said, "I have a man on the ground in Pakistan. Perhaps he could check it out, as you say. But that approach has not been successful of late. Raza is a man that moves around frequently, and seems to be always aware of our next move."

"He's a slippery bastard," Figueroa agreed.

"Tell me, is your tactical team ready?"

"The men are gung ho for an assignment," Figueroa said. "They'll jump at the chance of action."

"Good," said Smith. "Then let them know they're leaving tomorrow."

"So soon?" Figueroa seemed surprised.

"Do you anticipate a problem?"

"No," Figueroa said. "They'll do it."

Chapter 24

June 4
Islamabad

Peter Conley picked up the steaming teacup and inhaled deeply, noting the complex aroma of green tea, saffron, cardamom, and honey characteristic of *kahwah,* which he always made a point of drinking when he was in Pakistan. He sipped as he browsed intelligence reports on his phone—the latest one on the surge of reported sightings of Haider Raza, none of them particularly credible. As he set down the teacup, he noticed a striking pair of long-lashed blue eyes peering at him from the couch opposite his in the guest lounge of the Marriott hotel.

He shot back a smirk and sipped his tea again. When he raised his eyes again, she stole another glance and smiled. She was wearing a tan and green *shalwar khameez* that showed just a hint of her form underneath, wisps of dark red hair peeking out from under her headscarf. He checked the time on his phone—4:34 P.M. *All right, I have a couple of hours to spare.*

"You know," he said, "I have half a bottle of single malt up in my room that's just begging to be shared."

She set down the book she was reading, a biography of Imran Khan, a half-shocked, half-intrigued expression on her face.

"I don't even know you," she said in a tone that could have gone either way between offense and delight.

"I'm very friendly," he said.

"And sure of yourself." Conley could tell she was trying to suppress her smile. "It's not very safe, going to the room of a man you don't know."

"You're a beautiful woman working as a foreign correspondent in Pakistan," he said. "You're not afraid of anything."

She uncrossed and recrossed her legs. "How did you—"

"Come on," he said. "You've got *journalist* written all over you. Plus, you look too tough to be a diplomat, too sure of yourself to be a tourist, and too laid back to be private sector."

"I could be intelligence," she said, raising an eyebrow.

"For that," he said, "you look much too sensible."

She puckered her lips as she seemed to be considering something. "All right, big boy, I'll bite," she said, standing up off her couch without taking her eyes off him. "I'm Carolyn."

"Peter," he said, rising to meet her gaze.

"So about that single malt?" she said, turning to exit the lounge and looking back at him over her shoulder.

Conley woke up to the muffled vibrating of his phone. The bedroom was tinged in the orange light of dusk, and not bright enough to see anything. He stumbled out of bed and fumbled in the pocket of his pants until he found the buzzing cell. He looked at Carolyn, who stirred, wrapped in the bed's white sheets, then he crept to the bathroom and closed the door.

"Conley."

"We have a lead on Raza," said Smith, and then, "Were you asleep? It's barely seven p.m."

"Jet lag," he mumbled, blinking in the mirror. "What's that about Raza?"

"Air surveillance on a village in Northwest Pakistan. The data came from the CIA, but our analysts put it together. We want an operations-ready team on the ground to follow this lead, and you're going to be at its helm."

"That's a terrible idea," said Conley, pacing the tiny bathroom, keeping his voice low. "A tactical team is a bull in a china shop. Our chances are much better if we sneak up on them."

"Like what happened in Zhob?" asked Smith.

"Worse. That's just my point."

"I don't see it," said Smith.

Conley sat on the edge of the tub, then climbed in and lay in it. "I don't care whether you see it."

"The decision's been made, Agent Cougar," said Smith.

"So Bishop and the guys are coming to Afghanistan?"

"No. I'll be sending another team. Lambda Division."

"I never knew there was—"

"But you suspected, I'm sure," said Smith. "This is your confirmation. Project Aegis comprises more than one division. Lambda Division will be taking over our involvement in the investigation in Pakistan while the rest of Zeta turns their focus to Gunther Weinberg. We think he's behind the abduction. You'll remain involved since you're already on the ground. I'll put you in contact with their Division Head, Ken Figueroa. Set up the logistics, and help them with whatever they require."

"You got it," he muttered.

"And Cougar? Focus on the mission, please."

Conley hung up and stood in the tub, stretching and yawning. He splashed water on his face and opened the door to the room, where Carolyn stood fully dressed.

She leaned in and kissed him lightly on the lips. "Thanks for the tumble. You've been a doll."

"Do you want my number or anything?" he asked. She opened the room door and he hastily covered himself with a towel.

"I know where you're staying," she said with a wink.

Chapter 25

June 5
Boston

Morgan walked downstairs into the Zeta War Room in the late evening. The table was crowded, with Shepard lounging next to O'Neal by the head of the table, Kirby and Dietz conferring in a quiet huddle, and Bishop's hulking body reclining in a chair, his feet in gigantic black army boots resting on the table—boots that Morgan couldn't help picturing coming down to break a man's nose or solar plexus.

A tall, muscular black man who wore his hair close-cropped, military style, Bishop was a guy Morgan was glad to have on their side. It gave Morgan some comfort that Bishop was used to military obedience and following orders without question. CIA Black Ops wasn't the Army or the Navy, and he could barely stand all that *yes-sir-no-sir,* let alone deferring to some asshole with an insignia and a different title that came before his name.

Still, Morgan had to respect Bishop. He was never a pansy about making bold decisions, which made him a hell of a leader for the Zeta tactical team—certainly better than Morgan would have been, since he liked to give orders only marginally better than he liked receiving them. Apart from Conley, there was no one Morgan would rather have backing him up on a mission.

Bishop was a code name, as Morgan's was and had been Cobra ever since he'd been training with Conley on the Farm. Since he sure as hell wouldn't work with a group of strangers, Morgan ran him and everyone else through his Agency contacts. His real name—Morgan always remembered with a smirk—was Oliver Duffy.

"Is this everyone?" Morgan asked.

"Waiting on your ass," said Bishop. "Princess had to powder her nose?"

"I don't see you griping about Bloch not being here," said Morgan with a grin on his face.

"Hey," he said, holding up his hands chest high, "she's the one who pays me, she can come in whenever she likes."

"Cobra, good, you're here," came Bloch's voice, all business. Morgan looked up to see her at the door of her glass-walled office, to his right, dominating the entire room. Her footsteps echoed in the cavernous room as she made her way to the War Room floor. "Now settle down, everyone, and let's get this show on the road." She reached the head of the table, in front of the big screen on the wall, which was blank. Morgan settled in opposite Bishop. "The recent fiasco was a significant setback, but it wasn't the end of this investigation. We have some new information about the person who is ultimately behind the attack, and that will be our focus from here on."

"Sorry," said Bishop, half raising his hand, "but shouldn't we be hauling ass to Pakistan to go after the Secretary? Isn't it time we, you know, get in there?"

"It's being taken care of," said Bloch.

"By who?" asked Bishop. "It should be us out there."

Bloch looked down, and then spoke in a tone of formal authority. "As some of you know, and I suspect the rest might have guessed, we are not the only agency of our kind. One of our sister operations, Lambda Division, has been deployed to deal with the situation in Pakistan."

"Hey, as long as we're both stuck with a goofy Greek letter, they must be okay," piped in Shepard.

"They were sent, in fact, almost as soon as news of the failure of the most recent raid hit the wires," continued Bloch, ignoring Shepard. "They are coordinating with Cougar in Pakistan as we speak, and they will be helping Cougar with operations on the ground. In the meantime, I want your attention up here." She gestured at the screen. "Shepard, if you please."

A paparazzi photograph appeared on the screen. It showed a man lounging on a deck chair on a yacht, glistening white against the blue waters of what Morgan guessed had to be the Mediterranean. He was wearing a Panama hat, hiding a bright pink face from the sun, flanked by a bottle of Veuve Clicquot and a trim brunette half his age.

"Gunther Weinberg," said Bloch. "Fifty-six. German billionaire playboy. He and his sister, Lena, own a controlling interest in Himmel AG, the machine and auto parts manufacturer founded by their father, Tobias, as a military airplane builder for the Third Reich." Bloch cycled through a picture of old Tobias Weinberg shaking hands with a man Morgan recognized as Thomas Watson, president of IBM. "It is rumored that he further enriched himself by setting up a scheme to steal money and valuables from victims of the Holocaust."

"Peach of a family," said Morgan.

"Today, they are also responsible for a significant chunk of commercial shipping in Eastern Europe, South Asia, and the Middle East." She clicked to a new picture, this one of shipping containers piled high with HIMMEL stenciled on their sides.

"Yes, I read *The Economist* too," said Kirby. "I know who Gunther Weinberg is. What's his significance to our case?"

"Shepard and O'Neal have discovered that Weinberg is the man pulling the strings of Iftikhar Ali," said Bloch. "As such, he is likely the one behind the abduction as well."

"What do you mean?" asked Kirby. "What's supposed to be his involvement?"

"Bribery," said O'Neal. "He's been paying off Ali, probably in order to smuggle drugs out of Pakistan in supposed textile containers."

"Indeed," said Bloch. "It's more than a little suggestive of his deep involvement in this case."

"Even if that's true, I still don't get why we're focusing on this Weinberg right now, even if there are other people on it," said Bishop. "I mean, even if he is behind everything, we can deal with him later. Shouldn't we all be working on getting the goddamn Secretary of State back?"

"There are other angles to this that you perhaps don't appreciate," said Bloch. "Consider that the blame for the abduction is poised to fall—not entirely wrongly, I might add—on elements of the Pakistani executive branch. This is after a team of Navy SEALs was killed in a raid in their territory. Relations are strained to a breaking point. We are set on a clear path to war right now, Bishop. War with a nuclear power. No politician has dared say the word to the public yet, of course, but every moment that passes takes us farther along that path."

"And what does this Weinberg have to do with—"

"If we are able to show that this was his doing to the people in charge," said Bloch, "then perhaps it will avert war by giving the public someone to really hate in this story. Put a face to the villain. A face that isn't Pakistani. It might save a lot of lives and curb an international disaster."

"Sounds like a shaky proposition," said Kirby. "It relies on the alignment of a great deal of variables."

"Shaky's the best we've got right now," said Bloch. "O'Neal, you're up. What have you got for us?"

"Nothing in the way of any kind of financial motive," she said. "As you've already said, he was probably paying off Ali in order to smuggle drugs out of Pakistan. I can't think of any way in which the Secretary's abduction can play into that. Apart from it, as far as I can tell, he has no particular gain in throwing the United States and Pakistan into war. It seems like that kind of disruption could do a lot of damage to a shipping business. *But,*" she added, "war is a destabilizing force, and all destabilization has winners and losers in the market. I'm betting there's an angle to this where Himmel and Weinberg personally stand to make a lot of money from a war."

"Keep working and see what you can dig up," said Bloch. "Dietz, can you tell us anything about this?"

Louise Dietz, in tweed and glasses that covered half her face, began speaking and got immediately tongue-tied. She closed her eyes, took a deep breath, and started again, slowly and deliberately. "We have confirmation that Haider Raza is the one at least immediately behind the abduction of the Secretary. The assumed purpose is that of all terrorism—to intimidate, to expose the weakness of your target, to scare them into submission. Perhaps it is to lure us into war. Haider Raza would count it as a victory, as a fulfillment of his life's purpose, if it took the deployment of the US military apparatus to take him down. An invasion of Pakistan would also heighten anti-American fervor in the entire region. You can bet he's counting on that." She finished with an awkward nod, like a student finishing a presentation in class.

"How does Weinberg fit into that picture?" asked Morgan.

"That's the puzzle," said Dietz. "Strange bedfellows, those. The implication that there might be some practical gain for Weinberg is . . . sinister. I admit that I don't really know what to make of it."

"Thank you, Dietz," said Bloch. "I agree. It is disquieting. We need to keep digging on this to find out what Weinberg's ultimate purpose is."

"All right, I'm convinced that we need to go after this guy," said Bishop. "And, personally, I don't care why the man did it. I just care about nailing him. So what's our angle? How do we get at him?"

"I was getting to that," she said. "Gunther Weinberg is, of course, extraordinarily well protected. His schedule is carefully guarded, he never discloses where he will be next, and of course, he is never anywhere that doesn't have top-level security, in addition to his own bodyguards. But we may have an opening. He likes his expensive toys, cars in particular. He sponsors his own Formula One team. And he's a collector, a very avid one. Lately, he seems to have taken an interest in American muscle cars. This is where Cobra comes in." Morgan's cover job had always been as a classic car dealer, which he had taken up full time after he quit intelligence, years before. He'd had fairly significant success, and built a trusted name for himself in the business, and still did some dealing on his down time. "If you please," Bloch said, motioning for him to stand up.

Morgan moved to the head of the table, where Bloch took a seat to his right. "We are going to come at him through his love of cars," he said. "Which, by all accounts, is legendary. Lucky for us, this man has a hard-on for American muscle cars. I've made contact with one of Weinberg's known dealers, which just so happens to be one of my professional contacts. It seems he is on the market for a very particular specimen. Shep?"

The image came onto the big screen. It was a black car, sleek as a panther, a panty-dropper detailed with white racing stripes. Bishop whistled. "The chicks will cream, indeed."

"The 1970 Chevrolet Chevelle SS 454," Morgan continued. "A classic among muscle cars. A beast of the highway. All the raw American power that you might want. An engine that roars with the slightest push. A real head-turner."

"Okay, it's a car," said Kirby.

"It's not just a car," said Morgan. "This is the number-one pilot.

First out of the factory. Only driven one mile. All original parts, born in driveline with Concours-level restoration, original sale documentation, owner history—everything, and I mean *everything,* that a serious collector might want. Valued at two million dollars, it's one of the biggest catches out there."

Most of them—all but Bishop—seemed unimpressed.

"All right, I get it," said Kirby. "What's the next step then?"

"I sell it to him," said Morgan.

"So," began O'Neal, "we pretend to own this car, and—"

"There's no pretending," said Morgan. "We can't fool a man with Weinberg's means on something like this."

"So I suppose we now own this car?" asked Kirby.

"We bought it yesterday," said Morgan. "At asking price, but we needed to close before the seller found out about Weinberg. It was a major stroke of luck."

"And it cost us two million dollars," said Kirby flatly.

"How did you get to it before Weinberg's dealer?" asked O'Neal.

"It pays to have the right contacts," said Morgan. "Looking into Weinberg, I found out about his love of cars and this car in particular. I happened to know who owned it, and he was willing to sell."

"So, did it work?" asked Bishop. "Did Weinberg bite?"

"I've set the bait, and he's chomped on it hard," said Morgan. "He wants to meet in person."

"Is he coming here?" asked Kirby.

"No," said Morgan. "He's in Monte Carlo. We're leaving tomorrow night."

"Who's *we?*" asked O'Neal hopefully.

"Cobra, Shepard, Bishop, Diesel, and Spartan," said Bloch. The last two were members of the Zeta tactical team.

"And what's the plan, if I dare ask?" said Kirby.

"A man who's involved neck-deep in illegal activity like Weinberg doesn't keep his sensitive information locked away in a public server," said Bloch

"I checked," added Shepard.

"He'd be carrying around a hard drive," said Morgan. "Something big enough to store a heavy load of data, which means it's too big for him to haul around personally. That means it'll be with him, but not *on* him—which means his hotel room."

"Or the hotel safe?" interrupted Kirby.

"No," said Shepard. "He'll need to use it on a daily basis, and he wouldn't trust it with hotel personnel. It'll be in his room somewhere."

Morgan continued. "The plan is, I get in close enough to have access to that hard drive, and copy it. That way, Shepard can take the time he needs to beat whatever security the thing might have, and Weinberg's none the wiser that his data have been compromised. Meanwhile, tactical provides support and backup.

"The problem," he continued, "is that I'll have to use my real identity for this. I'm known in the classic car business, and it's the only way I can have the credentials to attract his attention. Which is why this needs to go down as a legitimate car sale. As far as he knows, I am nothing more than a classic car dealer, and that's as far as he'll know by the end of this operation. Bishop, Shepard—I'm counting on you guys to back me up on this."

"I'm just looking forward to my vacation in Monte Carlo," said Bishop. "I mean, we're going to a coastal paradise to sell a guy a car. How bad can it really get?"

Chapter 26

The sun shone harshly on the same airstrip where Harun had picked him up the week before as Peter Conley waited, standing with a dirty-white 1999 Honda Hobio van and its hired driver, Abbas. The plane, an oldish Beechjet 400 jet, landed in the late morning, an hour late but who was counting, and six boisterous men emerged from the sleek white aircraft. One of them strode ahead of the others with a swagger that marked him as the leader. He had short, hard blond hair, an angular nose and chin, face all sharp corners, and cocky blue eyes that cried out arrogance. *Asshole,* was Conley's first thought, the second being, *he's going to be trouble.*

"I'm Walker," he said, extending his hand. "And this here's Blue-jay, Mutt, Tex, Clutch, and Mantis." There was something fratty about them. Conley had not been a fan of Greek life in college. "You're—Cougar, right? You're supposed to be some kind of master spy? Some kind of Jason Bourne, back in the day?" This was a taunt, and Conley wasn't swallowing it.

"Listen, kid, you think you're hot shit because you get your orders, you come in and you clean up when guys like me go through all the trouble of handing it to you on a silver platter. I get it, I was a teenager once, too. But this is my territory now, and you and your posse here had better do what I tell you or you can get off my goddamn lawn."

"Jeez, chill," said Walker, with a smirk. "We'll be good, won't we, guys?" He gave Conley a pat on the back, dismissive masquerading as friendly. "Is this our ride?"

He took them first to a house that he had rented the day before for ten thousand dollars cash, no questions asked, to establish their base of operations. In the nice part of town, the part where they were used to foreigners, because he had thought, presciently, that Team Testosterone wouldn't have the sense to keep quiet and out of sight.

While the Lambda agents wrestled for beds, Conley went out to get them something to eat. He got takeout from a restaurant that Harun had taken him to a few days before. He got dirty looks from the people there, who easily identified him as an American. It was not a good time to be an American in Pakistan, even in relatively cosmopolitan Islamabad.

On his way back to the house, Conley called Harun and told him his impression of the team.

"This is bad news," Harun told him.

"It's firepower," said Conley in a halfhearted defense.

"We will stick out like a peacock in the desert," said Harun. "It will not be safe traveling with them into the countryside."

"We could've moved in on the house in Zhob if we'd had more people with us."

"We would not have gotten that far if we'd had more people with us."

"Harun, I need your help with this," said Conley. "We're going to need backup out there."

"Where is 'out there'?" asked Harun. "Back to Zhob?"

"No," said Conley. "Latest info puts Haider Raza out in the Chitral Valley."

"*Allah,*" said Harun. "That is practically Afghanistan. The roads are treacherous, and once there, there will be no other Westerner to be found for a hundred-kilometer radius. You will be sitting ducks."

"If Haider Raza's hiding out there—"

"Then he can't catch a whiff of any incoming Americans before they are standing behind him with a knife ready to slit his throat," said Harun. "Or else the Secretary of State is as good as dead."

"We can't do this just the two of us," said Conley. "We're going to need a team with us if we actually raid Raza." Conley didn't believe it, but he had to put a good show.

"It is madness."

"But at least it's the fun kind, right?"

"All right, all right," said Harun. "I will go. For you. But I don't think any good is going to come of this."

The Lambda tactical team greeted the food with ambivalence—grumbling from its foreignness but eating heartily from appetite. They were in a nice four-bedroom home furnished with a six-person table and chairs, along with mismatched silverware and chipped ceramic plates. Conley sat apart from them, watching their easy banter and stream of dirty jokes and one-liners with suspicion. He was never as lighthearted before a dangerous mission. After they ate, Conley pulled Walker aside to discuss strategy.

"Tomorrow, we'll move northwest into the countryside," said Conley. "In the direction of Peshawar through to the city of Dir. It'll be rough going, and your team needs to be hidden in the back of a truck. It'll be the better part of a day just to get to Dir, and from there, it's at least a full day's ride on a dangerous mountain road to the Chitral Valley. We're going to need satellite support once we get there. We don't want to linger long anywhere we can be found, either by Raza's men or by anyone else."

"I want to see any of these bastards messing with us," said Walker. "Six men, highly trained by the US military? I'd like to see anyone try to harm us."

"That kind of thinking works until you've got a Kalashnikov-wielding mob on your ass," said Conley.

"Yeah, whatever," said Walker.

"No, *not* whatever," said Conley. "I am not going to die for your idiocy. You are going to be *goddamn* careful, if not for your own sorry asses, then for what I'll do to you in Hell if we all get killed because of you."

"Fine, fine, I'll get in touch with Figueroa," said Walker. "He'll give us the support we need. And we'll *behave*."

"Good," said Conley. "I've spoken to a local asset I have here, Harun Syed. He's arranged for a truck to take us to Dir, where he's going to get us transportation over the Lowari Pass."

"Are you saying that he's coming with us?" said Walker with disbelief.

"Goddamn right he is, and we're lucky to have him."

"I don't like to . . . mingle with the locals," he said.

"Tough," said Conley. "He's our best shot at surviving this."

Walked scowled. "We don't need one of *them* with us."

Conley's face turned to a frown of puzzled consternation. "We need him," he said. "He knows the land, he knows the people. And he's Pakistani. Do you think anyone's going to talk to a bunch of Americans in rural Pakistan? We can't run any kind of investigation without him."

"They're all traitors," said Walker. "He'll turn on us. They all do."

"He's a friend," said Conley, stepping closer so his face was inches from Walker's. Conley, the taller man, looked down into his cold blue eyes. "He's *my* friend. And we need him. If you want me to lead you in this op, this is the way it will be."

Walker looked at Conley in menacing silence, then said, "Fine. Have it your way. But don't expect me to treat him with kid gloves when we find out he's a goddamn traitor."

Chapter 27

June 7
Monte Carlo

Dan Morgan arrived at the Hotel Oiseau in Monte Carlo in a silver Mercedes coupe that Zeta had arranged to wait for him at the airport, to the jealous looks of the others who were tagging along and had to take a van arranged by a local asset. Morgan didn't normally go for European cars, but he had to admit that it had plenty of power and handled beautifully. As he climbed out, he made a mental note to take it out on the Autoroute to see what it could do before the trip was over, if he had any time to himself.

It was a bright and sunny morning, and the sun glinted gloriously off the Mediterranean. The exterior of the Oiseau looked like a palace, done in classic Parisian style, with intricate designs and columns along its length. It stood on a low bluff overlooking the ocean, but the front entrance was on the inland side. He left his car for the valet under an overhang as ornate as the rest of the structure, and a porter took his bags and motioned him inside. The lobby was all done in white-and-pink marble. Elegantly dressed people, young and old, walked past, some headed for the beach, others for the town, everyone wearing designer sunglasses.

"Morgan," he said at the front desk. He didn't like using his real name—didn't like it at all. But it couldn't be helped this time.

"The arrangements have all been made by Mr. Weinberg, Mr. Morgan," said the young woman at reception, whose careful ponytail and muted makeup said quite clearly *at your service, but not that kind of service.* "The porter will take you to your suite. Would you like a brief description of our facilities, or perhaps a tour?"

"I'd just like to be taken to my room, please."

He followed a stiff young man in an unfortunate red uniform into an elevator and down a blue-carpeted hallway to an off-white door with branch and leaf patterns carved into its wood. The porter left his bags on the bed and Morgan gave the boy a folded-up ten-euro note discreetly, as they did, the money never seeing light of day.

"Thank you, sir," he said, and made himself scarce.

Morgan walked out onto the balcony, where he could see the ocean and the boardwalk far below. He had his sunglasses on, which cast the world in shades of yellowish brown, making the greens seem greener and everything else more vivid. It was beautiful, but he felt out of place. It wasn't there to be enjoyed, not for him. He wished that Jenny were there with him, that they were on vacation. He wondered how she was doing, and thought about calling her, but she probably wasn't up yet and he didn't want to wake her.

Morgan walked back into his room, opened his briefcase, and took out a device about the size of a cell phone with a small antenna attached—a bug sweeper, used to check the room for surveillance devices. Over the next twenty minutes, he thoroughly scanned the room, running the device along the walls from floor to ceiling, then the floor and ceiling themselves, then the bed and sofas and ornate wooden furniture, the old-fashioned rotary phone with the wood and brass finish and the Chinese-looking vase with the bouquet of tulips—all the fruity decorations there to impress fancy girls who trolled casinos and boardwalks for rich men and the same girls forty years later, now wives who had certain *expectations*. Morgan would toss it all out the window if they weren't going to charge his credit card, and then remembered that Weinberg was paying for the room and considered whether he wouldn't do just that. It would save him plenty of trouble scanning the room next time.

Jenny would have loved the room—or at least he thought so. It's not like he was the interior decorator.

Once he was satisfied that the room wasn't bugged, he opened his suitcase and took out his communicator, a tiny skin-colored earpiece that fit entirely into his ear canal, acting as microphone, earphone, and transmitter, all the while allowing him to hear perfectly out of his ear.

The room smelled of nothing with a hint of lavender, which he couldn't stand. He was sure they'd change the scent if he asked—

catering to the rich was all about meeting petty, absurd demands, and this was light in comparison. But he wasn't going to be the guy who complained about the *scent of his room,* so he went back to the balcony instead and sat down at a wicker chair to take in the scenery. He took out his cell phone and put it to his ear, so that anyone who happened to look at him wouldn't think it was strange that he was talking to himself.

"Tactical, come in," he said. He had to repeat it a couple of times until he got a response.

"This is tactical," came Bishop's voice in his ear. "Receiving loud and clear, Cobra. What's your status?"

"In the room, settled in, scanned for bugs," he said. "Awaiting first contact from the target. What's the word on your end?"

"We're all set up here," said Bishop. "How's the room?" For this last part, Bishop dropped the stiff formality of tactical communications and took on a conversational tone.

"Ridiculously large and fancy," Morgan said with a practically audible smirk.

"Lucky bastard. Meanwhile, I'm stuck sharing a bed with Diesel."

"Sorry, Bishop, I didn't know you had company."

"Screw you, Cobra," Bishop chuckled. "Next time, it's your turn to run support, and I'll get the fancy hotel room."

"Keep dreaming," said Morgan. "Cobra out."

Morgan went to his bag to pull out his tablet computer to access the mission dossier. He poured himself a Perrier from the minibar—fourteen euros, on Weinberg's dime—and sat on the balcony, going over the facts of the case and relevant photographs until the room phone rang.

He took the receiver off the hook.

"Hello."

"Is this Mr. Morgan?" The voice on the other end carried a heavy German accent, and a tone that didn't quite fit the posh surroundings.

"Mr. Weinberg?"

"This is Anse Fleischer. I am Mr. Weinberg's personal valet. Mr. Weinberg would like to meet you by the pool at your earliest convenience. Let us say, an hour?"

"I'll be there."

He hung up, then shed his traveling clothes—khaki pants and navy blue button-down. He walked into the bathroom, which also smelled of lavender, and ran the shower. The water poured from a sort of waterfall made of white marble, to match the rest of the bathroom. The cascade hit his back with nice, relaxing force, and he spent longer than usual under it, letting the pulsing streams massage his tense muscles. He dried off (big, white fluffy towels, because these people knew how to live) and put on a casual white button-down shirt, Bermuda shorts, and loafers. Not his outfit of choice, but he had to look the part, and the part was of a man of leisure.

He had some time before he had to meet Weinberg, which he spent discreetly scouting all the possible exit routes from the hotel, pretending to look at the facilities. It was the kind of information that he knew very well paid to have *before* you needed it. He then set up a few of his own motion-activated spy cameras in the room. It would catch any break-ins and transmit the video automatically to his phone—a system courtesy of Shepard.

"All right," he told Bishop over the communicator as he slipped on his special aviator sunglasses. Their thick rims concealed a listening device and a tiny still camera, activated by a button near his ear. "I'm going in."

"Good luck," said Bishop.

Morgan walked downstairs and out into the pool area. It was built on a deck overlooking the ocean, which he had spotted from the balcony earlier. Women reclined on deck chairs, their varying levels of beauty telling him whether the money came from their husbands or fathers. Waiters carried colorful, fruity cocktails, and towel boys rushed to attend to guests coming out of the pool. Morgan spotted Weinberg sitting on a deck chair at a table under a large umbrella, shirtless in a speedo. Morgan knew he was fifty-six, but he didn't look a day over forty—a result of a pampered lifestyle and never having a care in the world. He was pink and baby-faced, with a slight blond beard. He was not quite as lean as he used to be from pictures that Morgan saw, but he still had the body of a younger man, and the muscles of a swimmer. Sitting at the table with Weinberg, stiff and unrelaxed, was the man who Morgan took to be Anse Fleischer. Sitting down, he was still nearly a head taller than Weinberg, with thick broad shoulders under a casual light blue shirt, blond as well, with a face that might make a Neanderthal jealous, but only just. Had he been born some twenty years earlier, he might have made a better Terminator than Arnold.

Weinberg waved Morgan over.

"Mr. Weinberg," Morgan said.

"Ah, Mr. Morgan. A pleasure to make your acquaintance." Weinberg had a distinct German accent, though Morgan could tell even from a few words that the man's English was near perfect. "Please, sit down. Will you drink with me?" He motioned to a gin and tonic sitting on the table in front of him.

"I don't drink."

"Commendable, Mr. Morgan! Perhaps an Evian, or some fresh-made juice then?"

"I had a big lunch," he said, sitting down.

"So serious," he said, with a mock frown. "I did not know anyone could be so serious in Monte Carlo." He waved his arms to indicate the beauty of their surroundings.

"I'm here to do business, not enjoy myself," said Morgan.

"Look around you, Mr. Morgan! The sun, the beautiful women—or men, if that is your fancy. Is this the time or place to discuss business?"

"I thought that was the point of my coming here," said Morgan.

"Relax, my friend. This is on me. Have some fun."

"I like to keep business and pleasure separate."

"And how!" said Weinberg. "But there is nothing truly separate, is there, Mr. Morgan? What business can be separated from pleasure, and what pleasure is there without *some* business involved, don't you think?"

"I guess there are some of us who'd rather they didn't mix," said Morgan.

"Is that the talk of a master salesman, especially one who sells things of beauty and pleasure?" he asked. "I thought the secret to your business was that your client never believed himself to be a client, but rather a friend. I am a businessman myself, and the best business is done with a veneer of friendship."

"And let me guess, your friendships are deep down all about business?" Morgan said, leaning back in his iron-wrought chair, legs casually crossed.

Weinberg contained his look of annoyance. "Perhaps you are in the wrong line of business, Mr. Morgan. You have the makings of a psychiatrist, I think."

"I just think there are some things money can't touch," he said.

"An idealist, I see. Such a rare thing in a salesman. See, Mr. Morgan, it is my experience that, when you have billions at your disposal, you will be surprised at how little money cannot touch. How many people you can buy and sell."

"Are you in the business of buying and selling people, Mr. Weinberg?" asked Morgan, with a pointed raising of his eyebrows.

"I wouldn't be if they weren't so positively eager to be sold!" he said with his cackling laugh.

"And what about buying cars?" Morgan asked.

"I will pay asking price, Mr. Morgan, if only you will stop talking about business in this place! You will show me the car later, and we will close this deal. You have my word." Morgan caught Weinberg's eyes moving to a point behind him. "Now, please, relax. I do believe this is Ms. Harper coming our way."

Morgan twisted in his chair and saw a woman who had just emerged out into the sun from the inside of the hotel. She wore large black sunglasses and a wide-brimmed beach hat which sat at an angle on her head. Her hair was done up under the hat, but her bangs and a few loose wisps on the nape of her neck showed that she had brownish-red hair. She was wearing a green beach dress which hung off her shoulders, showing a white bathing suit and her alabaster skin underneath. Her features were delicate, like that of a porcelain doll, but she walked with a haughty self-assurance that gave her something of a Jackie Onassis quality. As she entered the shade of the umbrella, she drew off her sunglasses, revealing bright cat-green eyes.

Morgan reached his hand as if to scratch his ear, and discreetly took a few pictures of the woman using the hidden camera in his glasses. Weinberg stood up to greet her, and Fleischer did as well.

"I say," she said, giving Weinberg a kiss on each cheek, "this is rather nicer than where I'm lodged." She spoke in a precise high-class English accent, voice soft as velvet, at the same time seductive and distant, announcing that she was above anything that anyone might have to offer her. Morgan could tell right away that she was a man-killer and had built herself to be the perfect predator in this kind of environment.

"Elizabeth, my dear," said Weinberg. "Please meet Daniel Morgan." He stood up to greet her.

"A pleasure," she said as she kissed Morgan on the cheek, with just enough attention to kick Weinberg off his perch of most important man at the table while letting Morgan know that he could look, but never touch.

She stood by a chair and waited, until Anse pulled it for her and she sat.

It wasn't enough to say that she dominated their little group. She changed the power dynamics at whim. Morgan decided that he liked her. More important, he needed to find out who she was.

She turned back to Weinberg. "Please, Gunther, Elizabeth is what they called me at St. Theresa's, and I hardly need the memories of angry nuns wielding meter sticks. Do call me Lily."

"Excuse me," said Weinberg. "I am old-fashioned when it comes to formality. By all means, we shall call you Lily."

"And to what do we owe the pleasure of the company of the handsome Mr. Morgan?" she asked, pulling a cigarette from her purse.

"Strictly business," he said.

"Ah, a Yank," she said with a wink. Weinberg held out a lighter, and she leaned in to ignite the tip of her cigarette. She sucked lightly so that the flame took. She then let the smoke waft through her lips before exhaling "Always so strictly business."

"Mr. Morgan here is going to sell me a car," said Weinberg.

"I was under the impression that American car salesmen were all greasy little men that reeked of desperation," she said with a teasing flash of the eyes. "But there seems to be nothing little or desperate about you, Mr. Morgan."

"Mr. Morgan is helping me acquire a rather rare specimen," said Weinberg.

"Rare specimens are in no short supply around here," she said.

"I should say," said Weinberg, gesturing subtly toward her.

"I take it you're here in a more social capacity," said Morgan, gesturing toward Lily.

"I made Herr Weinberg's acquaintance last night at the Casino Versailles," she said, motioning for the waiter. "He asked me to blow on his dice, and I most kindly obliged."

"It is my experience that the most beautiful women carry with them most of the luck."

"Funny how that happens, isn't it?" said Lily. She took another drag from her cigarette, lowering her eyelids to a look that alluded to a different kind of pleasure. "When he rolled a hard six, he wouldn't let me leave his side for the rest of the night." Then, to the waiter who had approached, bearing an ashtray: "Be a dear and bring a girl a Bellini, would you, love? Möet. And it had better be Möet, because I'll know."

"Right away, mademoiselle," he said, leaving the ash tray and taking the order.

"I swear," she continued, her attention back on the table, "I've never seen anyone put the chips down on the craps table like that, Gunther. You really are in your own class of high roller, aren't you?"

"Ah, my dear Lily, don't you understand how boring it gets?"

"Oh, I'm *sure* it does, Gunther darling. Who could take such a charmless lifestyle?"

Gunther laughed. "You don't know. You can't know if you haven't lived a life like mine. All my money, my company, is all inherited. I have seen all the beauties of the world, many times over. Tasted the food of the finest chefs—as well as, if the delicacy of your presence will excuse it, the finest women. True excitement is a precious thing, and it takes a lot of money on the line to excite a man of my means."

"Oh, how wretched," she said, with a tone of exaggerated compassion. "Who will think of our poor, over-moneyed Gunther?"

"It does get boring, you comprehend? Ah, no, no one understands me."

"I'd think that being a billionaire would be a pretty good way to stave off boredom," said Morgan.

Weinberg laughed. "One would think, wouldn't one, Mr. Morgan? But alas, the toys seem to lose their sheen faster and faster these days, don't they?"

"What you're saying is that money doesn't buy happiness?" Morgan suggested.

"It does, Mr. Morgan, but it never *lasts*."

"Well, *I* think that I should have a *marvelous* time of it with a billion dollars," said Lily.

"I should think such a beauty would want for nothing," said

Weinberg. "All men should scramble to attend to your every desire."

"Fun as it is to keep men scrambling, Herr Weinberg, fawning grows tiresome *rather* quickly."

A cell phone rang, and Fleischer picked up. There were a few seconds as Fleischer listened to the phone, the table waiting expectantly. "Herr Weinberg," said Fleischer. Weinberg pushed back his chair and stood.

"I'm afraid I must go, my friends. Mr. Morgan, it seems the appearance of Ms. Harper has derailed our conversation. Might we continue this later? My dear sister Lena will be arriving here tonight. Perhaps you two will join us for a bit of gambling at the Palatine Casino."

"But of course, Gunther," said Lily.

"Capital!" he said. "And you, Mr. Morgan? Might you find a little time for pleasure on this trip after all?"

"I might make an exception," said Morgan.

"Fabulous!"

"I think I'll stick around and finish my drink," said Lily. "Plus, I would love to pick the brain of the enigmatic Mr. Morgan."

"Please," he said. "The drinks will be charged to my account. Friends, I take my leave."

Morgan watched as Weinberg walked away, into the hotel. Then he turned to Lily Harper, who was eying him inquiringly, with her smart, bright green eyes.

"I don't buy it," she said with a sly smile.

"What don't you buy?" he said, taken aback. This he didn't expect.

"You. Fancy car salesman. In service to the wealthy of the world." She tapped her cigarette against the ash tray. "There's something about it that I don't quite buy."

"And yet, here I am, selling a fancy car, as you put it, to a wealthy man. So the facts don't seem to line up with your theory."

"And still, it's not your place. It's not familiarity that makes you blasé about this. It's . . . something else. I can't quite put my finger on it. But there is something, I'm sure of it."

Her gaze lingered on his until the waiter brought her a peach-colored drink in a champagne glass. Did she know? She sipped her drink casually and flashed him a sly grin. Was she toying with him?

"Maybe I really am just here for business," Morgan said when the waiter had moved away.

"Businessmen are fawners," she said. "Especially those who sell personal luxuries to men like Gunther Weinberg. They love every minute of times like these. To please the client and make the sale, yes, of course. But also because every salesman is a climber, and every salesman of luxury is a class climber. They love luxury because luxury is what they wish they had."

"You don't know me."

"But I know people selling to the wealthy."

"Maybe from personal experience?" he suggested.

He thought she might have been irritated by the comment, but she emitted a trilling, titillated laugh instead. "What sort of woman do you take me for?"

"Not that kind," he said. "That would be too obvious for you."

"But ultimately it is that, isn't it? Even if the transaction is not explicitly about that, even if it is marriage, or companionship for a few days or weeks, that's what I'm selling. Isn't that what you're getting at? Well, Mr. Morgan, we all sell ourselves, ultimately. I just happen to know where my value lies."

No, thought Morgan. *You know perfectly well where your value lies, and it's in saying things like that to men who think you mean it.*

"I sell cars," he told her, holding his palms up.

"*Of course* you do," she said conspiratorially.

"What?" he asked, grinning.

"Just a flight of fancy, I'm sure," she said, with the same sly smile playing on her lips.

"I'm starting to think there's more to *you* than meets the eye, Ms. Harper."

"But of course there is," she said. "A lady *never* shows all her cards, Mr. Morgan. Mystery is the source of all her power."

"Well, neither does a gentleman," said Morgan. "I guess you'll just have to keep on wondering."

"I'm *certain* I will." She stood up, putting on her sunglasses. "Mr. Morgan, *such* a pleasure to make your acquaintance. Shall I see you at the casino tonight as well?"

"You can count on it."

He watched her as she walked away, and had to chuckle as she did. She was . . . something. He didn't know what, not yet. But she was something, all right.

He looked around, got up out of his chair, and made his way back to his room. He checked that the cameras he had set up were in place and nothing had been moved. Then he spoke aloud, "Bishop, come in."

"Getting you loud and clear, Cobra."

"Did you get all that?"

"I got you chasing tail when you're supposed to be on the job."

"I was *assessing*," said Morgan. "Do you think you can get an ID for me? Is Shepard there?"

"Right here," came Lincoln Shepard's voice.

"I took a picture on my glasses," said Morgan.

"Okay, downloading," said Shepard. "Hot damn, do I hate being the one with a desk job right now."

"You'll hate it less when I'm being shot at," said Morgan. "The woman—the name she gave was Lily—Elizabeth—Harper. Can you get me an ID?"

"Well, not everyone's in a database, and if she's interesting, she's using a fake name, so—yes. I can do anything, Cobra."

"Good. Make it snappy, then."

"What about Weinberg?" asked Bishop.

"He'll be at the casino tonight," Morgan told him.

"I know, I heard," said Bishop. "It'll be a good time to break into his room and see what you find."

"My thoughts exactly," said Morgan. "Tell Bloch I need some money. For tonight."

"Some?"

"Around fifty grand. I'm going to put in an appearance at the casino, and I need to put on a good show for Weinberg."

"Fifty grand? Jeez. Bloch's not going to like this. Why don't you just hit his room once he goes?"

"He'll be suspicious if I don't show up, and he might send that walking side of beef to come check up on me. I'd rather avoid concussions this time, all right? I'm going with him, and once I'm sure he's busy, I'll get the hell out of there and gain access to his room."

"Okay, Cobra, I'll run it by her, but she's going to want to talk to you."

"Then have her call me. Also, what do we have on Weinberg's sister?"

"Let me check," broke in Shepard. "Not much, Cobra. She's been involved in the family business, but she keeps to herself for the most part. Never been the public face of the company, and she shows none of Gunther's showboating, playboy behavior. Why do you ask?"

"Apparently she's dropping by this evening. I'm thinking maybe someone should keep an eye on her," said Morgan. "If Gunther is as rotten as he seems to be, what are the odds that the other apple is glowing waxy red and plump?"

"I'll have to do a little more digging," he said. "Speaking of digging, I've managed to tap into hotel security. We're getting a live feed from all the security cameras in the place."

"Fantastic," said Morgan. "What about the casino?"

"Getting to work on it now."

"Good. Hopefully you'll get it set up by tonight."

"People who know me know better than to bet against me," bragged Shepard.

"Yeah," said Morgan. "But Weinberg has a hell of a lot of money to bet with."

Chapter 28

June 7
Monte Carlo

"Zeta, this is Cobra, come in."

Morgan stood in front of a full-length mirror framed in carved wood covered in gold leaf, adjusting the lapel on his tuxedo.

"Shepard here," came the response.

"Just about ready," said Morgan. "Are we go on your end?"

"I'm in the fingerprint database to give you access to Weinberg's room," said Shepard. "I'm going to wait to grant you permission, so that no alarm bells go off and no one corrects it between now and then. I'm also ready to reprogram your key card."

Morgan walked to his suitcase and drew out the key-card writer he'd brought with him and set it down on the living room credenza. He then drew the key card from its slot by the door and inserted it into the device. "All right," said Morgan. "It's in."

"Give it two minutes," said Shepard. Morgan ran a comb through his hair and slipped on his Ferragamo wingtips using a shoehorn.

"All right," said Shepard. "That should do it."

Morgan stowed the card and then called the lobby and had his car brought around. It was a short drive through picturesque cobblestone streets to the Palatine Casino, an imposing building, full of old-Europe luxury and elegance. As he gave the valet his car keys, he saw a figure approaching, a woman in a sleek green gown with a leg slit that reached her upper thigh, with red hair and catlike eyes that matched the color of her dress.

"Ms. Harper," he greeted her tersely, as he might a confidante.

"Mr. Morgan," she said, giving him a kiss on each cheek. "It wouldn't have worked better if we had planned it. Will you escort me inside?" She extended her arm. Morgan gave her a look, and took her arm in his. They walked together into the casino.

The magnificence of its façade was more than matched by the interior, with thick, lush carpets, columns and ornate cornices everywhere. Jennifer sure would love this. He looked at Harper, wishing for a moment that his wife were there and that he weren't running this charade. Then again, much as he loved his wife, he loved the thrill of the danger, too.

"Not exactly Las Vegas, is it?" Ms. Harper said sarcastically. Indeed it wasn't. It had nothing of the brash, garish style of Sin City, none of its cheesy themed spaces, none of the constant cacophony of bells and whistles. This was a sober environment, the level of noise barely above that of a high-end restaurant. All the guests were dressed formally in gowns and tuxes.

Few things intimidated Morgan, but he never felt at home in this kind of scene. He could blend in fine, he always did, courtesy of his CIA training, but it wasn't his place. It wasn't real or raw, and hid who people really were instead of revealing them. Harper, on the other hand, seemed like she was born to walk among these people—and still, in some way, she seemed to be an outsider like him. He couldn't quite put a finger on why.

It didn't take them long to spot Weinberg, in a black velour tuxedo, his face tinged with a light pink flush, perhaps caused by the whiskey in his hand, or maybe the one before that. He was standing at the bar, talking to a tall woman who Morgan recognized.

"Ah, Mr. Morgan, Ms. Harper. Please, come meet my lovely sister. This is Lena."

Lena Weinberg was a towering blonde, taller even than Gunther and a few years his junior. She had angular features, with a sharp, prominent chin, a straight, thin, pointed nose. She was wearing a heavy gown that wouldn't have looked out of place at a funeral. Beautiful she was, but with nothing of the airy, seductive beauty of Lily Harper. Lena Weinberg's beauty was not inviting, not even in a teasing or manipulative way. Her look was harsh and aristocratic, something like a Roman statue, displaying naked superiority and nothing more.

"Mr. Morgan," she said, with feigned warmth that was all the more distant for its pretense. "A pleasure to meet you." She kissed him twice on the cheek, then turned to Lily Harper. "Ms. Harper," she said, with a more cutting tone to her voice.

"*Enchanté,*" said Harper, who detected the tone and responded in kind. They kissed with forced formality.

"I understand you and Gunther have become . . . acquainted," she said to Harper.

"You might say that," said Harper. "We were inseparable last night on the casino floor, weren't we, Gunther dear?"

"Ms. Harper here gave me quite the streak of good luck," Weinberg told his sister.

"Then I would suggest that Ms. Harper's luck has run out by now, Gunther." Something about how Gunther and Lena Weinberg acted around each other put Morgan off. There was something almost possessive in the way Lena clung to her brother.

"Lena, play nice now," said Weinberg. "How about a turn at the roulette table?"

"How about poker?" piped in Harper. "After all, we should strive to make Mr. Morgan feel at home in a strange land."

"Very well," said Lena, tight-lipped. "Gunther, would you find a waiter? A glass of Margaux, if they have it. If not . . . well, you know what I like."

"Certainly, dear sister. Ms. Harper, Mr. Morgan, can I tempt either of you for a drink? Ah, of course, Mr. Morgan, you don't partake. Ms. Harper?"

"I think the night is ripe for a Bloody Mary."

Weinberg gave a half-smile and went off in search of a waiter. Morgan, taking his cue, wandered off, pretending to look at the slot machines, but keeping close enough to be able to eavesdrop on the conversation.

As he walked seemingly out of earshot, Lena looked at Lily with murderous eyes and said in a low, menacing voice, "I know what you are. You do not fool me. There have been dozens like you before, and there will be more after. You will get nothing out of him or us, you hear?"

Morgan hid his reaction. So Lena saw something in Ms. Harper, too—some hidden cunning. She took the Brit for a gold digger, evidently. Morgan wondered if that was it, or whether something else was going on. As a spy, he'd learned to be suspicious.

"Whatever do you mean?" said Harper, with mock innocence.

"You know very well what I mean, you worthless—"

"Now, now," said Harper. "Dear brother will return at any second. I don't think he would like it if you were *rude* to his close personal friend, now, would you?"

"Do you know what I have already done to the likes of you, Ms. Harper? Do you think you're the first little whore that has had designs on my brother? I will destroy you before you can harm us."

"You could certainly try, love."

"You do not know how far the power of money goes in such matters," said Lena.

They stared into one another's eyes with looks that might have sizzled and sparked in their animosity. Their staring contest was interrupted by Weinberg's return, which caused the loathing on their faces to morph into a veneer of airy politeness. Morgan also rejoined the group. "They did not have the Margaux, alas," Gunther said. "I hope you can make do with a 2000 Chateau Lafite Rothschild." He handed her a crystal goblet.

"That will do fine, thank you," said Lena in a clipped tone, taking the glass by the stem and sniffing it with her sharp patrician nose.

"The waiter will find us shortly with your drink, Ms. Harper. Shall we make our way to the poker tables?"

Weinberg led the way across the casino floor, greeting people whom he seemed to recognize, and found a recently vacated poker table. The croupier, a thin, bony man with a shaved head in a red smoking jacket, greeted them. "How many players?" he asked.

"I believe I'll sit it out," said Lena. "Poker is a game for men in cowboy hats and mirrored sunglasses."

"Don't be a sourpuss, Lena," said Weinberg. She shot him a look. "Fine, fine, suit yourself," he said, throwing up his hands. "Ms. Harper, will you do us the honor of joining in our game?"

"The stakes are a little rich for my blood. I'd just as soon sit it out and watch." She perched on a stool by the table near Morgan and sipped her drink. "As it happens, I rather enjoy watching." She crossed her legs and her lips curled up on the left in a half smile.

Lena stood on the opposite side of the table, arms crossed and eyes made into slits of suspicion and hostility.

"What shall be the stakes?" asked Weinberg.

"I propose a gentlemen's agreement," said Lily Harper. "Gunther can certainly beat Mr. Morgan by betting higher and higher, and Mr. Morgan is sure to reach his limit much before Gunther reaches his."

"Intellect is such an attractive trait in a woman," said Gunther.

Harper continued without missing a beat. "I say you boys agree on a limit beforehand. That should make this game more fun."

"That is acceptable to me," said Gunther.

"To me, too," said Morgan, locking eyes with Harper. What was she playing at? "Let's say, a fifty-thousand-dollar limit?"

"That would be well covered by my account here," said Weinberg.

"Let me just make a phone call," said Morgan. He stepped away from the table and pretended to start a call on his phone. He then spoke into it, "Hello, this is Dan Morgan." He gave an account number and other identifying information. "I'd like to transfer fifty thousand dollars to my account at the Palatine Casino in Monte Carlo."

"Got it," said Shepard over the comm. "I'm putting it through now, Cobra." Morgan pretended to hang up and walked back to the table.

"My bank is making the transfer right now," he said to the croupier. Morgan took his seat once more across from Weinberg.

"You'll find I am not a man who likes to lose, Mr. Morgan," said Weinberg.

"Then you're going to hate playing against me."

"We shall see, we shall see." The waiter came, bringing Lena's wine and a gin and tonic for Weinberg. "Drink?" he offered Morgan. "Ah, apologies, again I forgot. That should perhaps give you an advantage, no?" He took a sip from his glass.

"You want me to tie my arms behind my back to make it fair?" Morgan said with a grin.

"Being cocky is not a winning strategy with me," said Weinberg, leaning forward against the table with a wolfish look of savage competition.

"What is the style, gentlemen?" asked the croupier.

"Texas hold 'em," said Morgan. "Aces high, no wild cards. Is that good for you?"

"A gentlemen's game," said Weinberg.

Lena snorted.

The croupier dealt the first hand. Morgan glanced at his cards, barely lifting them off the table. Mostly, he watched Weinberg's face intently. He knew well enough that, in poker as in spycraft, you play your opponent's cards rather than your own. He'd learned to play for stakes with the best in his group at the Farm, the CIA training facility, where the players used the deception techniques they were instructed in for the game. He had never played more difficult players, never encountered stronger poker faces, than those men, and in consequence, he won almost every poker game he ever entered. He wondered if the German's face would give anything away.

The flop gave Morgan a pair of jacks. He kept his eyes fixed on Weinberg—no sign of a reaction. Weinberg tossed in two thousand, and Morgan saw the bet. The croupier dealt the turn, which gave Morgan nothing. Another round passed where Morgan matched a low bet of Weinberg's, and still no sign of anything on his face. Morgan could tell he was no novice. The croupier then turned the river: jack of clubs. And he saw it: a slight twitch on Weinberg's lips, on the left. Bastard had a tell.

Weinberg raised him five thousand. Morgan had to know about the twitch, had to find out what it meant. It would be worth losing this that much. He saw the bet.

Weinberg showed his cards: a two and a four, which paired with a four on the table. The croupier dragged the chips over to Morgan. So that was his tell for a bluff. It meant he had nothing. Good to know.

"An auspicious beginning, Mr. Morgan," said Lily Harper. Both Morgan and Weinberg were too intensely involved in the game to respond.

Another hand was dealt, and the flop. Morgan had a king in his hand, another on the table. Eyes still on Weinberg, he made a three-thousand-dollar bet.

"Bold," Weinberg said. "But bold might lose you this game faster than otherwise."

"Maybe you should take a look at who has the bigger pile of chips," said Morgan.

The croupier showed the turn—another king. That was three kings. Morgan had a strong hand—and he had not taken his eyes off Weinberg. The croupier turned the river—queen, of no consequence to Morgan's hand. He just kept his gaze fixed on his opponent's face.

Morgan tossed in ten thousand.

"Very well, Mr. Morgan. I see your ten, and raise you twenty."

And there was the tell, the minuscule twitch of the lips. He was bluffing. He had to be.

"I'll see that bet," said Morgan.

Weinberg showed his cards. An ace and a two of spades. With three spade cards on the table—

Flush. A winning hand.

"Oh, goodness, Mr. Morgan," said Harper, "I think I am not clear on the specifics of this game, but that's bad news for you, isn't it?"

Morgan looked at Weinberg again, masking his suspicion. Had he been mistaken? Had he misread the twitch in Weinberg's lips? No, Morgan was sure of what he had seen. It could only mean one thing. Weinberg was playing a subtle game. He had pretended the tell at first, to lure Morgan into a greater bet. He knew how to wrap deception in the semblance of truth—even more, to disguise it as an involuntary betrayal. He was a clever one. But not clever enough—he had shown his hand too soon, so to speak. He might have saved his trick for a coup de grace, but now Morgan knew, and it wouldn't work on him again.

Weinberg smiled, as though he couldn't contain his self-satisfaction at his own cleverness. *Good,* thought Morgan. He was smart, but he didn't have the patience to take full advantage of it. He would throw away a dominant position just to gloat. It was a weakness to exploit—especially effective because Weinberg counted on it as a strength.

"Ah, I'll say, this hardly stings," said Weinberg. "Thirty thousand dollars, feh. Pocket change."

"Let's make this more interesting, then," said Morgan. He knew how men like Weinberg worked. Morgan wanted to impress him, to give him a thrill—something that would cloud his thinking, leave him high from a big win, and hence vulnerable to pride and care-lessness.

"Oh?" said Weinberg.

"Oh, good, I *like* interesting," said Harper excitedly, taking an-other sip of her Bloody Mary. Half the glass was gone now.

"The Chevelle is appraised at two million dollars, the full ticket price you promised to pay for it earlier today," Morgan said. "Cover me for that amount, and the car will serve as our collateral."

"Ah," said Gunther. Finally, something had surprised him. His interest was piqued. "I like that idea. At last, Mr. Morgan, you are letting loose a little bit. Allowing yourself to have a bit of fun."

"Gunther," said Lena in an admonishing tone.

"Oh, Lena, stop it," he said. "When is the last time you enjoyed yourself this much?"

"*Two million, Gunther.*"

"Precisely, my dear Lena. Two million."

"Cobra, what the *hell* are you doing?" asked Shepard through the communicator in Morgan's ear. Pretending to scratch his neck, Morgan pressed the tiny device through the cartilage of his ear and turned it off.

"*I* am not enjoying myself at all," said Lena. "And you are en-joying this altogether too much."

"You're right, I *am* enjoying myself." Weinberg cackled. "Mr. Morgan, I accept your offer. We will set the limit for this game at two million dollars. Croupier, would you make the arrangements with the casino? Permit a line of credit to be extended to Mr. Mor-gan from my account."

"Let's do this," said Morgan.

"I like you, Mr. Morgan. You have the—what do you Americans say? Stomach? Entrails? Balls. You have the balls, Mr. Morgan." Weinberg downed what was left of his drink and motioned to a waiter for another.

"You're not the first man to say that," he said.

"Nor the last, I'm sure. Are we ready, croupier?" Then, to Mor-gan, "What do you say? Ten thousand minimum bet, same for the big blind?"

"Sounds good to me," said Morgan, maintaining eye contact.

The game was a high-wire act for the both of them. Weinberg

had no tell, and Morgan knew he had none, either. Morgan lost two hundred thousand on the first hand, then won three hundred on the second. Bets continued to climb for five more hands, and the game remained even.

The cards were dealt, and he looked at his. Pocket aces. The croupier then dealt the flop—another ace. There was a round of betting, an inconsequential turn, and then the river: the last ace. Morgan had four of a kind.

"All in," said Weinberg, pushing his chips to the center of the table. The croupier deftly counted the chips.

"Two million, one hundred and sixty thousand from Mr. Weinberg."

Morgan had to finish the game, and he couldn't win. Weinberg had to end up on top, had to be left drunk on the victory. If he turned this bet down, he might not get a second chance any time soon.

"All in," said Morgan.

"That is one million, eight hundred forty thousand for Mr. Morgan," said the croupier. "All in."

Lily Harper visibly thrilled, a broad smile of perfect white teeth brightening her face.

Weinberg laughed out loud, attracting the attention of nearby tables. "Yes! Yes! Excellent!"

Weinberg showed his cards.

"Straight," said the croupier. "Ace high."

Less than a four of a kind. But Morgan had to lose. He placed his cards facedown on the table.

"Fold," he said in a dazed whisper, feigning the despair and sudden realization of a man who could not afford to lose two million dollars.

Weinberg broke out in uproarious laughter. "Brilliant! Ha ha!"

"Herr Weinberg wins," announced the croupier.

"Ah, *mein freund,*" said Weinberg, laughing, "you were foiled by American impulsivity. It did not serve you well this time."

"Wouldn't be the first time," said Morgan, looking grim.

"But if you don't go big, you never win big, right? Just not this time! Ha ha!"

"I'm sure that smarts, Mr. Morgan," said Lily.

"A drink to celebrate my new car?" asked Weinberg. "Ah yes, of course, you don't drink. But you won't mind if I do, certainly? Waiter! A Bollinger ninety-five, if you please!"

"Right away, sir."

"This is all awfully exciting, but I'm afraid I'm feeling none too well," said Harper. "The atmosphere might be a little too rich for my blood. If you'd please excuse me, I think I shall retire to my hotel."

"Seeing as I have no money left to play with, I think I'll escort Ms. Harper," said Morgan. He extended his hand to the German. "Gunther, well played."

"I'll be expecting you to bring my new car around the hotel in the morning, Mr. Morgan!" he said. "I am exhilarated by my victory. I believe my sister and I shall stay behind and work some of that out on the craps tables."

"Shall we, Mr. Morgan?" asked Lily, extending her arm. He took it, and they walked together toward the exit. "That must have hurt. Two million dollars? You are not a billionaire, from what I have gathered."

"And you're not embarrassed of walking out of the casino with a loser, Ms. Harper?"

"Well, Mr. Morgan, there are losers, and then there are *losers.* I get the feeling you are not of the type to be a loser for very long."

They walked past fancily dressed people and waiters in black and red.

"You know," she said, "someone might get the wrong idea, the two of us leaving together like this."

"Wrong idea? What could you be talking about, Ms. Harper?"

"Mr. Morgan, do be careful. A girl could fall for a man like you."

"One already has," he said. "I'm married."

"And still," she said, flashing him those vibrant green eyes, "I can't quite seem to care." He caught a whiff of her perfume, a scent, appropriately enough, of lilies. They were at the door to the casino now. She handed her ticket to the valet, and he handed his.

"Very flattering. A guy has to wonder why the feedback is so overwhelmingly positive from a girl like you."

"Are you concerned that I might be *interested* in you, Mr. Morgan?" she said, looking pointedly at his wedding ring.

"No, Ms. Harper. The problem with flattery is exactly when it's not the other *person* you're interested in."

"You've detected my stratagem then!" she said with a giggle.

By admitting it, she was still flattering him, but he didn't want to play the game to its ultimate level. "Home wrecker," was all he said, with a half-smirk.

"You don't know the half of it," she said with a lighthearted laugh. "So, big boy, how about it?"

"What do you think?" he said, holding up his left hand and offering an expression that said that he was not a man who could be seduced.

She looked at him with fake seriousness, then an exaggerated pouty frown. "Oh, all right. This is me, anyway." The valet had brought around a compact Aston Martin sports car. "Ta-ta, Mr. Morgan. Perhaps one day we shall meet again."

Morgan watched as she got into her car and sped away. His Mercedes was brought around next. He tipped the valet and got into the driver's seat. It was a few minutes before he made it back to the hotel. Once there, Morgan walked up to his room and turned on his communicator.

"Bishop, come in," Morgan said as he shed his tuxedo.

"This is Shepard," came the hacker's voice. "You know Bloch is flipping out over this million-dollar shenanigan."

"I made him feel like a winner," said Morgan. "He'll be riding that high all night on the casino floor while I do what I came to do. I know what these ops cost. I made a judgment call, and believe me, this was worth it. Speaking of," he said, taking a small electronic device and inserting it into the pocket of his khakis, "Time to disable those cameras for me."

"Stand by," said Shepard, with an almost audible shrug. Shepard was going to use his back door into the security system to loop old video on the security cameras as Morgan made his way to Weinberg's suite, so that there would be no record of the break-in, or even of Morgan leaving his room.

"All right," said Shepard. "Coast is clear and the camera feed's been overridden. Out you go."

Morgan walked out of his room and shut the door behind him. He made straight for the stairwell, then walked two flights up.

"Stop," said Shepard as Morgan reached the door to the top floor. "People in the hall." Morgan stood flat against the wall. He heard footsteps come closer, then recede. "Wait for it. . . . Go, now."

Morgan opened the door to the hallway and walked down to Weinberg's door. He inserted the key card he had made, and then placed his finger on the scanner. The LED light on the door flashed green, and the lock on the door opened. He wiped the scanner with the sleeve of his suit jacket and pulled out medical latex gloves from his inside breast pocket. He slipped them on and pulled the door open.

"All right," said Morgan, "going in."

"I see you, Cobra," said Shepard.

Once in the darkened room, Morgan pulled the door behind him, closing it with a light *click.*

"Restoring video feed," said Shepard. "In three . . . two . . . one . . . and we're back. Get to it, Cobra."

Morgan looked about the suite in the half light filtering in from the wide French doors to the balcony. It consisted of three spacious rooms. The living room was clean and neat, furnished in some sort of modern Louis XV fusion style, and to his right, wide-open French doors led to a dining area. He scanned these two rooms room for any computers, checking under furniture and in cabinets, finding none. Not that he thought it was going to be that easy. He turned a solid gilded doorknob to open heavy wooden doors that led into the bedroom, which held a wide four-poster bed of carved wood, sheer fabric draped from its canopy. Somewhere, there'd be a safe, and it would be close to Weinberg, near where he slept. He opened the closet, and found the black rectangular metal box with a keypad on its door.

"Shepard, what's the override code on the hotel safe?"

"Hold on," said Shepard, dragging the second word. "Four oh three nine."

He input the code and opened the safe. It was empty. He looked through the closet, then under the bed, then in the fireplace that adorned the wall next to the doors to the balcony. "Is there any other safe in this room? Any other hiding place?"

"Let me take a look," said Shepard. Morgan went to the desk in the other room, examining it for any hidden compartments. Then he went to the luggage, careful not to rumple any shirts, and checked for a false bottom. Nothing.

"Maybe you were wrong about the device," said Morgan.

"I wasn't wrong," said Shepard. "He needs to have somewhere to keep his data."

"Well, maybe you goddamn *were* wrong, Shepard," said Morgan as he checked every inch of the bed frame, running his hands underneath it for a latch of some sort. "Maybe it's all on his phone, or maybe—"

"Got it!" said Shepard. "The closet on the left side, farthest from the regular safe."

"Yeah?" said Morgan. "All I see is solid wood."

"Open the top drawer," he said. "Feel underneath. You'll find a latch."

He felt the smooth wood until his fingers grazed something small and metal. "Got it!" He clicked it, and the shelf above the top drawer opened upward, revealing a hidden compartment that jutted down, unseen, into the drawer's space, only about two feet across, one foot long, with a steel door and another keypad. The best safes weren't the ones that were hardest to crack, but the ones nobody ever knew existed.

"Tell me you have the override code for this one too," said Morgan.

"Of course! Can you imagine if some clown can't get his wife's jewels out because he forgot the combination?"

"Anytime tonight would be fine, Shepard," Morgan insisted.

"All right, all right, hold your horses," he said. "Okay, here goes. Five seven five three."

Morgan punched in the numbers as Shepard spoke. On pressing the three, he heard the mechanism whirring inside, and a green light flashed.

"Bingo," said Morgan. He pulled open the safe door. Laid out carefully inside were a number of paper documents, a pile of cashier's checks, and a small corrugated aluminum briefcase, about the size of a tablet computer. That was what he was after. He stood the briefcase up on the compartment and examined the four-digit lock, all wheels set to zero. Morgan closed his eyes and set to work.

He pulled the latch, as if to open the suitcase, and felt the tightness of the wheels. The first from the right was tight, and the rest loose. He turned the first wheel from zero to one, and felt the others again. Still tight. He continued turning the first wheel, one number at a time, until he felt that the next wheel over had grown tight. This meant that he had found the correct number for the first. He went on to apply the same process to the second wheel, then the third. With the fourth, he tried each number one at a time until he hit the right one, and the lock swung open with a heavy click.

Morgan opened his eyes, set the briefcase on its side, and pulled it open. Inside, tucked into a neat foam frame, was a black rectangular box, just slightly bigger than a paperback, with a keypad on it. This was the external hard drive, encrypted with a code, impossible for Morgan to guess. But luckily, he had help.

Morgan drew another device, a special thumb drive that was actually about twice the size of his thumb, from his inside pocket, which he connected to the hard drive via its USB port.

The thumb drive, specially prepared by Shepard, began downloading everything on the drive. The data would still be encrypted, but encryptions could be cracked with a powerful enough computer, which would be no problem at all, as long as they had enough time to run the program. The issue was getting access to the data in the first place. And by doing it this way, they could steal it without Weinberg ever knowing it was gone.

Morgan looked around the room once more. It was still dark, the only light coming from the pool area outside, wispy curtains flying in the breeze. In about a minute, the thumb drive blinked red to indicate that the download was complete. He removed it from the USB slot, then set the drive back exactly as he had found it in the briefcase. He then set all the wheels back to zero, closed the safe and locked it with the override code.

He heard the metallic *whir* of the lock resetting.

"Okay, now it's time to get the hell out of here," he said to Shepard through his comm.

Just as he was about to turn around, he heard the *click* of a gun being cocked behind him. He turned, holding up his arms, the thumb drive in his right hand.

Behind him, across the bed, was a figure dressed all in black with a black hood over its face and a ski mask covering everything but the eyes. From the outline, he could see that it was a woman, lithe like a cat. She was holding a snub-nosed Ruger LCR double-action revolver in her right hand. It was a tiny gun, almost comically small. But, even if it didn't have the stopping power of a

Desert Eagle, she could stop him well enough by plugging a couple of these bullets in his chest, and she seemed to be well aware of that. With her left hand, she pointed at the thumb drive, then motioned for him to give it to her.

"You don't want this, sweetheart," he said. "I can get you money. However much you want. This here isn't worth anything to you."

"Cobra?" asked Shepard. "What the hell is going on in there?"

Morgan couldn't answer directly, so he said to the woman, "Are you in Weinberg's room for his money? I can give you the combination to his safe."

She made a show of taking aim at his heart, and motioned once more for him to give her the thumb drive.

"Cobra, is someone in there with you? I'm paging Bishop as we speak, he'll come and get you."

Damn it, thought Morgan. All he needed was a tactical team barging into this situation. "I don't think you'll shoot me," he said. "It would be a damn shame if we attracted a lot of attention to ourselves and the owner of this room found out we were here." He hoped Shepard would take a hint.

"Do you want me to call it off?" asked Shepard. "Use the word 'bad' if you do."

"Looks like we've got ourselves in a bad situation here," said Morgan.

"Okay," said Shepard, "calling them off. They'll be circling the hotel. I hope you know what you're doing."

The woman made an emphatic gesture for him to give her the thumb drive.

The bed was between them. He couldn't rush her, not without taking three bullets to the chest. Running away was equally out of the question. Call her bluff? Dodge her bullets? Or live to fight another day?

"All right," Morgan said. He tossed it to her, too hard, trying to get her to fumble, but she caught it like a pro, and put it into a pocket in her pants. She then took a bow and started walking backward, to the balcony door.

"Shit!" cried Shepard. "Cobra! It's Fleischer! He's on your floor!"

Goddamn it. Well, there was no saving this op now. "Fleischer is coming," said Morgan to the woman. "He's going to be in through that door any second now. Let's get out of here, you and me, before he catches us."

The woman stopped moving, as if startled, and trying to figure out what to do.

"It's true," said Morgan. "We've got to get out of here." He inched closer to her. He had to get that thumb drive.

"Cobra, I'm going to deauthorize his card, but that'll only hold him so long."

The figure continued her inching walk toward the door to the balcony, gun trained on his chest. He inched along with her, keeping a constant distance between them. He cleared the bed, so that nothing blocked his way to her.

They both heard the sound of a card being inserted into the reader at the door, and a fumbling at the knob. The thief turned her head to look. Morgan took advantage of the distraction by dodging to the left and then rushing her. He knocked the gun out of her hand, but she avoided his tackle. The gun hit the hardwood floor with a heavy *thunk* and went sliding to the corner of the room.

Morgan swung a punch, and she ducked out of the way. She grabbed a poker from the fireplace and swung at him. It connected painfully with his side, strong enough to crack a rib. She swung again, this time at his head, but he grabbed it and pulled it out of her hand. She staggered forward as he did, and he got her into a half nelson. At the door, Fleischer was rattling the doorknob.

Morgan could feel her hair on his face, bunched up and covered by the black hood. Up so close, he could even make out her scent, almost neutral, but with just a hint of—

"Lily?" he asked. The hesitation was all she needed to kick him in the shin and swing her head back hard, hitting him in the cheek. That was going to leave a mark. His grasp slipped just enough for her to wrest herself free.

She dashed out to the balcony, and Morgan ran after her. He followed her down the length of the balcony, past the three French doors to the other rooms of the suite.

"Nowhere to go from here!" he yelled out.

"Nowhere to go but up!" she answered, clambering with incredible, catlike speed onto the railing, then a cornice, then pulling herself up to the roof. She looked down at him, gloating. "Sorry love," she said, "but Weinberg's *mine*." She disappeared into the darkness, taking the thumb drive with her. *Goddamn it!* He examined the walls, amazed—there was no foothold he could possibly use to follow her up.

"She's on the roof," said Morgan.

"Who's she?" asked Shepard. "What?"

"Lily Harper's on the goddamn roof! I want Bishop and tactical on it! And check out where she's staying. She drives a blue Aston Martin sports car. She's got the thumb drive. Find her!"

Morgan heard a loud crack. Through the door to the balcony, he saw that Fleischer had just broken down the door, and was standing at the doorway.

"*Scheisse,*" whispered Morgan.

Morgan looked at that mountain of a man. He didn't like the odds of a fair fight against him, and he didn't have a gun on him. He looked back, but the odds of not breaking his legs in the fall were even worse. Morgan ran forward, grabbed the poker that Lily had dropped and took a running swing at Fleischer. He was big and slow, and didn't react fast enough. Morgan hit him square in the face. He doubled down and held his face in his hands, crying out in pain. Morgan ran right past him and out the door.

He ran down the stairs, skipping steps at a time, straight to the lobby and then out the door.

"Mr. Morgan," said the valet as he approached, "Shall I get your car?"

Morgan ran right past him, ignoring the question.

"Shepard, I need someone to pick me up."

"Where are you?"

"Running along the hotel."

"Bishop's coming around with the tac team in the van," he said. "I've got you on GPS. I'm sending him your way."

Morgan kept on running until a black van pulled up alongside him. The side door opened, and he saw Spartan and Diesel, from Zeta tactical, inside. He hopped into the van without its coming to a stop, and it kept right on moving with him inside. They closed the side door, and Morgan fell back against the seat, exhausted.

"So what's the status?" asked Spartan.

"I lost it, and I got made. Total bust. Any sight of her?"

"We were just about to spread out and make our search," she said.

"It's too late," said Morgan. "She'll be gone by now. Let's regroup."

"And then what?" asked Bishop from the front seat.

"Then we find Lily Harper and get that thumb drive back. Did you hear, Shepard? *Find out where she's staying.* Because if we don't, we've lost the only thing we've got on Weinberg, and our only connection to the location of the Secretary."

Chapter 29

June 8
Monte Carlo

"Have you got anything on Lily Harper?" asked Morgan, poking at his rib where she had whacked him with the iron poker.

He was back at the temporary base of operations that they had set up in Monte Carlo. It was a two-story house, up the hill and far from the beach. Shepard was at his computer, as usual, and Morgan was pacing the room. Bishop and the tactical team were out looking for Lily Harper at the hotel where they had found out she had been registered. Morgan wasn't hopeful that she'd be there.

"Nothing," said Shepard. "Nothing yet, anyway."

"You have a picture, can't you use face recognition software to match it to an ID?" Morgan asked as he looked at his reflection in the mirror. He had an ugly black-and-blue bruise on his left cheek where she had head-butted him.

"Yes, but it takes time to run a picture through every known database in international intelligence!" Shepard said.

"All right, all right," said Morgan, backing off.

He stepped out onto the balcony, looking at the breathtaking beauty of the Monte Carlo sunrise. A longing crept up from the back of his mind to be here with his wife, Jenny. He pictured what it would be like to be there without responsibilities, an actual vacation—

Some movement below caught the corner of his eye, and he turned his head down to look. It was a blue compact Aston Martin, driving down the road.

Lily Harper.

"Is the car fueled up?" Morgan asked Shepard.

"What?" asked Shepard.

"The car," said Morgan. "The Chevelle. Is it fueled up?"

"Yeah, we had it ready for Weinberg to turn on the engine and test it out."

"Good. Where are the keys?"

"They're in the garage, hung up on a hook," said Shepard. "What—"

"No time!" said Morgan. "Send Bishop and the rest after me!"

Morgan ran downstairs and burst into the garage. He took the keys and pushed the button to open the garage door. He then got behind the wheel of the car. He turned the ignition, and the car came to life.

It was sacrilege, he knew. The car was mint condition. There was no other car like it. He looked down at the odometer, which read only one mile, as the garage door rolled open. Simply driving it would ruin it, let alone the kind of driving that Morgan tended to do. It was physically uncomfortable for him to do this. But the mission was more important. It was the most important, more than any car. Even a two-million-dollar, one-of-a-kind car. He took a deep breath.

Morgan tore out of the garage. The driveway was practically nonexistent, and he drove right out onto the road. Harper was on a different street, over and down, and with the glimpse he had caught, he formed a mental map. He maneuvered and turned right, then a second right to follow her. She'd be ahead of him now, but he had a hunch that she'd be getting out of town at that very moment, and there was one way out from where they were.

Morgan picked up speed, but was still not going fast enough to attract attention from the police. In under a minute, he was within sight of the Aston Martin. He coasted the car, letting it slow down to keep a fair distance from her.

She picked up speed. *Damn,* Morgan thought. He figured he'd be able to follow her for longer before she caught on. She was good. She'd had training, that much was obvious. And he supposed the racing stripes on the Chevelle didn't exactly help.

Harper sped on down the avenue, forcing cars off the narrow road. She was driving a small sports car with excellent steering, while Morgan's vehicle was broader and heavier, made for the open

American road and not narrow European streets. Morgan had to swerve left and right to keep up, dodging compact European cars and leaving angry, honking drivers in his wake. To his right was a short cliff, and Morgan knew that going off of it would mean serious injury, possibly death. He pressed on.

Up ahead, Harper turned into the highway, which was not much wider than the avenue they had been on, but gave them a bit more room to maneuver. He stepped on the gas, leaning on the horn so that other drivers would get out of the way. She was putting a lot of distance between them. He had to speed up, or he was going to lose her, and the very thing that he'd come to Monte Carlo to retrieve.

Ahead he saw a sharp, upward-inclined curve. Morgan knew that if he slowed down here, he'd lose her. *Let's go then, you bastard.* He floored the accelerator, going for a drift, and the car roared. He turned, but the tires didn't hold. The car spun out, the world becoming a blur until he felt the impact with a boulder on the passenger's side, just in time to see Harper's Aston Martin disappearing in the distance.

Morgan blinked twice. He felt woozy. He blinked again, and had the impression he had blacked out, not knowing how much time had passed. Seconds? Minutes? Though the car was still, the world still seemed to be spinning.

"Shepard?" he said. Had he put in the communicator or had he left it? He couldn't remember. "Shepard? Come in." He tried to feel for it in his ear, but the task seemed to be beyond him.

He tried to open the door, but it took several pushes before he could get it open. He staggered out of the car, but his knees buckled and he fell to the ground.

Morgan turned on his back, and looked up to see a man looking down on him. His vision was blurry, so it took a moment for the face to resolve into that of Anse Fleischer. The world darkened as the enormous German picked him up. Morgan was dragged into a navy blue BMW sedan. Morgan lost consciousness just as the door shut out all the light from the outside.

Chapter 30

June 8
Monte Carlo

Dan Morgan woke up facing the wall in a suite he did not recognize in a hotel that was, judging by its decor, most definitely in Monte Carlo. The red-and-gold wallpaper told him that it was not the Oiseau. Oddly, the patterns seemed to be moving. His arms and legs were bound with strong packing tape to a heavy upholstered chair, made of hardwood and thus impossible to take apart if he wanted to make a quick escape. *Bad.* He looked to his right to see the room door, and then to his left to find Weinberg sitting back on an armchair that matched the wallpaper, drinking a gin and tonic out of a tall glass. *Worse.*

Morgan felt thick meaty hands grab his chair, and he thought he might lose his lunch as the man—it could only be Anse Fleischer—swiveled the chair so that Morgan was facing Weinberg.

"You seemed to have crashed my car, Mr. Morgan," he said, taking a sip from his drink. "I'm afraid I must ask you for your insurance information. And—oh, yes, you broke into my room and stole something from me."

Weinberg took a cigarette from a golden cigarette case and set it aflame it with a matching lighter. "I don't smoke, did you know that? Not usually." He took a deep, needy drag from his cigarette. "Except when I am very, very angry."

He made a waving signal with his hand. Anse Fleischer appeared from behind Morgan and stood in front of him, the massive German's abdomen taking up Morgan's entire field of vision. Morgan didn't literally see it coming, but he was expecting the back-handed slap delivered across the face. His cheek stung, especially where the stroke had caught the bone. He looked up at Fleischer's face, towering above him. There was a nasty cut running from his left cheek to his nose from where Morgan has struck him with the poker.

"Oh, good," said Morgan. "We're practically matching. Maybe we can sing together later." Weinberg gestured, and Fleischer hit him again.

"Mr. Morgan, perhaps you should sing now, alone," said Weinberg. "Was there anyone else working with you?"

Morgan spat blood on the carpet at Weinberg's feet.

"Of course you did not act alone," he said. "This was not a job for just one man. The question now is, who do you work for, Mr. Morgan?"

"I'm self-employed, actually," said Morgan. "The hours are great, but they really hose you with the tax—" *Thwack.* Fleischer's hand fell heavily again.

Morgan heard the room door swing open behind him. "Shall I bother to say 'I told you so,' Gunther?" came Lena Weinberg's cold, haughty voice from behind Morgan.

"Indeed you did, little sister," said Weinberg. "I should listen to you more often."

"That's what I keep saying, but do you listen?" she said humorlessly.

Weinberg sipped his drink with affected nonchalance, but Morgan saw that his grip on the glass was leaving him white-knuckled, and he had sucked down his cigarette with urgent rage. Weinberg was angry, angry enough to be very dangerous in the short term. Morgan looked around the room. The tycoon was sitting in front of wide bay windows. Morgan could see nothing but sky from his vantage point. But that meant that they were probably still facing the sea, still on the bluff, and thus not far from the Oiseau Hotel.

"I had a feeling," said Lena, walking around Morgan's chair to crouch in front of him, "that you were up to something. I just wasn't sure what. At first, I thought you were simply a con man, here to cheat Gunther out of money. God knows, there have been plenty of *those* vultures circling my family fortune ever since we were children. But

I did not know about *you,* not for sure. So I asked to the croupier, with a very generous tip, for him to reveal your cards. And what did you think we found?"

"That card dealers at the Palatine are incorruptible?"

Weinberg leaned forward met Morgan's eyes straight on. "What sort of a man folds a winning hand of two million dollars?" he growled. "That is my question, Mr. Morgan. I might, perhaps, on a whim. But you are *not* me, Mr. Morgan. Two million is not a fun night out for you, it is the difference between retiring tomorrow and having to work into your eighties so that you can have a roof over your head. So when does a man like you fold on two million dollars?"

"When he wants something other than money," said Morgan.

"When he's not paying the bills," said Weinberg. "Which leads me to ask you again, Mr. Morgan, who do you work for?"

Morgan turned to Fleischer. "I'll give you one million dollars cash to turn on them and help me escape," he said. "You know I'm good for it." Fleischer walked to him, towering above him. In a flash, Morgan felt the sting of the man's hand against his cheek. Weinberg laughed.

"Anse has been with our family since he was born," he said, "as his father was before him. This is not a loyalty that can be bought, Mr. Morgan."

"No, just cultivated," said Morgan. "Instilled in the family dog."

Fleischer moved to strike Morgan, but Weinberg stayed him by raising his hand. "He is merely trying to anger you, now that he has found that he cannot turn you. Keep your calm. And remember that you will have the opportunity to kill him *after* we are done questioning him."

"Well, *that* puts you in a weak bargaining position, doesn't it?" said Morgan. "Letting on that you're going to kill me."

"He speaks of death without fear," said Lena. "I can tell." She leaned in close to him so that he could almost smell her breath. There was nothing seductive about her proximity, only menace. "You have been acquainted with death, haven't you, Mr. Morgan?"

"I will not suffer those who cross me to live," said Weinberg, lighting a second cigarette. "But believe me, Mr. Morgan, there are things worse than death. I have not told Anse *how* to kill you. If you cooperate, perhaps I will give him specific instructions to make it quick and painless. If not..." He drew deeply on the cigarette. "Anse does like to get creative in his killing, don't you, Anse? It is a trait we like to encourage."

"No way I can bargain for my life then?" asked Morgan. "After all, I might have something you want."

Weinberg raised his left eyebrow. "And what would that be?"

"I can tell you everything about who sent me. The people who are after you. It won't stop with me, you know."

"Who is it?" Weinberg demanded.

"Not unless you let me go," said Morgan.

"Your life is not necessary to get me what I want," said Weinberg. "There is nothing Anse can't torture out of you."

This wouldn't have been the first time Morgan had been on the rack, and he knew he could hold up, at least for a couple of days. But he'd known of stronger men than him that had broken under continual, sustained torture. The important thing was not to get spooked. If he could keep thinking and talking, he could delay his death long enough to plan his escape.

"That might work," said Morgan. "Of course, as soon as my people figure out that I've been captured, they're going to start covering their tracks. Soon, any trail I can lay out for you is going to have gone cold." Morgan leaned forward as far as his restraints permitted him. "And even if you can get everything out of me eventually, I can guarantee you that you won't be able to get it all out of me quickly." He sat back, in a relaxed position. "I can tell you what you want to know, but only if you let me go."

Weinberg looked at his sister, then back at Morgan. "And I suppose just my promising to release you is not going to be enough?"

"No, not really," said Morgan.

"Okay," said Weinberg. "Tell me what you have—give me some idea of the information you can offer me—and I will tell you whether it is worth your life."

"Just kill him and be done with it!" insisted Lena.

"Let him speak," said Weinberg.

"I guess I can do that, if Eva Braun here gives me a chance," said Morgan, shooting a glance at Lena. She was smart. Smarter than Gunther, even. He wondered if she was the true brains behind the company. "I happen to work for a competitor—no, I will not tell you which. I'm a contractor, ex-US intelligence. My specialty is industrial espionage. I will not tell you any more than that until I have some manner of guarantee that I will be let go."

"Telling me who your boss is will not be sufficient for that," said Weinberg. "I know I have enemies who would like to steal my secrets, to discredit me, and even to have me killed. The information you are attempting to entice me with is nothing to me. Do better."

"Okay," said Morgan. *Just keep talking until something sticks.* "I can give you data—information that I have gathered already, and what others like me have gathered."

"Are you suggesting that you're going to tell me about *myself,* and that will save you?" Weinberg smiled. "I thought that you were better than that."

"It's not only that," he said. "You'll know what they know. And there's other data, about other companies—things that I can guarantee will be valuable to you. You would be able to strike back and deal a crippling blow to my employers. It would, at the very least, set our industrial espionage program back months."

"You turn rather quickly on the hand that feeds you," said Lena.

"Like I said, I'm a contractor," said Morgan. "Not a company man. What, you think I'd die for someone just because they cut me a check?"

"You yourself said that some things cannot be bought," said Weinberg, finishing off a second cigarette. "Not with money, anyway." He mashed the stub into a brass ashtray. "Let's suppose that this deal is advantageous to me. How do we make a trade? I will not let you go until you show it to me, and once you have, that is the whole game, no?"

"I guess that is a problem, isn't it?" said Morgan. "But there might be a solution to our little conundrum. The information I am offering you is accessible on an encrypted server. I can give you access to this with a password. We go out to a public place, where I can be sure you will not shoot me, and—"

"And you can run away to safety," said Lena. "Kill him. He is a liar, and is probably lying again."

"Hmm, yes," said Weinberg, stroking his beard. "It does pose a problem. Still, we need not take his word for it. What he said is easily verifiable. Anse, will you get my computer for me, please?"

"No," said Morgan. "Not here."

"Here, Mr. Morgan. That is my best offer."

"I'm not giving it to you here. I don't have any guarantee you won't kill me if I give it to you here."

"Anse," said Weinberg. "Give Mr. Morgan a little incentive."

Fleischer bent down and grabbed Morgan's left hand. He took Morgan's pinky finger in his thick paw.

I hate this part.

Fleischer bent Morgan's finger back until it cracked. Morgan screamed through gritted teeth, squirming wildly in his chair, straining against the restraints.

"You will give me the information now," said Fleischer. "Or you will give me the information after you have no fingers left. The decision is yours."

"Someone will hear," he said, panting with pain.

"The room is soundproofed," said Weinberg. "One of the benefits of paying an ungodly daily rate. Mr. Morgan, tell me how to access the server."

"Not until—"

"Anse," said Weinberg. "Again."

Fleischer grabbed Morgan's ring finger and pulled it back. Morgan roared with pain.

"Are you ready to talk?" said Weinberg.

"Eat shit," said Morgan, through heavy breaths and a fog of pain. The bastard just sat back and sipped his drink like he was watching the opera. Morgan looked at his two mangled fingers bending backward at sickeningly wrong angles, and wondered if they had been broken or just dislocated.

"That is not very polite," said Weinberg. Morgan spat at him, the bloody gob landing on Weinberg's suede loafers. Weinberg looked down with disgust, then motioned to his valet. "Anse."

Fleischer grabbed Morgan's middle finger. Morgan winced. "Okay, okay!" Morgan exclaimed. Fleischer held his finger but didn't bend it back. Weinberg held up his hand. "I'll tell you. Open the browser and input exactly what I tell you."

Lena picked up the computer. She had been standing and pacing, but now she sat next to Weinberg and waited for the laptop to start up. "Shoo," said Morgan at Anse, who scowled in response.

"Okay," said Lena. "I am ready. Let's see what Mr. Morgan has for us."

Morgan dictated the address of one of Zeta's shared servers, staring at the thick patterned carpet as he did, with a look of shame and defeat. In the meantime, he prayed that Shepard had an alert for strange activity on the server.

"Okay," said Lena Weinberg. "It is asking me for a password."

"Listen carefully," said Morgan. "The password is . . ." Morgan spoke a long string of numbers, letters and symbols, and Weinberg typed them in, one by one.

"Is that it?" she asked.

"That's it," he said.

She hit Enter on the keyboard.

"The password is incorrect," said Lena. "Kill him."

"I think I agree with you this time," said Weinberg.

"No! No!" said Morgan. "You must have written it wrong. The password is right. I swear!"

"Okay, Mr. Morgan," said Weinberg. "You have one more try. One more chance to prove to me that you are not lying."

"Okay, listen carefully this time." Morgan repeated the string, and Weinberg typed it in once more.

"Failed again," said Lena.

"They've changed it! They must have found out I was taken and changed the password!"

"He is playing with us," said Lena.

"No, I swear!" Morgan said. "Look, I'll tell you everything if you let me go! Whatever you want to know!"

"I'm afraid I must agree with my sister this time," said Weinberg. "You have wasted enough of my time, and I must be going. I have a busy day in Vienna ahead of me. Anse, take him away. Torture him and find out what he knows. And be careful. He is tricky. Take Gert to help keep an eye on him. After you have found what he knows, kill him."

Weinberg held a gun on him while Fleischer cut Morgan loose from the chair. Morgan kicked Fleischer downward on the shin and then pivoted for an uppercut to the jaw, but Fleischer deflected and grabbed him in a choke hold. Another man came in, presumably Gert, almost as bulky as Anse, with dark hair slicked back into a ponytail. He bound Morgan's hands with plastic cuffs as Fleischer held him. Then Fleischer released him and set him walking.

"I have a gun to your back," he said to Morgan in a thick, drawling voice. "It will be hidden, but it will be there. If you try to run away, you will die."

Morgan, Fleischer, and Gert marched out the room and to the elevator.

"I'll give you a million dollars to kill him and let me go," Morgan said to Gert.

"Don't listen to him," said Fleischer in German. Gert remained silent.

They reached the hotel garage. Morgan looked for a possible way out, but there was no way he could run without risking getting shot. They escorted him to Weinberg's Beemer, and sat him in the front passenger seat. Gert sat behind him, and Morgan could practically feel the gun in his back. Fleischer took the driver's seat.

"Do anything," Fleischer admonished, nose inches from Morgan's, "and you will die."

Fleischer pulled out, and then steered out the garage.

"So, where are we going?" Morgan asked in his best conversational tone. It was received with stony silence.

Morgan winced at the sudden light as they drove outside. He did not recognize the street they were on, but he spotted the Saint Nicholas Cathedral, and knew they were not far from their base of operations.

That's when he saw it: a black van, coming toward them on the opposite side of the street. His plan had worked, sort of. Shepard had found him, traced his location based on the strange attempt to access the Zeta remote server. *I'll have to remember to buy him a beer,* Morgan thought.

Then the thought occurred to him that they would be going to the hotel. They weren't looking for Morgan in a car, and wouldn't be able to see through the tinted windows, anyway. He had seconds to act.

In a calculated move, Morgan pulled the hand brake. The car skidded and fishtailed on the cobblestones until it came to a stop. Fleischer hit his head against the steering wheel, and Morgan felt the impact of Gert hitting the seat back. Without missing a beat, Morgan clicked open his seat belt and opened the passenger door.

He hit the ground rolling, and used the momentum to get to his feet. He then ran in front of the van, which was just about to pass the BMW. It screeched to a halt to avoid him. Diesel was behind the wheel, and Morgan saw the whites of his eyes as he stared in disbelief and yelled something. Morgan ran to the side door of the van as it opened from the inside. He jumped in, next to Bishop and Spartan.

"Go! Go!" he yelled. "Let's get the hell out of here!"

The van began moving. He heard gunshots outside, and there were several dull thuds as bullets hit the back of the van. Morgan allowed himself to breathe once they had been driving for thirty seconds and the sound of gunfire had died out.

"You guys sure like to cut it close," said Morgan.

"Shepard said there was some weird activity in the servers, and traced it back to here," said Bishop. "I didn't want to come at all. Said it was probably some kind of fluke. You can thank him later."

"Oh, I will," he said, catching his breath. "I will."

"Oh, and one more thing," he said. "You'll be interested to know he got a hit on your girl."

"You mean the thief who stole the thumb drive?" asked Morgan.

"Yeah. This Lily person. Looks like he found out who she is."

Chapter 31

"Her name really is Elizabeth," said Shepard. "Elizabeth Louise Randall."

Morgan was sitting in an old and stained wicker chair that groaned when he shifted his weight. On Shepard's screen he saw the unmistakable green eyes and red hair. Lily. They were in one of the rooms of the base of operations. It was decorated Mediterranean style, with white walls, tile floors, and rounded arches on the doors, which vaguely recalled Middle Eastern styles. On another computer was the face of Diana Bloch, on a video conference call.

Diesel, who was the best of them at first aid, had taken care of Morgan's fingers by setting them back and bandaging them. They hurt like hell, but they weren't broken.

"What is she, some kind of scam artist?" asked Morgan. "Grifter? Notorious cat burglar?"

"Not quite," said Shepard. "She's MI-5."

"You're *kidding,*" said Morgan. "British intelligence?"

"No doubt about it," said Shepard. "Field operative. Got a list of skills to match yours, Cobra. With the added bonus of being a lot easier on the eyes."

"Lily's a spy?" said Morgan, still incredulous. "What the hell was she doing there?"

"That's the thing," said Shepard. "No one knows. She's gone AWOL. Hasn't checked in over the past two weeks."

"Any chance that's all plausible deniability?" asked Morgan, rubbing his bandaged fingers and testing for pain. "Could be they sent her on a covert op, and want to play it off as a rogue agent and wash their hands of her."

"Unlikely," said Bloch. "They'd be burning an agent for nothing if they did that. They might do it for a high-value assassination, but not for this kind of thing."

"So, what, she's gone rogue?" asked Morgan. "Working for the highest bidder?"

"Who knows," said Shepard.

"It's our best working theory," said Bloch. "Any indication of possible sedition in her file?"

"No," said Shepard. "She was a model agent before she disappeared. No indication that she would do something like this."

"We still need to figure out what 'something like this' is," said Morgan. "We still have no idea what her ultimate mission was in Monte Carlo."

"Could be blackmail, sabotage . . ."

"Maybe," said Morgan. "But she said something to me. After I found out it was her in Weinberg's suite, as she left. *Weinberg's mine.* I get the feeling this wasn't about stealing the data."

"Assassination after all?" asked Bloch.

"Well, that's one way to put it," said Morgan. "But the feeling I got is that it was personal. Like she wanted to—"

"Hold on—now this is something," Shepard interrupted. "I've just got a hit on one of her identities. She's just taken off on a commercial flight to Vienna."

"That's where Weinberg is headed," said Morgan. "She's going after him."

"If she kills him, our lead goes cold," said Bloch.

"Shepard, I need you to find out exactly where Weinberg is going to be in Vienna," said Morgan. "I've got to stop her before she pulls the trigger. And I'm going to need a fast car."

Chapter 32

Peter Conley looked through a slit on the side of the truck. After his eyes adjusted to the light, he could see the endless rocky mountains circling the road. It had been a very awkward drive so far. The whole Lambda team had bristled with suspicion from the moment they laid eyes on Harun, who was now sitting shotgun with the driver. The rowdy energy of the group had chilled, and everyone sat quietly, hardly speaking to one another, in the dark and bumpy ride. It didn't help that the box they were in formed a natural steam room.

The vehicle in question was what was locally called a jingle truck. It had intricately carved wooden panels covering the entire trailer and the door, all painted in bright clashing colors. This particular specimen was yellow, red, and green, with tchotchkes hanging all along its grille and sides. The driver of the truck was a man named Yasir, who had agreed to carry this dangerous cargo only after significant cash-based exhortations, and was grumpy the whole way there.

By Conley's estimation, they should be arriving in Dir at any minute. The city was an isolated town of twenty thousand inhabitants tucked away in a small valley in Northwestern Pakistan. Most of the people working in the town were truck drivers, which was good news for them. It might be tricky finding a driver somewhere unfamiliar, but that kind of supply helped, and they would likely go unnoticed in the swarm of trucks coming in and leaving town.

The trouble came in getting to their final destination, Chitral

Valley, on the border with Afghanistan. The problem was less hostiles than that this was one of the most dangerous roads in the world. Narrow and treacherous, the twisting two-laner regularly claimed the lives of drivers who chanced it in their rickety, decorated trucks.

Conley opened up his satellite phone and sent a message to Ken Figueroa, the head of Lambda Division, asking for updates on Raza. He quickly got a message back that there had been none.

"That rat's going to sell us out," said Walker. "I can't believe you'd lead us into a situation like this, trusting one of *them*." Conley didn't need to make out Walker's face in the dark to know who the *you* of that sentence was.

"I trust Harun," he said, "and Harun is managing the driver."

"Should have taken a goddamn chopper," said Walker.

"Let's not go over this again," said Conley.

They did not see the city of Dir except brief glimpses. Yasir parked the truck at a garage where other truck drivers were waiting for work. Harun haggled with a driver and then another. Money, of course, was no object, and even then it wouldn't cost too much, because these drivers normally made something to the order of thirty dollars a month.

Eventually, the back door opened, and the Lambda tactical team had their semiautomatics at the ready. But it was only Harun.

"What are you doing?" he scolded. "Come on, I've got us transportation into the Chitral valley."

They were in a closed garage. Yasir was there, as well as another man.

"Our driver," said Harun. "Akram. He's been driving the Lowari Pass for over ten years, never a wreck." Akram was a man no older than thirty, with a jet-black moustache and a loose-fitting light brown button down shirt. He had his hands clasped in front of him and bowed, in a subservient manner. Walker and the Lambda team were visibly displeased, but didn't say anything.

"I will get you food," said Harun, "and then we go."

Harun left them to lounge outside of a truck for once. The Lambda Tactical team spread out, stretching their limbs, a couple of them taking advantage of the limited space in the garage to exercise. Conley took the opportunity to inspect Akram's truck, which was in poorer condition than Yasir's, and then talk to Akram himself, who was standing silently beside his vehicle.

"How old are you, Akram?" Conley asked in Urdu.

"Twenty-nine," said Akram. His Urdu wasn't great, but he seemed to understand it fine, and seemed gratified that Conley spoke a language he was at least somewhat conversant in.

"You started doing the pass when you were nineteen?"

"Driving," he said. "Before, I went with my brother. I helped to get the truck unstuck, remove rocks from the way, things like that."

"So you know the road pretty well then?"

Akram smiled. "I do, sir. I certainly do."

"How long do you think it'll take us to get across, with the weather the way it is?" Conley asked.

"We can make it in one day, if we are lucky."

"Good, good." Conley looked around the room, arms akimbo. "Akram, are you married?"

"I have a wife," he said, smiling. "Children soon, inshallah."

"Do you have a picture of her?"

Akram smiled as he called Conley up to the truck's cab to show a picture that had been pasted onto the dashboard in a colorful frame.

Conley asked him if he liked chocolate, and he answered yes. "Hold on a second," he said.

Conley drifted away from Akram toward the back of Yasir's truck, where he had left his pack. Walker stopped him with a hand to the chest. "We're supposed to kill 'em," he said. "Not talk to 'em."

"Take your hand away or you lose it, pretty boy," said Conley.

Walker did, with a gesture of childish arrogance. "You're going native, old man."

Conley fumed. "Forget about being a decent goddamn human being for a second," he said. "That man over there"—he motioned toward Akram—"just smiled at me. He sees me as human now. If he was ever planning on double-crossing us, well, I just made that a whole lot less likely."

"You know what would make him a lot less likely to betray us?" said Walker. "A bullet to the brain."

"And then you're stranded in a strange town surrounded by people who hate you," said Conley, anger rising. "Tell me, Walker, were you dropped as a child or were you born this stupid?"

Bluejay, a short Hispanic man with a round nose, stepped in. "Why don't you both back off?" he said.

Walker scoffed. "Whatever. But we'd better get to killing soon, 'cause my trigger finger's getting itchy." He glowered at Akram, who shrunk to a corner.

Chapter 33

Morgan flew down the smooth, well-kept highways to Vienna in his black Mercedes coupe, keeping the line of communication with Zeta open the whole way. Shepard, meanwhile, was looking into where Weinberg might be in the city, and where Randall might intercept him. Weinberg kept his schedule out of networked devices, but this wasn't necessarily true for the people he was meeting with. Shepard ran a search that got him the information he was looking for.

"He has a five o'clock with an Austrian steel baron," he told Morgan through the communicator, which was set up on a remote connection through Morgan's phone.

"Can you send me satellite images for the location?" Morgan asked.

"It'll be on your tablet in seconds," said Shepard. "That's where their offices are, and that's where they're going to meet."

Morgan took the tablet computer from his bag, which was on the passenger seat, and held it in his right hand as he drove with his left. On the screen there appeared a 3-D model overlaid with satellite images of tall buildings on a broad street. He tossed the tablet aside to pay attention to the road, weaving through traffic.

"What do you think?" asked Shepard.

"She'll be there," said Morgan.

"How do you know?"

"It's where I'd be."

Shepard worked on getting everything he could about the area as Morgan continued to speed the rest of the way to Vienna. From the target location, the modern office building called the City Tower, in Vienna's business district, Morgan guessed that there was one of two ways she'd do this—sniper rifle or poisoning. Given that Weinberg knew her face, Morgan had gone with sniper as most likely course.

From there, it was a matter of finding the best place to set up— the place that he would choose. And the choice here was obvious.

"The parking garage," said Morgan. "That's where she'll set up." Morgan was within the city limits by now and starting to hit traffic. "I need you to find everything you can about that parking garage," said Morgan. "Look for security cameras and anything that might tell us if her car is in there." A light turned yellow, and the car in front of him stopped. "Shit!" He banged the steering wheel in frustration. "And get surveillance on the streets!"

He gripped the steering wheel as traffic moved, slowly, so slowly.

"Already did," said Shepard. "Weinberg is due to arrive in ten minutes."

Morgan swore. "Okay," he said. "Traffic laws just turned optional." He passed the car in front of him in wrong-way traffic and ran a red light, narrowly avoiding a scrape. "How are we doing with eyes in the parking garage?" Morgan asked.

"Coming, coming," said Shepard. "It's got them, now just a matter of gaining access . . ."

"Make it snappy," said Morgan, to the honk of a car that he cut off to shave a few milliseconds off his time.

"Okay, got it," said Shepard. "Feeds coming in—holy hell, that's a lot of cameras. It's going to be a while to sort through all of them."

"Can't you just work some computer magic to—"

"No, Cobra, I cannot write a program from scratch to search these video feeds for Randall or her car."

"Is Bishop there?"

"Here," came Bishop's deep voice through the communicator. "Diesel and Spartan, too."

"I need all eyes on those cameras. Top floors first, Shepard. She's likelier than not to be up high. She's going to have a car with her to make a getaway, but it might not be the same."

"Then what are we looking for exactly?" asked Bishop.

"I don't know, just see if you find something!"

Morgan was stuck behind a crowd of tourists crossing the road. They cleared, and he hit the gas. Within a minute he could see the City Tower, and shortly after the far less impressive parking facility.

"In view of target," he said.

Traffic was heavier here, and the slow crawl with his destination in plain sight was worse than all the rest. So close, so close.

Finally, he made the turn into the parking garage, with three cars ahead of him for the electronic ticket booth.

"What's up with that camera?" came a woman's voice—Spartan.

"What are you talking about?" said Morgan. The line of cars moved ahead.

"It's just dark," said Shepard, "it's nothing."

"Wait, dark like broken? Or working and dark?"

"Looks like it's working," said Shepard.

That had to be her. Disabling or blacking out the camera was the first thing he'd do if he were setting up. Morgan reached the ticket dispenser and pushed the button.

"What level?" he asked.

"Fifth."

"Where on the fifth level?"

"Southwest—well, I'd say corner, but the building's an oval," said Shepard.

"Good enough."

Morgan sped along the spiral ramp faster than even he was comfortable with. Twice the side of his car scraped against the guard walls—a bigger slip would break the concrete and send him sailing into the air to a sudden and dramatic stop. He kept a steady curve, tires squealing.

"Weinberg's car is pulling up," said Shepard. "Get your ass up there!"

The Mercedes turned screaming onto the fifth level of the parking garage. The direct route was closed off, and he was forced to go around the level to get to the location Shepard had given him. He was making a racket, but it didn't matter. If she was there, he'd already announced his presence.

"Cobra, he's getting out of the damn car!"

Morgan brought the car to a screeching halt and stepped out, leaving the door open behind him, his Walther in his right hand. He ran down the aisle, looking from car to car until he spotted the top of her head through the windshield of a VW sedan. He could just tell that she was facing inward, waiting for him to pass, probably to shoot him and then get to Weinberg.

Morgan took a hard right and jumped up onto the VW, rolling on the roof of the car and sliding down behind Lily. Before she figured out what the hell had just happened, he had his Walther against her head.

"We have to stop meeting like this," he said.

She tensed up in surprise at hearing his voice. She was holding a sniper rifle, which he recognized as an AS50 BMG—not his first choice, but respectable for its portability. "The car salesman," she said without looking at him.

"Not quite."

"So I see," she said. "You are full of surprises, Mr. Morgan. Although I suppose that's not your real name, either."

"Drop the rifle and hands up, Agent Randall."

She didn't move. "Oh, we've gone all formal now, I see. I think I liked you better as a car salesman."

"No you didn't," he said.

"Cocky aren't we?"

"*Drop it,* Lily. I don't want to kill you."

"But for some reason you so very much want to save the life of Gunther Weinberg. Tell me, how much did he pay you to make you turn? How much are you worth, Morgan?"

"I do have my reasons," he said. "But none of them have to do with wanting to protect him. I can explain, just toss the rifle. You won't be able to make the shot now. Not with me here."

"Are you sure?" He caught her eye in the rearview mirror of the VW, and there was a glint of challenge and mischief. She swung the rifle backward by its barrel, apparently betting that Morgan wouldn't shoot her. She was right. The rifle's stock missed his head by half an inch and got him in the shoulder. The blow didn't do much except throw him off balance, but that's all she needed. With a kick, she knocked the Walther from his hand, grabbing it from the air in her left and, in a move he had to respect, grabbed the two bandaged fingers in his left hand. He cried out in pain.

Taking the opening, she picked up the rifle again. Morgan

braced for the deadly shot, but instead she made straight for the guardrail at the edge of the garage, right behind him. She hastily set up the rifle and looked through the scope.

"You're kidding," said Morgan.

She pointed his Walther at him with her left. "I'm very much not."

"You couldn't possibly hit him like this."

"I was top of my class in sniper training," said Randall. "Don't tell me what I can't do with one of these."

"Okay," said Morgan. "Suppose you can. It doesn't mean you should."

"And why is that, Mr. Morgan?"

"Because I'm asking you to."

She scoffed. "You've got to do better than that, love."

"Okay, then. I will. Don't shoot Weinberg because he's our only lead in the abduction of the American Secretary of State."

Her grip on the handle of the rifle loosened. "You have got to be kidding me. Weinberg?"

"We've got it on good authority," said Morgan. "Might have been able to confirm it if I only had the contents of that thumb drive you stole off of me."

"Sorry about that," she said. "I've got it here in my pocket. You can have it, soon as I kill him."

"If you kill him, there's no going back," said Morgan. "You'll never work in intelligence again. And if anyone catches you, it's life in prison."

"Somehow, I think I'll survive."

"Think about this, Lily."

"I'm already burned," she said. "I've got nothing to go back to. This is all I've got left. So why don't you leave me to it?"

"It's not all lost," said Morgan. "We can help."

"How would you possibly be able to help? And who the bloody hell is 'we'?"

"We are . . . a nongovernmental organization with friends in high places. Let's just leave it at that. We can smooth things over with MI-5. Hell, with your skills, I'm confident we can even give you a job if you'd like."

"What I'd like is to kill that bastard Weinberg."

"We can arrange for that," said Morgan. "I'll personally do it if you'd like. God knows the world would be better off with him dead. But not today. Right now, I need you to put away the rifle. We need him alive."

"He's right there," she said. Morgan saw. He had Fleischer next to him, and his car was coming around. "All I have to do is pull the trigger . . ."

"Don't," said Morgan. "Whatever reason you have to kill him, it can wait. Just until this crisis is over. Then I promise you—"

"All right," said Randall, exhaling and backing away from the rifle. Morgan watched as Weinberg entered his car. "I'll hear what you have to say. And if it helps to stop whatever Weinberg is up to, then good. But afterward, I get him, and you help me do it. Is that clear?"

"Crystal," said Morgan.

"Christ, I need a beer," she said, taking apart her sniper rifle. "You're buying."

Chapter 34

"So what did he do to you?"

Morgan asked the question over a circular table at a dim Vienna bar. The waitress had just set a tall half-liter glass of a cloudy light yellow beer on the table in front of Morgan, who pushed it across to Lily Randall, and pulled the mineral water to his own side of the table.

"Do?" she asked, tilting the glass for a long draught of beer. She was in the same black turtleneck she had been wearing for the assassination—a turtleneck that said both "cat burglar" and "German sophisticate" at the same time. Her hair had been in a tight bun, which she now undid, letting her locks flow loosely down to her shoulders.

"This is about revenge, isn't it?" said Morgan. "This whole thing with Weinberg."

Her bright green eyes seemed smarter somehow. There was more than just the quick wit she demonstrated in Monte Carlo—her intelligence had depth. "What makes you so sure?"

"Nothing else would drive someone to do what you did," said Morgan. "Leave your life and job behind. Risk losing everything, getting nothing better in return. What, you weren't doing enough good at MI-5, you had to go after some random German billionaire, bad as he might be? *Please.* There's only one thing that makes a person act that way. So it's revenge. Got to be."

"You sound like you know something about the subject." Her eyes were defiant as always. She didn't have the same manner as she had put on in Monte Carlo—the sex wasn't turned on nearly as high, and he didn't get the feeling that every word out of her mouth was meant to manipulate him now. But she was still hiding behind irony, deflecting honesty. Given that he had been pointing a gun at her not half an hour earlier, it was hardly any surprise.

"I might," he said. "But I asked you a question. Answer me. Was this about revenge?"

The bar was filling up with people getting off work. The bar skewed younger than Morgan, but Lily, apart from not looking a bit German, fit in just fine.

"I just want him dead," she said, not looking him in the eye.

"And I'm sure you have good reason. Hell, I've known him a few days and I already want him dead."

She emitted a hollow laugh and drank. "Maybe that has something to do with those." She pointed to Morgan's bandaged fingers. The reminder made them throb with pain. "Or that shiner on your face."

"No, that last one was you," he laughed.

"Oops," she said, not sounding particularly sorry.

Morgan ran his fingers gently over the bruise. "Look, Lily, whatever your reasons, we can't let you kill him. At least not yet. We need to know what he knows and what he's doing. But you can help us stop him. I could use someone with your skill to watch my back."

"I haven't forgotten that you kept me from killing him today," she said. Then, relenting, she added, "It's not like I'm doing anything right now, anyway. I suppose I'll take any way that I can stick it to Weinberg. Okay, I'll come with you."

"It's not the same, I know," said Morgan. "But it's *something.* And once this all blows over, well . . . I can tell you I wouldn't miss the bastard if someone happens to off him. I might even come along for the ride. Provided you don't hold me at gunpoint this time." He shot her a teasing grin.

"No promises," she said, smiling, warmth seeping in to her expression. "I might still have to shoot you before this is over."

"You wouldn't be the first to try," he said. "Now, if you don't mind, I'll take that thumb drive off of you."

Maintaining eye contact with him, Randall reached into her

shirt, slipped her fingers under her bra, pulled out the small plastic device, and handed it across the table to Morgan. He picked it up, and the plastic was warm to the touch. He attached the thumb drive to a device he had in his pocket and turned it on. Then he turned on the transmitter on his comm.

"I've got the drive," he said. "I'm transmitting the data now."

"You're the man," said Shepard. Randall finished off the rest of her beer.

"You might feel better if you pace yourself," said Morgan.

"I think more beer is what's going to make me feel better right now," she said, raising her hand to call over the waitress. "So now that you've got what you want, are you going to give me the brush-off?" she asked.

"I happen to be a man of my word," he said. "I meant what I said when I invited you to come along. I could really use you."

"I'm sure you could," she said with a sly grin.

"Married. Remember?"

"Oh, you're no fun." The waitress came by, and Randall ordered a second beer.

"So what's in this thing, anyway?" Morgan asked, holding the thumb drive between his index and middle fingers.

"No idea," said Randall.

"What do you mean?"

"I mean, I was interested in exactly one thing: his schedule. Hoped to catch him off guard. There was a little too much in there for me to bother looking at everything. Plus, a lot of the files are individually encrypted. I didn't have the time to go over each one, what with planning an assassination and all."

"Right," said Morgan. "The assassination. You still haven't told me what that's all about."

"Haven't I?" she said, feigning absentmindedness.

"Oh, please," said Morgan. "I know it's revenge. What I don't know is, revenge for what?"

"You really don't know when to quit."

"You say that like it's a bad thing."

Her beer came, and she downed half of it in one go and put the glass down. "All right," she said. "I'll tell you." She took a deep breath. "Gunther Weinberg killed my parents."

"Oh," said Morgan. "I'm sorry to hear that."

"Look, it's fine," said Randall. "I mean, it's not fine. I hate it. But the fact that they're dead—what else is there but to reconcile myself to it and move on?"

"Doesn't sound like the words of someone who left everything behind to get revenge," said Morgan.

"Grief is one thing, revenge is another," said Randall. "Living in the past won't bring my parents back. I know. I don't think it'll bring any kind of satisfaction or . . . or closure or whatever. And hating him for ruining my childhood won't do me any kind of good. I know all that. So don't tell me any of this, all, right? Don't tell me it's not worth it, that it'll be hollow once it's done. I know the whole speech. I've given the speech."

"I wasn't going to say any of that."

"This isn't about me, you understand?" she continued. "It's about *them*. What good am I if I don't get justice for my parents?"

Morgan didn't quite see it. She was being too rational, too cool about this, and going AWOL to a rogue assassination mission was not the action of a cool and rational person. But he decided to let it slide.

"How did it happen?" he asked.

Randall took another deep swig of beer. "My parents were investigative journalists, and they had some dirt on his company." Morgan caught a hint of a slur in her voice. "They were going to expose a whole slew of criminal activity perpetrated by Himmel. You know, his corporation. And then a car ran them off a cliff."

"Damn," said Morgan.

"Of course, I didn't know it at the time," she continued. "I was only six when it happened. I always thought it had been an accident, and nobody disabused me of that notion. Then, as a teenager, I read the newspaper and police reports and discovered that there were suspicious circumstances around the whole thing. Some paint transfer on the car, tire marks on the road. I knew by then that it had been a murder, but I had no idea who had done it. I went a little crazy for a while there. Did the kinds of stupid things that teenage girls do, and then some."

"Vandalism? Shoplifting?"

"Car theft, and a couple of other things besides. But it didn't take. In the end, I turned my pain into determination. Doubled down on my studies. Went to a fancy boarding school on scholarship—and let me tell you, the upper-class girls never let you forget where you came from. They tormented me for a year. That is, until I broke the queen bee's nose and threatened to slit their throats in their sleep."

"You sound like you could make that threat believable," he grinned.

"Helps when you have a reputation for being the crazy one. After that, I just focused on doing my work, getting the marks. Got into an MI-5 trainee program, and the rest is history."

"Except that's not all, right?" said Morgan. "Something changed. Something made you go after Weinberg."

"About six months ago, I found out what my parents were doing when they were killed. Investigating Weinberg's company for illegal trafficking. Discovered it totally by accident, doing some desk work one day. I came across a report on Weinberg's company, and there, I found a reference to some research done by my parents—apparently they'd shared some of it with British Intelligence in the course of their investigations. I put two and two together. That's when I started researching all I could about him. His family history, what his company had done under his leadership. Suspicions of piracy on the Black Sea, of massacring union leaders in Romania, of rigging local elections in Georgia—that's the country, not the state with the peaches. So I decided to kill him—I just needed to figure out when, where and how. You know how it went from there." She finished the last of her beer. "God, here I am, telling you my whole life story."

"To be fair," he said, "I did ask."

"And what about you?" asked Randall. Her eyelids drooped slightly. "What makes the enigmatic Mr. Morgan tick?"

"I'm not really a complicated man—"

"Said the international man of mystery."

"Ah," he said. "I guess there is that."

"Yes, there is that."

"I admit, that is complicated. But I'm not."

Morgan's phone beeped, and he looked down at the screen.

"What's that? Message from the wife?"

"That's our cue to get to work," said Morgan. "My people have something on Weinberg. And from the looks of it, it isn't good." He stood up and dropped a couple of bills on the table for the beers and the water. "You still have time to back out."

"Oh, please," she said, walking out ahead of him. "Like I'm going to be outdone by a bloke who won't even drink a pint."

Chapter 35

"It seems things are a lot worse than we imagined," said Bloch.

Morgan and Randall had gotten themselves a room at the Hotel Sacher in Vienna—Morgan had been adamant about getting two beds—and had set up a three-way video call with Diana Bloch at Zeta Headquarters and Lincoln Shepard, still in Monte Carlo. Morgan and Lily sat side by side at the room's hardwood desk, made hasty introductions, and they jumped right into the business at hand.

"Do you know what an EMP is?" asked Shepard.

Morgan was about to respond when Randall preempted him. "Electromagnetic pulse. An expanding wave of electromagnetic radiation." Any sign of drunkenness had completely left her voice and posture, and Morgan wondered whether that had been a put-on as well. "If it's strong enough, it can pretty much wipe out any electronic device for miles. They were discovered as a side effect of nuclear detonation in the forties. There have been several attempts to create an EMP-only weapon, some of them successful, but never deployed in the field."

"Someone was head of her class," said Shepard.

"So what's this about, Shepard?" asked Morgan.

"The EMP device," said Shepard. "We found specifications to one on the contents of Weinberg's hard drive. A Russian prototype weapon."

"So he's trying to get this weapon?" Morgan asked.

"He already did," said Bloch.

"What?"

"He stole it from a train yesterday as it was being transported to Siberia for testing. We just found out when Shepard looked into the whereabouts of the thing."

Morgan swore. "That's bad news."

"Aren't you sorry you didn't let me kill him now?" asked Randall.

"What can he do with the EMP?" asked Morgan.

"Take your pick," said Shepard. "Shut off the lights in any major city in the world. Hit the Pentagon, NORAD, even take out the entire US electrical grid, with a well-placed strike."

"Jesus Christ," said Morgan. "Do we have any idea what he's planning? Any idea what the hell this has to do with the Secretary of State?"

"None whatsoever," said Bloch. "Although I think it's probably safe to assume that, given the abduction of the Secretary, the target is likely to be in the United States."

"Something's bothering me," said Randall. "Why is he doing this? What the *hell* kind of connection could these things have with each other?"

"Opportunity?" ventured Shepard. "Because they're there? Sometimes it's as simple as that. The chicken just wants to get to the other side."

"I don't buy it," said Randall. "Not for one minute. Weinberg's a clever bastard. There has got to be some angle here."

"Do you know what I think?" cut in Morgan. "I think he's bored. I think he just ran out of better things to do with his fortune. I think we have a man who thinks he can slap America in the face. Who does something because it's just the next logical step. The next thing he can do to assert his power. I think he got tired of *just* being president of a multibillion-dollar corporation. He wanted more. And now he has the US Secretary of State and a dangerous weapon on his hands. He wants to bring America to its knees. And, do you know what? *We won't let him.* I don't care why he's doing it. I'm going to stop him."

"Hear, hear, Mr. Morgan," said Randall. "So I suppose the question is, what *are* we going to do about it?"

"We don't know where the EMP is," said Bloch. "We don't know where Secretary Wolfe is. But we know where Weinberg is."

Randall perked up at this. "Oh?"

"Weinberg's left Vienna," said Shepard. "He's on a plane, on a flight path to the Greek island of Santorini. He owns a villa there."

"I say it's time to take action," said Morgan. "No more nibbling around the edges, no more undercover. Let's take the fight to him. Bring him in and put the screws on him, and find both the Secretary and the EMP."

"I have to agree with you this time, Cobra," said Bloch. "We tried subtlety, and it failed. We can't afford to wait this time. We need to take decisive action right away. I'm deploying the tactical team to Santorini to go after Weinberg. Cobra, I want you to meet up with them there. Ms. Randall?"

"Yes?"

"I understand you have some kind of vendetta against Weinberg. But you also appear to have some very valuable skills. If you can put aside your thoughts of revenge, perhaps we can use you in this mission."

"I'll help if I can," said Randall.

"Good," said Bloch. "Then you two had better get ready. You board your flight to Greece in two hours."

Chapter 36

Night fell on the blue Mediterranean Sea as Morgan and Randall's taxi dropped them off at the small dock where an aging Greek in a ratty polo shirt was waiting for them with a small speedboat.

"Come on, I don't have all night," he said hoarsely, breath smelling of alcohol with a hint of anise.

Morgan stepped down onto the boat and held his hand out to help Lily. She scoffed and hopped gracefully off the pier. The Greek gunned the engine, and the speedboat carried them along the darkening waters to a schooner about a mile off shore.

"Welcome aboard!" said Spartan as she helped Randall up onto the boat, then Morgan. Spartan was already in a black wetsuit. Its passengers delivered, the speedboat roared off into the black Mediterranean waters. "You made it. And this is Randall?"

"Who else?" she said. "And you must be the famous Spartan."

"Built like a twig, aren't you?" said Spartan, shadowboxing the air in front of Lily. "You sure you can tangle with the big boys?"

Spartan didn't have Lily's greyhound physique. She was more solidly built, with a squarer face and a stronger jaw. Her wetsuit clung to her body, revealing its outlines. They were far from delicate, but they were powerful. While she was attractive in her way, she could not match Lily's eye-turning beauty, the curves revealed by her sheer floral dress.

"Maybe you'd like to try me, blondie," said Lily.

"Let's save the violence for Weinberg, all right?" said Morgan.

They walked down the wooden steps into the cabin, which was

lit by a dim, flickering light that swayed to the movement of the boat.

"Glad you could join us, Cobra," said Bishop, who was in his wetsuit as well. Next to him was Diesel, reclining on the wooden seat of the schooner, his naked torso exposed to the cool night breeze. "I take it that this lovely lady is Ms. Randall."

"Enchanté," she said.

"I hear you gave Cobra a little bit of trouble back there," said Bishop.

"I heard you kicked his ass," said Spartan, shooing Diesel away to take a seat next to him.

"That's not quite how it happened," said Morgan.

"He's just bitter that he got beat up by a girl," said Randall.

"She had a gun on me," Morgan grumbled.

"All right, big guy," said Bishop. "We have your wet suits here. Ms. Randall—"

"Lily will do fine," she said. "Ms. Randall makes me sound like a frumpy secretary or a librarian or something."

"I don't think *anyone* would mistake you for either of those things," said Bishop. He handed her the neoprene suit. "We got your size from the MI-5 employee database."

"How indiscreet of you," she said.

"I'll leave you to change," said Bishop, moving toward the wooden stairs.

As he, Diesel, and Spartan walked up and out of the cabin, Morgan shuffled through the canvas bags to find his own wetsuit and was about to leave when he noticed out of the corner of his eye that Lily had already pulled her dress down, her black bra exposed.

"Jesus!" he said.

"Oh, you prude," she teased, and continued to undress. Morgan turned around and unbuttoned his shirt, glad he never shared any of the details of his work with his wife. As he pulled down his pants, he caught a glimpse of Lily's reflection on one of the portholes, and made a point to avert his eyes from that as well. Careful not to bend the injured fingers on his left hand, he pulled on the neoprene suit, which clung tightly to his skin. He moved around so that the elastic material would settle comfortable on his skin—and to kill time until he was sure he wouldn't see Lily Randall's bare chest.

"It's okay, you can turn around now," she said. He did, to find her sporting a gently mocking grin, the black suit clinging to her form, revealing her flat stomach and the curve of her waist.

"It's a bit of a tight fit," she said. "Don't you think?"

Morgan rolled his eyes and banged his good hand a couple of times against the wooden side of the cabin, calling out to the others that they were dressed.

They all converged on the open-air deck of the schooner. The captain cut the lights and started the engine, and they rumbled in the darkness under the stars and the nearly full moon. Morgan reclined, laying his head on his pack, resting his back on the hard wood, which felt as cozy as a bed. The others got comfortable too, and they shared war stories in the dark until they were in sight of Weinberg's villa. The captain cut the engine, and all they could hear was the creaking of the boat as it gently rocked from side to side.

It was built high on a steep and otherwise empty and barren hill, dimly lit by the light of the moon. It was typical of what they called Cycladic architecture, bearing whitewashed, round-edged walls, climbing the slope in boxy, steplike segments. A high wall circled the entire property, although they could see the house itself because of the angle. The dimensions of the villa were as expected for a man like Weinberg—at least eight bedrooms, spacious verandas, a large backyard hidden by the angle, and a helicopter on a landing pad—a two-seater, but Morgan couldn't tell what kind from that distance.

"Damn," said Diesel. "Must be nice, being a millionaire."

"That's billionaire," said Spartan. "With a *b*."

"Yeah, well, either way."

Morgan took a pair of night-vision binoculars from the field pack that they had brought for him and examined the house. His vantage point prevented him from assessing whether Weinberg was in there, although the armed guards patrolling the property told him that was more than likely.

"How many do you count?" Morgan asked Bishop.

"Six."

"I count seven," said Morgan.

"Two by the pool, two at the side of the house, two circling the perimeter," said Diesel, joining the party. "That's six."

"There's one on the roof," said Morgan. "On the far end, near the window that has the light on."

"I see him," said Bishop. "All right. Diesel takes sniper duty. We take it in teams of two. Scale the walls on either side. On the right there's a small gap in the bushes against the house itself. On the left there's a covered, out-of-sight sconce. Diesel keeps us informed about the location of the guards as much as he can. One team secures the first floor while another moves on to the second. We converge on Weinberg's room and take him away while Diesel provides cover."

"What are the teams?" asked Morgan.

"Since you and Lily are already acquainted, you can team up," said Bishop. "Mistrust is a tactical disadvantage."

"Mistrust?" said Lily, with mock outrage. "Of little old me?"

"Might have something to do with you stealing the thumb drive off Cobra and leaving him to get caught," said Spartan.

"Teaming up with Lily will be fine," said Morgan. "Are we ready?"

"Let's go," said Bishop.

They assisted each other in putting on their scuba gear and waterproof rucksacks and dropped off the back of the boat. Morgan was last to jump in, the cool water enveloping him. He looked at the compass strapped to his wrist, and swam in the dark water due south. He continued for about ten minutes until he could just make out the outlines of the land rising in front of him. He found the ridge that he was aiming for, and came out of the water on the other side of it, shielded from view of the house. He spotted Bishop, Lily, and Diesel already there, crouching and unstrapping their gear. A few seconds after he got out of the water, Spartan's head emerged, snorkel first. They stashed their gear behind a rock, put on boots and bulletproof vests. They strapped on their sidearm holsters—Morgan with his Walther PPK—shouldered their backpacks and slung their HK MP5s across their chests—all but Diesel, who had his M39 sniper rifle instead. They then tested their communicators.

"Zeta, we are in position," said Bishop.

"Mission is go," said Shepard. "I repeat, mission is go."

"All right, move out," said Bishop.

They lowered their night-vision goggles and ran in a line with the ridge on their left, shielded from view. When they were level with the lower wall of the villa, they turned to make their approach—except Diesel, who broke off from the group and continued climbing to find a suitable sniper nest.

They ran under the cover of darkness over the uneven rocky terrain, Bishop taking the lead, Morgan bringing up the rear behind Lily. Upon reaching the whitewashed outer wall, they stood up against it so that they couldn't be seen by anyone above. Morgan signed to Lily to follow him along the ocean-facing wall, while Bishop and Spartan ran up the slope.

They ran about three hundred yards, negotiating the tricky footing of the rock at the foot of the four-yard wall. They rounded the corner and Morgan signed for them to halt. "In position."

"Ready here, too," said Bishop.

"Hold in position," said Diesel. "Wait for it. . . . Okay, move out."

The wall was too high to climb unaided, but they had brought along a tactical ladder for that purpose. This was a device with a square hook at one end attached to Kevlar rungs. He reached back to retrieve it from his pack. He then swung up the hook and tossed it over the wall, then pulled the ladder down. The hook found purchase at the top of the wall, and he pulled the ladder taut.

"Cover me," he told Lily, and began the climb. It took him seconds to reach the top and jump over the wall, landing on the deck as lightly as he could. Here, he was in the spot chosen for insertion—covered by an awning, a dark corner which turned into a spacious deck and Olympic-sized swimming pool illuminated by floodlights.

Leaning over the side, he signaled for Lily to follow. He raised his night-vision goggles and stood against the side of the lowest boxy unit of the house, drawing his combat knife. Lily soon swung her body in a smooth fluid motion over the wall, landing at his side. She pulled the ladder up and stashed it in Morgan's rucksack. It was surprisingly compact when bunched up.

"Diesel, we're up here. Give me the position of the guards?"

"There's one right above you. Keep flat against the wall. Another one is about to round your corner in just over ten seconds. Bishop and Spartan, there are two there, facing away from you about eight feet from the corner. I want you all to make your move on my mark."

Morgan gripped his knife.

"Three," counted Diesel, "two, one . . ."

The guard appeared at the corner right at Diesel's mark. He appeared to be looking out at the moonlit ocean, oblivious to the death that awaited him. Morgan let him walk to the edge of the wall, so that he had his back to him. In a quick and precise motion, Morgan grabbed the man's forehead and slit his neck. He gurgled, and Morgan nudged him so that he slumped over the wall. The man spun in the air to land on his back on the ground below. Morgan then heard the whistle of a sniper's bullet, and the dull impact above. The guard from the roof tumbled down and hit the deck around the corner from Morgan and Lily, blood and brains splattering around his head.

Thanks, Diesel.

Morgan signaled for Lily to go. She took the lead this time, and he followed behind.

"Lily, you've got a man behind the glass at the entrance nearest to you." He was referring to the enormous French doors that faced the swimming pool. "Bishop and Spartan, there are two bad guys coming around from the front on your side."

"How do you want to take this one?" Morgan asked.

"Follow my lead," she told him. She dropped her gear, undid her bulletproof vest, and then unzipped her wetsuit, pulling off the top so that it hung limply at her front and Morgan could see her exposed back.

"What the hell are you doing?" She walked out, in full view of the glass door, and continued to walk forward.

He heard the door unlock, slide open, and another of the guards, Uzi in hand, emerged from the interior. The man whistled to call her attention, and she turned around, looking innocent.

"Oh, dear, am I in trouble?" she said innocently.

Morgan was so stunned by what she had done that he almost forgot to take action. He approached from behind and plunged his tactical knife into the man's neck. Holding on to his torso and still gripping the knife, Morgan pulled him backward, setting him gently down in the darkness where he wouldn't be spotted.

"I'd like to see you try that trick," said Lily.

"Let's get inside," Morgan told Lily, who had followed him. "And for God's sake, put a shirt on."

She pulled on her wetsuit and re-strapped her vest. They rounded the corner once more, Bishop and Spartan showed up from the far end of the house. They met at the open French doors, and Bishop took the lead, spreading wispy white curtains as he entered.

They had come into a sort of lounge, with sprawling couches all done in wicker and white leather. Morgan couldn't help thinking that Jenny would adore it.

"We'll get Weinberg upstairs," said Morgan. "You two secure the first floor."

"Roger," said Bishop. Morgan lowered his night-vision goggles and signaled for Lily to follow him, clutching his MP5. They crept up the wooden staircase and found a hallway upstairs with five doors, all on their left, facing the ocean, ending in another curving staircase. Lily guarded their back as Morgan checked the rooms one by one. The first four came up empty. The door to the fifth was closed.

Morgan pushed the door, which opened with a creak. Beyond it was a suite furnished with a rustic hardwood bed with matching closet and dresser. White curtains billowed from the door to the balcony, on the opposite wall. Weinberg was lying on top of the comforter on the bed, naked, curled up facing away from them. Morgan raised the MP5 and unlocked the safety catch.

"Weinberg!" Morgan shouted.

The German sat up, confused and blinking in the darkness.

"No sudden movements," said Morgan, "or I'll shoot. Get slowly out of bed. Put on some—"

"Stop!" came a sharp, imperious female voice from behind them, and light flooded the room from the hallway. "I have a gun on you, and I can shoot you both before you turn around." Lena Weinberg. *Shit.* They had no idea she was here. "Don't move a muscle. Guns on the floor. Both of you." Morgan looked at Lily, who seemed about ready to turn around and shoot Lena. He mouthed *no.*

"I see your bulletproof vests," said Lena, "and I raise you a lifetime of instruction as a sharpshooter. I am pointing my gun at you, Ms. Randall. If either of you move a muscle, you'll be dead within half a second. And I have to say, the odds will not look good for you, either, Mr. Morgan. Now, *guns on the floor!*"

Morgan unslung the MP5 and set it on the floor. Lily scowled but followed suit.

"Handguns!" Lena exclaimed.

They unholstered their sidearms and let them drop to the floor.

"Good. Now back up against the window." They circled the bed, arms up. "Gunther! Come on behind me!"

They heard the groan of the bed as Weinberg stood. "Shoot them, Lena."

Morgan was calculating the probability of being able to break through the window when a loud crash of something made of glass or china shattering reverberated from downstairs.

"Ah, so they are not alone," said Lena.

"That's right," said Morgan. "Toss the gun and we might let you live."

Heavy steps thudded on the stairwell. All four of them tensed up. *Come on, Bishop! Spartan!*

From the hallway appeared the hulking frame of Anse Fleischer.

It was enough of a distraction for Morgan to make his move. In one swift movement and a grunt of exertion, he lifted the bed on its side, pushing it against the door. He and Lily pivoted out of the way as Lena shot through the mattress, bullets hitting the window and far wall. Morgan picked up his MP5 and kicked Lily's over to her.

Now what? Morgan couldn't risk killing Weinberg. He loosed a hail of bullets into the bed, aiming high. That would keep them away, but time was on their side, not Morgan's. The Weinbergs could simply call the police—if they hadn't already. All they could do was hold their ground.

Except—the balcony. They still had the Kevlar ladder.

"Lily, get that open," he said, motioning toward the balcony door. He pulled out the ladder from his rucksack.

"Spartan," he said, fixing the hook on the ledge, letting it unroll down to the deck. "Bishop. Report in."

"They're not responding," said Diesel over the comm.

"I need to get to them," said Morgan. "Can you provide a distraction?"

"Like a big explosion?" asked Diesel. "I've got two very large gas tanks in my sight."

"That'll do," said Morgan.

"On your mark," said Diesel.

"No time like the present," said Morgan. He motioned for Lily to climb out onto the balcony, while he let fly a barrage of covering fire at the room door. Then, to Lily: "When you touch down, go directly inside and look for them."

"Leave no man behind," said Lily, who disappeared out the window.

"Good. Okay, Diesel," said Morgan, "we're ready for you."

"Hold on to your asses," said Diesel. Morgan heard a distant gunshot, then another. The house shook, and the backyard was lit up in orange by the unseen fireball.

Morgan climbed over the parapet and down on the ladder. He clambered down, rung by rung, until he touched down on the deck again. Lily was already inside the house.

"They're here!" she called out. "And alive! Give me a hand!"

Morgan ran in the house, into the foyer. Bishop and Spartan were laid out on the floor. They had been beaten, and the furniture around them was broken. Half of Spartan's face was red and swollen, with a deep cut on her cheek. Bishop was bleeding from the forehead, where several pieces of glass were embedded. A large framed mirror that hung on the wall was badly cracked.

"I got her," said Lily, lifting Spartan with considerable difficulty. Spartan, half conscious, was at least able to support part of her weight on her own feet, but Lily looked like she might fall any second.

Morgan turned his attention to Bishop, who was mumbling incoherently. "Okay, buddy, come on, let's get up." Bishop, tall and muscular, was heavy as hell. "Come on, let's go."

As they walked back to the living room, Morgan's eyes were drawn to the stairs. The Weinbergs would be coming down any second now. He and Lily, carrying their injured comrades, could do little to defend themselves. He picked up the pace, but Lily was lagging behind. Morgan made it outside and carried Bishop around the corner of the house, where he and Lily had originally scaled the wall. He then went back for Lily and Spartan. They had not yet crossed the living room. He reached them and held Spartan up himself.

"Here, let me," he said to Lily. "You get out of here."

He picked Spartan up—she was solid, but still a lot smaller than Bishop. He heard footsteps on the stairwell. Fleischer and his employers were coming downstairs. Morgan had to get out with Spartan. Knees burning, he ran outside, hearing gunfire behind him. A bullet whizzed past his ear. He carried Spartan toward the side of the house, where Lily was standing over Bishop. She had her gun out.

"Get out of the way!" she yelled, but he couldn't. Moving away from the side of the house would expose him to gunfire from inside. But Fleischer would reach the glass doors to the outer deck in seconds. Morgan looked back and saw him emerge, gun in hand. He raised it to shoot, and—

A shot rang out and hit the side of the house, inches from Fleischer's head. He doubled back inside.

Diesel!

"Get the hell out!" said Diesel through the comm.

"I'm working on it!"

He ran over to the others. "There's no ladder," said Lily.

"We'll just use the same—" he trailed off. That ladder was hanging over the glass door, exposed to the inside of the house.

He turned to Bishop. "Come on, buddy" he said, close to the man's face. He slapped him, and he seemed to stir.

"Cobra . . ." he said, barely getting the word out.

"He's out of commission," said Morgan. Lily, meanwhile, was bent over Spartan, trying to wake her. Spartan stirred, and then opened her eyes.

"Wake up!" Lily said. "We're not out of the woods yet. Can you stand up?"

"I think so," said Spartan. Groaning, she got up. "Bishop—"

"Alive," said Morgan. "But unconscious. We need to get out of here, and the way out is down there." He pointed to the wall with the long drop.

"That's got to be eight feet," she said. "Do we have a ladder?"

"No," said Morgan. "We'll have to jump. After we drop Bishop down."

"I was afraid you'd say that."

"Come on," he said, "help me with him."

The three of them together hoisted Bishop onto the wall, which was low on their side, and sat him down. "Now," said Morgan, "we're going to hold on to him for as long as possible, and lower him as far as possible. Got it?"

Morgan pushed Bishop over, and grunted from the weight. Lily nearly went over with him. Holding him by the arms, they managed to lower him far enough that the drop was a mere three feet.

"Sorry, buddy," said Morgan. Then, to Spartan and Lily, "Okay, let go."

Bishop dropped, his feet hit the ground, and he fell on his side.

"Spartan, you next," said Morgan. "I've got you." She held his hand until she was low enough, then let go.

"Lily—"

"I got this," she said, and swung over the wall, hanging by her hands, and turned loose.

Morgan looked down at the three of them, then back at the house. "I'm going back," he said. "I can't let them get away."

"That's suicide!" said Lily. "Even I can tell you that!"

"I can't let them slip through our fingers again."

"We can't carry him without you!" said Lily, motioning to Bishop. "We need you here. He needs your help. He'll die if he doesn't get medical attention."

Morgan looked back again. They were right. He couldn't leave Bishop to die. He dropped from the ledge, a stab of pain shooting through his right knee as he hit the ground. He then bent down to lift up Bishop. "Let's go!" he said. "Diesel, you there? What do you see?"

"They're still in the house," said Diesel. "I fired a couple more warning shots, and they seemed to get the picture and stay out of sight. Hold on, I see something. Police cars on the road—get the hell out of there, Cobra!"

"Go on," he said. "Lily, watch her back. I'm not sure she's one hundred percent yet."

"What about you?" Lily asked.

"Carrying Bishop is going to slow me down," Morgan told her. "There's no reason for you to wait. Go!"

Morgan watched them run off into the darkness, and carried Bishop along, one step at a time, Morgan's knee pulsating with pain with every footfall. The tactical team leader was wavering on the edge of consciousness. "You—are—going—to have—to buy me—something *extra*—nice—when we get—back," Morgan said through his ragged breaths. "Bishop! *Wake—up!*"

Bishop murmured as they walked together, dragging his feet.

It took interminable minutes of pain until Morgan reached the sconce where they had stashed their equipment. Spartan was waiting there for him.

"Lily's gone to the boat," she said. "She said she'd bring back the dinghy for Bishop. And me too, I guess."

Morgan slumped against the ridge, catching his breath. "Diesel," he said, "we're clear, get your ass down here."

The police had brought searchlights, but they were far enough away that the cops would take a long time getting there. They heard the sputtering of the dinghy's engine some ten minutes later. They loaded Bishop first onto the dinghy floor.

"I got this," said Spartan, but her hand slipped and she fell on the rock, crying out in pain. Morgan and Diesel helped her on, then they pushed it out onto the water, climbing in when it had cleared the beach.

As they rode back to the darkened schooner in gloomy, defeated silence, Morgan heard the rotors start up on Weinberg's chopper. It was the sound of him once again slipping through their fingers.

Chapter 37

Chapman's phone rang. Caller ID told him that it was Rose, and he fiddled with a paper clip until the call went to voice mail. He'd been dodging her calls out of guilt. Instead, he sent brief text messages informing her that he was okay but couldn't pick up the phone, and asked about her and Ella.

A knock came at his door, and Cynthia Gillespie opened it without stepping through the threshold.

"Hey, look, I thought you should know. That alert you had me place on Weinberg? Well, we got a hit. He arrived at JFK airport this morning by private jet. Looks like he's here to attend some charity gala in New York City. Shall I send you the details?"

"Please do," he said. "Cyn?"

"Yeah? Do you need something else?"

"Could you just come in here and talk to me for a minute?"

She exhaled with nervous weariness, and sat down on a chair across from his desk. "All right, I'm here."

"Listen," he said. He swallowed, working up his nerve. "Cyn, we have to talk about what happened."

"Nothing happened, Buck," she said. "We have nothing to talk about."

"Something did happen," he insisted.

"Buck . . ."

"We need to talk about it, Cyn."

"We really don't," she said.

"Cyn," he said. "Come on."

"What the hell do you want me to say? You're *married*, Buck. It can't happen, and that's that." She stood up, and then he did as well.

"I know it can't, I just feel like . . ."

"Like what, Buck?" she said.

"Like we need to clear the air. Look, clearly, this was a mistake—"

"I know," she said, with irritation. "It was, and there's nothing else to say. Consider the air cleared."

"I don't believe you," he said. "I don't think that's true."

"Shit, Buck, *what do you want me to say? You* kissed *me,* remember?"

"I know," he stammered. "I just— Listen, you're the best analyst in this office, and just about the only person I can trust in this entire agency. Damn it, I need you, Cyn, and I need to know that you'll be around and we can work together."

Her face turned to an expression that he couldn't read, and there was something between them he couldn't understand. It was interrupted by the cell phone on his desk ringing. Caller ID displayed his wife's name in large, clearly visible letters.

Cynthia looked down at the phone, then back up at him. "I need to go, Buck. I have work to do. *We* have work to do. Let's leave the high school drama aside and just do our jobs, all right?"

She turned around and shut the door behind her. Buck listened to the phone ringing, wondering what had gone wrong in that conversation.

The phone stopped ringing, and the call went to voice mail. Buck took his other phone from his coat pocket and dialed Smith.

Chapter 38

Morgan walked into his home through the garage door in the late afternoon, in dire need of a shower. The team had been picked up by a helicopter from the schooner and gone straight to the airport, where a jet had brought them to America. Lily had been put up at the downtown Hilton, and Spartan had been sent to the hospital with Morgan. He got his fingers properly immobilized and was checked for fractures and internal damage—just one, a hairline on a right rib—and then was discharged. He took a cab home.

"Bishop is stable, but he's not out of the woods yet."

That's what Bloch had told them. Bishop had been airlifted by another helicopter and taken to a hospital in Munich, where he'd have the best medical care that money could buy. But Fleischer had really pounded on him. Slammed his head hard into a mirror. Others had gotten brain damage from less than that, Morgan knew. Bishop could drop dead at a moment's notice at this stage.

The other thing Bloch had told them was that they could find no sign of Weinberg or the EMP device. It had come to Greece, that much they knew. From there it might have gone anywhere in the world.

Morgan opened the garage door, which led into the kitchen. Nieka was on the other side, whining and waiting to greet him. She licked his hand, and stood up on her hind legs to try to lick his face.

"Down, girl!"

Morgan heard footsteps running down the stairs, and his daughter, Alex, entered the kitchen at a jog.

"Dad, you're back!" She ran over and threw herself on him, hugging him as hard as she could.

"Hey, kiddo," he said, hugging her back. "Good to see you."

"You look like hell," she said. "Your face . . ." Her hand went up to her cheek, mirroring the spot where his skin was still darkly bruised.

"I'll survive," he croaked. He opened the refrigerator and pulled out some fruit.

"Mom's at the store," she said. "I should call her to let her know you're back."

"No," he said, taking the blender from the cabinet. "No need to do that. I'll see her when she gets home. I just need to lie down for a bit."

"Oh—okay," she said, disappointed. "They still haven't found the Secretary, I guess."

"I know." Morgan was too preoccupied to talk. His answers came out as curt and uninterested. He selected a plump red apple from the fruit basket, took a knife from the block, and started chopping it.

"They're saying there might be a war," said Alex, crossing her arms in front of her.

"They're probably fueling up the aircraft already," said Morgan.

"Are you serious?" she asked with alarm.

"No. No," he said, rubbing his face. "Not as much as that, I think. But plans are being drawn up, I'm sure. As a precaution, if nothing else." He tossed the apple pieces into the blender cup, then peeled a banana.

"Pakistan has nuclear weapons, right?" she asked.

"Right," he said.

"Could they hit us here in the States?"

"Probably not," Morgan said. "Their missiles don't go that far, at least as far as we know. But they could attack others. Israel wouldn't be out of the question. Maybe our allies in Europe."

"Do you think things might go nuclear? If we invade?"

"It's a possibility," said Morgan. He poured in the milk, then ran the blender.

"Dad! Please! I'm scared! Talk to me!"

He looked at her again and his eyes focused. He was brought away from his haze, and he saw his daughter, fragile and in need of him. "I'm sorry, Alex. Things haven't been easy. I've had a lot of things on my mind."

"How do you think things have been *here,* Dad?" she said, with resentment in her tone. "We're scared stiff! I know you're in danger out there, but Mom and I are here, afraid that we're going to lose you!"

"I'm sorry," he said.

"Don't be sorry, Dad. Just talk to me."

Morgan poured the smoothie into a tall glass. "All right," he said. "Come with me to the living room. I'll tell you what I can."

Morgan sat down on the couch, and Alex sat in an armchair so that they were facing each other. Neika walked over to them and sat at Alex's feet, and she petted the dog absently.

"I want you to be honest," she said. "What are the chances that the Secretary is going to be found?"

"The more time passes, the less likely it is that we'll find him alive," said Morgan.

"Okay," she said, biting her lip in apprehension. "Why was he taken?"

"I honestly have no idea," he said. "I can't make any sense of it."

"I thought it was just terrorists," said Alex.

"It's more complicated than that," said Morgan.

"Like how?"

"I can't tell you that," he said.

"All right. I can respect that." She looked him in the eyes. "Dad, do you think there's going to be war?"

"Honestly? I don't know. Everything's up in the air right now, and neither I nor anyone else knows where the chips are going to fall."

"I see." She ran her hand down Neika's back. "I don't really feel any better," she said.

"Sometimes the truth doesn't make us feel better," said Morgan. "All we can hope for is to be able to do something about it."

Alex sat up taller. "How can you do it, Dad? *Why* do you do it? Why choose this life?"

"It's not a choice," he said. "Not anymore."

"Do you really love the thrill of it that much?"

"No," he said, thinking of their defeat in Santorini and Bishop in the hospital. "I just have something to protect."

Alex was about to speak again, but was interrupted by the sound of Jenny's car pulling up to the driveway. Morgan waited for her in the kitchen. She opened the door and broke out into a wide smile when she saw him. He hugged and kissed her.

"My God, Dan, have I missed you," she said as he pulled her tight against him. "Are you back for good? Is it over?"

His face told her that it wasn't. "I'm just waiting for the call," he said.

She disguised her disappointment with a tearful smile. "That's my man," she said. "Out there saving the world. I'm proud of you, did you know that?" He kissed her again, but they were interrupted by a beep from his phone.

It was a message from Bloch. *We've got something. Come in right now.*

"I need to go," Morgan said.

"Already?" said Jenny.

"I'll be back," he said. "I promise. Before you know it."

Jenny put her hands on his shoulders. "Go do what you do," she said. "You know that I'll always be waiting for you at home." She kissed him deeply, the way a sailor's wife kisses her husband before a long voyage.

Chapter 39

June 10
Chitral Valley, Pakistan

Akram's truck broke down twenty miles from the Chitral Valley. Conley and the rest didn't know it at first, huddled in the back of the truck. It had been a slow ride, during which the truck tipped to this side and that, going over terrain so uneven they wondered whether they were on roads at all.

This truck was entirely enclosed, so they didn't get a chance to peek out at the majestic beauty of the landscapes that Conley had seen in pictures as he researched the location of the mission. They just sat in the dark, hot, smelly interior, bumping into each other every time the truck lurched.

The vehicle stopped.

"Are we there?" asked Clutch, a short and thickly built black man with a round face, the team's sniper. "I gotta take a piss."

"Why don't you use a bottle like the rest of us?" asked Mantis, the curly brown–haired explosives expert who Conley placed as Midwestern from his accent.

"Ain't no way for a man to relieve himself," he said.

Conley banged on the wall that adjoined the truck's cab. He heard the passenger door open, and then the back door was unlocked. Blue-gray light poured in from outside together with a rush of cool fresh air.

"We've broken down," Harun told them. "Akram's going to take a look. It's not a rare occurrence. If any one if you could help, it might get us moving faster."

"Any of you clowns mechanics?" asked Conley. None of the

others moved. Conley turned back to Harun. "I can fix a car in a bind."

"Does that mean we can come out?" asked Clutch.

"We are hidden here from the main road," said Harun. "But—"

"I'm gonna go piss off the mountain," said Clutch.

The others moved to get out as well. Conley dropped off the edge of the truck last. Walker radioed their status to the support crew at Lambda headquarters.

Harun looked doubtfully at the others spreading out around the truck, but Conley said, "Let them. They're going to kill each other if they don't get some air."

They were on a rocky ledge overlooking the Chitral valley, and it occurred to Conley that he lived for sights like these. They were high on the mountain, and the verdant valley spread out below in a patchwork of cultivated plots like something out of the Middle Ages. At the far end of the valley he saw the Kunar River, its water an astonishing light blue against the gray rocky riverbed.

It felt good to have the hard ground beneath his feet, after sitting on the metal floor of the truck for so long. Everything ached, and worse now that he was moving and in the cooler outside air. He stretched and jogged in place to get his circulation flowing.

"All right, let's take a look at that engine," he told Harun.

Akram had already opened up the hood of the truck and had his head buried inside.

"Have you checked the battery?" asked Conley in Urdu. He realized that he didn't have the vocabulary to talk car mechanics in the language. They worked by pointing, miming and showing, trying to figure out different possible causes of the breakdown.

After half an hour of trial and error, Conley took a break and found Walker smoking on a boulder and sat next to him. He took a deep swig of water from his canteen. "I think it's time we went over the coordinates to where Haider Raza is supposed to be and lay out our plan of attack," he said.

Walker put out his cigarette on the rock and stood up. "All right," he said. "My stuff's on the back of the truck."

Conley got up and they walked over together. "Listen," said Conley as Walker rifled through his bag. "I think we got off on the wrong foot before. Maybe if we just—"

"I don't want to know you, man," Walker interrupted. "I just want to be done with this mission and get out of this shit hole. All right? Now, let's get this done."

"All right, let's." *Asshole.*

Walker pulled out a plasticized map and laid it out in front of them. Conley recognized the Chitral valley. "This is where we are," he said, pointing at the map.

"Yeah," said Walker. "I see it. Raza's supposed to be at a farmhouse here." He pointed to a location to the northeast of where they were—not too far as the crow flew, but the road down the mountain was winding and treacherous. "We have to get close without being seen. There's mountains here, maybe there's somewhere for us to hide. I've got some satellite pictures, hold on . . ." Walker shuffled through his bag.

Conley scratched his chin. "Akram!" he called out. "Come here a second." The Pakistani got down from the truck and jogged over to Conley. Conley waved him over to look at the map, and pointed to the corner of the map where the farmhouse was located. "Do trucks go here?" he asked in Urdu.

He seemed to need a minute to decipher the map, then it seemed to dawn on him. "Yes, sir, they do."

"Have you ever been there?"

"Many times."

"Good. Sorry to interrupt you. I'll be back to help you with the engine in a second."

Akram walked away. Walker asked, "What the hell was that?"

"He says it's not rare for vehicles to go that way," said Conley. "We can ride this truck almost to their doorstep."

"Okay," said Walker. "Look." He had found the satellite images. "The terrain is higher along here—there's a small ridge, some rocks. It's right by the farm. We can hide out and run surveillance."

Walker had a good eye for strategy, Conley thought. It was a good position, and it took wit to find it on the satellite photo. "Sounds like a plan. Get close, then watch for any sign of the Secretary."

"If we ever get there," said Walker, motioning toward the truck. "If we get this piece of crap moving again."

Conley looked around once more. The Lambda team was lounging, a couple of them playing cards. The sun had disappeared behind the mountains, but the sky was still blue. They still had hours of light left. If the problem was fixable, they'd make it. If not—well, they'd cross that bridge when they had to.

He went back to help Akram and Harun with the engine. After another twenty minutes of tweaks and Akram trying to start the engine, Harun found the problem and Akram fixed it with duct tape, which made Conley nervous about what else might have been fixed with duct tape. But there was no use worrying about that—they had no other options. This time, when Akram turned the key, the truck came back to life.

Before they departed, Conley showed Harun, on the map, a spot beyond the ridge where they could stop, and Harun coordinated with Akram to get them there. Then, everyone piled back into the back, Conley last, and Harun closed them in. They were off. It was a short, bumpy ride to the valley floor, and then another hour of mostly smooth sailing. The Lambda team sang dirty ditties until Harun banged on the back of the truck cab, either because they were near civilization or because he just wanted them to shut up.

When they came to a stop and heard the engine cut off again, no light was coming in from the tiny cracks in the truck anymore. Harun opened the back door, and they saw that night had fallen.

"This is where you get off," said Harun, "And I turn back."

"You're not coming?" asked Conley as he hopped off the truck and pulled his pack along with him.

"I've done my part," said Harun. "Akram and I want to be as far away from this as possible when it happens. Come here, old friend." He pulled Conley in close for a hug. As they embraced, he whispered, "Watch out for these men. I do not trust them, and you should not, either."

Harun climbed into the back of the truck and Akram executed a ponderous U-turn, returning from where they came.

"Watch them go straight to Raza and tell him where we are," said Walker as they watched the truck roll away.

"We should have killed them and left their bodies in a ditch," said Mantis.

"Let's move out," said Conley.

It was a dark and moonless night. They had been left in a crook of rock that shielded them from prying eyes. They would have to walk about a mile in open farmland to reach Raza's villa, and the night would provide the cover.

They walked a couple hundred yards up the side of the mountain, single file, and found a protected outcropping to hide out behind and run surveillance. Walker radioed in their position to headquarters. "Have the evac chopper ready. Tell them to home in on this location." He was promised that it would be within two minutes of them at all times.

"Who's running our getaway?" Conley asked.

"A couple mercenaries with a Mil Mi-8." That was unsurprising. The Soviet-designed Mil Mi-8 was one of the most popular helicopters in the world, and was in wide civilian use. It was certainly easier to get and less regulated than a Black Hawk.

"Who are they?" Conley pressed.

"Who cares?" said Walker, and that was that.

The team got out their night vision and remote surveillance gear. Conley had his binoculars, which would serve. They were within a mile of the house, with a wheat field the stretched nearly all the way to their location. The lights were on and the windows plainly visible against the darkness. Conley looked through the binoculars.

The house was not small, probably boasting some four or five bedrooms and having some touches of ornamentation like a row of simple columns and rounded arches, but it was mostly plain, single-story and built of exposed stone. Conley saw two men inside, and thought he saw a Kalashnikov leaning against a wall. They spent nearly twenty minutes surveying the compound, in silence except for a few brief exchanges.

It was Mutt who spotted him first. "That's him. Holy shit, that's him! Second window on the left, look fast!"

Conley looked through his binoculars. The beard had been trimmed, but the face was unmistakable.

Haider Raza.

"We've got the bastard," said Bluejay.

"Call it in, Walker," said Conley.

Walker already had the radio in his hand. "We have positive identification. I repeat, we have positive identification. It's Raza. We've got the bastard."

"Copy. Proceed with caution, Walker," came the crackling voice from the radio communicator.

The excitement was palpable, but the team's eagerness made Conley uneasy. "We need a plan of attack," he said.

"The plan is we go in and kick ass," said Walker, inspecting his sidearm.

"We need to confirm that the Secretary of State is in there," said Conley.

"We'll do that *after* Raza and his men are dead."

"Walker, Jesus Christ—" started Conley, losing his patience.

"We're going in now," said Walker. "You want to stay behind, you go right ahead. Team, move out."

They filed out around the outcropping and out of sight. "Goddamn it," Conley whispered. He found his tactical vest in his pack and strapped it on over his rumpled white button-down shirt. Then he fished out his Beretta M9, pocketed two extra magazines, put his seven-inch tactical knife in its leather sheath, and set off after them.

The night was dark, and he could hardly make them out about twenty yards ahead. It took them less than a minute to reach the wheat field. Walking through the wheat was noisy and the stalks whipped at Conley's hands. A rising wind made the plants bow and blew dust in his face, but at least masked whatever sound they might make. The house loomed larger and larger up ahead.

A low stone wall marked the edge of the wheat field about thirty yards from the house. The team crouched against it, looking over at the three windows that faced them. Figures walked past the windows too often to allow an approach this way. Walker signaled for them to move north along the stone wall. They crept forward, crouching to keep out of sight. Conley unsheathed his knife and clutched it in his hand.

Walker stopped up ahead, and made a sign that a hostile lurked outside beyond the wall. He signed for Bluejay to take care of it. Bluejay drew his handgun, which had a suppressor attachment. Even with the suppressor, it could very well have alerted the whole house to their presence. Conley motioned to Walker and held up his knife. Walker understood and motioned Bluejay to stand down.

Conley peeked over the wall and saw the man walking a few feet beyond the corner of the house, where a row of arches began. He had an AK-47 in his hands, slung over his shoulder, and was looking in the direction of the road—away from them. This would be child's play.

Conley propelled himself over the low stone wall and landed on the other side with hardly a tap of his feet. He crept to the side wall of the house to stay clear of the line of sight of the windows. On reaching the corner, he looked around it to make sure this was the only hostile. The side of the house was otherwise empty.

Conley made his final approach in five quick strides. The man heard, but had no time to react before Conley pulled his head back and slit his throat. He held the man firm as he fell, setting him on the ground. He got a look at the man's face as he gurgled his last with his darkness-adjusted eyes. By his wispy beard, he couldn't have been older than twenty. The man's blood soaked Conley's tactical vest down to his white shirt.

He signaled to Walker, and the team moved out toward him. Conley skulked along the row of columns at the side of the house. He pointed to the door nearest them. It was wooden and looked weak and partly rotted. Walker signed for Mutt, Clutch, and Mantis to go around and take the windows, while he, Bluejay, and Conley took the door. He gave them the count of ten to make their move.

Conley braced for entry, sheathing his knife and pulling out his Beretta. Bluejay was poised to kick the door in, while Walker had his Uzi submachine gun ready to fire. Conley counted the numbers off in his head.

Walker gave the signal after the ten seconds had elapsed, and Bluejay kicked the door. It swung open with a bang. Conley heard gunfire from the side of the house—outside, and not inside. It was a good sign.

Walker took the lead, with Conley following and Bluejay in the rear. In the small foyer, a simple chandelier hung from the ceiling, and a tattered carpet covered the floor. It was dark, but another door, closed, seemed to lead deeper into the house. Walker opened the door to reveal a corridor, in which a man who Conley had seem through the window was scrambling out of one of the rooms that were being attacked from the outside, a Kalashnikov rifle in his hands. His face contorted into shock when he saw Conley, but didn't have time to react before Conley plugged him twice in the chest with his Beretta.

Another man emerged from the farthest room on the left, but Conley could not get a shot out before he disappeared into the back bedroom. Conley advanced, with Walker close behind. The door to the back bedroom had been left partly open. Conley plunged inside, gun out and ready to shoot any threats. He was shocked by what he found.

Raza had not armed himself, nor made any defenses for himself.

The terrorist was on the floor, kneeling, arms stretched at an upward angle, palms facing upward, in a position of prayer. His eyes were transfixed in some sort of religious ecstasy.

Walker, who had been right behind Conley the whole time, barged into the room.

"Where's Wolfe?" Conley demanded of Raza.

"He is not here," said Raza serenely. There was victory in his tone, in his expression.

Walker stepped forward, drawing a Desert Eagle semiautomatic. "Time to say good night, asshole."

"Allahu akb—" Raza began. He never finished.

"No!" Conley yelled. But it was too late. Walker pulled the trigger. Raza's head erupted in blood, and he slumped to the ground.

"Walker, what did you *do?*" Conley demanded.

"Clear!" he heard someone shout from the other rooms. "Clear!" called out another voice.

"Just exterminating a pest off the face of the Earth," he said, with contempt in his voice. He spat on Raza's corpse.

"Goddamn it, Walker, we *had* him. He wasn't resisting, he didn't have a gun."

"He deserved to die."

"He could have told us where to find the goddamn Secretary of State!" Conley yelled, exasperated.

"Are you giving me crap about killing a goddamn *terrorist,* Cougar?" Walker demanded, chest out like a rooster in a cockfight. Blood was pooling around Raza's mangled head. "Maybe you'd like to die a martyr like him. Is that it?"

"Hey, hey!" said Bluejay, getting between them. "We've done the mission. Now, let's get the hell out of here."

"You watch yourself, *Cougar,*" said Walker. "Just watch yourself." He drew his radio. "This is Walker. Requesting extraction, over." He turned back to Conley. "We're leaving. If there's anything you don't like, you're free to stay here with *him.*"

The Lambda team filed out of the room and down the hallway. Conley took one last look at Raza's corpse before following them.

Chapter 40

Dan Morgan picked up Lily at her hotel and led her to the garage door that opened into Zeta Division headquarters.

"Nifty," she said, as he opened the circuit breaker panel and put his hand on the fingerprint scanner.

"Bloody hell," she said when they reached the War Room. "You work *here?* This is a lot nicer than our facilities across the pond."

"Agent Randall." Diana Bloch, looking imposing in a white starched blazer that looked vaguely Japanese, walked forward to greet her. "Welcome to the fold. We're glad to have you."

Seeing her there was strange and uncomfortable, kind of like having your father-in-law meet your ex-fiancée. But she was good, and they needed good people. At the very least, he was glad as hell that she was no longer against them.

Morgan took his usual seat at the table and Lily took the cue to sit next to him. Diesel was there looking dour, and Spartan too, with half her face bruised and raw, but looking strong and self-possessed. Shepard had his seat flanking Bloch on the right, as usual. To her left was a seat whose emptiness was palpable. It was where Bishop usually sat.

"So, you want to tell them?" Shepard asked Bloch, who stood at her place at the head of the table.

"He's in the country," she announced. "Weinberg is in the United States. His sister, Lena, too."

"Excuse me?" said Morgan.

"We have a record of him entering the country," said Shepard. "He arrived this morning at JFK airport."

"Why weren't we there to catch him?" asked Morgan, banging on the table. "We almost died trying to get him. Bishop's in the hospital! And now we had his goddamn location *in this country!* If we could have stopped him at the airport, all we'd have had to do was bring him in!"

"It's not that simple," said Kirby. "We didn't have real-time monitoring of customs and immigration services, nor the manpower to stay on top of it. We got this from one of our guys at the CIA."

"And now we have a terrorist on American soil," Morgan snarled.

"We're all aware of the gravity of the situation," said Bloch.

"Yeah, I hope you are," he said. "Well, can we track him now, at least?"

"Weinberg has been a lot more careful," said Shepard. "His name hasn't turned up in any government or private databases that we have access to—no hotel registries or reservations, no transportation beyond his initial entry into the country, no wireless communication, nothing. No hits on any of his credit cards or bank accounts. Whatever we were using to find him before, it's no good now."

"Great," said Morgan. "What about the EMP? If Weinberg is here, is the EMP here as well?"

"It's our working assumption," said Bloch.

"Any chance of finding it?"

"We're looking into it," said Kirby. "But we've got thirty thousand shipping containers arriving in this country *every day.*"

"Plus," said Shepard, "Weinberg's in the shipping business. If there's one thing he knows, it's how to get something past customs."

"So for all we know—" Morgan began.

"It's already here, yes," finished Bloch.

"Fantastic."

"We do have one lead," said Bloch. "It's weak, but it's something."

"What?" said Morgan.

"The Governor's Charity Gala at Liberty Island. Weinberg is one of the guests. That was supposedly his reason for being in the country."

"And why the hell do we think he's going to show up, being as he's in hiding and all?" asked Morgan sarcastically.

"He RSVP'd," said Shepard. "Look, Cobra, I know it's unlikely, but it's really all that we have to go on."

"It's thin," said Morgan.

"It's what we have," said Kirby.

"Weinberg has been reckless before," added Bloch. "He may be getting reckless again."

Morgan looked at his hands, rubbing his bandaged fingers and finding that they still hurt like hell. "All right, so what's the plan?" he asked.

"We send in you and Agent Randall," said Bloch. "As guests to the gala to try to find him among the crowd."

"He knows us," said Morgan. "Our faces. That'll tip him off."

"We're counting on it," said Bloch. "We'll have a team doing surveillance. If and when he leaves the party, we'll have people on him."

"What people?" said Morgan. "I'm sorry, but we're a couple of soldiers short of a tactical team. With Bishop in the hospital, Spartan in no condition to go out in the field, Lily and me inside, you're left with—"

"It won't be the Zeta tactical team," said Bloch. "That's the other piece of news."

"Bad news?" asked Lily.

"It's more of a good news, bad news situation," said Shepard.

"Haider Raza is dead," said Bloch. "He was killed by the Lambda tactical team and Cougar late yesterday."

Good, Morgan thought. *Hope the bastard suffered.* "What about the Secretary of State?"

"That's the bad news. He wasn't there. He was at least two days gone from Raza's hideout when Lambda moved in. Raza and his men were killed without interrogation."

The people around the table moaned in frustration.

"At least it's another terrorist dead," said Morgan.

"The upshot of this," continued Bloch, "is that the Lambda tactical team is returning from Pakistan."

"And Cougar?" asked Morgan.

"Cougar, too. They will be running support for the gala, and will move in on Weinberg when it's time. They will stand by with a surveillance van and a helicopter, and Shepard back here commanding satellite surveillance. If Weinberg's there, he won't escape us."

"And we have to work with a team we've never even met," Morgan said.

"You've done plenty of ops with assets you barely knew," said Bloch. "You know how the game is played. Plus, we'll have one of ours on their side."

"So we're abandoning the search for the Secretary?" Morgan asked.

"It's been a dead end so far," she said. "Let the government agencies work on finding Wolfe. It's better to focus our efforts on finding Weinberg, and the EMP. Much as I hate to say it, if he detonates it on American soil, we'll have a much bigger problem on our hands than a missing cabinet member."

Chapter 41

June 11
Langley

"Haider Raza is dead," said Smith without averting his eyes from the road.

"Jesus," said Chapman, squirming in the passenger's seat of Smith's Hyundai. The car looked, inside and out, like it had just rolled out of a factory, with not a smudge or personal touch in its interior. "Thank God. The Secretary—"

"Was not there," said Smith. "Although he had been."

Chapman held up his hands, like he was attempting to grasp at something. "Where? How?" he asked.

"In the Chitral valley, on the border between Pakistan and Afghanistan."

Smith had called him earlier in the day and had asked him to wait at the curb at the northwest corner of Twenty-Fifth and Pennsylvania at 5 P.M. sharp. He'd made his excuses and been there when Smith's jet-black Azera pulled up.

"Your people?" Chapman asked.

Smith ignored the question, which was answer enough for Chapman. "I see," he said.

"This information needs to get to the regular government intelligence channels," said Smith. He drove carefully, following every traffic regulation to the letter. "Open the glove compartment."

Chapman did. In it was a manila envelope.

"Go ahead and open it," Smith said. "You'll find a report from an asset of yours in Pakistan." Chapman undid the metal clasp and upturned the envelope, letting the documents inside slide out. "The story is that this was a raid from the Pakistan Taliban—motivated by some arcane theological or political dispute over what kind of fundamentalist Islam is the best. Don't worry about the details. All you, and anyone else, need to know is that this was Jihadi-on-Jihadi—and, of course, that the Secretary is likely nearby."

Chapman leafed through the papers. They included eyewitness accounts written in Urdu and photographs of the bloody scene. This was thorough. "What if someone asks around and discovers that something about this is off?" asked Chapman.

"They won't," said Smith. "And it's in your best interest to assist in that."

"Right," said Chapman. If the Agency knew he was passing on information to Smith . . .

They drove without speaking, until Smith spoke. "I know that the matter of payment is a touchy subject for you—"

"So let's not, okay?" said Chapman. "You don't own me. I help you and you help me. That's how it works. Got it?"

Smith offered only tacit assent.

"Good," said Chapman. "Now, take me back to where you picked me up. I've got work to do."

Chapter 42

Dan Morgan examined his face in the mirror in the morning light. The bruising was mostly gone now, and the cut on his cheek was scabbed over. He ran his tongue over his sliced lip.

He thought of Bishop, still in the hospital in Germany. That *bastard* Anse Fleischer. Morgan resolved that he'd get him, one way or another. When they got Weinberg, Fleischer would not escape.

Jenny had freaked about his injuries, as usual, when she saw him come home beaten and bruised. At one time this would have caused endless arguments between them about his recklessness and about how being a spy would eventually kill him. She had come to terms with it and understood the importance of what he did for a living. But that didn't mean that she wouldn't freak out anyway.

The way she usually freaked out was by cooking compulsively, and this time was no exception. She had started making pasta from scratch, and the kitchen table was now dusted with flour and covered with drying tagliatelle. She was also baking, giving bushels of pies and cakes to the neighbors who shared the sleepy little cul-de-sac they lived in, one at a time.

He disrobed and took his morning shower, then got dressed in jeans and a polo shirt. He had slept late, still a bit jet-lagged from the trip, so when he went downstairs he found his wife already working the stand mixer, a chili-pepper-patterned bandanna on her head and a floral apron tied around her waist. Thanks to the noise, she had not heard him approaching, and emitted a little yelp of surprise when he put his arms around her.

"It's only me," he said, leaning in to kiss her. Her cheek was dusted with white flour.

She gave him a peck on the lips without turning around. "Hey, you," she said. "I'm baking a Christmas cake for the Rosens."

"Honey, it's June."

"I know, I know," she said. She picked up a knife and started chopping up dried apricots. "But Sandra really loves them. I think they'll appreciate it just the same."

"I'm sure they will," he said.

"And it's always a good idea to practice neighborliness," she added.

"Be careful they don't think you're secretly trying to give them diabetes," said Morgan.

"Very funny," she said. "You're dressed. Are you going out?"

"Just a quick errand in the city," he said. He was going to check in on Lily, but Jenny didn't need to know that.

"Before you go," said Jenny, turning around to face him, "Dan, you have to talk to your daughter. She's out and about on that motorcycle of hers at all hours. I have no idea where she *goes,* Dan, or what she's doing. She won't listen to me, she thinks I'm square. But she'll listen to you. She worships you."

Morgan stroked her cheek with his right hand. "Let the kid have a little longer leash, Jenny dear. It'll do her good."

"Longer leash? Dan, Alex is most definitely *off the leash.* She's doing exactly as she pleases, and she is *too young* for that."

"Eighteen's old enough to move around on your own," he said. "I did it. Isn't it kind of a double standard to treat her differently than I was?"

"I don't care about double standards, I care about my daughter," she said. "*Talk to her, Dan.*"

"All right," he said. "I'll talk to her."

"Thanks," said Jenny. "She's over in the den. Go say good morning."

"I don't have to talk to her *right now,* do I?"

Jenny shot him a scolding look. "Today would be better," she said.

"All right, all right." He popped into the den to give his daughter a kiss and told her he'd be back later if she wanted to do something.

Then he walked to the garage, got into the Shelby, and set off in the direction of Boston.

On I-93 he looked in his rearview mirror and noticed something that made him frown, although he couldn't figure out why. It was a motorcycle some ten cars behind him, ridden by a woman in a black helmet. It made him think of Alex, although of course *her* helmet was pink. *Could it be . . .*

He had to find out.

He took the next off-ramp, and watched. She had hung back, but when he was at ground level, he could see the motorcycle getting off the ramp way up behind him. He turned into McGrath Highway, and on seeing that she had followed him there, turned into Broadway.

After a few minutes he made a right into a narrow, one-way side street, which was deserted, as expected. He parked the Shelby about seven yards from the corner, completely blocking the street. He pulled the hand brake and got out of the car. He waited with arms crossed, leaning against the car for about twenty seconds until a familiar Ducati Streetfighter turned onto the street and screeched to a halt, turning sideways and almost tipping over.

In front of him was his daughter Alex's bike, being ridden by none other.

"Busted," he said.

She took off her helmet to reveal a face that was half ashamed, half proud.

"Just what in the hell do you think you're doing?" he asked her.

"You know what I'm doing," she said with a confident grin.

He had to respect her, and hell, he was even proud. It was like something he would've done, back in the day. But he couldn't say *that.* This was a parenting moment. He had to admit, Jenny was right. Alex *was* going too far.

"I do," he said, and her grin faded away. It pained him to take this away from her, but he had to be a parent. "You're getting in *way* above your head."

"Dad, I was just—"

"This isn't a game, Alex. I agreed to teach you what I knew, and you agreed to stay out of trouble."

"Dad, I'm not—"

"If you can't honor that deal, I won't teach you a single other thing. And that's a promise."

She looked at him with humiliated rage, tears welling in her eyes. She hid her face in her helmet and turned on the ignition on her Ducati.

"And one more thing!" he yelled out as she turned around to speed away. "I catch you following me or anyone else again, and you can kiss that fancy bike good-bye!"

Chapter 43

The day of the gala had arrived. Morgan, dressed in a well-tailored tuxedo, took Lily's arm in his. He had considered telling Jenny the nature of the night's mission, on the off-chance that he and Lily were caught in the background of a photograph of a famous couple and ended up in the society pages. It seemed, however, implausible enough that he shrugged it off. With a little luck, Jenny would be none the wiser.

Lily was wearing a corseted red gown and shoes to match—something she called Manolo Blahniks, as if he were supposed to know what those were. They came out of their limousine at Battery Park, where an illuminated red carpet led to the docks. There, a small fleet of luxury speedboats was ferrying guests to and from the island.

They gave their names at the pier. Bloch, likely through the shadowy, well-connected Smith, had gotten them on the guest list alongside scores of high-ranking politicians, A-list celebrities, and assorted people who were wealthier than God. A security guard ran a metal detector wand over them. As expected, it missed the nearly invisible earbuds that were inserted into each of their left ears.

The speedboat took them and a handful of other guests toward the island, where the Statue of Liberty was fully lit in all her glory. Four searchlights lit the sky above her, the light shining bright then fading into the fog.

The speedboat reached the pier on Liberty Island, which was

decked out with the same kind of pomp and circumstance they had found at Battery Park.

Morgan didn't recognize the pop singer onstage, but he had a feeling that Alex might if she were there. The crowd was fancy, but not as homogenous as it was in Monte Carlo. People dressed with the same sober elegance as those in the European casino mingled with less-formal guests—movie stars and artists in open collars, with disheveled hair, and Silicon Valley billionaires with the relaxed casualness of people who had no family name to uphold and too much money to need to maintain a respectable image.

"Do you see him anywhere?" asked Morgan.

"No, but I think I see David Bowie."

"Lily, focus," he said. "We're here for Weinberg."

"All right, " she said, pouting. "Has anybody ever told you you're no fun at all?"

Scanning the crowd, Morgan couldn't spot Weinberg, but he did pick out one familiar face.

"Excuse me," he said to Lily, and walked toward a woman in her early middle age, with short brown hair and a respectable demeanor, wearing a black shawl over a sober dress of the same color. She was talking to an older man, bearing an expert look of feigned attention and interest.

"Senator," he said, interrupting her conversation.

Lana McKay turned to him, and then her eyes grew large and she covered her mouth in surprise. "Oh, my goodness." She turned to the man she had been talking to. "If you'd excuse me, Roger. I need to exchange a few words with this gentleman. His appearance here is—somewhat shocking, to say the least." She turned back to Morgan. "My apologies, Mr. Morgan. I never thought that I would see you again. I have to say, the experience is not entirely unlike seeing a ghost."

"I do prefer to stay out of sight," he said. "Although sometimes I do get to come to events like these. Are you enjoying yourself, Senator?"

"Not really, no," she said with a confidential smile. "But political exigencies bring me here. They're an unfortunate part of Washington culture that every freshman senator with a head full of ideas comes to accept and rue."

"Really?" he asked. "I kind of hoped that you'd be above that."

"Yes," she said. "Me too. You judge me, Mr. Morgan, and I can understand that. You're a man of action. Your approach to getting things done is direct. No bullshit, if you'll pardon my language. Just do what needs to be done. But to try that in Washington is to beat your head against a brick wall. You hit up against a system of one hundred people with one hundred different agendas. Good intentions and good ideas mean nothing by themselves."

"Instead, you play the game and you lose yourself," he said.

"Well, you do get to the point rather fast, don't you?" She sighed. "There's a lot I would rather do. I lot a really need to do. I don't have to tell you that the outcome of our current crisis with the Secretary can have deep ramifications to our safety and integrity as a nation. In particular, what we decide to do about it. This could could plunge the nation into permanent war and push us closer to a police state."

"You wouldn't know it from looking around this crowd," said Morgan, gesturing at the revelers around them, the colorful flashing lights of the stage where the pop star was lip-synching a tune, the servers carrying trays of champagne and tiny canapés.

"You really wouldn't, would you?" she said. "The world could be coming down around them, and they might not even notice as long as there's a waiter handy to top off their dry martinis."

"Meanwhile, we're at the same party, lamenting the state of the world," said Morgan.

"What does that say about us?"

Morgan laughed.

"I have to admit that your presence here is ominous, Mr. Morgan" said McKay, lowering her voice. "I hope it doesn't mean that someone intends to blow up the Statue of Liberty or anything like that."

"No, nothing like that," he said. "Not as far as I know, anyway."

Morgan noticed a presence through his peripheral vision, and saw that his date had caught up to him. "My word, those Wall Street types can be rather crass," she said, looking back in the direction she had come from. She turned to face McKay. "Good evening, Senator. Lily Randall. *Enchanté.* It's an honor, really. I'm a *huge* fan of your early work."

"There seems to be a lot of that going around," said McKay.

"Mr. Morgan, it has truly been a pleasure seeing you again., but duty calls." McKay walked off into the crowd to make conversation with the jet set.

When Morgan saw the intruders out of the corner of his eye, it was already too late. The sound of gunfire tore through the revelry. Bodyguards and security personnel were dropping all along the perimeter of the party area. Figures in black were emerging from the edges of the party and swarming into the center, firing semiautomatic weapons in short bursts.

Weinberg! It had to be! What was his plan? To eliminate a rival? A political opponent?

It didn't matter. Morgan just had to get to safety.

He scanned the crowd until he found McKay. "Senator! Get behind me!" He looked around for cover, but the party was out in the open. He wheeled around and came face-to-face with the answer, all three hundred feet of it. "Come on. We're going into the statue."

In the commotion, he spotted one of the gunmen, dangerously close, who in his black mask seemed to be looking directly at him. He spoke into a communicator that seemed to be on his sleeve, and walked in their direction. Were they after him? Had Weinberg identified him to them somehow? Was this all about him?

He looked at the terrified woman on his right. No, of course this was not about him. It was about *her.* The senator.

The man raised the semiautomatic, ready to shoot, when a flash of red appeared behind him. Lily Randall, who had somehow gotten behind him, swung a heavy silver platter at his unprotected head. The metal hit with a clang, and he fell forward with an *oof.* Lily crouched and relieved him of his PP-90 nine millimeter. Then she jogged over to Morgan and McKay.

"Let's get out of here!" she said.

"To the statue," said Morgan, leading McKay with them. Between them and the statue was an enormous tent that held an extensive bar and dance floor. They ran behind the bar and out the back of the tent, emerging not far from the entrance to the statue museum, which was ensconced between two points of the star-shaped base. This corner of the party was quiet, at least for the time being. They ran over to the museum doors. Morgan reached them first and pulled the handle. Locked, of course. He tried kicking it, but they were too heavy. He kicked again, putting the force of his entire body behind the blow. The door barely budged.

"Morgan!" Lily yelled. He looked behind him, as two gunmen had appeared in their line of sight, one who had followed them through the tent and another who had made his way around. "I've only got so many rounds to fend off both of them!" She shot off a burst toward the nearest one, and he ducked for cover behind a tub of ice.

Morgan kicked the door vigorously, but it did no good.

"Morgan!" Lily repeated.

"Behind us, Senator," Morgan said, stepping forward to protect her. The two men were moving closer, and soon they would be close enough to overwhelm any covering fire Lily could provide. She let out another burst of bullets, which made them stop. Then another man emerged from behind the tent.

A single submachine gun had no hope of holding off three armed men. They were cornered, and all was lost.

The door behind them opened and someone yelled, "Get inside!"

Morgan ushered McKay in, then Lily. The man who had admitted them, a security guard, closed and locked the door behind them. "Step away!" he yelled. Morgan moved out of the line of sight of the door panes, and motioned for McKay to do the same.

Morgan surveyed the room they were in—he'd never visited the statue before. It was a large foyer, square and two stories high, with a balcony enclosing a spacious central area. The old torch, with its intricate verdigris copper frame, was mounted right in the middle of the chamber, tall enough to be partly obscured and only wholly visible from the balcony.

"What the hell is happening?" asked the guard. He looked like he was pushing seventy, pudgy and balding, but there was something sturdy in him, too. He was not a guy who let himself be pushed around. Clarke, his badge read.

"Shooters," said Morgan. "A lot of them."

"I have a gun," Clarke said, pulling out a Ruger revolver. "They're not coming in here."

Morgan had to admire this guy's guts. "You can't do much with that," he said. "There are too many them, and they're armed like marines. This door won't hold for long."

Right on cue, there was a bang on the door as the gunmen tried to kick it in.

"We've got to get out of here," Morgan said.

"Where is there to go?" asked Lily. "We're trapped."

"Up," said Morgan.

Chapter 44

Buck Chapman saw the commotion through the blinds of his office windows as everyone clustered around a TV that was mounted on the wall. His heart sank. Clustering around the TV, he knew, was particularly bad. Certain kinds of bad news were learned of through more discreet channels, and later passed on to the news media. It took a disaster of a certain magnitude for TV news to scoop the CIA.

He ran outside and struggled to see through the crowd and hear past the cacophony of talking and crying. He made out the Statue of Liberty and heard the newscaster mention gunfire.

"What's going on?" he shouted over the din.

"The governor's gala is being held hostage by armed men," said Gillespie, who had a more direct view of the TV, without looking away.

"Governor's gala . . . Jesus, Weinberg was supposed to attend!" he said to her. "That can't be coincidence, can it?"

Heads shifted and he got a clear view of the picture on the screen. Bodies in tuxedoes and gowns lay strewn on the ground at Liberty Island, and people were being herded into the open center by figures in black. Flashes of gunfire were rendered as faint pops in the helicopter video.

"Is there something we need to be doing?" she asked.

He searched his mind. Surely they needed to be doing something. Right?

But he came up empty. He could only watch the TV in horror and desperation.

Chapter 45

Alex Morgan sat at a café in a lobby across from the Hampton building, watching the comings and goings of the parking garage, pretending to read a book on the history of the Secret Service.

She'd been feeling restless at home, sick of reading and exercising and everything else. She took off on her motorcycle, driving up and down the highway for nearly an hour until she took the ramp into the city and made her way there. She'd driven past it many times in that week, and sat down for a stakeout twice before. It had never yielded anything, but she still stayed, trying to catch a glimpse of something, notice a pattern, identify a person.

If she were asked *why* she was doing this, she might not know. She had a vague fantasy that she would find out something interesting, something only a skilled spy could have caught, and her father would be impressed by her daring and resourcefulness. At the same time, after his scolding the other day, she wanted to defy him, to do anything that would make him mad. If she were confronted with these fantasies, she would deny them, embarrassed. But there they were nonetheless.

She continued to eye the street, not paying much attention—it was late at night and she didn't really expect any movement—until she did actually see something. A white van drove to the gate of the parking garage. Two men got out and crouched down at the gate opening mechanism. Within less than twenty seconds, the gate had been raised.

Strange, thought Alex. She tossed a couple of bills on the table, put the book back in her messenger bag, got up and walked off toward the Hampton building garage. She slinked in, squeezing past the closing gate like she had that first time, and ran down the ramp to the area of the parking garage where she had seen her father walk through the mysterious door.

She stopped at the corner, where she stood flat against the wall and peeked around the edge. The van had parked near the door, and two men were bending over at a panel on the wall, while two more stood near the vehicle. They had black masks concealing their faces, and were wearing dark colors.

Seconds later, the door opened. The two men went inside, while the other two opened the back doors to the van. The rear of the vehicle was turned away from Alex, but as they walked a few feet away from it Alex saw that they had taken out something the size of a carry-on bag and were hauling it between the two of them.

Alex took out her phone and called her father. By some miracle, she caught a signal, underground. The phone rang several times; no answer.

Come on, Dad, pick up! She tried again, and failed in the same way.

She looked at the van. Something was happening. Something important, something bad, and she could not stop it. She considered rushing the men, but she had no weapons except for a small pocket-knife.

She bit her lip. This battle was lost, but perhaps there was something that she *could* do.

Alex turned around and ran full tilt toward the exit.

Chapter 46

"What the hell is going on out there?"

Diana Bloch had emerged from her office to the War Room, where Shepard was hunched over his computer and Spartan was saying repeatedly into her headset microphone, "Cobra, come in." On the big screen was a grid of TV broadcasts from the scene. O'Neal watched in horror, while Louise Dietz seemed to be trying not to look at all.

"No idea, Boss," said Spartan. "Cougar's in the dark too, and Cobra isn't responding."

"I'm trying to raise whatever I can, but no one has anything about what's happening on Liberty Island," said Shepard. "All we know is what's on TV."

"That's not much," said Bloch.

Shepard shrugged. "They're on the scene." He motioned to the big screen. "Any new developments, we'll catch live."

"Get ahold of Morgan!" she insisted. "I want a report on what's happening. *Immediately.*"

"We're trying," said Spartan.

She turned to see Kirby approaching from an inner corridor.

"Bloch," said Kirby. "Look, it's probably nothing, but it's strange. I thought I should run it by you. Just in case."

"This isn't exactly a good time, Kirby," said Bloch.

"It's fine, I can come back, I just—"

Bloch rubbed her index finger and thumb against her forehead. "Just spit it out, Kirby. What is it?"

"The security system's been offline for three minutes," he said. "Camera feeds in the garage are down, as well as the door authentication systems."

"Not the first time that's happened," said Bloch. "Probably just a glitch. Louise," she said to Dietz, who was still sitting at the table, frozen by the urgency of the situation. Bloch figured that giving her something to do might help. "Go check the elevator. The security system sometimes has this issue when there's something blocking the door. Make sure nothing is in the way." Louise took off at a nervous run toward the entrance to Zeta Headquarters. "Kirby, you get Shepard to run some diagnostics—*after* we've resolved the current crisis, please. This is not the time to pull him off—"

A loud, muffled *clang* came from down the hall, in the direction of the elevator.

"What the—" began Kirby. All eyes turned to the entrance hall. And then the explosion hit.

A hundred things seemed to happen at once. The walls, ground, and ceiling shook. All the glass walls to Bloch's office shattered, raining tempered glass down on the floor. The lights went out just as fire shot out of the entrance hall into the War Room.

Everything went black, except for the glow of the fireball, which mushroomed up to the ceiling and died against the concrete.

Bloch blacked out. When she came to, she saw the War Room by the light of flames on the walls and floor. How long had she been unconscious? It couldn't have been longer than a few seconds, could it? She looked around, but she was disoriented, her vision hazy.

"Is anyone conscious?" she asked out loud. Every word sounded muffled. She noticed a ringing in her ears. She repeated the question, trying for a steadier and louder voice. Out of the corner of her eye, she saw Shepard stumble to his feet.

"Shepard! Over here!" It took a fair bit of shouting before she caught his attention and he limped over to her. His cheek was scratched, his shirt torn and sooty.

"Are you hurt?" she asked. He seemed dazed, even more out of it than usual.

"No." He patted himself down, examining himself in the flickering light of the flames. "I don't think so."

Bloch detected more movement in her peripheral vision and turned around. "Spartan. Thank God. Are you okay?"

The solidly built Spartan was still on the ground, shaking her head and blinking hard. "I'm alive," she said.

"Listen," said Bloch, "I need you to check the entrance, make sure we're not being invaded. See what you can gather about the explosion." She turned to Shepard. "Give me a status on the electronics."

He walked over to his console, still trembling. He pushed a few buttons, then took a look under the hood.

"Everything's fried," he said. "I might be able to recover something from the servers, but I won't be able to access any of it before we get more equipment down here."

Spartan returned from the entrance corridor with tears in her eyes. "My God . . . Louise . . . The bomb was dropped from the elevator shaft. She was right there. She didn't stand a chance."

"Damn," said Bloch, tears welling in her eyes. Louise Dietz was talented and young. It was a real loss. But she couldn't mourn for her right now. "We just have to focus on the survivors. How many of us were there? Oh my God, Kirby."

He had been standing mere feet from her. She looked around and saw him, facedown, across the room. He must have been caught in the shock wave. She rushed over as fast as she could, but her legs were heavy and sluggish. Spartan reached him first.

"He's alive," she said. "Barely breathing. He needs medical attention."

"Okay," said Bloch. "Let's find a working cell phone, or some other way of communicating with the outside."

"There might be something further inside," said Shepard. "Problem is, this place was built to keep wireless communications *out.*"

"We'll worry about that when we have a cell phone to work with," she said. "There are flashlights in the maintenance closet in the East hallway. Go!" He walked off. Bloch turned to Spartan. "Go see if anyone else was hurt and if you can . . . move . . ." Bloch's vision grew faint and her legs felt weak.

She collapsed.

"Bloch!" cried Spartan, lunging to catch her.

"I'm fine," Bloch said, except she was now on the floor, with Spartan holding her back so her head wouldn't knock against the hard stone. She looked down at her abdomen, and just then noticed that her suit was soaked and sticky, a dark stain. "I'm . . ." Her mind was hazy, her thoughts clouded. She blacked out for a second, and then opened her eyes to see Spartan's face over hers. "How long was I out just now?" she asked.

"A few seconds," said Spartan, choking back tears. "Gave me a bit of a scare, boss."

"Nonsense," said Bloch. "I'm fine. I don't need your help. But there might be others who do. Go and see if anyone else is hurt."

"Bloch . . ."

"I'll *be* fine," she said. "O'Neal was in here somewhere. Find her. Then get the word out. Help Shepard find some way to communicate with the outside. We've got work to do. Go!"

Spartan gently laid Bloch's head on the ground, and then stood and walked down the east corridor, disappearing into the bowels of Zeta headquarters. Bloch looked down at her own wound. She was bleeding too much, and knew she needed a doctor soon, perhaps as soon as poor Kirby. But she didn't want anyone fawning over her when there was work to be done.

Bloch tried to get up, but had to hold down a cry of pain, and then frustration. This was a crisis. The country needed her, her troops needed her. She tried again, and this time roared with the searing in her gut. No, she was in no condition to get up. This time, she'd have to trust everything to others, even her life itself.

She lay back. So tired. All she needed was a little rest. To close her eyes.

Just a little rest.

Chapter 47

Morgan led the way up the stairs of the base of the Statue of Liberty, followed by Lily, McKay, and Clarke, the security guard. He stopped at a locked door, which led into the pedestal of the statue. Clarke took the lead and unlocked the door. Behind them, Morgan could hear the assailants banging against the outer door.

Going through the door to the pedestal, they emerged into a square space with wide, spacious, carpeted stairs running along the walls in a spiral that wouldn't be out of place in a nice office building.

"Cougar!" Morgan said out loud as he ran. "Cougar, come in!"

"Cobra, would you tell me what the hell is happening?" he responded through the communicator.

"There was a raid of some kind on the party," said Morgan, without breaking stride. "Men with semiautomatics. My guess is amphibious commandos. They took out the security and moved in on the guests. Killed plenty. Body count's in the dozens, I'm betting, but I think now they're just rounding them up. I think they were after Senator McKay."

"My God," said Conley. "Where are you? Did Lily make it?"

"She's here with me, and so is the senator," said Morgan. "We're in the statue. Listen, Cougar, we've got to get the senator out of here. Is there any chance of a daring escape here?"

After a pause, Conley said, "Can you get to the crown?"

Morgan repeated the question to Clarke. He gave a thumbs-up.

"That's an affirmative, Cougar."

"Get there as fast as you can. I'll send the chopper for you."

"Roger," said Morgan. "Over."

Within some two minutes they reached the door to the statue, which Clarke unlocked for them with his thick set of keys. Inside was a narrow spiral staircase that led upward, apparently without end. Each sound they made reverberated all through the length of the colossus.

Below, Morgan heard shouting. The attackers had gotten into the base of the statue, and they were in the pedestal now.

"Clarke," said Morgan, "I need you to escort the senator to the crown, and get her on the chopper that's coming for her. Can you do that?"

McKay objected. "Aren't you coming?"

"I need to stay to keep them from getting to you," he said. "Lily, do you have my back?"

"You know it, Cobra," she said.

"Can't you protect me better by coming with me?" asked McKay.

"Those guys meant business," said Morgan. "They're out for blood. If I let them get near you, it's you they're going to be shooting at. At least on the stairs, they'll have a different target. Clarke, can I borrow your gun?"

"Brother, you need it more than me," the guard said, and handed it out, handle first. Morgan took it. It had a nice heft to it. He recognized it as a Ruger SP101.

"It packs a punch," said Clarke.

"I'll bet," said Morgan. ".357 Magnum?"

"Believe it."

"No extra bullets?"

"Just the six in the drum," said Clarke.

"It'll do," said Morgan. "Now go! Get to safety. We'll hold them off here."

They hurried up the steps, their footsteps against the metal echoing up and down the statue. Morgan and Lily turned toward the stairs that led up to the pedestal. "How much have you got left?" he asked her.

"Half clip, if that much," she said.

"It's going to be a challenge," he said.

"If it's a Bolivian army ending for us, at least it'll be a good death," she said.

He cocked his Ruger. "Let's do this."

They crouched at the top of the stairs, guns at the ready. Morgan stretched out his hand, keeping a steady aim. The first man appeared at the base, rushing forward. His eyes went wide as he saw the gun aimed at his head. Morgan shot him in the forehead before he could raise his submachine gun. The Magnum bullet did its damage and he fell forward, splayed out on the stairs.

He was easy because he'd been careless. The others would be more wary. But Morgan thought he might be able to push the element of surprise further.

Morgan jumped over the railing, landing on the dead man's back to break his fall, and turned a corner on the landing to fire three shots toward two commandos who were approaching. They pivoted out of his line of sight. Morgan looked down at the man he had killed. He had fallen on his semiautomatic, and there was no way for Morgan to pick it up without making himself vulnerable. But he did have a sidearm in a hip holster, a black Glock .22. Morgan drew it from the holster with his left hand and raised it so that both guns were at chest level, bracing for more. He had no hope for accuracy shooting double-handed, but the point here was suppressing fire.

He inched back upstairs, sights trained on the landing below. The men could come around at any second, guns blazing. He continued his way back up.

"Who are you?" came a voice from around the corner. Morgan couldn't quite place the accent, but it sounded Eastern European. Probably a mercenary, he guessed. Morgan didn't respond. He looked up at Lily, who was breathing heavily, beads of sweat trailing down her forehead. "There are five of us here. More to come," the intruder yelled.

"You're not coming in here," said Morgan, as he reached the top of the staircase.

"We just want the senator," he said. "Send her out and we will go away."

"We have the higher ground," Morgan said. "We can hold this position as long as we want."

"Against a few of us, maybe," said the man. "But we have the numbers and the guns."

"I'll give you each a hundred thousand dollars to fight for me," Morgan said. The answer was laughter.

"You can't outbid our employer, buddy."

"Two hundred and fifty."

"Oh, yeah? You gonna write us a check right now, or what?"

There was no way he was going to convince them, but he'd encountered hired guns stupid enough to believe it before.

"Just come out," said another one. "You don't have to die here today."

"No," said Morgan. "But you will." He looked up—McKay and Clarke were almost at the top of the stairs. He turned to Lily. "Let's move up," he whispered. She glided ahead of him onto the narrow spiral staircase that led up to the statue's head. Morgan followed close behind. Both tried to keep their footsteps as soft as possible so as not to announce their movements to the enemy, but it was nearly impossible to achieve any kind of stealth.

Morgan heard the attackers coming up, at first in slow, careful footsteps, and then at full tilt once they realized Morgan and Lily were no longer holding their position. Morgan and Lily had ascended twice around the central shaft when several bursts of gunfire came from below—covering fire as the men climbed up into the statue. The noise reverberated inside the hollow giant.

The gunmen must have seen Morgan and Lily running up, because they fired up at them. The railing was solid up to Morgan's waist, which offered them some protection. A bullet hit the vertical shaft that supported the staircase, directly above Morgan's head.

"Down!" he cried. He and Lily crouched so that they were hidden by the railing. They continued moving ahead, but much more slowly now that they couldn't stand. There were a couple of more bursts from below, bullets hitting the railing and sailing above it. Then Morgan heard the clangs of metal footsteps as men mounted the stairs.

"Cobra, come in!" came Conley's voice over the comm. "The chopper's going to be there in just about a minute," he said.

"The Senator should already be in the head of the statue," said Morgan. "Tell them not to wait for me."

"Morgan—"

Another burst of gunfire. "You heard me!" Morgan yelled. "Out!"

Morgan and Lily continued their ascent of the steep staircase, the men below hot on their heels. Morgan knew that, as long as he and Lily were forced to crouch, the men would catch up with them before they reached the top.

"Lily," he yelled to her over the deafening noise, "I want you to keep going, understand? I'm going to hold them back. Don't argue with me, just go. If you reach the top before the chopper leaves, go and don't wait for me."

She looked back with sad eyes and nodded. He stopped and turned around, lying back against the stairs. The footsteps drew closer. He held up both handguns at his abdomen and listened, feeling the vibration of the metal steps underneath him. As he heard them just feet away, he held his breath and raised the weapons.

The first commando ran headlong into his field of vision. He was not expecting Morgan, and didn't have time to react before Morgan fired the two bullets remaining in the Ruger into his head. He was close enough that he nearly fell on top of Morgan, who pushed the body with his feet so that he fell backward, against the next man on the stairs. Morgan threw the Ruger at the assailant, moved the Glock to his right hand, and leapt down a few more steps to shoot the man who was trying to extricate himself from the dead weight that had fallen on top of him.

Morgan couldn't press the attack any more without exposing himself. He turned around and resumed his ascent, holding the mercenary's Glock in his right hand. He checked the magazine— thirteen rounds left. He heard banging noises that reverberated through the stairs, then a soft, dull thud below. They were throwing their fallen comrades over, clearing the way. Then they continued to climb, at least five more by the sound of it. But Morgan had moved far enough ahead that he'd reach the top well before they would.

He ran up the final flight of stairs to the crown until he was standing, gasping for air, among the others. Clarke was doubled over from the effort, panting. McKay stood apart, wide-eyed and terrified but composed, apparently ready to take action if necessary. Lily moved to close the trap door to the head as Morgan caught his breath.

"It doesn't lock," she said.

"There's only one way out," said Clarke. He motioned toward the windows that lined the crown of the statue.

"You've got to be kidding me," said Morgan.

"You want to get to the top of the crown?" he asked. "That's the way."

"I'll go first," said Lily. "Morgan, cover us here." She handed Morgan the semiautomatic, which he held in his left, then raised herself up like a gymnast by a structural beam and kicked out the window, which fell out into emptiness. A gust of wind pushed its way inside, whipping Morgan's hair against his forehead. Lily wriggled out the window opening, standing up on the ledge in her high-heeled shoes, and her legs disappeared upward.

"All right, Senator," Morgan said to McKay. "You're next."

"I can't do that!" she exclaimed.

"I'll help," he said. "I'll hold you and Lily'll help pull you up." She looked at Morgan with panic. "There's no choice, Senator. If you want to live, this is what you're going to do."

She turned to the window, trembling. "Okay," she said. "Let's go."

"Clarke," said Morgan. He handed the guard the PP-90. "Hold the fort while I help her up, all right?"

"You got it," Clarke said, taking the submachine gun and positioning himself over the trap door, holding the weapon with both hands.

Morgan walked to the open window and called up to Lily. "I'm sending McKay up."

"Come along now!" Lily yelled down over the roaring wind. "I think I see the chopper coming!"

Morgan held McKay as she stepped up to the open window. She was shaking uncontrollably. She took off her shoes and climbed onto the ledge with Morgan holding her hips. She slowly stood, her body outside the statue, reaching up to Lily.

"I've got her!" said Lily. Morgan leaned out the window, giving McKay a leg up as Lily pulled her from the other end. He watched as the senator disappeared onto the crown. Then he turned back to Clarke, who was watching the stairs.

"Your turn," said Morgan.

"They're gonna be here any second," said Clarke.

"Then let's get the hell out of here!" Morgan said.

"I'm not getting up on the head and you know it," said Clarke. "I'm too old. Could barely walk up these stairs."

"Come on," said Morgan. "I've got you. I'll push you up, and Lily will help from the other side."

"That ninety-pound girl? No way, José. Take a look at this gut." He patted his stomach. "I'm staying right here. I spent thirty years guarding this old statue, and I'm not about to stop now."

"Then I'll stay with you," said Morgan. "We can hold them off together."

"Now, don't argue," he said. "You're young and I'm old. I'm staying, and you're going."

Morgan looked up at the low ceiling of the statue's head. McKay was up there. All this had been at least partly about her. Weinberg, responsible for this and possibly more, was still at large and had a dangerous weapon in his hands. Morgan's honor told him he had to stay and help Clarke, but he had more important things to do.

Morgan held out the Glock to Clarke. "Are you okay using these?" he asked.

"Boy, I was in 'Nam before you were even in diapers," he said. "Give that here." Clark held the submachine gun in his right hand, the Glock in his left. "Get the hell out of here. I'll hold them off for you."

"You're a good man, Clarke."

"No," he said with a smile. "Just old. But I've got some use in me yet."

Morgan faced the opening and took a deep breath. *Goddamn heights.* He hated them more than he hated facing down the barrel of a gun. He climbed up on the window, forcing himself not to look down, then stood up, this time on the outside of the statue. He held on to one of the spokes of the crown. Winds whipped his body, but he held firm. He had to shut his eyes tight to avoid looking down.

He heard gunfire below as he pulled himself up to the top of the crown. He thought he might slip when his feet were raised off the ledge, but his arms held. Lily and McKay were already there, crouching and clutching each other for support. Morgan could see the chopper now too, nearing fast from the west. He held on to a spoke of the crown and looked down.

He saw innumerable dead bodies, of security personnel and guests alike. The survivors were all huddled around the center of the square, with about ten gunmen standing guard around them. *What was the point of this?* Morgan thought in horror. *It can't have been all about McKay. But what the hell* was *it about?*

Morgan felt the wind of the chopper's blades and turned around to see it hovering over the head of the statue. The side door opened, and a ladder unrolled until it was within their reach.

McKay climbed up onto the chopper first, followed by Lily and then Morgan. Clearing the top rungs, he thought he heard an exchange of gunfire within the head of the statue. As the chopper flew away, it seemed as though all the shooting had stopped. Clarke had fallen, but he had died saving them.

Chapter 48

June 15
New York City

The Eurocopter AS365 Dauphin carrying Morgan, Lily, and Lana McKay touched down on an empty parking lot outside an abandoned department store on a dark suburban street in Newark. The rotors were still turning when three sedans maneuvered into the lot and formed a rough semicircle around the chopper. Conley got out of the driver's seat of the first car, a maroon Toyota Corolla, and six other men came out of the other two, all large with an air of ex-military about them. Morgan stepped down off the chopper first, and helped Senator McKay off.

"What the hell happened back there?" asked Conley. Morgan told him the story as quickly as he could, from the time the armed men emerged from the sea until their ascent to the crown of the statue. He then asked, "Do you have any news about what's happening on the island?"

"Well, the truth is," said Conley, "they disappeared."

"What do you mean?"

"A serious attack was being mounted," said Conley. "Four teams of Navy SEALs, two in helicopters and two in boats, were about to launch a coordinated raid when the attackers just walked away. Went right back into the sea, according to the guests, and didn't come up again."

"Is anyone going after them?" asked Morgan.

"Sure," said Conley, "but there's been nothing yet. These guys knew what they were doing. My bet is that they had an airtight exit strategy."

"Christ," said Morgan. "What now?"

One of the men who had come with Conley stepped forward. He was a thin, angular man, with a pointed nose and a pointed chin with thin, short blond hair.

"This is Agent Walker," said Conley. "He's the head of Tactical at Lambda Division." Morgan got the feeling that Conley didn't care much for Walker.

"A pleasure to meet you, Cobra," said Walker. "That was a hell of an escape back there. My hat's off to you." Even giving a compliment, Walker seemed to be sneering.

"Thanks," Morgan grumbled.

"First order of business is getting the Senator out of here and somewhere safe," said Walker.

"I'll take care of that," said Morgan. "I can take her into hiding, somewhere no one will find her."

"I appreciate your intentions here, but we're taking her back to Lambda Headquarters," said Walker. "We have a secure facility where she'll be safe."

"Like at a party with full security personnel?" said Morgan. "Whoever did this will stop at nothing to get at her. There's no guaranteed safe place. The best option is to hide somewhere as far away from major centers as possible."

"A place where she'll be completely vulnerable if she's found out?" said Walker.

"I think we just saw," said Morgan, "that *any* place will be vulnerable if she's found out."

"Excuse me," McKay spoke up. "I'm very glad everyone is so interested in my well-being, but I really ought to have a say in this, don't you think? I'd rather go with Mr. Morgan."

"With all due respect, ma'am, we need you where we can best protect you," Walker said.

"She's coming with *me*," said Morgan. "You'll force her to go with you over my dead body, do you understand?"

"If that's what it comes to," hissed Walker.

"Hey, *hey!*" Conley hollered. "We don't need this pissing contest right now. Walker, you and your team have your hands full. Senator McKay trusts this man. Let her go with him."

"All right," said Walker, "but if something happens to her because she was with him and not with us, this is on *your* ass."

He drew a phone and walked out of earshot. Conley moved in closer and spoke in a low tone.

"Look, Morgan, there's something else. We lost communication with Zeta about half an hour ago. There are some reports, very sketchy, that there's been an explosion."

"Are they alive?" asked Morgan.

"We don't know anything yet," said Conley. "Police and fire-fighters are on the scene, but they haven't even started to clear away the debris yet, so it's going to be awhile."

"Goddamn it," said Morgan. "So this means—"

"We're on our own for the time being. Listen, you take Lily and get McKay somewhere safe. Use my car."

"You got any trackers on that?" Morgan asked.

"No," he said. "But I can't promise you one of the Lambda people didn't bug it. There's a bug sweeper in the glove compartment, though. Stop for gas a few miles out and give it a once-over."

"You don't trust these people?" Morgan asked.

"I maintain a healthy skepticism at all times," said Conley. "Keeps me alive and in one piece."

"Got it. We're going to need a couple of guns, too."

"I've got two Colts stashed in the car," he said. "One strapped under the seat, another in the trunk, under the spare tire. Don't tell me where you are going, and keep your cell phone off. I keep an encrypted sat phone in the glove compartment, too. Completely untraceable. Call me every thirty minutes for updates."

"Got it," said Morgan. "Keep me in the loop. Weinberg's still at large with the EMP. This isn't over yet."

Morgan got into the driver's seat, with Lily in the passenger seat and McKay in the back. He took out the back panel of his phone and removed the battery without taking it out of his pocket, then drove out of the parking lot and toward I-78.

Chapter 49

Alex Morgan had been following the van for nearly an hour when it stopped for gas.

She had run out of the building when she had saw them take in the bomb—she knew it was a bomb, of course, once the ground shook with the explosion. She panicked, not knowing what to do. Her father's car was not there, so at least he was not hurt.

Not knowing how to proceed, she called 911 and continued with her original plan. She reached her motorcycle, which was parked around the corner, and turned it on. When the van peeled out of the garage, she took off after it, keeping the safe tailing distance that she had learned from her father. And so she followed them, to the Mass Pike due west, for a mostly uneventful tail, during which she tried and failed repeatedly to call her father.

Now they were stopping for gas. Alex couldn't stop with them without blowing her cover. And, she noted, looking down at the fuel gauge, she'd need to stop pretty soon, too. It looked like they might be going a long while yet, and she didn't want to run out of fuel mid-pursuit.

She sped on ahead, flying as fast as she dared down the highway until she found the next gas station, some five miles down the road. She filled up, paid with a few crumpled bills she had stuffed in her pocket, and guided her bike to a dark corner of the parking area, killing her lights. She tried to call her father again three more times, but got only voice mail. She sent him a message this time—*911 call me.*

A few minutes later, the van drove by. At this time, there were too few cars on the highway. Not wanting the driver to notice he was being followed, she kept the lights on her motorcycle turned off. As she drove onto the highway, it was much darker than she had imagined it would be. Apart from the pool of light of the van ahead, she was riding on a sea of blackness. She kept her eye fixed on the van's lights, making a mental map of the road as it weaved ahead of her—if she didn't, she felt sure that she would drive off the road and into a tree.

They drove like this for another hour or so. Alex nearly got run down by a speeder, who missed her by mere inches. Eventually, the van turned off the highway onto a local road. This proved tricky, as the byway's sharper turns were more difficult for her to follow with the headlights off. Before long, the van turned into a dirt road in a forested area.

Alex stopped. There was no way she'd be going in there without headlights. So she stayed at the side of the road for about ten minutes—as long as she could stand waiting. Then, hoping that she had given the van enough time to reach its ultimate destination, she turned on her lights and drove into the woods.

The road was tolerably smooth for being a dirt road. She moved along it carefully, wary of running into the parked van. But she didn't have to worry, because she spotted its destination a half mile away. Floodlights lit up an entire clearing ahead. She took the bike off the road and parked it out of sight, behind a thicket. She approached the rest of the way on foot.

When she drew close enough to get a clear view, her jaw dropped. An entire runway had been built here, in the middle of the forest, extending over a mile away from where she was standing. On the end closer to her was a large military-looking cargo plane. Its back door was open. The van was parked behind it, near a small refrigerated truck and a Jeep. At least a dozen men moved about busily, and the door to the back of the refrigerated truck was open. Alex stayed in the darkened tree line, out of sight, and moved in closer to get a better look.

The men were pulling out a large, heavy box from the truck. It took six men to carry it, and they seemed to be struggling. One man seemed to be in charge—large, blond, and muscular, almost handsome if he weren't so intimidating.

She looked at her phone. Why wasn't her father answering?

Chapter 50

Diana Bloch clutched her abdomen as she walked down the hallway of the fifth floor of the Boston Mandarin Oriental, closely followed by the contrasting figures of O'Neal and Spartan. O'Neal seemed smaller than usual, and her typical life and energy seemed drained from her. Spartan had, characteristically, turned defiant in the face of tragedy. To her, it was a personal affront, the attack on Liberty Island as much as the one on Zeta. Her face was bruised, but she kept her chin up.

Bloch slipped in the key card, opened the door and turned on the lights to suite 411. "Ladies," she said as she walked through the room, "this is going to be our base of operations for the time being." It was a spacious room, boasting, in addition to the irrelevant bed, a spacious desk, a small round dining table with four chairs near the window, and a large L couch upholstered in yellow.

"Let's get all surface spaces cleared up," Bloch said. "Push the beds against the wall. Leave the desk for Shepard—you know how he likes his space. Set up a phone charging station over here on the coffee table—I don't want anybody running out of batteries." She turned. Spartan was carrying a large desktop computer under one arm and a monitor under the other that they had salvaged from the wreckage at Zeta headquarters. O'Neal was hugging her laptop against her chest.

Bloch took out a second key card and held it up. "This is the card to the room next door. You'll want a shower, I'm sure, and we can take shifts for twenty-minute naps. I know you're tired but we can't spare anyone any longer than that. Now, let's get set up."

Spartan took the table by the window, setting the desktop on the floor and then looking for an outlet. O'Neal chose the couch, nearly collapsing on it, then opening up her computer on her lap. Bloch found the remote and turned on the TV to a news channel, which was showing an aerial feed of Liberty Island. There seemed to be nothing new.

Bloch set the TV on mute, walked into the bathroom, and locked the door. She pulled up her shirt to expose her bandages. She still felt intense, stabbing pain. But she saw no bleeding, which meant that the sutures were holding.

She caught a glimpse of herself in the mirror. She looked so tired, so disheveled. Her hair was out of place. She hadn't had time to reapply makeup or to fix her hair. She had changed out of her shirt, which had been bloodied from her injury, but that the one she wore was rumpled and unkempt. The sight distressed her. This loss of her professional demeanor intensified the sense that things were spiraling out of control.

Spartan had managed to climb up the elevator shaft and call emergency services. It turned out to have been unnecessary, though—the explosion had been heard from the outside, and firemen and paramedics had already been on their way. The emergency workers climbed down to Zeta Headquarters—Bloch thought of Smith and the nightmare that it would be to cover this up—put out the fires and took out the injured and dead. They'd taken Bloch to the hospital, where doctors wanted to keep her overnight. She refused to stay after she'd received emergency care, and nobody seemed to be in the mood to stop her.

Of the others, only Kirby had remained in intensive care, and—

Bloch turned away from the mirror, but then forced herself to confront what she wanted to forget. The name formed brightly and painfully in her imagination. *Louise Dietz.* She had accepted the job with a sense of adventure that overrode her natural meekness. Now she was dead, killed by the blast, the person closest to the elevator when it hit. The terrible responsibility of putting Dietz in harm's way was weighing heavily on Bloch.

Hearing a knock on the hotel room door, Bloch was drawn away from her guilt. She walked out of the bathroom and checked the peephole to find Lincoln Shepard holding two enormous shopping bags filled with boxes. She opened the door.

"I come bearing gifts," he said, holding up the bags. He walked in and examined the room. "Hey, great digs. It's got a great no-rubble-or-burning-debris thing that I like. Very modern."

Shepard set the boxes down on the table by the windows and unpacked the equipment. He gave Spartan instructions in setting up her computer so that they could share information. When she looked at him blankly, he did it himself. Relieved, Spartan used her cell phone to reach out to a Homeland Security liaison.

"Okay, I've got a link to the emergency responder network," said Spartan, looking at her computer. "They have a list of casualties being updated in real time. . . . It's up to fifty-six so far."

"Look for anything that could give us a hint of Weinberg's purpose," said Bloch.

"The list of the dead just keeps growing," said Spartan. "Two senators, the CEO of . . . look, the Speaker of the House."

"Hmm . . ." said Bloch. "Cougar said that they targeted Lana McKay specifically. And she's—"

"President pro tempore of the Senate," said Shepard. "Elected this year. Youngest senator to hold that position in many, many years. Do you think it's significant?"

"Weinberg is not playing around," said Bloch. "They had an agenda. They're after something specific. Keep trying to connect the dots."

Chapter 51

June 16
Pennsylvania

The night wore on as Morgan drove west on I-78. They stopped at a gas station near Bridgewater, where Morgan took the gun from the trunk and gave it to Lily. As the tank was filling up, he ran the bug detector under the bumper. It beeped as Morgan swept the rear right wheel. He ran his hand under the car until he found what he was looking for.

He pulled the device off the chassis, to which it was magnetically attached, and examined it. It was definitely a tracker, black with a blinking LED light. *Bastards.* Apparently the distrust was mutual. Morgan walked over to a truck that had come from the opposite side of the highway and stuck it to the inside of the truck's rear bumper.

As he drove off, Morgan wondered where they would stop. Farther would be better, but he couldn't afford to be too far from the action—he might be called on to do something on short notice. He took the phone that Conley had left in the car and fingered it.

"Do you have anyone you'd like to call?" Morgan asked McKay. "The call would be untraceable."

"No, I'd rather not," said McKay. "There's nobody that I'm very close with. I'd just as soon not risk talking to anyone."

"Lily?" he asked.

"I'm good."

Morgan looked at the clock on the dash. It was past 2 A.M. Jenny would be sleeping by now, but. . . . He dialed his home number.

"Hello?" Her voice was sleepy and slightly hoarse.

"Hi, honey, it's me. Sorry to call so late."

"That's all right," she said. "I'm glad you did. Is everything all right?"

"I'm okay," he said. "But Liberty Island has been attacked. It's on the news."

"Oh, God," she said. "I haven't been watching TV today, and all the computers are off. Where are you, Dan?"

"I can't tell you. But I'm safe. I won't be coming home tonight, though."

"I figured," she said.

"Now, I don't want you to be scared," he said, "but I want you to stay home tomorrow. You and Alex need to stay indoors, okay? I can't tell you why, but please, just do it."

"Okay," she said. "I'd better tell Alex, she might get up earlier than me." He heard her footsteps, and the creaking of the bedroom door.

"Dan," she said, her voice panicked. "Dan, where is Alex?"

"What do you mean?" he asked.

"She's not here, Dan." He heard her running downstairs. "Her motorcycle's gone."

"Oh, God. Let me call her," he said. "I'll call you right back." He hung up and dialed his daughter. She picked up before the second ring. "Alex?"

"Dad? Is that you?"

"Alex, is everything okay? Where are you? Your mother just found your bed empty and your motorcycle gone—"

"Dad, I need to talk to you."

"Alex, things are a bit crazy right now, I can't really talk. But you have to call your mother. She's worried sick about you. You should be with her right now, she needs—"

"Dad, you gotta listen to me. There was an explosion. At the place you go. Where you work. Someone planted a bomb."

"I've already been—how do you know where I work?"

"I—I followed you one time."

"You what?" he said. "You— We're going to have a very serious talk about this, young lady."

"*Fine,* Dad, I don't care, just *listen.* I was watching the street, and I saw this van go into the building. . . . They tossed a bomb or something."

Morgan struggled to contain his anger. This was no time to lose his cool. "Are you safe? Were you hurt?"

"I wasn't hurt," she said. "I—I just saw it happen. But, uh . . . I'm not so sure I'm safe."

"What do you mean?"

"I followed them. The people who blew up the place."

Jesus Christ, the reckless child. "Followed them where?"

"Somewhere off 287. Here, I'll send you a pin."

"You'll send me what?"

"A pin, Dad. My location on GPS." Conley's phone vibrated, announcing that it had received whatever it was she'd sent.

"Are you still where they are?" he asked.

"In the woods, just out of view. Look, Dad, that's not all. There's a landing strip here, out in the middle of nowhere. Also a plane. It looks like one of those military cargo aircraft. They've loaded something into it. A big box of some kind. Something's happening here, Dad."

Oh, God, the EMP. "Get out of there, Alex. I've got the location. I'll take care of it."

"Dad, no."

"Alex, *get out of there.*"

"Something might happen. I need to be here. Look, I'll keep out of sight. No one is going to see me. But I'm not leaving."

She was as stubborn as he was. Arguing would accomplish nothing. "Okay. *Fine.* But stay out of sight. And *don't do anything.* I'm on my way. I'll be there in no time."

"Dad, it took me four hours to get here."

"I'll be there in two." Then he added, "And Alex? Call your mother."

Chapter 52

Smith was waiting in the underground hotel parking garage when he saw Ken Figueroa's car pull in and find a spot about fifty feet away.

Smith checked his Kel-Tec P-32 in its holster attached to his left ankle, and then stepped out of his car and walked toward Figueroa, who was already stepping out of his. Smith hated meeting in person at a time like this, but certain protocols had to be followed. With Zeta out of commission, Lambda was the only resource he had left on the East Coast. As the head of Lambda, Figueroa was the man to see.

"It's time to declare a state of emergency," said Smith. "Things are out of control. We need to get top-level officials and the Aegis board to secure locations. I'm going to need your help with this, Ken."

"I know," said Figueroa. "Procedures are already underway. There's only one thing missing."

With veiled trepidation, Smith reached into his inner jacket pocket and produced a folded printed list of names on heavy paper stock. He had never held a more valuable piece of paper in his hands. It was the single biggest secret that Smith, a man of so many secrets, was privy to.

"Here it is," said Smith. "The list of board members of Project Aegis."

Figueroa took the list from Smith and unfolded it, looking at its contents. Smith could swear that a smirk played on Figueroa's face, a disturbing smile of triumph, or perhaps even glee. But Smith's attention was diverted to a subtle movement around Figueroa's waist.

Smith heard the gunshot before he saw the gun, which had been concealed in Figueroa's blazer pocket. Sudden sharp pain made him clutch his torso, and he toppled to the ground, falling first to his knees and then sideways against his right arm. In the darkness, he saw only the gray of Figueroa's pants leading to his polished brown patent leather shoes.

"It's hard for me to express exactly how goddamn *tired* of you I am," said Figueroa. He waved the gun, and Smith thought he might shoot to kill this time, but he didn't seem to be done talking. "I'm sick of all your secrecy bullshit, your orders, and this goddamn *mystique* you put on about yourself." He kicked Smith in the shoulder. A sharp pain reverberated through his body. "So goddamn self-serious. So mysterious. The ridiculous *name* you chose for yourself."

Smith's mind went to the tiny pistol in its ankle holster. The garage was dark, and he didn't think Figueroa had seen it. He resisted looking at it—it might just draw Figueroa's attention. But so would reaching for it.

"You're a power broker, Smith," spat Figueroa. "That might sound big, but it just calls attention to the fact that you have no power of your own. You might move the pieces here and there. And men like me are forced to live in your shadow."

The foot swung again, this time hitting Smith in the gut. Smith doubled into the fetal position on the ground. It was almost too much to bear.

"But I know your secret," said Figueroa. "You've actually got no power. You give orders, you act like the boss, but you're *middle management,* Smith. You're an errand boy."

As the pain wafted away, Smith took note of his position, his back arched, legs bent to protect his abdomen. All he had to do was reach.

"After all this, Smith, all you are is an impotent, ineffectual—"

Smith stretched his left arm until his hand wrapped around the handle of his semiautomatic. It took the space of two words for Smith to draw the gun from its holster and align the sight with Figueroa's head. He pulled the trigger. The bullet entered Figueroa's brain through his eye, killing him mid-sentence. He fell heavily backward.

That was that.

The shot reverberated in the parking garage. Smith gritted his teeth against the pain and looked at his wound, which was gushing blood. It looked bad. He wondered if it might be fatal. He crawled over to Figueroa's corpse to check for a phone. Just moving this small distance nearly caused him to cry out in pain. He found the phone, but it was password-locked. No use.

Smith looked at his car, where his own phone was. It was only about twenty yards' distance, but it seemed impossibly far away. He couldn't walk. He could hardly move from the pain. It might have been useless even to try. He might very well die halfway there.

Doing his best to stanch the wound with his left hand, Smith crawled, inch by inch, toward the car.

Chapter 53

Morgan drove into one of the small towns bordering the highway and got McKay a room at a motel. He did the registration himself so that she wouldn't be recognized, then handed her the key and a slip of paper with the number to his cell phone written on it.

"If anything happens, call this number, and *only* this number. Stay put. Nobody knows you're here, so you'll be safe. I need to go take care of my daughter, but I'll be back for you, or I'll send someone I trust. I promise."

She looked at the number. "Thank you, Morgan. Thank you for saving my life."

He and Lily walked back to the Corolla and took off once more, streaking down the highway toward the coordinates Alex had given him. They drove side by side, silently, the whole way, and made the turn into the dirt road in just under two hours. He drove slowly until he caught sight of the floodlights Alex had described to him. He took the car off the road, finding a spot that would hide it well enough in the dark, about a hundred feet away. He and Lily took out their guns and walked out.

"I would kill for some proper shoes right now," Lily said. She was still in her high heels.

"Or a flashlight," said Morgan. They stumbled in the dark toward the light in the clearing, all the way to the tree line.

"Dad!" It was a loud whisper. "Dad! Over here!" Morgan saw Alex's faint silhouette some twenty feet away and walked over to her.

"Young lady!" He hugged her. "We're going to have a talk when we get home."

"Dad! This is important. Look!"

Morgan examined the plane and the two vehicles parked near it.

"And the box is inside already?" Morgan asked.

"I saw them carry it in," said Alex. "Look! That guy! I think he's the leader or something. They all seem to take their orders from him."

The features and the bulk of the man were familiar, even from far away. "That's Fleischer," said Morgan.

"Who's Fleischer?" she asked. "Do you know that man, Dad?"

"Weinberg's definitely behind this," said Morgan, ignoring her. Another of the men had gotten into the Jeep and was maneuvering in into the airplane cargo hold through the ramp.

"Bastard. This is Lily, by the way," said Morgan.

"Nice to meet you, kid," said Lily. "You wouldn't happen to have an extra pair of shoes on you, would you?"

Alex looked at Lily's high heels and frowned. "You two aren't exactly dressed for a top-secret mission, are you? Were you at a party or something? Were you on a *date?*"

"Undercover," said Morgan. "But at a party, yes. Turned out the hors d'oeuvres were no good. Plus, these men came along and shot half the guests."

"What?" Alex asked.

"We're thinking it might have something to do with these guys," said Morgan. He watched the men as they talked on the edge of the ramp to the airplane. "It would really help if we knew what they were saying."

The words were barely out of his mouth when Alex took off, running along the tree line.

"What the hell—"

He saw her shoot out of the light toward the men. He clutched his gun, ready to run out and help her, when he saw that the angle at which she was running kept the van between the men and her. She reached the van and stood flat against it, ear cocked.

"I have to hand it to you, Morgan," said Lily. "That is one *hell* of a girl you raised."

"That she is," he said with grudging respect.

They watched as Alex listened to the men's conversation. This lasted a few minutes, until the men walked onto the airplane. Alex ran back to the darkness of the trees, then back over to Morgan and Lily.

"That was—" Morgan began angrily.

"Awesome, I know," said Alex. "Listen, they were talking about something. 'The weapon,' they kept calling it."

"That would be the EMP," said Morgan. "The box you told us they carried into the plane earlier."

"Okay," she said. "Well, they had a plan that they kept referring to. Said they had to get the timing just right." The engines of the plane came to life with a roar.

"Timing for what?" asked Morgan, raising his voice to be heard above the noise. "What else did you hear?"

"Something about an aircraft," Alex said. "Bringing it down. That targets 'one' and 'two' would be on it."

"Oh, God," said Lily. "Morgan. The attack on Liberty Island. The government would go into a state of emergency. In a situation like that, they'd definitely airlift the President out of DC. He's going to be in the air. It's Air Force One. They're bringing down the goddamn Air Force One."

Morgan took Conley's phone out of his pocket. "Lily, I want you to take this phone and call Peter Conley. It's in the phone's memory as the last call made. Then call Smith—that should be in the phone's memory, too, by name. Tell both of them what we heard here. And stay with Alex. I need you to get her to safety. Get her to where we left McKay. Here are the keys to the car. Will you do that for me?"

"Count on it," said Lily.

"Where are you going?" asked Alex, alarmed. He didn't answer. "Dad?"

"I'm going to stop them," he said. "I love you, Alex, and I'm proud of you."

He ran straight for the plane, jumping onto the ramp as it was closing. He pulled himself up and into the plane. All the passengers were in the seats near the cockpit, which were turned forward. No one saw him as he slid down the ramp and crouched behind the Jeep, bracing for takeoff.

Chapter 54

June 16
Washington, DC

Hoisting himself onto the driver's seat of the car was the hardest part. Smith's legs were hardly working. Pulling himself up felt like a screwdriver was tearing at his insides. Blood flowed freely as he used both arms to hoist himself. But with gritted teeth and purpose of mind, he managed.

He reached a slumped position on the driver's seat, with his face near the hand brake. Pressing against the wound with his right hand, he picked up the phone and tried Bloch, but hers was apparently off. He tried a few numbers for Zeta, but they wouldn't go through, either. He was thinking of other numbers he could dial when the phone rang so unexpectedly that he nearly dropped it.

"Who is this?" said Smith, doing whatever he could to keep his voice steady

"This is Lily Randall."

"The British agent?" he asked.

"Is this Smith?" she demanded.

"This is he." Smith was holding his breath now to keep from screaming in pain, and it slowed his speech.

"Are—are you okay? You sound awful."

"Just—say what you—called me to—say."

"Cobra says the EMP is meant to for the President," she said. "It's going to take out Air Force One tonight."

Goddamn it. That is bad. "Is—that—all?" he asked, with the painful pauses in his speech.

"That's it," she said.

"I want—you to call—a number for me. Tell them—what you told me. Explain—everything. Can you—do that?"

"Yes, yes, of course," she said. "Just for God's sake tell me who to call."

He gave her the name and number as fast as he could.

"Okay," she said. "I'll call now."

Hanging up, he turned on the interior light of the car and looked at the bullet hole. It couldn't wait for an ambulance. He reached for the glove compartment and pulled it open. In there was a special first aid kit he'd put together for this kind of emergency.

First, he cleaned the area with a gauze pad. Then he took out a packet of chemical hemostat, which should help control the bleeding, and applied it to the wound. He couldn't hold back the howl of pain. He opened three more packets of gauze and pressed them against the bullet hole, then took a roll of bandage and rolled it around his torso, pulling as tight as he could. He held it in place with a thick piece of surgical tape.

He pulled himself up again, so that he was sitting upright in his seat. Feeling himself weakening, he used all the will he could muster to hold out against unconsciousness. He tested his feet, and found that he could move them enough to operate the gas pedal with his right and the brake with his left. He turned the key in the ignition.

He pushed the accelerator too far backing out, and crashed against the car behind him. He shifted the car into drive, turned the steering wheel, and let go of the brake, applying the least pressure that he could. The car lurched forward. He managed to get it to move in the right direction. He scraped the entire right side of the car turning a corner a little further ahead, but in this stumbling style, he managed to leave the parking garage and get out into the street.

The hospital was only four blocks away. All he had to do was get that far. He felt his consciousness fading as he moved ahead in lurches, past one block, two, three. He could see it. The entrance to the emergency room lay one block ahead, its white fluorescent light seeming to be at the end of a long tunnel.

He pushed the gas pedal with his foot. It seemed so heavy, he could hardly control it, and the car picked up speed. His hands were weak now, so weak that he couldn't hold on to the steering wheel.

So close. So close. The car turned, from the open street into the grille of a storefront. The window held dark gray men's suits, mannequins lit even this late at night.

He noticed the car wasn't moving anymore, even though he could hear the roar of acceleration. As his mind faded, he thought he could hear voices of men screaming something that sounded like "hell, hell, hell."

Chapter 55

Buck Chapman left the live feed of reporting from Liberty Island streaming on his computer. Hostages were now being ferried off the island, and the dead were being arranged in rows of black body bags. He listened to the news as he read reports coming in from both civilian news agencies and blogs and official secret channels within the US government.

In the outer office, people were still crowded around the TV. Others were at their workstations, probably doing the same thing as Chapman. He was startled by the vibration of Smith's phone in his inner breast pocket.

He picked up the call and held the phone to his ear.

"Hello?"

"Is this Philip Chapman?" It was a woman with an English accent.

"Who are you?" he demanded. "How did you get this number?"

"I'm calling on behalf of a Mr. Smith. He—I think he's injured."

"What happened to him?"

"It's complicated. Listen! I have a message for you. It's from Smith. There's going to be a terrorist attack. They—tonate an EM—"

"I'm sorry, you're breaking up," he hollered. "Repeat that."

"—M—P!"

"Did you say EMP?"

"Yes!" The call was suddenly clear. "An EMP is going to be detonated tonight over DC! It's meant to take down Air Force One!"

Chapman's heart sank. "When?"

"Soon!" she exclaimed. "The plane is already in the air!"

"Dear God. Is there anything else?"

"No! Are you someone who can do something about that?" she asked. "Because maybe you should see to that now."

He felt a surge of adrenaline and hung up the phone. "Cyn!" he yelled out. "Cyn, in here, now!"

She ran to his door, breathless and alarmed. "What is going on, Buck?"

"An EMP device is going to detonate over DC. Spread the word. The primary target is the Air Force One and the President, but we need to get the word out to as many people as possible. Enlist everyone here to make calls. Get in touch with FEMA first. They have emergency protocols in place. Then call every other government agency you can, starting with Homeland Security. I'll take care of warning the President."

"But how do you—"

"Cyn, *now*. Oh, and tell them to use speakerphone and take their cell phones out of their pockets. No one should be holding *any* electronic equipment when the blast hits. Spread the word."

She turned to the office and banged on the wall for attention. "I'm going to need everyone's attention here!"

Chapman turned his attention to making the most important call of that day.

Chapter 56

Morgan waited, crouched behind the Jeep in Weinberg's cargo plane, as the Airbus Beluga got off the ground. He held the straps on the right side of the plane against the g-force of takeoff, hoping that the Jeep would not skid and crush him—although the vehicle was secured to hooks on the airplane's fuselage.

He didn't have much time to make his move. Soon enough, Weinberg's men would get up and move around. He counted six of them, and their semiautomatics were close by, hanging from the side of the plane near the seats. At least one was bound to have a handgun on him. Plus, gunfire in an airplane was never a good idea, although the option of bringing down the plane would always be there as a last resort.

He looked around at the other cargo. There were some boxes that might have contained weapons, but Morgan couldn't reach them without exposing himself. On the ground was a box of heavy duty buckled canvas straps, like the ones that were holding the Jeep in place. Emergency flotation devices and military-grade parachutes lined about ten feet of the floor across from the Jeep.

In the middle of the cargo hold, on the conveyor belt that led to the ramp in the back, was the EMP device. It was painted a dark, purplish blue to blend in with the night sky. It consisted of a sturdy metal frame about the size of a refrigerator with an ovoid shape suspended inside—the device itself, with what seemed to be a thick enough protective metal shell to make it impervious to bullets. It had a control panel with an LCD display on the side and a large flat box on top that had some kind of opening mechanism. Morgan surmised that it was a parachute to keep the device aloft as the airplane put some distance between itself and the blast.

The Jeep that had been loaded into the plane was outfitted for military use, which meant it probably contained a box in the back. Morgan raised his head just enough over the spare tire to confirm that it was there. Then, slowly, gingerly, he opened the latch and lifted the lid. *Jackpot.* Inside were two M16s and a row of magazines.

He looked at the men, but their heads were obscured by the seats. He reached over the back of the Jeep and pulled out one of the rifles, then two magazines. As he did, he caught the glint of something moving side to side—the key to the Jeep was in the ignition. He took another magazine and crouched behind the Jeep again. He loaded one magazine into the M16 and slipped the other into the waist of his pants in the back. The third he left on the floor, safely ensconced between two slats.

Morgan felt the forces shift—the plane was leveling off, ending its ascent. He could hear the men speaking, though he couldn't hear what they were saying. He peeked around the Jeep and saw that two of the men standing. It was time for action.

Morgan picked up the spare magazine and leapt onto the Jeep. He turned the key in the ignition, put the car into gear, and put the magazine on the accelerator. The straps still holding on tight to the vehicle, the motor roared furiously and the tires skidded on the floor.

All six of the men heard this. Those who were sitting down stood up to look backward with fear on their faces, while those already standing lunged for their guns. Not fast enough. Morgan bounded off the back of the Jeep and released the buckles on both safety straps. The car charged forward, the curve of the airplane turning it toward the center of the cargo hold. It missed the EMP by several feet and hit the seats head-on, plowing through them and stopping against the cockpit door, its still rotating tires raised off the floor by the debris.

Two of the men were caught in the seats when the Jeep hit, and two had managed to dodge to each side. The plane rocked upon the impact of the Jeep, and everyone was sent sprawling. Morgan tumbled forward, crashing against one of the men on the right front corner of the cargo hold.

In the chaos, Morgan saw that the man who had cushioned his fall had a Glock semi tucked into a hip holster. Morgan pulled it out and fired the first bullet into that man's gut, then two into the torso of the other man who had fallen just a few feet away. On the other side of the Jeep were another man and Anse Fleischer.

Morgan stood up and ran around the Jeep and the debris of the seats, but the tumble had left him dazed. He fell forward and rolled onto his side. He pushed himself into a standing position and, a little more carefully, made his way around the Jeep. He saw the other soldier first, struggling to get up, and fired. His aim was not as good as usual—the first three bullets were embedded harmlessly into the fuselage. The last hit home on the man's neck.

Morgan barely saw the hulking shape of Anse Fleischer barreling toward him and tackling him backward toward the EMP device. Morgan lost his grip on the Glock and smashed backward into the floor of the plane, with his own weight combined with Fleischer's. The meaty white left hand came down hard with two punches to Morgan's temple. Morgan grabbed for anything too use as a weapon, and his hands closed on a jagged and pointed piece of metal from the mangled seats. He thrust the makeshift knife just as Fleischer's fist came for another punch, and the metal plunged deep into the German's hand. The man bellowed.

Morgan held tight as Fleischer jerked away, and the shard came free in Morgan's hand. Fleischer had pulled his torso away instinctively, giving Morgan the opening to stab the jagged metal into his abdomen and push it up into his rib cage, trying to drive it through his heart. Morgan evidently missed, and Fleischer emitted a gurgling scream.

The giant got up. He lifted Morgan clear off the ground and shoved him hard against the floor. Morgan blacked out. When he came to, he saw Fleischer kneeling by the EMP device, operating the LCD panel with his still-intact right hand. He was obviously weakened, his fingers shaking, his breathing ragged.

Morgan staggered toward him. His mind was clear enough to know that he couldn't kill Fleischer if he wanted any hope of disarming the EMP. His eyes fell on the security straps, which were now strewn all over the floor. He picked one up, then grabbed Fleischer's right hand. Fleischer was too weakened to shake Morgan off. Morgan secured his hand to the EMP's armature, then took his mangled left hand and did the same.

"You're stuck," said Morgan.

"It's armed," Fleischer said, and smiled with reddened teeth. Blood oozed from his lips to the floor. Morgan looked at the display on the EMP device. It was counting down from seven and a half minutes. He tried pressing a "cancel" button on the touchscreen, and it prompted him for a six-digit code.

"Disarm it!" cried out Morgan.

Fleischer laughed.

"You're tied to it!" yelled Morgan. "If it goes off, you die!"

"I am already dead!" Fleischer exclaimed.

"Tell me how to disarm the bomb! Give me the code!"

"You can't stop it," he said. "The EMP will detonate, and there is nothing you can do!"

"You have the opportunity to do one last good thing!" Morgan roared. "Of not dying a mass murderer!"

"I die serving the Weinberg name!" he said in ragged, gasping breaths. He spat out a wad of blood, but he was so weak that it dribbled off his lips and down his chin. His head lolled on his shoulders, and he slumped against the EMP device.

Morgan tried to input random codes, and only got as far as three when the keyboard locked and wouldn't allow him to try any more. He tried to remove the panel from the frame, but it was welded in place, and all the wires ran through the steel armature. He looked around for some way to destroy the device. Bullets wouldn't do it, explosives would just set it off.

This thing was going to be triggered, no matter what he did.

He looked back at the Jeep, which trapped the pilot in the cockpit. There was nothing Morgan could do for him, either.

Morgan stumbled to the left side of the cargo hold, which held the parachutes. He took one down and hit the button to open the back ramp as he strapped himself into the pack. A crack of blackness appeared, widening, a powerful gust of wind enveloping Morgan's bruised and aching body. As soon as the opening was large enough, he jumped off the back into emptiness. He let himself fall, getting as far away from the plane as possible.

Morgan felt the shock wave first, almost hot enough to melt his skin, and the hairs on his body stood on end with static electricity. Below, all the lights went out for miles, as far as the eye could see, all the way to the brightly lit cluster of DC itself. He pulled the ripcord and felt the violent upward tug as the parachute deployed. He looked up at the airplane, high above him already, and saw it sputter in the moonlight and fall out of the sky.

Chapter 57

Chapman made his first call to the Secret Service. The top priority had to be to save the President, if possible.

He, along with everyone else in the office, contacted government agencies, then radio and TV stations, then airports and then hospitals. Once the most urgent calls had been made, they all took the time to call their families. Rose was brave and resourceful, as usual. She was frightened, but she kept her head and took his instructions down.

Chapman was on the speakerphone with a head nurse at an ICU when the blast hit. The phone flashed blue, along with every other piece of electronic equipment in his line of sight. He heard screams and the sound of shuffling in the outer office. Within seconds, candles were lit—some people had evidently been prepared.

Chapman sat back in his chair. As the adrenaline subsided, the full fatigue, stress, and horror of the past day set in. He heard people crying in the outer office. He slumped off his chair to the floor and leaned against his desk. He focused on steady breathing as a way of keeping from falling apart.

He heard a delicate knock on his door, but he didn't have the energy to respond. The door creaked open and light footsteps came around his desk. The shadow of Cynthia Gillespie loomed before him.

"Buck," she said in a voice that tried to be comforting but ended up sounding fragile. She lowered herself until she was sitting on the floor with him.

"I'm scared," she whispered.

He nodded, as a way of saying, *so am I.*

"I need you close," she said. He moved over so that she could sit next to him, her back against his desk. He took her hand in his. She shifted her body so that she could face him. In the darkness, he could see her eyes, wide and frightened. She kissed him.

"Don't say no," she whispered into his ear. "I need this right now."

"I won't," he whispered back, and kissed her, getting lost in her warm, soft lips.

Chapter 58

June 16
Kunar Province, Afghanistan

The sun was high in the sky. Sergeant Dwayne Davenport looked out the window of his Humvee into the mountainous, rocky terrain of the Kunar province of Afghanistan. It was a routine patrol, filled with both boredom and dread, typical of the war, which had bursts of violence interspersed with long stretches of absolutely nothing.

Looking into the distance, he thought he could see—no, it definitely was a person, a man, dressed in rags, running and motioning to them.

"Stop the car!"

He took out the binoculars and stood up through the sunroof. He looked at the man. There was something strange about him, something Davenport couldn't quite place.

"Identify yourself!" Davenport called out, then said the same in Pashto and Dari, the two major languages of Afghanistan. The man was too far away to hear, but continued to run toward them.

"Just shoot him!" cried out Flowers, the newest member of their squad. Davenport didn't want to, not yet. He was nervous, too. A patrol being approached could always mean an attack, and other unfriendlies could be hidden around them. Davenport scanned the area with the binoculars. If this was an ambush, he caught no sign of it. He yelled out to the man again. No response.

The man did seem to be yelling something that Davenport couldn't catch. He was closer now, too close for comfort. Davenport took aim, and at that moment heard what the man was saying.

"Help me! Help me, please!"

In English.

"What are you waiting for? Shoot him!" yelled out Flowers.

"Shut up!" said Davenport.

The man approached the vehicle, then dropped to his knees in exhaustion. With a weak but firm voice, he intoned:

"My name is Lee Erwin Wolfe. I'm the Secretary of State of the United States of America. For God's sake, please get me out of here."

Chapter 59

"DC is dead," said Shepard, reading from his computer. "No power anywhere in the city."

"Then it happened," Diana Bloch whispered. She sat down on the bed of the suite at the Mandarin. She could only stare at the wall in horror. "Do we have estimates for casualties?"

"We'd need to figure out how many planes were airborne within the blast radius of the device," Karen O'Neal said. "There could have been twenty, thirty even more. That's going to be the lion's share of the deaths. Next is people hooked on some kind of life support, pacemakers. There would be accidents from cars' electronics going haywire." She spoke quickly. "And we don't actually know how big a surge is going to flow through certain electronic equipment—whether a person holding a cell phone against their ear would be electrocuted, for instance. And what about people stuck in vehicles like cars or elevators or—"

"Okay," Bloch cut her off. "That's enough, Karen. Let's all calm down."

"My sister lives in DC. She has a husband and a son. I can't call them to know that they're okay and—"

"Stop," said Bloch. "As soon as we get communication, we'll do whatever we can to contact them."

"Do you think the president was on Air Force One when the EMP went off?" asked Spartan. She was slumped over the desk, fighting back tears.

"No clue," said Shepard. "All my *goddamn* connections to DC have been severed." He banged his fist on the hardwood desk, scowled in pain, and then clutched it protectively.

"But someone was warning the public," said Spartan. "It was on TV, on the radio, on the Internet. . . . Someone managed to warn a lot of people. Maybe the President got away, too."

"There has to be something we can do," said O'Neal, tears flowing from her eyes.

"Well, how do we find out about the President?" asked Spartan.

"The flight plan would have been logged," said Bloch. "It will take the right person to have access to it, and it'll be hard with DC—and more important, Langley—in the dark."

Karen O'Neal broke down in sobs. Bloch comforted her with a hand on her shoulder.

Spartan glanced at her computer, and something seemed to catch her eye. "Holy shit," she said.

"What?" asked Shepard.

"The Secretary's been found," said Spartan.

"*What?*" exclaimed Bloch.

"The story's just being relayed among the agencies," said Spartan. "Here we go. He was found by an army patrol in Paktia Province. He was in bad shape. Beaten and bloody, dehydrated, walking out in the mountains. It was sheer dumb luck that he happened to run into a US patrol vehicle. He's on his way back to the country now. One piece of *goddamn* good news in this hell-on-Earth of a day."

"How did he get free?" Bloch asked.

"They haven't said," Spartan said. "Maybe it's still classified."

"It is good news that he's alive," said Bloch. "Wolfe is a strong figure. Even if the President is alive, he's MIA. We need someone to bring the country together, to remind people of our shared values, of our responsibilities to one another."

"What now?" asked Shepard. "We lost. Weinberg won. What do we do next?"

"Are you kidding?" asked Bloch, with anger in her voice. "No, Shepard, we haven't lost. We've lost people, and they will be mourned. Weinberg struck at the heart of our country. But Gunther Weinberg cannot destroy us. He can't, not without killing every last one of us and every idea that we stand for. We haven't lost, because our work isn't done."

"Bloch . . ." said O'Neal in disbelief.

"No," said Bloch. "I won't accept defeat. Now is when we rally our troops, pool what resources still exist, and bring Weinberg to justice while the wound is still fresh. Who's staying here and fighting?"

The others in the room stared at her blankly. Then O'Neal, swallowing her tears, raised her hand.

"I believe that my sister and my nephew are alive," she said. "But they were there. They are probably feeling scared and helpless. If I can help, in whatever way I can, I'll do it for them."

"I'll stay," said Spartan. "Of course."

Bloch looked over at Shepard. "It's funny," he said. "Karen's staying because she has people, but I have no one, really. No family, no friends that I care about that much." He sat up straighter. "But that's exactly why I'm staying. I won't do any good anywhere else."

"Then it's settled," said Bloch. "We stay here and we work through this. Shepard, I want you to reestablish a link with DC. Langley in particular. Spartan, you're on communications. I'm going to give you a list of people to contact, and you're going to get in touch with them. O'Neal, get me data. The more we know about this, the better." Bloch took a deep breath. "We need to be another line of defense when others have failed. A lot depends on what we do. And it's far from over."

Chapter 60

Suspended below his parachute, Morgan floated toward the pitch-black ground of the Washington, DC, region. As his eyes grew accustomed to the light of the moon, he was able to make out individual features of the landscape. He had seen two passenger airplanes fall out of the sky when the EMP was deployed, and the flaming wreckage of another one that had been behind him. As he drifted, all he felt—apart from the pains and aches of being tossed like a ragdoll first by the plane and then by Anse Fleischer—was how powerless he was to help anyone.

The wind carried him to a developed suburb, which posed many dangers for landing, from roofs to trees to pools and even power lines, which though not currently electrified could tangle his chute and leave him hanging.

Morgan steered into the middle of a street. He landed first on a stalled car, putting a sizable dent on the roof, but was carried upward by a gust of wind. He hit the asphalt a few yards ahead, barreling down on his feet and then stumbling to his knees. He released the parachute, and it flew away like a giant bat, carried by the night's winds. Having made sure that he was still in one piece, he stood up and looked around.

A few people had emerged on the streets and were offering to help others. Some were trying to profit from the situation, as in the case of a man who had set up a portable gas stove and was offering to rent it out to people who had electric stoves at home. Just down the street, another man seemed to be offering the same thing for free. Many who were out in the streets looked scared and aggrieved, but more seemed to be helping.

He passed one young man who offered assistance—Morgan certainly did look in need of first aid, he realized, but he declined. He heard the same young man offer help to the next person he crossed. Another was holding a clipboard and trying to figure out if there were any dead, and whether people needed anything. *This is America,* Morgan thought with a warm glow. *Neighbors helping each other out.* An old man approached him on the sidewalk.

"It's all blacked out," he said. "People are saying it might be World War Three. Like we're being invaded. But I don't see any enemy bombers."

"It's not World War Three," said Morgan. "You're going to be fine. We're all going to be fine."

Morgan ran down the street, looking for the thing he needed most: transportation. Modern cars depended on electronics to start and run, and all of those would be as good as gigantic paperweights. He'd have to find a car from the eighties or earlier. He dashed, block by block, looking for a car that might be functional.

It took him about ten blocks, but he knew it was the one as soon as he had seen it. It was a 1969 Camaro, vivid red. He looked up and down the street, seeing no one. He had to work fast. The owner might be watching from a window.

Morgan took off his tuxedo jacket and wrapped it around his elbow. "Sorry," he said, and shattered the glass of the back driver's-side window. He reached into the car and unlocked the driver's side door.

Once behind the wheel, he reached toward the backseat and found an ice scraper, which he used to pry open the cover under the steering wheel. He stripped the wires with his teeth and touched them together. The car came to life.

Morgan laughed out loud when he shifted into gear. He set out. It was slow going in that area, as he had to maneuver around countless vehicles that had stopped dead in the middle of the street. He apologized under his breath for every yard he ran over, every lawn ornament and bush he crushed.

He found his way to the highway north. Police were already shutting down the way *into* DC, but nobody thought of closing off the way *out* of it. Morgan had the highway to himself for several miles northward before he found working electricity again. He stopped at a gas station and used the pay phone to call Alex, who had Conley's phone.

"Did you make it there?" he asked. "Are you with McKay?"

"Jesus, Dad, are you okay? I heard that the EMP was detonated, and Washington's in the dark. Is that true?"

"It's true," said Morgan. "A lot of people were hurt. But I'm okay. I'm coming for you, okay honey? But I need you to do something for me now."

"Shoot, Dad."

"I want you to send out a message to Zeta," said Morgan. "Lily can help you with that. Tell them what happened, and that I'm alive. I'll be there in a few hours."

Chapter 61

June 16
Boston

The TV was on in the makeshift Zeta headquarters at the Mandarin Oriental, and everyone was glued to the screen. The Secretary of State, newly returned from captivity, was preparing to go before the cameras. A news anchor was offering regular updates on information out of DC. No one had yet found the President or the Vice President. The Speaker of the House had been killed at Liberty Island, and president pro tempore of the Senate Lana McKay was missing.

"McKay's alive," said Bloch, coming in from the hallway. "So are Morgan and Lily Randall. Lily has McKay and Morgan's daughter somewhere safe and secret, and Morgan was in DC when the EMP hit. He's on his way north now."

"Wait, hold on," said O'Neal. "Shh. Listen." She pointed at the TV.

"The line of succession in case of the death of the president," said the blond news anchor, "goes vice president, speaker of the House, president pro tempore of the Senate, and secretary of state. If those missing government officials have indeed been killed, then Secretary of State Lee Irwin Wolfe will be our president."

"It's a good thing Wolfe's alive," said Shepard. "The next in line was Secretary of the Treasury. Not exactly inspiring."

"But even if the President and the Vice President are dead, McKay's still alive," said Spartan. "It's a moot point."

"Yeah," said O'Neal. "But you don't think—"

"Are there any leads on Weinberg's location?" asked Bloch.

"Not a thing," said Shepard. "But we do have a silver lining in terms of communications. They're flooding working satellite broadband devices into DC. They'll allow people at least to send messages to their loved ones, and to get government agencies up and running again, even if at severely limited capacity. Meanwhile, we have helicopters scouring the area for the President and the VP."

"Good," said Bloch. "Meanwhile, the search for—"

"Listen!" cried out O'Neal. "It's all starting to make sense. It's coming together, just be *quiet* for a second."

Everyone sat in stunned silence as Karen O'Neal scrunched up her face deep in thought. "Weinberg's plot," she said. "It's an attack on the presidential line of succession. The President, Vice President, Speaker of the House, President pro tempore of the Senate, and the Secretary of State."

"So Weinberg wants the US President to be the Secretary of the Treasury?" asked Shepard.

"Sounds like a plan to weaken the US by elevating to the presidency a person who has none of the relevant experience," said Bloch.

"No! No! Listen," O'Neal said. "Secretary of State Lee Irwin Wolfe. He was the first. Why was he the first? And why was he *kidnapped?* Why does he return a hero at the exact moment when the nation most needs one?"

"The Secretary . . ." Bloch didn't finish the thought.

"Exactly," said O'Neal. "The thought had occurred to me before, but all suspicion had been deflected by the fact that he had been abducted. But it was all orchestrated perfectly, to give him the perfect opportunity to seize the presidency."

"It makes sense," said Bloch, her eyes wide with the realization. "How does Weinberg fit in?"

"He wants a US President in his pocket," she said. "Someone he could blackmail and control."

"Well, terrible as it is," said Spartan, "It's not quite so bad, is it? I mean, we know Senator McKay is alive, and for all we know the President and Vice President are, too. Let Wolfe have his speech. It's only a matter of time before evidence of this gets out."

"Yeah," said Shepard. "Except . . . Weinberg's not out of the picture yet, McKay's in hiding, and the whereabouts of the President and VP are unknown."

"You're saying—" began Bloch.

"He may try to kill them yet," said Shepard.

"We need to warn Cougar," said Spartan. "McKay needs more protection. She needs to be brought in, she needs to be on TV. Everyone needs to know that she's alive!"

"You're right," said Bloch. "This needs to happen as soon as possible. I'm going to get Cougar on the phone. Finding Weinberg is back to being our number-one priority."

Chapter 62

June 16
North Carolina

Peter Conley was driving right behind Walker and the rest of the Lambda team in a metallic Nissan Versa along a forested stretch of road in North Carolina on their way to Washington, DC, when he got the call from Bloch. She explained Karen O'Neal's theory about Wolfe's complicity and Weinberg's ultimate plan.

"It's time for McKay to come out of hiding," said Bloch. "We think you should go get her."

Conley flashed his high beams for Walker to pull over, and then pulled in behind him on the shoulder. A car tore down the highway, bobbing Conley's car in its wake as it passed. "I'm going to need her location," said Conley.

"Sending it now," said Bloch.

Conley pulled the hand brake and got out of the car. He breathed in the invigorating cool night air, made fresh by the dark, dense forest that bordered the highway. Walker, out of his own car, strode over to him.

"I've just spoken to Bloch," said Conley. "She thinks I should collect McKay and escort her to a major city."

"No problem," said Walker. He squinted as a car approached with its high beams on. It passed them with a *whoosh*. "Why don't I send one of the cars with you? We can spare a couple of guys to make sure she gets there safely."

Clutch, who had been in the car with Walker, also emerged out onto the shoulder. Conley's instincts made him uncomfortable. There was something shifty about him. "It's fine," he said. "There's no need for either of you to come along. We have Lily Randall. And it's best not to attract too much attention to myself."

"Fair enough," said Walker with a shrug. "Are those the coordinates on your phone?"

"Yes," said Conley in a drawn-out syllable, holding his phone closer to his chest.

"Can we take a look?" asked Walker.

"I think I'd better just go," said Conley.

Clutch drew a handgun from the back waistband of his pants and pointed it at Conley.

"How about now?" asked Walker.

"Hey, guys," said Conley, bringing his hands up to his chest. "I don't know what this is about, but I'm not your enemy here."

"Give him the phone," said Clutch.

"What's your angle here?" asked Conley. "Do you want to be the big hero? 'Cause I can give you credit if you want."

"I think the guy with the gun makes the rules," said Clutch. "Now, are you going to hand it over?"

Both of them squinted at a coming headlight, and a deep bass horn told Conley that it was a semi truck.

"Shoot him," said Walker, with eyes half-closed.

"With plea—"

Conley reared up and kicked Clutch hard in the chest exactly two seconds before the truck that had been barreling toward them passed. Clutch was thrust backward onto the highway, firing a wild shot upward, and was bashed by the truck's grille. The driver slammed the brakes, and the acrid smell of burning tires wafted through the air.

Conley took advantage of Walker's astonishment to throw a left hook, but Walker dodged and returned with a punch to the gut. He kicked Conley so that he fell over, and stepped on his hand until he relinquished the phone.

"You're gonna pay for that," said Walker.

"Hey!" someone shouted. It was the truck driver. Two shots rang out, and he was hit twice in the chest by one of Walker's teammates.

The poor guy. But a distraction was a distraction. Conley kicked Walker's leg hard once, then twice. Walker toppled backward, and the phone tumbled toward Walker's Hyundai.

The entire Lambda team was emerging from their two vehicles. Conley stared at the phone for a single beat, but it was lost. He had no hope of getting to it now.

He turned and dashed into the dark woods, hearing gunshots behind him. He ran as fast as he could without risking breaking his legs until he could no longer see the road. He felt confident that they wouldn't come after him. They were in a hurry to get to McKay, and that stretch of road now resembled a butcher shop.

No, they would be going. But not before they had sabotaged his car and left him without a phone. Conley tried to remember where the last gas station was, but couldn't. It must have been far away. He was stranded, with no transportation, no means of communication. And he was the only one who knew that a team of murderous bastards was on its way to kill Lily, Alex, and Senator McKay.

Chapter 63

June 16
Washington, DC

Buck Chapman was awoken, partially clothed and with his arms embracing Cynthia Gillespie, by a sudden bustle in the outer work area. Cynthia opened her eyes as well, and pulled her clothes on without a word to him. Once she was dressed, but still turned away and with downcast eyes, she asked, "What the—?"

Chapman walked out of his office to find that two young people carrying heavy shopping bags had come into the outer office.

"What's this?" Chapman asked the young man.

"Satellite-enabled smart phones," he said. "We're here to bring you out of the dark ages. We're also leaving instructions here for you to log on to a secure network with the specific purpose of sharing information in the DC area. Congratulations. You're all connected again."

Chapman turned his on and followed the setup instructions. The network was a simple and clever system where anyone could share, though certain special subnetworks were only accessible to those with security clearance. As he looked it over, it seemed that the damage had not been quite as bad as he had imagined. He logged on to the secure network, and saw the top item on the list.

"Oh my God," he said.

Chapter 64

"It's the President," Shepard announced, raising a fist in victory. "And the Vice President. They've been found. They were on Marine One, the presidential helicopter, when they got the warning."

The room in the Mandarin Oriental came alive with a burst of enthusiasm.

"Why hasn't this information been released to the public?" asked Bloch.

"They made an emergency landing in the middle of the woods," said Shepard. "They were incommunicado for hours. It's been only minutes since a reconnaissance helicopter spotted them, and the pilot hasn't found a way to land there yet. They're holding off on releasing the information until they're at a secure location."

Bloch flopped into her chair with relief. The casualties of the day had not been as catastrophic as she had thought it had been. With the President located and Conley on the way to pick up McKay, this series of events might be drawing to a close.

Her phone rang: unknown number.

"This is Bloch," she said, adopting her usual businesslike tone. "Who is this?"

"This is Cougar," came the voice on the other line. She sat up, alarmed.

"Where are you? What is this number?"

"I'm at a gas station," he said. "It's Lambda. They're working for Weinberg."

"What?" she exclaimed, incredulous.

"I can't explain it, either," he said. "But they took my cell phone at gunpoint, along with the coordinates of McKay's hiding place. They tried to kill me, and they mean to kill her, too. You need to warn them."

"Hold on," she said, while motioning for Shepard to lend her his phone. She dialed the phone in Lily's possession. It rang once, twice, three times.

"Hello." It was a man's voice.

"Who is this?" she demanded.

"Bloch," said the voice, in a reassuring tone. "It's me. It's Morgan."

"Morgan, thank goodness. Are you still at the hotel?"

"Yeah, we're here."

"Get out," she said in her commanding voice. "Get out right now. Lambda—they're working for Weinberg and they know where you are. Get out and get as far away from there as possible."

"I could do that," he said. "But I think it's better to end this right here, right now."

"Morgan, the safety of Senator McKay—"

"Won't be in jeopardy," he said. "She'll be far away when anything goes down. But I'm not running anymore. This ends tonight."

Chapter 65

Walker was in a pissy mood, and when he was in a pissy mood, he drove too fast. Although, the truth was, he always drove too fast. Not that he loved the speed, but he resented the road and others on it.

He had lost Clutch, and he was not happy about that. Cougar had gotten away, and he was even less happy about *that*.

He was aching for the feel of his Uzi in his hands. His mood had been improving as they approached their destination. In fact, Walker was downright giddy as he turned into the Ellery. The rest of his team followed in the other car.

The Ellery was a plain two-story motel with the corridor exposed to open air on one side. They parked in the lot, and everyone emerged from the cars with semiautomatic machine guns drawn and ready.

"We don't want any survivors," said Walker. "We'll kill the entire damn motel if necessary. But out primary target is room twenty-one."

He took the lead, going up the stairs and all the way down the hallway, with four of his team following him. He stopped at the door and tried to peek in through the large window, but the blinds were drawn. The lights were off inside. He signed for Bluejay, who kicked like a mule, to get it open. The former linebacker positioned himself in front of the door and stomped it in.

Walker let the others go in first, and then entered the room. In the light from outside he saw two beds and a cot, all of them occupied. He gave the signal to fire at will, and Lambda team let fly a hail of bullets into each of the figures in the beds.

Something was not right. There was no blood, no parts, just foam and feathers. Walker turned on the lights. Goddamn decoys! Pillows and blankets! They'd been fooled by elementary-school level deception.

"What the hell is that smell?" asked Bluejay.

Morgan stepped out of room 26 of the Ellery Motel. On his daughter's cell phone, he dialed 911. Phone in hand, standing halfway down the upstairs hallway, he drew a Zippo lighter from his pants pocket.

"Nine-one-one, please state your emergency," came the voice on the other line.

"I'd like to report a fire at the Ellery Motel," he said. "Send help right away." With this, he hung up, flicked the lighter, and dropped it.

Morgan had always appreciated the way that flames traveled on alcohol, in a way that was beautiful, smooth, almost elegant. He watched as the iridescent blue spread down the hall. It was a beauty to behold.

Of course, some rather more explosive materials were beautiful, too.

The door to room 21 erupted in a spout of flame, and this would not be the mild burning of alcohol. He felt the heat singeing his hair. He would rather not have to think about what it might be like for someone who was in that room.

It couldn't have been pleasant.

Chapter 66

As soon as Smith's gunshot wound had stabilized, his connections had gotten him out of the hospital and into another: Johns Hopkins. He limped down the antiseptic corridor, as walking any faster would have hurt like hell, until he came to the checkpoint where Secretary of State Lee Irwin Wolfe's security detail was standing guard.

"He's expecting me," said Smith, flashing one of his many fake identities.

One of them checked a list while the other spoke into his communicator. "Follow me," the one with the communicator said after a few seconds. He led Smith farther down the hallway to a wide door that opened into a spacious private room. There lay the Secretary of State, haggard and unshaven but clean and in apparent health. He looked up at Smith, showing a weary and suffering expression with a hint of relief.

"Smith," he said.

Smith looked to his right, where a bodyguard sat vigil on a chair. Wolfe took the cue.

"Give us a minute, Ryan, would you?" The man left the room. "Smith," Wolfe repeated. "What happened? You're hurt."

"I was double-crossed," said Smith. He watched Wolfe's expression, but saw no sign of a reaction. "By Ken Figueroa, of all people."

"Are you kidding?" said Wolfe, looking surprised. "Ken *shot* you?"

"Right." Smith pulled the chair in which the bodyguard had

been sitting to a spot on Wolfe's bedside. "And then I shot him. And now I'm here, and he's in a body bag."

"Why the hell would Ken shoot you?"

"That's a good question," said Smith. "I've been asking myself that for the past twenty-four hours. Why the hell would Ken Figueroa shoot me? Why would his tactical team turn on my people and try to kill Senator Lana McKay? Why would they kill Haider Raza, unarmed, when he is the only person who could tell us about your whereabouts?"

Smith saw the alarm dawn on Wolfe's demeanor.

"Do you have something tell me, Lee?"

"Listen, Smith, I—I don't know what you're getting at here."

"All, coincidentally, as Gunther Weinberg attacks, simultaneously, the President, the Vice President, the Speaker of the House, and President of the Senate. Who, if all dead, would clear up the line of succession to the presidency directly to, well, *you*. Just, coincidentally, as you return from being held captive and tortured by America's public enemy number one to receive a hero's welcome. Am I leaving anything out, Lee?"

Wolfe chuckled. "You're losing it, Smith. You're so far into your own conspiracies that you're seeing them everywhere."

"Is that a fact?" Smith said.

"Yes, it is," Wolfe said, anger creeping into his tone. "I'm back to my home country after going through hell in Pakistan, and you—"

"Save it," said Smith. "I know you planned the attack on the line of succession. I know you planned your own abduction to make yourself into some kind of hero. But it's over, Wolfe."

"You pathetic little man," said Wolfe. " Do you know who you're talking to? I will bury you. I will—"

"No," broke in Smith. "You won't. The Aegis board have been notified. They are unanimous on this issue. You're done. You have two choices. You bow out and keep out, letting America keep thinking that you're a hero—"

"What, no justice to be served? Aren't you going to ask me to fall on my sword or something? Commit seppuku?"

"I do not care about justice," said Smith. "I care about outcome. You are done, whether or not you live. No good can come of bringing this all to light. You have a choice. Leave public life forever. Retire, citing your recent captivity. Go to a ranch in Texas and spend the rest of your days hunting or horseback riding or whatever it is you do. Or die in the next few days."

Wolfe stared out into the middle distance, abstracted. There was no guilt in his demeanor, Smith noticed. Only a hint of shame, and he had been given a way out to avoid it. That was what motivated people like Wolfe, all they would respond to—shame, and the drive to avoid it.

"I have just one question," Smith said. "How does Gunther Weinberg fit into all of this? What was in it for him? Influence?"

Wolfe shook his head. "No. I mean, yes, that, too, but something else. He was . . . *bored,* I think." He stared into the distance, as if he were somewhere far away. "I know how it sounds, but it's true. He already had all the money he could possibly use. There was nothing he couldn't buy. But it wasn't enough for him. He needed more. He needed—something like this. A grand plan, something truly extra-ordinary. The way he talked about it, like it was going to be his masterpiece." Wolfe turned his head to look at Smith. "This isn't over yet."

"If you're going to threaten me, Lee—"

"No, not at all," said Wolfe. "I mean Weinberg. He's not done. He won't let this failure stop him."

"I'm sure we can manage—"

"You don't understand," said Wolfe. "He's here, he's still in the country, and he has a tactical nuclear weapon in his possession. He's going to make his mark, and he'll raze an American city if he has to."

Chapter 67

June 17
Boston

"All right, this is the situation," Bloch told Shepard and Spartan in their suite at the Mandarin Oriental, with Morgan, Conley, and Lily on speakerphone. "We have to find a tactical nuclear weapon that's located somewhere on American soil. We have zero leads as of right now, and this is a race against the clock. Run a search for Weinberg's names on every database."

"We've tried that," said Shepard. "No go. No hits for his own name and ID or his sister's, no known aliases. . . . It looks like money can buy you real anonymity."

"Shipping manifests?" suggested Lily. "Anything that can help us determine how he got the bomb here?"

"Not in the time that we have," said Shepard.

"Can we do a satellite sweep for the bomb's radiation signature?" asked Conley.

"It's possible in theory," said Shepard. "But not in our time frame."

"Why not?" asked Morgan.

"Making a general sweep of the whole country, for starters, would take days that we don't have," said Shepard. "Also, there's nothing unique about the signature on a nuclear bomb. We'd be poring over satellite readouts for weeks trying to weed out all the CT scan and X-ray machines."

"What if we narrowed down the search parameters?" suggested Bloch. "Give you a target area to run the search?"

"That might work," said Shepard. "What are we looking for?"

"What would he need to launch a missile?" asked Bloch.

"Highway access to get the equipment in, enough space to set up the rig," said Conley.

"And privacy," added Morgan. "You don't want the neighbors catching sight of your nuclear missile."

"Let's not forget that Weinberg travels in style," said Lily. "He wouldn't settle for any old place."

"So let's see..." said Shepard. "Properties larger than fifty acres...rented or bought in the past year....Let's set a price threshold....There!" His screen displayed a list of real estate properties. "All right," he said. "Now, I'm going to input their coordinates into our instructions for the satellite sweep, and see if something comes up."

Everyone watched Shepard's computer screen as it blinked through a blur of images and numbers. After about thirty seconds, Shepard said, "You know, this is probably going to take awhile. Why don't you all go get a cup of coffee or something?"

Bloch sat back down on the room's sofa, and noticed how tired she was. There was a deep ache in her muscles, and her eyelids grew heavy. The pain in her torso was dulled, but still hurt constantly, always at the edge of her consciousness. She was tired, so tired. If only she could rest her eyes—

"We've got a hit!" came Shepard's voice.

Bloch's eyes shot open. "How long was I out?" she asked.

"About an hour and a half," said Spartan.

"Why didn't you wake me up?" she said.

"Boss, you're burning the candle at both ends," said Shepard. "We thought you could use the rest."

"All right, no matter," said Bloch. "What do we have?"

"Manor house in South Carolina," said Shepard, showing her a satellite photo of a green property. "One hundred and fifty acres, colonial style. Rented out six months ago to an anonymous holding company, and look at what we have on the front lawn!" He pointed to a rectangular red smear overlaid on the satellite picture of the house and property. "Radiation signature. That's our bomb."

"All right," said Bloch. "It's time to move out. Cobra, Cougar, Lily, get moving. I'm sending Diesel your way as well. We'll work on getting you access to the mansion from here."

Chapter 68

It was nighttime when Morgan pulled the Corolla carrying Conley and Lily into a narrow roadside stop where Diesel was waiting for them. They were a mere four hundred yards from the edge of Weinberg's property.

"I've brought us some firepower," said Diesel. He popped his trunk and displayed a wide array of weapons, as well as bulletproof vests and night-vision goggles for everyone. "Gear up," he told them. "We're moving out right away."

Morgan surveyed the weapons—automatics and semiautomatics, handguns, tactical knives, and—

"I call dibs on *that* one," said Morgan.

"I thought you might," said Diesel. "That we use in case we need to destroy the missile."

"Won't it cause the warhead to go nuclear?" asked Morgan.

"If you hit the rear of the rocket, it'll be disabled without setting off the bomb," said Diesel. "Just be careful to aim for the butt."

They left the cars where they had parked and walked into the woods with Conley navigating, the terrain rendered green by the night vision. They reached the perimeter wall to Weinberg's property within ten minutes. It was the most remote corner they could find, where it bordered public land. Morgan slung a FIM-92 Stinger portable surface-to-air missile launcher, a particularly heavy weapon, across his back. It weighed him down as he climbed the tactical ladder to the top.

Once in, they spread out on the forested area, taking cover as they moved across the terrain. They soon neared the expansive lawn in front of the house. It was an enormous colonial mansion, red brick with majestic white columns and entablature. But impressive as it was, it garnered less attention than the missile, more than half as tall as the house, illuminated by the floodlights that lit up the entire area.

From behind the tree line, Morgan counted twelve men in black—the same hired guns, he surmised, that had carried out the attack on Liberty Island. Four were patrolling the edge of the lawn and two held sniper positions on the balcony, while the rest were scattered around the missile. They carried an assortment of submachine guns—Morgan saw three Uzis and two MP5s and a Colt nine millimeter among them. He clutched his own suppressed Remington sniper rifle and stood with his back to a mossy beech trunk.

"We're outnumbered three to one, at least," said Morgan over the radio communicator. "Our one advantage is the element of surprise. Let's use it wisely."

"Roger," said Diesel. "I'll take the sniper on the left, and you the one on the right, you figure?"

"Confirmed," said Morgan. "Conley, Lily, give us covering fire. Remember not to stay in one place—you stay put, you let them know where we are and how many we are. Let's keep them guessing."

Morgan rested the Remington on a low bough of the beech and found his first target lying behind the white banister of the corner of the balcony. Taking stock of the wind, he adjusted the shot.

"Do you have your shot, Diesel?"

"Standing by," he said.

"On my mark. Three. Two. One."

The gunshots rang out nearly simultaneously. Morgan's target jerked at the impact of the bullet.

Immediately, the remaining ten commandos sprinted out toward the woods, fanning out over the lawn. He heard the suppressed fire from Lily's and Conley's MP5s. Morgan took aim with his rifle again, waited for another burst of bullets—from his right, Lily—and took the shot, hitting one of the running men in the neck. With this second shot, his location would certainly be made, so Morgan ran parallel to the tree line, taking cover now behind a bush.

"Morgan!" Gunther Weinberg bellowed from the house's veranda. "I know you're out there!"

Forgetting about the approaching hostiles, Morgan took aim at Weinberg, but he was too hasty. The bullet sailed over Weinberg's head to hit the ceiling.

"Launch!" Weinberg exclaimed. "Launch now!"

The first of the guards had reached the tree line to Morgan's distant left, but Conley was waiting for him and took him out with four discharges of his Beretta Storm .45. Morgan ran again, leaving the position he'd given away while Diesel took out another hostile with his sniper rifle.

Morgan took cover behind a boulder and lifted the bulky Stinger surface-to-air launcher he had carried with him onto his shoulder. The tactical nuclear missile lit up with a deafening roar, shooting a jet of blue fire into the lawn.

"Ready to neutralize the weapon," said Morgan. "Cover me."

"Aim carefully," said Diesel. "We've got one chance at this."

Morgan was taking aim when something blocked his view—two commandos entering the forest directly between him and the missile.

Damn it.

"Need backup!" he called out. He laid aside the launcher. His sniper rifle would be of no use at such close quarters. He unholstered his Walther PPK nine millimeter and crouched behind the boulder.

"Morgan, you need to take out that missile!" said Conley.

He heard the cracks of the men's footsteps—they were flanking him on either side of the stone. He transferred his weapon to his left hand and unsheathed his combat knife with his right. It was a stupid, desperate move, but it was his only option.

Morgan emerged from behind the boulder, the two hostiles no more than three yards away. As he raised his left hand to shoot and drew his right to make the throw, gunfire rang out from his right and a single shot on his left, and the two men collapsed inward.

"That works too," said Morgan, sheathing his knife and holstering the PPK.

"You said you needed backup," said Diesel.

"You're welcome," said Lily.

"Appreciated," he said, picking up the rocket launcher. The missile began rising in the air. One shot. That's all that stood between him and the detonation of a nuclear weapon on the homeland.

Morgan pulled the trigger. The rocket fired out of the cylinder, burning bright, and hit the missile between two of its rear fins. The steel cylinder exploded in a red fireball that rose up past the roof. What was left of the missile flew two hundred feet to land on the far end of the lawn.

Morgan smirked.

"Spread out!" he yelled. "We're taking Weinberg tonight!"

"Cobra, Cougar, flank the house on—"

A single distant gunshot rang out, and Diesel cried out in pain. "I'm hit!" he said. "I took one in the leg."

By eyeballing the rough angle of entry, Morgan knew the bullet had come from the house. He looked through the scope of his rifle and found the shooter, positioned at the attic window above the central cornice. All he could see were pale, feminine hands.

"That's Lena Weinberg," said Morgan, back against a broad maple.

Lily's eyes narrowed. "I'll get her."

"Hold that thought." Morgan took a shot. He had no hope of making it, but he hit the window, shattering the glass, and saw her withdraw.

"How many hostiles left on the ground?" Morgan asked.

"Three," said Conley.

Another gunshot. "Two," corrected Diesel.

"You two fend them off," said Morgan. "I'm off to get Weinberg." He looked at Lily. "Let's go together. Ready?"

Without responding, Lily took off across the lawn. He sprinted after her, keeping his distance, dodging left and right at random intervals. He made it across the grass in ten seconds flat and reached the safety of the front door, where Lena couldn't shoot them from the balcony.

Lily opened the door and walked in, Morgan following. The house was filled with hunting trophies and bodies of taxidermied critters, which filled the spacious entrance hall with ominous shadows.

"Morgan!" came Weinberg's voice from beyond a door ahead.

Morgan turned to Lily. "Go find Lena!" He stepped forward, rifle in hand, to take cover behind a grandfather clock. "Weinberg!"

he shouted. "You're not leaving this house alive if you don't come out with your hands up right *goddamn* now."

"I have a different idea," said Weinberg. "You might have taken my Anse, but I am not defenseless, you know."

Automatic fire tore through the door, from at least six guns. Morgan hugged the wall and let the clock take the brunt of it.

"You are the one who will die, I think," said Weinberg.

Lily ran upstairs. She heard heavy footsteps coming from the balcony and along the upstairs corridor, toward the back of the house. She only saw a dark shadow of Lena Weinberg disappearing into a dark threshold—no, not entirely dark. There was a flickering light inside. Lily ran headlong down the hall, gun drawn, and into the door after Lena.

She heard the low whistle of wood flying through the air before something hit her hand, knocking the handgun onto the floor. Before she could react, another blow caught her in the back and sent her flying forward on her knees. In the dim light, which emanated from a fireplace in the far wall, she saw as her eyes adjusted the upraised aristocratic chin of Lena Weinberg and her cool, deadly eyes. She was holding a quarterstaff in both hands.

"I thought you might come," she said. "I've been reading up on you. I didn't know who you were then, but I do now."

She swung the staff. Lily rolled out of the way just as it whipped by her and thwacked the hardwood floor.

"Poor little orphan girl," Lena said. "Out for revenge on the man who killed her parents."

"It was revenge before," said Lily. "Now, I just want the pleasure of seeing you dead." They circled each other. Lena lunged, and Lily dodged again.

"Oh, the cold-blooded killer. Quite a departure from the Monte Carlo floozie, don't you think, Miss Randall?"

"And you're not quite the proper lady you pretend to be, are you?"

"It is entirely proper for a lady to learn to defend herself," Lena said.

Lily scanned the room for a possible weapon. She spotted one: a basket of canes near the door through which she had come in. She stepped back as Lena advanced again, keeping Lily away from the door. This was going to take some risk.

Lily feinted forward and left, and Lena swept her quarterstaff at her. Lily then rolled right, and in one fluid motion as she got up, she picked up a cane from the basket.

"Well done!" Lena laughed. "Perhaps we are more evenly matched than I thought."

The cane had a nice heft to it. Lily practiced swinging it a few times as Lena looked for the right moment to pounce. Lily made the first move, striking low at Lena's legs, and missing. Lena landed a sharp blow against Lily's left arm, and she cried out in pain.

Lena swung down this time, and Lily rolled away. Not backing down, Lena swung again, and this time Lily parried with her cane. However, with the blow, the cane seemed to break, suddenly much lighter in her hands. She was about to toss it aside when she looked at it and was surprised.

Lena's blow hadn't broken the cane, merely unsheathed the sword that was hidden inside.

"Oh, this should be interesting," said Lena. She pressed forward, sending blow after blow. Lily knew the sword-cane couldn't parry one of those blows, so she was left to dodge one after the other. At one point she nearly lost her balance, and Lena took advantage of it to kick her in the chest. Lily knocked against a table, dropping a number of unseen objects backward toward the flickering fire. Again the staff came down, and Lily dodged aside.

"You know, there's more to Gunther and me than meets the eye," Lena said, pressing forward. "Gunther, the playboy, is infinitely more than that."

"A psychopath and a terrorist?" asked Lily, lashing out with the sword but coming up short.

"Gunther has the vision," Lena said, offended. "The grand ideas. I admit, he is better at that than me. But he would be nothing without me. He would have accomplished little, because he has no knack for the practical. I was the planner. The one who took care of business."

The light in the room had grown brighter. Risking a look, Lily turned her head to the fireplace and saw that the cloth from the table she had knocked down had fallen into the flames, which had spread to the carpet and the drapes.

"Do you think I care about the dynamics of your sick little family?" said Lily.

"I do have a point, you idiot girl."

"That being?"

"Who do you think killed your parents? I mean, do you really think Gunther would concern himself with trifling details? Two insignificant British journalists? *I* arranged for the accident."

"Bitch," Lily said through gritted teeth.

Lena laughed. "I suppose I am. Does it make you angry? Does it make your face hot, your blood boil? Do you want to kill me more than ever now?" She swung the quarterstaff, and Lily narrowly avoided having her skull crushed.

The fire seemed to be galloping now. This old house was ripe for the flames, full of dusty tapestries and hardwood.

"I just wanted to see your face when I told you," Lena said. "Before you die."

She launched an attack. Lily rolled under it, getting on the other side of Lena—the side near the door. Lightning quick, she slashed at Lena's calves. The woman bellowed in pain but did not even stumble. Lily backed out the door, letting Lena swing at her furiously but ineffectively. She was getting enraged and tired. Hers was a heavier weapon that Lily's, and its weight was taking a toll.

With the next swing, Lily evaded easily and stuck again, opening a deep cut in Lena's right arm. Lily's anger was fading, leaving her alert. She saw that downstairs, Morgan was pinned down by several gunmen. The steady gunfire kept him from coming out.

Another blow from Lena, another dodge. Lily tipped a heavy chair with her foot and pushed it against Lena. It was enough to make her stagger back. Lily slashed at her hands, so that she dropped her staff. Then Lily kicked Lena against the banister and plunged the sword into Lena's heart. She gasped, more surprised than in pain. Blood gushed out of her chest, and she went limp.

"Weinberg!" Lily hollered into the cavernous entrance hall to the house. "Your sister is dead. *I* killed her. I wanted you to know that before you die." She shoved Lena's body over the railing. The corpse flipped over and fell on the antlers of a mounted deer, hanging with her arms out and the sword sticking out of her chest, with an expression of wide-eyed horror.

"Lena!" It was a nearly animalistic wail. Weinberg ran into the hall, screaming, and stood in front of his sister's body, looking up at her. He turned around, with a handgun aimed at Morgan.

Morgan shot a single bullet, which caught Weinberg square in the center of the forehead. He tipped forward and fell on the floor with a *thud*.

"You've got two choices," Morgan yelled out to Weinberg's gunmen. "You can stay where you are, following the orders of a dead man, so I can pin you down in this house until you burn to death. Or you can toss your guns and come out with your hands up."

The automatics came sliding from the door into the hall, then the five men, single-file, with their hands up. Lily jogged down the stairs and took one of their rifles. They marched out of the house, where the spreading conflagration would soon consume the bodies of the two Weinbergs, into the cool night air.

Chapter 69

Morgan walked up the stairs to the temporary Zeta offices on Charles Street. He opened the outer door with a key, which seemed quaint and antiquated, and walked past the empty reception and through the unfurnished, undecorated halls to Bloch's office. He knocked.

The door opened, and there was Bloch, as unruffled as usual. Although, Morgan observed, not quite: her movements showed a certain stiffness from the wound that still hadn't healed. Bloch winced as she motioned for him to sit down. Morgan knew she must be in a lot more pain than she showed.

She took her seat. "How are you, Morgan?"

He exhaled. "Well. My daughter's safely at home. And I went to see Bishop in the hospital. He tells me he'll be out by the end of the week."

"And up and about in no time," said Bloch.

"So why am I here?" asked Morgan. "Am I getting chewed out?"

Bloch chuckled. "Nothing like that. I'd just like to let you know a couple of things. First, Elizabeth Randall has proven a capable and valuable agent. We have invited her to stay with us as a permanent addition to the team, and she has accepted."

"Glad to hear it," said Morgan. "I'll be glad to have her watching my back, and I think she'll be better off having someone sensible watching hers."

Bloch raised an eyebrow at the adjective, but said nothing. "Then there is the matter of your daughter."

"Oh," said Morgan, casting a sidelong glance at nothing in particular.

"Yes," said Bloch. "She knows not only about our existence, but also the location of our headquarters."

"Look, I'm sorry, I—"

"That's not what this is about," Bloch broke in. "I'm not here to talk about you, Morgan. I'm here to talk about *her.*"

"Wait, *what?*"

"She has proven resourceful in a crisis. She has demonstrated valuable skills in the field. And, as I understand it, she herself is interested."

"Absolutely not," said Morgan. "I won't allow it. Jenny would kill me."

"I am not asking *you,* Morgan. The offer will be extended to her, and if she accepts, she will begin training. I am merely *informing* you so that you don't break down my door later and tell me I didn't warn you."

Morgan slumped in his chair. "I don't even have the energy to fight you on this," he said. "Or her. I suppose I brought this on myself by starting to teach her in the first place."

"She's a talented young woman," said Bloch. "She deserves her chance to do what she wants to. And what I suspect is what she will do best."

"That girl can do whatever she wants," he said.

"And it surprises you that she chose to follow in her father's footsteps?"

Morgan chuckled, then sighed. "What now, Bloch?"

"Now, we rebuild," she said. "Bigger and better. Zeta's far from over, Morgan, and it will take more than Gunther Weinberg to stop us."

Morgan laughed. "I don't know how many more of them *I* can survive," he said.

"I know you, Morgan. And for you, the answer will always be 'as many as it takes.'"

ACKNOWLEDGMENTS

I would like to thank my agent, Doug Grad of the Doug Grad Literary Agency in New York, for all his hard work, dedication, and guidance over the past three years. His knowledge of the industry has been a huge help and he is a pleasure to work with.

I would also like to thank my local publicist, Skye Wentworth of Skye Wentworth Public Relations in Newbury, Massachusetts, who has encouraged me to follow my dream and has worked hard to get many radio and newspaper interviews as well as book-signing events.

I also want to thank my good friend and bestselling author John Gilstrap, who has been a mentor to me since we met three years ago. He has provided me with invaluable advice.

A very special thank-you to my editor at Kensington Publishing, Michaela Hamilton. Michaela has had faith in me, guided me, and fought for me and helped me to write the best book I possibly could. She is not only my editor, but a true friend.

Special thanks, too, to Caio Camargo, whose input has been essential in the writing of the Dan Morgan thrillers.

Coming soon from e-Pinnacle

TWELVE HOURS

A Dan Morgan Thriller—e-Book Exclusive!

Kippy Goldfarb / Carolle Photography

ABOUT THE AUTHOR

LEO J. MALONEY was born in Massachusetts, where he spent his childhood, and graduated from Northeastern University. He spent over thirty years in black ops, accepting highly secretive missions that would put him in the most dangerous hot spots in the world. Since leaving that career, he has had the opportunity to try his hand at acting in independent films and television commercials. He has ten movies to his credit, both as an actor and behind the camera as a producer, technical adviser, and assistant director. He lives in the Boston area. Visit him at www.leojmaloney.com.

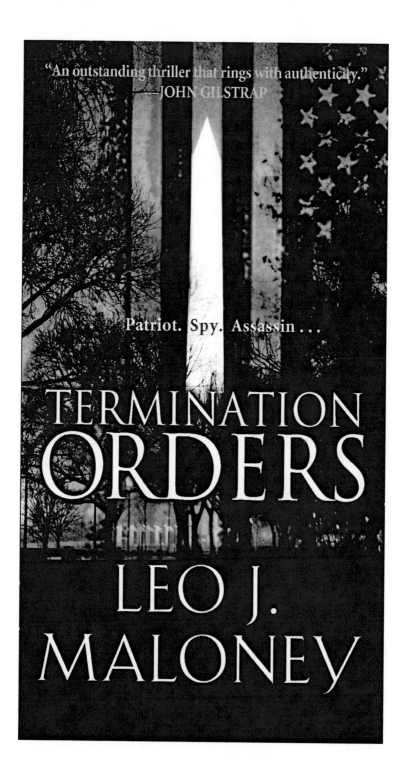

"An outstanding thriller that rings with authenticity."
—JOHN GILSTRAP

Patriot. Spy. Assassin . . .

TERMINATION
ORDERS

LEO J.
MALONEY

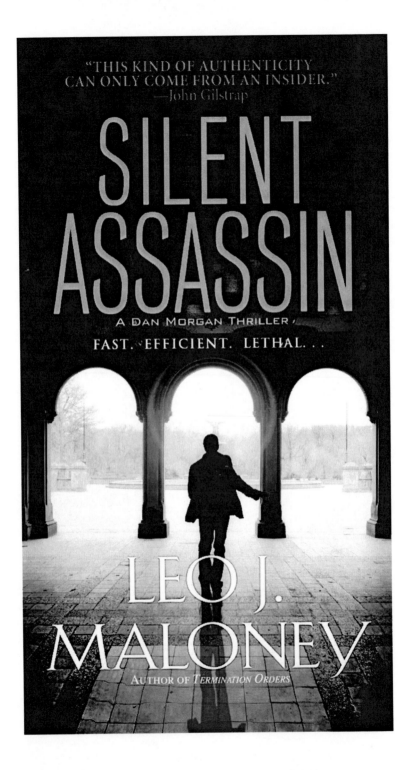

SILENT
ASSASSIN

A DAN MORGAN THRILLER

FAST. EFFICIENT. LETHAL. . .

LEO J.
MALONEY

AUTHOR OF *TERMINATION ORDERS*